G.A. Henty

The Curse of Carne's Hold

G.A. Henty

The Curse of Carne's Hold

1st Edition | ISBN: 978-3-75238-613-4

Place of Publication: Frankfurt am Main, Germany

Year of Publication: 2020

Outlook Verlag GmbH, Germany.

Reproduction of the original.

THE CURSE OF CARNE'S HOLD
BY G. A. HENTY

CHAPTER I.

HOW THE CURSE BEGAN.

There was nothing about Carne's Hold that would have suggested to the mind of the passing stranger that a curse lay upon it. Houses to which an evil history is attached lie almost uniformly in low and damp situations. They are embedded in trees; their appearance is gloomy and melancholy; the vegetation grows rank around them, the drive is overgrown with weeds and mosses, and lichens cling to the walls. Carne's Hold possessed none of these features. It stood high up on the slope of a hill, looking down into the valley of the Dare, with the pretty village of Carnesford nestling among its orchards, and the bright stream sparkling in the sunshine.

There was nothing either gloomy or forbidding about its architecture, and the family now simply called their abode The Carnes; the term "Hold" that the country people applied to it was indeed a misnomer, for the bombardiers of Essex had battered the walls of the old fortified house, and had called in the aid of fire to finish the work of destruction. The whole of the present structure was therefore subsequent to that date; it had been added to and altered many times, and each of its owners had followed out his own fancies in utter disregard of those of his predecessors; consequently the house represented a medley of diverse styles, and, although doubtless an architectural monstrosity, was picturesque and pleasing to the eye of men ignorant of the canons of Art.

There were no large trees near it, though a clump rose a few hundred yards behind it, and took away the effect of bareness it would otherwise have had. The garden was well kept, and bright with flowers, and it was clear that no blighting influence hung over them, nor, it would be thought, over the girl, who, with a straw hat swinging in one hand, and a basket, moved among them. But the country people for six miles round firmly believed that a curse lay on Carne's Hold, and even among the county families no one would have been willing to give a daughter in marriage to an owner of the place.

Carnesford, now a good-sized village, had once been a tiny hamlet, an appanage of Carne's Hold, but it had long since grown out of leading strings, and though it still regarded The Carnes with something of its old feudal feeling, it now furnished no suit or service unless paid for so doing. Carnesford had grown but little of late years, and had no tendency to increase. There was work enough in the neighbourhood for such of its inhabitants as wanted to work, and in summer a cart went daily with fruit and garden produce to Plymouth, which lay about twenty miles away, the coast road dipping down into the valley, and crossing the bridge over the Dare at Carnesford, and then climbing the hill again to the right of The Hold.

Artists would sometimes stop for a week or two to sketch the quaint old-fashioned houses in the main street, and especially the mill of Hiram Powlett, which seemed to have changed in no way since the days when its owner held it on the tenure of grinding such corn as the owners of The Hold required for the use of themselves and their retainers. Often, too, in the season, a fisherman would descend from the coach as it stopped to change horses at the "Carne's Arms" and would take up his quarters there, for there was rare fishing in the Dare, both in the deep still pool above the mill and for three or four miles higher up, while sea-trout were nowhere to be found plumper and stronger than in the stretch of water between Carnesford and Dareport, two miles away.

Here, where the Dare ran into the sea, was a fishing village as yet untouched, and almost unknown even to wandering tourists, and offering indeed no accommodation whatever to the stranger beyond what he might, perchance, obtain in the fishermen's cottages.

The one drawback to Carnesford, as its visitors declared, was the rain. It certainly rained often, but the villagers scarcely noticed it. It was to the rain, they knew, that they owed the bright green of the valley and the luxuriousness of their garden crops, which always fetched the top price in Plymouth market; and they were so accustomed to the soft mist brought up by the south-west wind from over the sea that they never noticed whether it was raining or not.

Strangers, however, were less patient, and a young man who was standing at the door of the "Carne's Arms," just as the evening was closing in at the end of a day in the beginning of October, 1850, looked gloomily out at the weather. "I do not mind when I am fishing," he muttered to himself; "but when one has once changed into dry clothes one does not want to be a prisoner here every evening. Another day like this, and I shall pack up my traps and get back again on board."

He turned and went back into the house, and, entering the bar, took his seat in the little sanctum behind it; for he had been staying in the house for a week, and was now a privileged personage. It was a snug little room; some logs were blazing on the hearth, for although the weather was not cold, it was damp enough to make a fire pleasant. Three of the landlord's particular cronies were seated there: Hiram Powlett, the miller; and Jacob Carey, the blacksmith; and old Reuben Claphurst, who had been the village clerk until his voice became so thin and uncertain a treble that the vicar was obliged to find a successor for him.

"Sit down, Mr. Gulston," the landlord said, as his guest entered. "Fine day it has been for fishing, and a nice basket you have brought in."

"It's been well enough for fishing, landlord, but I would rather put up with a lighter basket, and have a little pleasanter weather."

The sentiment evidently caused surprise, which Jacob Carey was the first to give expression to.

"You don't say, now, that you call this unpleasant weather, sir? Now I call this about as good weather as we could expect in the first week of October—warm and soft, and in every way seasonable."

"It may be all that," the guest said, as he lit his pipe; "but I own I don't care about having the rain trickling down my neck from breakfast-time to dark."

"Our fishermen about here look on a little rain as good for sport," Hiram Powlett remarked.

"No doubt it is; but I am afraid I am not much of a sportsman. I used to be fond of fishing when I was a lad, and thought I should like to try my hand at it again, but I am afraid I am not as patient as I was. I don't think sea life is a good school for that sort of thing."

"I fancied now that you might be a sailor, Mr. Gulston, though I didn't make so bold as to ask. Somehow or other there was something about your way that made me think you was bred up to the sea. I was not sure about it, for I can't recollect as ever we have had a sailor gentleman staying here for the fishing before."

"No," Mr. Gulston laughed, "I don't think we often take to the rod. Baiting a six-inch hook at the end of a sea-line for a shark is about the extent to which we usually indulge; though sometimes when we are at anchor the youngsters get the lines overboard and catch a few fish. Yes, I am a sailor, and belong, worse luck, to the flagship at Plymouth. By the way," he went on, turning to Jacob Carey, "you said last night, just as you were going out, something about the curse of Carne's Hold. That's the house up upon the hill, isn't it? What is the curse, and who said it?"

"It is nothing sir, it's only foolishness," the landlord said, hastily. "Jacob meant nothing by it."

"It ain't foolishness, John Beaumont, and you know it—and, for that, every one knows it. Foolishness indeed! Here's Reuben Claphurst can tell you if it's nonsense; he knows all about it if any one does."

"I don't think it ought to be spoken of before strangers," Hiram Powlett put in.

4

"Why not?" the smith asked, sturdily. "There isn't a man on the country-side but knows all about it. There can be no harm in telling what every one knows. Though the Carnes be your landlords, John Beaumont, as long as you pay the rent you ain't beholden to them; and as for you, Hiram, why every one knows as your great-grandfather bought the rights of the mill from them, and your folk have had it ever since. Besides, there ain't nothing but what is true in it, and if the Squire were here himself, he couldn't say no to that."

"Well, well, Jacob, there's something in what you say," the landlord said, in the tone of a man convinced against his will; but, indeed, now that he had done what he considered his duty by making a protest, he had no objection to the story being told. "Maybe you are right; and, though I should not like it said as the affairs of the Carnes were gossiped about here, still, as Mr. Gulston might, now that he has heard about the curse on the family, ask questions and hear all sorts of lies from those as don't know as much about it as we do, and especially as Reuben Claphurst here does, maybe it were better he should get the rights of the story from him."

"That being so," the sailor said, "perhaps you will give us the yarn, Mr. Claphurst, for I own that you have quite excited my curiosity as to this mysterious curse."

The old clerk, who had told the story scores of times, and rather prided himself on his telling, was nothing loth to begin.

"There is something mysterious about it, sir, as you say; so I have always maintained, and so I shall maintain. There be some as will have it as it's a curse on the family for the wickedness of old Sir Edgar. So it be, surelie, but not in the way they mean. Having been one of the officers of the church here for over forty year, and knowing the mind of the old parson, ay, and of him who was before him, I always take my stand on this. It was a curse, sure enough, but not in the way as they wants to make out. It wouldn't do to say as the curse of that Spanish woman had nowt to do with it, seeing as we has authority that curses does sometimes work themselves out; but there ain't no proof to my mind, and to the mind of the parsons as I have served under, that what they call the curse of Carne's Hold ain't a matter of misfortune, and not, as folks about here mostly think, a kind of judgment brought on them by that foreign, heathen woman. Of course, I don't expect other people to see it in that light."

This was in answer to a grunt of dissent on the part of the blacksmith.

"They ain't all had my advantages, and looks at it as their fathers and grandfathers did before them. Anyhow, there is the curse, and a bitter curse it has been for the Carnes, as you will say, sir, when you have heard my story.

"You must know that in the old times the Carnes owned all the land for miles and miles round, and Sir Marmaduke fitted out three ships at his own expense to fight under Howard and Blake against the Spaniards.

"It was in his time the first slice was cut off the property, for he went up to Court, and held his own among the best of them, and made as brave a show, they say, as any of the nobles there. His son took after him, and another slice, though not a big one, went; but it was under Sir Edgar, who came next, that bad times fell upon Carne's Hold. When the troubles began he went out for the King with every man he could raise in the country round, and they say as there was no man struck harder or heavier for King Charles than he did. He might have got off, as many another one did, if he would have given it up when it was clear the cause was lost; but whenever there was a rising anywhere he was off to join it, till at last house and land and all were confiscated, and he had to fly abroad.

"How he lived there no one exactly knows. Some said as he fought with the Spaniards against the Moors; others, and I think they were not far from the mark, that he went out to the Spanish Main, and joined a band of lawless men, and lived a pirate's life there. No one knows about that. I don't think any one, even in those days, did know anything, except that when he came back with King Charles he brought with him a Spanish wife. There were many tales about her. Some said that she had been a nun, and that he had carried her off from a convent in Spain, but the general belief was—and as there were a good many Devonshire lads who fought with the rovers on the Spanish Main, it's likely that the report was true—that she had been the wife of some Spanish Don, whose ship had been captured by the pirates.

"She was beautiful, there was no doubt about that. Such a beauty, they say, as was never seen before or since in this part. But they say that from the first she had a wild, hunted look about her, as if she had either something on her conscience, or had gone through some terrible time that had well-nigh shaken her reason. She had a baby some months old with her when she arrived, and a nurse was engaged from the village, for strangely enough, as every one thought at the time, Sir Edgar had brought back no attendant either for himself or his lady.

"No sooner was he back, and had got possession of his estates, being in that more lucky than many another who fought for the Crown, than he set to work to rebuild The Hold; living for the time in a few rooms that were patched up and made habitable in the old building. Whatever he had been doing while he was abroad, there was no doubt whatever that he had brought back with him plenty of money, for he had a host of masons and carpenters over from Plymouth, and spared no expense in having things according to his fancy. All this time he had not introduced his wife to the county. Of course, his old neighbours had called and had seen her as well as him, but he had said at once that until the new house was fit to receive visitors he did not wish to enter society, especially as his wife was entirely ignorant of the English tongue.

"Even in those days there were tales brought down to the village by the servants who had been hired from here, that Sir Edgar and his wife did not get on well together. They all agreed that she seemed unhappy, and would sit for hours brooding, seeming to have no care or love for her little boy, which set folk more against her, since it seemed natural that even a heathen woman should care for her child.

"They said, too, there were often fierce quarrels between Sir Edgar and her, but as they always talked in her tongue, no one knew what they were about. When the new house was finished they moved into it, and the ruins of the old Hold were levelled to the ground. People thought then that Sir Edgar would naturally open the house to the county, and, indeed, some entertainments were given, but whether it was that they believed the stories to his disadvantage, or that they shrank from the strange hostess, who, they say, always looked on these occasions stately and cold, and who spoke no word of their language, the country gentry gradually fell away, and Carne's Hold was left pretty much to its owners.

"Soon afterwards another child was born. There were, of course, more servants now, and more state, but Lady Carne was as much alone as ever. Whether she was determined to learn no word of English, or whether he was determined that she should not, she at any rate made no attempt to acquire her husband's language, and many said that it was a shame he did not get her a nurse and a maid who could speak her tongue; for in the days of Charles there were foreigners enough in England, and there could have been no difficulty in procuring her an attendant of her own religion and race.

"They quarrelled more than ever; but the servants were all of opinion that whatever it was about it was her doing more than his. It was her voice to be heard rising in passionate tones, while he said but little, and they all agreed he was polite and courteous in his manner to her. As for her, she would walk for hours by herself up and down the terrace, talking aloud to herself, sometimes wringing her hands and throwing her arms wildly about. At this time there began to be a report among the country round that Lady Carne was out of her mind.

"She was more alone than ever now, for Sir Edgar had taken to making journeys up to town and remaining for weeks at a time, and there was a whisper that he played heavily and unluckily. So things went on until the third child was born, and a fortnight afterwards a servant from The Hold rode

7

through the village late at night on his way for the doctor, and stopped a moment to tell the news that there was a terrible scene up at The Hold, for that during a momentary absence of the nurse, Lady Carne had stabbed her child to death, and when he came away she was raving wildly, the efforts of Sir Edgar and two of the servants hardly sufficing to hold her.

"After that no one except the inmates of The Hold ever saw its mistress again; the windows in one of the wings were barred, and two strange women were brought down from London and waited and attended on the poor lady. There were but few other servants there, for most of the girls from about here soon left, saying that the screams and cries that rang at times through the house were so terrible that they could not bear them; but, indeed, there was but small occasion for servants, for Sir Edgar was almost always away. One night one of the girls who had stayed on and had been spending the evening with her friends, went home late, and just as she reached the house she saw a white figure appear at one of the barred windows.

"In a moment the figure began crying and screaming, and to the girl's surprise many of her words were English, which she must have picked up without any one knowing it. The girl always declared that her language made her blood run cold, and was full of oaths, such as rough sailor-men use, and which, no doubt, she had picked up on ship-board; and then she poured curses upon the Carnes, her husband, the house, and her descendants. The girl was so panic-stricken that she remained silent till, in a minute or two, two other women appeared at the window, and by main force tore Lady Carne from her hold upon the bars.

"A few days afterwards she died, and it is mostly believed by her own hand, though this was never known. None of the servants, except her own attendants, ever entered the room, and the doctor never opened his lips on the subject. Doubtless he was well paid to keep silence. Anyhow, her death was not Sir Edgar's work, for he was away at the time, and only returned upon the day after her death. So, sir, that is how the curse came to be laid on Carne's Hold."

"It is a terrible story," Mr. Gulston said, when the old clerk ceased; "a terrible story. It is likely enough that the rumour was true, and that he carried her off, after capturing the vessel and killing her husband, and perhaps all the rest of them, and that she had never recovered from the shock. Was there ever any question as to whether they had been married?"

"There was a question about it—a good deal of question; and at Sir Edgar's death the next heir, who was a distant cousin, set up a claim, but the lawyer produced two documents Sir Edgar had given him. One was signed by a Jack Priest, who had, it was said, been one of the crew on board Sir Edgar's ship, certifying that he had duly and lawfully married Sir Edgar Carne and Donna Inez Martos; and there was another from a Spanish priest, belonging to a church at Porto Rico, certifying that he had married the same pair according to Catholic rites, appending a note saying that he did so although the husband was a heretic, being compelled and enforced by armed men, the town being in the possession of a force from two ships that had entered the harbour the night before. As, therefore, the pair had been married according to the rites of both Churches, and the Carnes had powerful friends at Court, the matter dropped, and the title has never since been disputed. As to Sir Edgar himself, he fortunately only lived four years after his wife's death. Had he lived much longer, there would have been no estate left to dispute. As it was, he gambled away half its wide acres."

"And how has the curse worked?" Mr. Gulston asked.

"In the natural way, sir. As I was saying before it has just been in the natural way, and whatever people may say, there is nothing, as I have heard the old parson lay down many a time, to show that that poor creature's wild ravings had aught to do with what followed. The taint in the blood of Sir Edgar's Spanish wife was naturally inherited by her descendants. Her son showed no signs of it, at least as far as I have heard, until he was married and his wife had borne him three sons. Then it burst out. He drew his sword and killed a servant who had given him some imaginary offence, and then, springing at his wife, who had thrown herself upon him, he would have strangled her had not the servants run in and torn him off her. He, too, ended his days in confinement. His sons showed no signs of the fatal taint.

"The eldest married in London, for none of the gentry of Devonshire would have given their daughter in marriage to a Carne. The others entered the army; one was killed in the Low Countries, the youngest obtained the rank of general and married and settled in London. The son of the eldest boy succeeded his father, but died a bachelor. He was a man of strange, moody habits, and many did not hesitate to say that he was as mad as his grandfather had been. He was found dead in his library, with a gun just discharged lying beside him. Whether it had exploded accidentally, or whether he had taken his life, none could say.

"His uncle, the General, came down and took possession, and for a time it seemed as if the curse of the Carnes had died out, and indeed no further tragedies have taken place in the family, but several of its members have been unlike other men, suffering from fits of morose gloom or violent passion. The father of Reginald, the present Squire, was of a bright and jovial character, and during the thirty years that he was possessor of The Hold was so popular in this part of the country that the old stories have been almost forgotten, and it is generally believed that the curse of the Carnes has died out."

"The present owner," Mr. Gulston asked; "what sort of a man is he?"

"I don't know nothing about him," the old man replied; "he is since my time."

"He is about eight-and-twenty," the landlord said. "Some folks say one thing about him, some another; I says nothing. He certainly ain't like his father, who, as he rode through the village, had a word for every one; while the young Squire looks as if he was thinking so much that he didn't even know that the village stood here. The servants of The Hold speak well of him—he seems kind and thoughtful when he is in the humour, but he is often silent and dull, and it is not many men who would be dull with Miss Margaret. She is one of the brightest and highest spirited young ladies in the county. There's no one but has a good word for her. I think the Squire studies harder than is good for him. They say he is always reading, and he doesn't hunt or shoot; and natural enough when a man shuts himself up and takes no exercise to speak of, he gets out of sorts and dull like; anyhow, there's nothing wrong about him. He's just as sane and sensible as you and I."

After waiting for two days longer and finding the wet weather continue, Mr. Gulston packed up his rods and fishing tackle and returned to Plymouth. He had learned little more about the family at The Hold, beyond the fact that Mrs. Mervyn, who inhabited a house standing half a mile further up the valley, was the aunt of Reginald and Margaret Carne, she having been a sister of the late possessor of The Hold. In her youth she had been, people said, the counterpart of her niece, and it was not therefore wonderful that Clithero Mervyn had, in spite of the advice of his friends and the reputation of the Carnes, taken what was considered in the county the hazardous step of making her his wife.

This step he had never repented, for she had, like her brother, been one of the most popular persons in that part of the county, and a universal favourite. The Mervyn estate had years before formed part of that of the Carnes, but had been separated from it in the time of Sir Edgar's grandson, who had been as fond of London life and as keen a gambler as his ancestor.

The day before he started, as he was standing at the door of the hotel, Reginald Carne and his sister had ridden past; they seemed to care no more for the weather than did the people of the village, and were laughing and talking gaily as they passed, and Charles Gulston thought to himself that he had never in all his travels seen a brighter and prettier face than that of the girl.

"Charles Gulston thought he had never seen a prettier and brighter face than that of the girl."

He thought often of the face that day, but he was not given to romance, and when he had once returned to his active duties as first lieutenant of H.M.S. *Tenebreuse*, he thought no more on the subject until three weeks later his captain handed him a note, saying:

"Here, Gulston, this is more in your line than mine. It's an invitation to a ball, for myself and some of my officers, from Mrs. Mervyn. I have met her twice at the Admiral's, and she is a very charming woman, but as her place is more than twenty miles away and a long distance from a railway station, I certainly do not feel disposed to make the journey. They are, I believe, a good county family. She has two pretty daughters and a son—a captain in the Borderers, who came into garrison about a month ago; so I have no doubt the soldiers will put in a strong appearance."

"I know the place, sir," Gulston said; "it's not far from Carnesford, the village where I was away fishing the other day, and as I heard a good deal about them I think I will take advantage of the invitation. I dare say Mr. Lucas will be glad to go too, if you can spare him."

"Certainly, any of them you like, Gulston, but don't take any of the midshipmen; you see Mrs. Mervyn has invited my officers, but as the soldiers are likely to show up in strength, I don't suppose she wants too many of us."

"We have an invitation to a ball, doctor," Lieutenant Gulston said after leaving the captain, to their ship's doctor, "for the 20th, at a Mrs. Mervyn's. The captain says we had better not go more than three. Personally I rather want to go. So Hilton of course must remain on board, and Lucas can go. I know you like these things, although you are not a dancing man. As a rule it goes sorely against my conscience taking such a useless person as one of our representatives; but upon the present occasion it does not matter, as there is a son of the house in the Borderers; and, of course, they will put in an appearance in strength."

"A man can make himself very useful at a ball, even if he doesn't dance, Gulston," the doctor said. "Young fellows always think chits of girls are the only section of the female sex who should be thought of. Who is going to look after their mothers, if there are only boys present? The conversation of a sensible man like myself is quite as great a treat to the chaperones as is the pleasure of hopping about the room with you to the girls. The conceit and selfishness of you lads surprise me more and more, there are literally no bounds to them. How far is this place off?"

"It's about twenty miles by road, or about fifteen by train, and eight or nine to drive afterwards. I happen to know about the place, as it's close to the village where I was fishing a fortnight ago."

"Then I think the chaperones will have to do without me, Gulston. I am fond of studying human nature, but if that involves staying up all night and coming back in the morning, the special section of human nature there presented must go unstudied."

"I have been thinking that one can manage without that, doctor. There is a very snug little inn where I was stopping in the village, less than a mile from the house. I propose that we go over in the afternoon, dine at the inn, and dress there. Then we can get a trap to take us up to the Mervyns', and can either walk or drive down again after it is over, or come back by train with the others, according to the hour and how we feel when the ball is over."

"Well, that alters the case, lad, and under those conditions I will be one of the party."

CHAPTER II.

MARGARET CARNE.

Ronald Mervyn was, perhaps, the most popular man in his regiment. They were proud of him as one of the most daring steeplechase riders in the service, and as a man who had greatly distinguished himself by a deed of desperate valour in India. He was far and away the best cricketer in the corps; he could sing a capital song, and was an excellent musician and the most pleasant of companions. He was always ready to do his friends a service, and many a newly-joined subaltern who got into a scrape had been helped out by Ronald Mervyn's purse. And yet at times, as even those who most liked and admired him could not but admit, Ronald Mervyn was a queer fellow. His fits were few and far between, but when they occurred he was altogether unlike himself. While they lasted, he would scarce exchange a word with a soul, but shut himself in his room, or, as soon as parade was over, mounted his horse and rode off, not to return probably until late at night.

Mervyn's moods were the subject of many a quiet joke among the young officers of the regiment. Some declared that he must have committed a murder somewhere, and was occasionally troubled in his conscience; while some insisted that Mervyn's strange behaviour was only assumed in order that he might be the more appreciated at other times. Among the two or three officers of the regiment who came from that part of the country, and knew something of the family history of the Mervyns, it was whispered that he had inherited some slight share of the curse of the Carnes. Not that he was mad in the slightest degree—no one would think of saying that of Ronald Mervyn— but he had certainly queer moods. Perhaps the knowledge that there was a taint in his blood affected him, and in course of time he began to brood over it.

When this mood was on him, soon after joining the regiment, he himself had spoken to the doctor about it.

"Do you know, doctor, I am a horrible sufferer from liver complaint?"

"You don't look it, Mervyn," the surgeon replied; "your skin is clear, and your eye is bright. You are always taking exercise, your muscles are as hard as nails. I cannot believe that there is much the matter with you."

"I assure you, doctor, that at times for two or three days I am fit for nothing. I get into such a state that I am not fit to exchange a word with a human being, and could quarrel with my best friend if he spoke to me. I have tried all sorts of medicines, but nothing seems to cure me. I suppose it's liver; I don't know what else it can be. I have spoken about it to the Major, and asked him if at any time he sees me look grumpy, to say a word to the mess, and ask them to leave me to myself; but I do wish you could give me something."

The doctor had recommended courses of various foreign waters, and had given him instructions to bathe his head when he felt it coming on; but nothing had availed. Once a year, or sometimes oftener, Ronald retired for two or three days, and then emerged as well and cheerful as before.

Once, when the attack had been particularly severe, he had again consulted the doctor, this time telling him the history of his family on his mother's side, and asking him frankly whether he thought these periodical attacks had any connection with the family taint. The doctor, who had already heard the story in confidence from one of the two men who knew it, replied:

"Well, Mervyn, I suppose that there's some sort of distant connection between the two things, but I do not think you are likely to be seriously affected. I think you can set your mind at ease on that score. A man of so vigorous a frame as you are, and leading so active and healthy a life, is certainly not a likely subject for insanity. You should dismiss the matter altogether from your mind, old fellow. Many men with a more than usual amount of animal spirits suffer at times from fits of depression. In your case, perhaps due, to some extent, to your family history, these fits of depression are more severe than usual. Probably the very circumstance that you know this history has something to do with it, for when the depression—which is, as I have said, not uncommon in the case of men with high spirits, and is, in fact, a sort of reaction—comes over you, no doubt the thought of the taint in the blood occurs to you, preys upon your mind, and deeply intensifies your depression."

"That is so, doctor. When I am in that state my one thought is that I am going mad, and I sometimes feel then as if it would be best to blow out my brains and have done with it."

"Don't let such a fancy enter your head, Mervyn," the doctor said, earnestly. "I can assure you that I think you have no chance whatever of becoming insane. The fits of depression are of course troublesome and annoying, but they are few and far apart, and at all other times you are perfectly well and healthy. You should, therefore, regard it as I do—as a sort of reaction, very common among men of your sanguine temperament, and due in a very slight degree to the malady formerly existent in your family. I have watched you closely since you came to the regiment, and, believe me, that I do not say it solely to reassure you when I affirm that it is my full belief and conviction that you are as sane as other men, and it is likely that as you get on in life these fits of depression will altogether disappear. You see both your mother and uncle were perfectly free from any suspicion of a taint, and it is more than probable that it has altogether died out. At any rate the chances are slight indeed of its reappearing in your case."

"Thank you, doctor; you can imagine what a relief your words are to me. I don't worry about it at other times, and indeed feel so thoroughly well, that I could laugh at the idea were it mooted; but during these moods of mine it has tried me horribly. If you don't mind, I will get you to write your opinion down, so that next time the fit seizes me I can read it over, and assure myself that my apprehensions are unfounded."

Certainly no one would associate the idea of insanity with Ronald Mervyn, as upon the day before the ball at his mother's house he sat on the edge of the ante-room table, and laughed and talked with a group of five young officers gathered round him.

"Mind, you fellows must catch the seven o'clock train, or else you will be too late. There will be eight miles to drive; I will have a trap there to meet you, and you won't be there long before the others begin to arrive. We are not fashionable in our part of the county. We shall have enough partners for you to begin to dance by half-past nine, and I can promise you as pretty partners as you can find in any ball-room in England. When you have been quartered here a bit longer you will be ready to admit the truth of the general opinion, that, in point of pretty women, Devonshire can hold its own against any county in England. No, there is no fear whatever of your coming in too great strength. Of course, in Plymouth here, one can overdo the thing, but when one gets beyond the beat of the garrison, men are at a premium. I saw my mother's list; if it had not been for the regiment the female element would have predominated terribly. The army and navy, India and the colonies, to say nothing of all-devouring London, are the scourges of the country; the younger sons take wings to themselves and fly, and the spinsters are left lamenting."

"I think there is more push and go among younger sons than there is in the elders," one of the young officers said.

"They have not got the same responsibilities," Ronald laughed. "It is easy to see you are a younger son, Charley; there's a jaunty air about your forage cap and a swagger in your walk, that would tell any observant person that you are free from all responsibilities, and could, as the Latin grammar says, sing before a robber."

There was a general laugh, for Charley Mansfield was notoriously in a general state of impecuniosity. He, himself, joined merrily in the laugh.

"I can certainly say," he replied, "'He who steals my purse steals trash;' but I don't think he would get even that without a tussle. Still, what I said is true, I think. I know my elder brother is a fearfully stately personage, who, on the strength of two years' difference of age, and his heirship, takes upon himself periodically to inflict ponderous words of wisdom upon me. I think a lot of them are like that; but after all, as I tell him, it's the younger sons who have made England what it is. We won her battles and furnished her colonies, and have done pretty nearly everything that has been done; while the elder sons have only turned into respectable landowners and prosy magistrates."

"Very well, Charley, the sentiments do you honour," another laughed; "but there, the assembly is sounding. Waiter, bring me a glass of sherry; your sentiments have so impressed me, Charley, that I intend to drink solemnly to the success of second sons."

"You are not on duty, are you, Mervyn?"

"No, I am starting in half an hour to get home. I shall be wanted to aid in the final preparations. Well, I shall see you all to morrow night. Don't forget the seven o'clock train. I expect we shall keep it up till between three and four. Then you can smoke a cigar, and at five the carriages will be ready to take you to the station to catch the first train back, and you will be here in time for a tub and a change before early parade."

The ball at the Mervyns' was a brilliant one. The house was large, and as Mr. Mervyn had died four years before, and Ronald had since that time been absent on foreign service, it was a long time since an entertainment on a large scale had been given there to the county. A little to the disappointment of many of the young ladies in the neighbourhood, the military and naval officers did not come in uniform. There were two or three girls staying in the house, and one of them in the course of the evening, when she was dancing with Ronald, said:

"We all consider you have taken us in, Captain Mervyn. We made sure that you would all be in uniform. Of course those who live near Plymouth are accustomed to it, but in these parts the red coats are rather a novelty, and we feel we have been defrauded."

"We never go to balls, Miss Blackmoor, in uniform, except when they are regular naval or military balls, either given by our own regiment or some of the regiments in garrison, or by the navy. That is generally the rule though perhaps in some regiments it is not so strictly adhered to as with us."

"Then I consider that it is a fraud upon the public, Captain Mervyn. Gentlemen's dress is so dingy and monotonous that I consider it distinctly the duty of soldiers to give us a little light and colour when they get the chance."

"Very well, Miss Blackmoor, I will bear it in mind; and next time my mother gives a ball, the regiment, if it is within reach, shall come in uniform. By the way, do you know who is the man my cousin is dancing with? There are lots of faces I don't know here; being seven or eight years away makes a difference in a quiet country place."

"That is Mr. Gulston; he is first-lieutenant of the flagship at Plymouth. I know it because he was introduced to me early in the evening, and we danced together, and a capital dancer he is, too."

"He is an uncommonly good-looking fellow," Ronald said.

Margaret Carne seemed to think so, too, as she danced with him two or three times in the course of the evening, and went down to supper on his arm.

Ronald having, as the son of the house, to divide his attentions as much as possible, did not dance with his cousin. Lieutenant Gulston had been accompanied by the third-lieutenant, and by the doctor, who never missed an opportunity of going to a ball because, as he said, it gave him an opportunity of studying character.

"You see," he would argue, "on board a ship one gets only the one side of human nature. Sailors may differ a bit one from another, but they can all be divided into two or three classes—the steady honest fellow who tries to do his work well; the reckless fellow who is ready to do his work, but is up to every sort of mischief and devilment; and the lazy, loafing fellow who neglects his duty whenever he possibly can, and is always shamming sick in order to get off it. Some day or other I shall settle on shore and practise there, and I want to learn something about the people I shall have to deal with; besides, there's nothing more amusing than looking on at a ball when you have no idea of dancing yourself. It's astonishing what a lot of human nature you see if you do but keep your wits about you."

In the course of the evening he came up to the first-lieutenant.

"Who is that man you have just been talking to, Gulston? I have been watching him for some time. He has not been dancing, but has been standing in corners looking on."

"He is Mr. Carne, doctor; a cousin, or rather a nephew, of our hostess."

"Is he the brother of that pretty girl you have been dancing with?"

The lieutenant nodded.

"Then I am sorry for her," the surgeon said, bluntly.

"Sorry! What for?"

The surgeon answered by another question.

"Do you know anything about the family, Gulston?"

"I have heard something about them. Why?"

"Never mind now," the surgeon said. "I will tell you in the morning; it's hardly a question to discuss here," and he turned away before the lieutenant could ask further.

It was four o'clock before the dancing ceased and the last carriage rolled away. Then the military and naval men, and two or three visitors from Plymouth, gathered in the library, and smoked and talked for an hour, and were then conveyed to the station to catch the early train. The next day, as they were walking up and down the quarter-deck, the first-lieutenant said: "By the way, doctor, what was it you were going to say last night about the Carnes? You said you were sorry for Miss Carne, and asked me if I knew anything about the history of the family."

"Yes, that was it, Gulston; it wasn't the sort of thing to talk about there, especially as I understand the Mervyns are connections of the Carnes. The question I was going to ask you was this: You know their family history; is there any insanity in it?"

The lieutenant stopped suddenly in his walk with an exclamation of surprise and pain.

"What do you mean, Mackenzie? Why do you ask such a question?"

"You have not answered mine. Is there insanity in the blood?"

"There has been," the lieutenant said, reluctantly.

"I felt sure of it. I think you have heard me say my father made a special study of madness; and when I was studying for my profession I have often accompanied him to lunatic asylums, and I devoted a great deal of time to the subject, intending to make it my special branch also. Then the rambling fit seized me and I entered the service; but I have never missed following the subject up whenever I have had an opportunity. I have therefore visited asylums for lunatics whenever such existed, at every port which we have put into since I have been in the service.

"When my eye first fell upon Mr. Carne he was standing behind several other people, watching the dancing, and the expression of his face struck me as soon as my eye fell upon him. I watched him closely all through the evening. He did not dance, and rarely spoke to any one, unless addressed. I watched his face and his hands—hands are, I can tell you, almost as expressive as faces—and I have not the smallest hesitation in saying that the man is mad. It is possible, but not probable, that at ordinary times he may show no signs of it;

18

but at times, and last night was one of those times, the man is mad; nay, more, I should be inclined to think that his madness is of a dangerous type.

"Now that you tell me it is hereditary, I am so far confirmed in my opinion that I should not hesitate, if called upon to do so, to sign a certificate to the effect that, in my opinion, he was so far insane as to need the most careful watching, if not absolute confinement."

The colour had faded from the lieutenant's face as the doctor spoke.

"I am awfully sorry," he said, in a low tone, "and I trust to God, doctor, that you are mistaken. I cannot but think that you are. I was introduced to him by his sister, and he was most civil and polite, indeed more than civil, for he asked me if I was fond of shooting, and when I said that I was extremely so, he invited me over to his place. He said he did not shoot himself, but that next week his cousin Mervyn and one or two others were coming to him to have two or three days' pheasant shooting, and he would be glad if I would join the party; and, as you may suppose, I gladly accepted the invitation."

"Well," the doctor said, drily, "so far as he is concerned, there is no danger in your doing so, if, as you say, he doesn't shoot. If he did, I should advise you to stay away; and in any case, if you will take the advice which I offer, you won't go. You will send an excuse."

The lieutenant made no answer for a minute or two, but paced the room in silence.

"I won't pretend to misunderstand you, Mackenzie. You mean there's no danger with him, but you think there may be from her. That's what you mean, isn't it?"

The doctor nodded.

"I saw you were taken with her, Gulston; that is why I have spoken to you about her brother."

"You don't think—confound it, man—you can't think," the lieutenant said, angrily, "that there is anything the matter with her?"

"No, I don't think so," the doctor said, gravely. "No, I should say certainly not; but you know in these cases where it is in the blood it sometimes lies dormant for a generation and then breaks out again. I asked somebody casually last night about their father, and he said that he was a capital fellow and most popular in the country; so if it is in the blood it passed over him, and is showing itself again in the son. It may pass over the daughter and reappear in her children. You never know, you see. Do you mind telling me what you know about the family?"

19

"Not now; not at present. I will at some other time. You have given me a shock, and I must think it over."

The doctor nodded, and commenced to talk about other matters. A minute or two later the lieutenant made some excuse, and turned into the cabin. Dr. Mackenzie shook his head.

"The lad is hard hit," he said, "and I am sorry for him. I hope my warning comes in time; it will do if he isn't a fool, but all young men are fools where women are concerned. I will say for him that he has more sense than most, but I would give a good deal if this had not happened."

Lieutenant Gulston was, indeed, hard hit; he had been much struck with the momentary glance he had obtained of Margaret Carne as he stood on the steps of the "Carne Arms," and the effect had been greatly heightened on the previous day. Lieutenant Gulston had, since the days when he was a middy, indulged in many a flirtation, but he had never before felt serious. He had often laughed at the impressibility of some of his comrades, and had scoffed at the idea of love at first sight, but now that he began to think matters seriously over, the pain the doctor's remarks had given him opened his eyes to the fact that it was a good deal more than a passing fancy.

Thinking it over in every light, he acknowledged the prudent course would be to send some excuse to her brother, with an expression of regret that he found that a matter of duty would prevent his coming over, as he had promised, for the shooting. Then he told himself that after all the doctor might be mistaken, and that it would be only right that he should judge for himself. If there was anything in it, of course he should go no more to The Hold, and no harm would be done. Margaret was certainly very charming; she was more than charming, she was the most lovable woman he had ever met. Still, of course, if there was any chance of her inheriting this dreadful thing, he would see her no more. After all, no more harm could be done in a couple of days than had been done already, and he was not such a fool but that he could draw back in time. And so after changing his mind half-a-dozen times, he resolved to go over for the shooting.

"Ruth, I want to speak to you seriously," Margaret Carne said to her maid two days after the ball. Ruth Powlett was the miller's daughter, and the village gossips had been greatly surprised when, a year before, they heard that she was going up to The Hold to be Miss Carne's own maid; for although the old mill was a small one, and did no more than a local business, Hiram was accounted to have laid by a snug penny, and as Ruth was his only child, she was generally regarded as the richest heiress in Carnesford. That Hiram should then let her go out into service, even as maid to Miss Carne at The Hold, struck every one with surprise.

20

It was generally assumed that the step had been taken because Hiram Powlett wanted peace in the house. He had, after the death of his first wife, Ruth's mother, married again, and the general verdict was that he had made a mistake. In the first place, Hiram was a staunch Churchman, and one of the churchwardens at Carnesford; but his wife, who was a Dareport woman—and that alone was in the opinion of Carnesford greatly against her—was a Dissenter, and attended the little chapel at Dareport, and entertained the strongest views as to the prospects and chances of her neighbours in a future state; and in the second place, perhaps in consequence of their religious opinions, she was generally on bad terms with all her neighbours.

But when Hiram married her she had a good figure, the lines of her face had not hardened as they afterwards did, and he had persuaded himself that she would make an excellent mother for Ruth. Indeed, she had not been intentionally unkind, and although she had brought her up strictly, she believed that she had thoroughly done her duty; lamenting only that her efforts had been thwarted by the obstinacy and perverseness of her husband in insisting that the little maid should trot to church by his side, instead of going with her to the chapel at Dareport.

Ruth had grown up a quiet and somewhat serious girl; she had blossomed out into prettiness in the old mill, and folks in the village were divided as to whether she or Lucy Carey, the smith's daughter, was the prettiest girl in Carnesford. Not that there was any other matter in comparison between them, for Lucy was somewhat gay and flirty, and had a dozen avowed admirers; while Ruth had from her childhood made no secret of her preference for George Forester, the son of the little farmer whose land came down to the Dare just where Hiram Powlett's mill stood.

He was some five years older than she was, and had fished her out of the mill-stream when she fell into it, when she was eight years old. From that time he had been her hero. She had been content to follow him about like a dog, to sit by his side for hours while he fished in the deep pool above the mill, under the shadow of the trees, quite content with an occasional word or notice. She took his part heartily when her stepmother denounced him as the idlest and most impertinent boy in the parish; and when, soon after she was fifteen, he one day mentioned that, as a matter of course, she would some day be his wife, she accepted it as a thing of which she had never entertained any doubt whatever.

But Hiram now took the alarm, and one day told her that she was to give up consorting with young Forester.

"You are no longer a child, Ruth, and if you go on meeting young Forester down at the pool, people will be beginning to talk. Of course I know that you are a good girl, and would never for a moment think of taking up with George Forester. Every one knows what sort of young fellow he is; he never does a day's work on the farm, and he is in and out of the 'Carne Arms' at all hours. He associates with the worst lot in the village, and it was only the other day that when the parson tried to speak to him seriously, he answered him in a way that was enough to make one's hair stand on end."

Ruth obeyed her father, and was no more seen about with George Forester; but she believed no tale to his disadvantage, and when at times she met with him accidentally, she told him frankly enough that though her father didn't like her going about with him, she loved him and meant to love him always, whatever they might say. Upon all other points her father's will was law to her, but upon this she was firm; and two years afterwards, when some words young Forester had spoken at a public-house about his daughter came to his ears, Hiram renewed the subject to her, she answered staunchly that unless he gave his consent she would not marry George Forester, but that nothing would make her give him up or go back from her word.

For once Hiram Powlett and his wife were thoroughly in accord. The former seldom spoke upon the subject, but the latter was not so reticent, and every misdeed of young Forester was severely commented upon by her in Ruth's hearing. Ruth seldom answered, but her father saw that she suffered, and more than once remonstrated with his wife on what he called her cruelty, but found that as usual Hesba was not to be turned from her course.

"No, Hiram Powlett," she said, shutting her lips tightly together; "I must do my duty whether it pleases you or not, and it is my duty to see that Ruth does not throw away her happiness in this world and the next by her headstrong conduct. She does not belong to the fold, but in other respects I will do her credit to say she is a good girl and does her duty as well as can be expected, considering the dulness of the light she has within her; but if she were to marry this reprobate she would be lost body and soul; and whatever you may think of the matter, Hiram Powlett, I will not refrain from trying to open her eyes."

"I am quite as determined as you are, Hesba, that the child shall not marry this young rascal, but I don't think it does any good to be always nagging at her. Women are queer creatures; the more you want them to go one way the more they will go the other."

But though Hiram Powlett did not say much, he worried greatly. Ruth had always been quiet, but she was quieter than ever now, and her cheeks gradually lost their roses, and she looked pale and thin. At last Hiram determined that if he could not obtain peace for her at home he would elsewhere, and hearing that Miss Carne's maid was going to be married he decided to try to get Ruth the place. She would be free from Hesba's tongue there, and would have other things to think about besides her lover, and would moreover have but few opportunities of seeing him. He was shy of approaching the subject to her, and was surprised and pleased to find that when he did, instead of opposing it as he had expected, she almost eagerly embraced the proposal.

In fact, Ruth's pale cheeks and changed appearance were not due, as her father supposed, to unhappiness at her stepmother's talk against George Forester; but because in spite of herself she began to feel that her accusations were not without foundation. Little by little she learnt, from chance words dropped by others, that the light in which her father held George Forester was that generally entertained in the village. She knew that he often quarrelled with his father, and that after one of these altercations he had gone off to Plymouth and enlisted, only to be bought out a few days afterwards.

She knew that he drank, and had taken part in several serious frays that had arisen at the little beershop in the village; and hard as she fought against the conviction, it was steadily making its way, that her lover was wholly unworthy of her. And yet, in spite of his faults, she loved him. Whatever he was with others, he was gentle and pleasant with her, and she felt that were she to give him up his last chance would be gone. So she was glad to get away from the village for a time, and to the surprise of her father, and the furious anger of George Forester, she applied for and obtained the post of Margaret Carne's maid.

She had few opportunities of seeing George Forester now; but what she heard when she went down to the village on Sundays was not encouraging. He drank harder than before, and spent much of his time down at Dareport, and, as some said, was connected with a rough lot there who were fonder of poaching than of fishing.

Margaret Carne was aware of what she considered Ruth's infatuation. She kept herself well informed of the affairs of the village—the greater portion of which belonged to her and her brother—and she learnt from the clergyman, whose right hand she was in the choir and schools, a good deal of the village gossip. She had never spoken to Ruth on the subject during the nine months she had been with her, but now she felt she was bound to do so.

"What is it, Miss Margaret?" Ruth said, quietly, in answer to her remark.

"I don't want to vex you, and you will say it is no business of mine, but I think it is, for you know I like you very much, besides, your belonging to Carnesford. Of course I have heard—every one has heard, you know—about your engagement to young Forester. Now a very painful thing has happened.

On the night of the dance our gamekeepers came across a party of poachers in the woods, as of course you have heard, and had a fight with them, and one of the keepers is so badly hurt that they don't think he will live. He has sworn that the man who stabbed him was George Forester, and my brother, as a magistrate, has just signed a warrant for his arrest.

"Now, Ruth, surely this man is not worthy of you. He bears, I hear, on all sides a very bad character, and I think you will be more than risking your happiness with such a man; I think for your own sake it would be better to give him up. My brother is very incensed against him; he has been out with the other keepers to the place where this fray occurred and he says it was a most cowardly business, for the poachers were eight to three, and he seems to have no doubt whatever that Forester was one of the party, and that they will be able to prove it. I do think, Ruth, you ought to give him up altogether. I am not talking to you as a mistress, you know, but as a friend."

"I think you are right, Miss Margaret," the girl said, in a low voice. "I have been thinking it over in every way. At first I didn't think what they said was true, and then I thought that perhaps I might be able to keep him right, and that if I were to give him up there would be no chance for him. I have tried very hard to see what was my duty, but I think now that I see it, and that I must break off with him. But oh! it is so hard," she added, with a quiver in her voice, "for though I know that I oughtn't to love him, I can't help it."

"I can quite understand that, Ruth," Margaret Carne agreed. "I know if I loved any one I should not give him up merely because everybody spoke ill of him. But, you see, it is different now. It is not merely a suspicion, it is almost absolute proof; and besides, you must know that he spends most of his time in the public-house, and that he never would make you a good husband."

"I have known that a long time," Ruth said, quietly; "but I have hoped always that he might change if I married him. I am afraid I can't hope any longer, and I have been thinking for some time that I should have to give him up. I will tell him so now, if I have an opportunity."

"I don't suppose you will, for my brother says he has not been home since the affair in the wood. If he has, he went away again at once. I expect he has made either for Plymouth or London, for he must know that the police would be after him for his share in this business. I am very sorry for it, Ruth, but I do think you will be happier when you have once made up your mind to break with him. No good could possibly come of your sacrificing yourself."

Ruth said no more on the subject, but went about her work as quietly and orderly as usual, and Margaret Carne was surprised to see how bravely she held up, for she knew that she must be suffering greatly.

24

CHAPTER III.

TWO QUARRELS.

Three days later the shooting party assembled. Several gentlemen came to stay at the house, while Ronald Mervyn and his party, of course, put up at Mervyn Hall. The shooting was very successful, and the party were well pleased with their visit. Reginald Carne was quiet and courteous to his guests, generally accompanying them through the day, though he did not himself carry a gun. After the first day's shooting there was a dinner party at Mervyn Hall, and the following evening there was one at The Hold.

Lieutenant Gulston enjoyed himself more than any one else, though he was one of the least successful of the sportsmen, missing easy shots in a most unaccountable manner, and seeming to take but moderate interest in the shooting. He had, very shortly after arriving at the house, come to the conclusion that the doctor was altogether mistaken, and that Reginald Carne showed no signs whatever of being in any way different from other men. "The doctor is so accustomed to us sailors," he said to himself, "that if a man is quiet and studious he begins to fancy directly there must be something queer about him. That is always the way with doctors who make madness a special study. They suspect every one they come across of being out of their mind. I shouldn't be at all surprised if he doesn't fancy I am cracked myself. The idea is perfectly absurd. I watched Carne closely at dinner, and no one could have been more pleasant and gentlemanly than he was. I expect Mackenzie must have heard a word let drop about this old story, and of course if he did he would set down Carne at once as being insane. Well, thank goodness, that's off my mind; it's been worrying me horribly for the last few days. I have been a fool to trouble myself so about Mackenzie's croakings, but now I will not think anything more about it."

On the following Sunday, as Ruth Powlett was returning from church in the morning, and was passing through the little wood that lay between Carnesford and The Hold, there was a rustle among the trees, and George Forester sprang out suddenly.

"I have been waiting since daybreak to see you, Ruth, but as you came with that old housekeeper I could not speak to you. I have been in Plymouth for the last week. I hear that they are after me for that skirmish with the keepers, so I am going away for a bit, but I couldn't go till I said good-bye to you first, and heard you promise that you would always be faithful to me."

"I will say good-bye, George, and my thoughts and prayers will always be with you, but I cannot promise to be faithful—not in the way you mean."

"What do you mean, Ruth?" he asked, angrily. "Do you mean that after all these years you are going to throw me off?"

Ruth was about to reply, when there was a slight rustling in the bushes.

"There is some one in the path in the wood."

George Forester listened for a moment.

"It's only a rabbit," he said, impatiently. "Never mind that now, but answer my question. Do you dare to tell me that you are going to throw me over?"

"I am not going to throw you off, George," she said, quietly; "but I am going to give you up. I have tried, oh! how hard I have tried, to believe that you would be better some day, but I can't hope so any longer. You have promised again and again that you would give up drinking, but you are always breaking your promise, and now I find that in spite of all I've said, you still hold with those bad men at Dareport, and that you have taken to poaching, and now they are in search of you for being one of those concerned in desperately wounding John Morton. No, George, I have for years withstood even my father. I have loved you in spite of his reproaches and entreaties, but I feel now that instead of your making me happy I should be utterly miserable if I married you, and I have made a promise to Miss Carne that I would give you up."

"Oh, she has been meddling, has she?" George Forester said with a terrible imprecation; "I will have revenge on her, I swear I will. So it's she who has done the mischief, and made you false to all you promised. Curse you! with your smooth face, and your church-going ways, and your canting lies. You think, now they are hunting me away, you can take up with some one else; but you shan't, I swear, though I swing for it."

And he grasped her suddenly by the throat; but at this moment there was a sound of voices in the road behind them, and dashing Ruth to the ground with a force that stunned her, he sprang into the woods. A minute later the stablemen at The Hold came along the road and found Ruth still lying on the ground.

"He grasped her suddenly by the throat."

After a minute's consultation they determined to carry her down to her father's house, as they had no idea what was the best course to pursue to bring her round. Two of them, therefore, lifted and carried her down, while the other hurried on to prepare the miller for their arrival.

"Master Powlett," he said as he entered, "your girl has hurt herself; I expect she slipped on a stone somehow, going up the hill, and came down heavy; anyhow we found her lying there insensible, and my two mates are bringing her down. We saw her two or three hundred yards ahead of us as we came out of the churchyard, so she could not have laid there above a minute or so when we came up."

Ruth was brought in. Mrs. Powlett had not yet returned from Dareport, but a neighbour was soon fetched in by one of the men while another went for the doctor, and in a few minutes Ruth opened her eyes.

"Don't talk, dear," her father said, "lie quiet for a few minutes and you will soon be better; you slipped down in the road, you know, and gave yourself a shake, but it will be all right now."

Ruth closed her eyes again and lay quiet for a short time, then she looked up again and tried to sit up.

"I am better now, father."

"Thank God for that, Ruth. It gave me a turn when I saw you carried in here, I can tell you; but lie still a little time longer, the doctor will be here in a few minutes."

"I don't want him, father."

"Yes, you do, my dear, and anyhow as he has been sent for he must come and see you; you need not trouble about going up to The Hold, it was three of the men there that found you and brought you down; I will send a note by them to Miss Carne telling her you had a bad fall, and that we will keep you here until to-morrow morning. I am sure you will not be fit to walk up that hill again to-day. Anyhow we will wait until the doctor comes and hear what he says."

Ten minutes later the doctor arrived, and after hearing Hiram's account of what had happened, felt Ruth's pulse and then examined her head.

"Ah, here is where you fell," he said; "a good deal of swelling, and it has cut the skin. However, a little bathing with warm water is all that is wanted. There, now, stand up if you can and walk a step or two, and tell me if you feel any pain anywhere else.

"Ah, nowhere except in the shoulder. Move your arm. Ah, that is all right, nothing broken. You will find you are bruised a good deal, I have no doubt. Well, you must keep on the sofa all day, and not do any talking. You have had a severe shake, that's evident, and must take care of yourself for a day or two. You have lost all your colour, and your pulse is unsteady and your heart beating anyhow. You must keep her quite quiet, Hiram. If I were you I would get her up to bed. Of course you must not let her talk, and I don't want any talking going on around her, you understand?"

Hiram did understand, and before Mrs. Powlett returned from chapel, Ruth, with the assistance of the woman who had come in, was in bed.

"I look upon it as a judgment," Mrs. Powlett said upon her return, when she heard the particulars. "If she had been with me at chapel this never would have happened. It's a message to her that no good can come of her sitting under that blind guide, the parson. I hope it will open her eyes, and that she will be led to join the fold."

"I don't think it is likely, Hesba," Hiram said, quietly, "and you will find it hard to persuade her that loose stone I suppose she trod on was dropped special into the road to trip her up in coming from church. Anyhow you can't talk about it to-day; the doctor's orders are that she is to be kept perfectly quiet, that she is not to talk herself, and that there's to be no talking in the room. He says she can have a cup of tea if she can take it, but I doubt at present whether she can take even that; the poor child looks as if she could scarce open her eyes for anything, and no wonder, for the doctor says she must have fallen tremendous heavy."

Mrs. Powlett made the tea and took it upstairs. Any ideas she may have had of improving the occasion, in spite of the doctor's injunctions, vanished when she saw Ruth's white face on the pillow. Noiselessly she placed the little table close to the bed and put the cup upon it. Ruth opened her eyes as she did so.

"Here is some tea, dearie," Hesba said, softly. "I will put it down here, and you can drink it when you feel inclined." Ruth murmured "Thank you," and Hesba stooped over her and kissed her cheek more softly than she had ever done before, and then went quietly out of the room again.

"She looks worse than I thought for, Hiram," she said, as she proceeded to help the little servant they kept to lay the cloth for dinner. "I doubt she's more hurt than the doctor thinks. I could see there were tears on her cheek, and Ruth was never one to cry, not when she was hurt ever so much. Of course, it may be because she is low and weak; still I tell you that I don't like it. Is the doctor coming again?"

"Yes; he said he would look in again this evening."

"I don't like it," Hesba repeated, "and after dinner I will put on my bonnet and go down to the doctor myself and hear what he has got to say about her. Perhaps he will tell me more than he would you; he knows what poor creatures men are. They just get frighted out of what wits they've got, if you let on any one's bad; but I will get it out of him. It frets me to think I wasn't here when she was brought in, instead of having strangers messing about her."

It came into Hiram's mind to retort that her being away at that moment was a special warning against her going to Dareport; but the low, troubled voice in which she spoke, and the furtive passing of her hand across her cheek to brush away a tear, effectually silenced him. It was all so unusual in the case of Hesba, whom, indeed, he had never seen so soft and womanly since the first day she had crossed the threshold of the house, that he was at once touched and alarmed.

"I hope you are wrong, wife; I hope you are wrong," he said, putting his hand on her shoulder. "I don't think the doctor thought badly of it, but he seemed puzzled like, I thought; but if there's trouble, Hesba, we will bear it together, you and I; it's sent for good, we both know that. We goes the same way, you know, wife, if we don't go by the same road."

The woman made no answer, for at that moment the girl appeared with the dinner. Hesba ate but a few mouthfuls, and then saying sharply that she had no appetite, rose from the table, put on her bonnet and shawl, and, without a word, walked out.

She was away longer than Hiram expected, and in the meantime he had to answer the questions of many of the neighbours, who, having heard from the woman who had been called in of Ruth's accident, came to learn the particulars. When Hesba returned she brought a bundle with her.

"The doctor's coming in an hour," she said. "I didn't get much out of him, except he said it had been a shock to her system, and he was afraid that there might be slight concussion of the brain. He said if that was so we should want some ice to put to her head, and I have been up to The Hold and seen Miss Carne. I had heard Ruth say they always have ice up there, and she has given me some. She was just coming down to inquire about Ruth, but of course I told her she couldn't talk to nobody. That was the doctor's orders. Has she moved since I have been away?"

Hiram shook his head. "I have been up twice, but she was just lying with her eyes closed."

"Well, I will go and sit up there," Hesba said. "Tell that girl if she makes any noise, out of the house she goes; and the best thing you can do is to take your pipe and sit in that arbour outside, or walk up and down if you can't keep yourself warm; and don't let any one come knocking at the door and worriting her. It will be worse for them if I has to come down."

Hiram Powlett obeyed his wife's parting injunction and kept on guard all the afternoon, being absent from his usual place in church for the first time for years. In the evening there was nothing for him to do in the house, and his wife being upstairs, he followed his usual custom of dropping for half an hour into the snuggery of the "Carne Arms."

"Yes, it's true," he said in answer to the questions of his cronies, "Ruth has had a bad fall, and the doctor this afternoon says as she has got a slight concussion of the brain. He said he hoped she would get over it, but he looked serious-like when he came downstairs. It's a bad affair, I expect. But she is in God's hands, and a better girl never stepped, though I says it." There was a murmur of regret and consolation among the three smokers, but they saw that Hiram was too upset for many words, and the conversation turned into other channels for a time, Hiram taking no share in it but smoking silently.

"It's a rum thing," he said, presently, during a pause in the conversation, "that a man don't know really about a woman's nature, not when he has lived with her for years and years. Now there's my wife Hesba, who has got a tongue as sharp as any one in this village." A momentary smile passed round the circle, for the sharpness of Hesba Powlett's tongue was notorious. "It scarce seemed to me, neighbours, as she had got a soft side to her or that she cared more for Ruth than she did for the house-dog. She always did her duty by her, I will say that for her; and a tidier woman and a better housewife there ain't in the country round. But duty is one thing and love is another. Now you would hardly believe it, but I do think that Hesba feels this business as much as I do. You wouldn't have knowed her; she goes about the house with her shoes off as quiet as a mouse, and she speaks that soft and gentle you wouldn't know it was her. Women's queer creatures anyway."

There was a chorus of assent to the proposition, and, in fact, the discovery that Hesba Powlett had a soft side to her nature was astonishing indeed.

For three days Ruth Powlett lay unconscious, and then quiet and good nursing, and the ice on her head, had their effect; and one evening the doctor, on visiting her, said that he thought a change had taken place, and that she was now sleeping naturally. The next morning there was consciousness in her eyes when she opened them, and she looked in surprise at the room darkened by a curtain pinned across the window, and at Hesba, sitting by her bedside, with a huge nightcap on her head.

"What is it, mother, what has happened?"

"You have been ill, Ruth, but thank God you are better now. Don't talk, dear, and don't worry. I have got some beef-tea warming by the fire; the doctor said you were to try and drink a cup when you woke, and then to go off to sleep again."

Ruth looked with a feeble surprise after Hesba as she left the room, missing the sharp, decisive foot-tread. In a minute she returned as noiselessly as she had gone.

"Can you hold the cup yourself, Ruth, or shall I feed you?"

Ruth put out her hand, but it was too weak to hold the cup. She was able, however, slightly to raise her head, and Hesba held the cup to her lips.

"What have you done to your feet, mother?" she asked, as she finished the broth.

"I have left my shoes downstairs, Ruth; the doctor said you were to be kept quiet. Now try to go to sleep, that's a dear."

She stooped and kissed the girl affectionately, and Ruth, to her surprise, felt a tear drop on her cheek. She was wondering over this strange circumstance when she again fell asleep.

In a few days she was about the house again, but she was silent and grave, and did not gain strength as fast as the doctor had hoped for. However, in three weeks' time she was well enough to return to The Hold. Hiram had strongly remonstrated against her doing so, but she seemed to set her mind upon it, urging that she would be better for having something to think about and do than in remaining idle at home; and as the doctor was also of opinion that the change would be rather likely to benefit than to do her harm, Hiram gave way.

The day before she left she said to her father:

"Do you know whether George Forester has been caught, or whether he has got away?"

"He has not been caught, Ruth, but I don't think he has gone away; there is a talk in the village that he has been hiding down at Dareport, and the constable has gone over there several times, but he can't find signs of him. I think he must be mad to stay so near when he knows he is wanted. I can't think what is keeping him."

"I have made up my mind, father, to give him up. You have been right, and I know now he would not make me a good husband; but please don't say anything against him, it is hard enough as it is."

Hiram kissed his daughter.

"Thank God for that news, Ruth. I hoped after that poaching business you would see it in that light, and that he wasn't fit for a mate for one like you. Your mother will be glad, child. She ain't like the same woman as she was, is she?"

"No, indeed, father, I do not seem to know her."

"I don't know as I was ever so knocked over in my life as I was yesterday, Ruth, when your mother came downstairs in her bonnet and shawl, and said, 'I am going to church with you, Hiram.' I didn't open my lips until we were half-way, and then she said as how it had been borne in on her as how her not being here when you was brought in was a judgment on her for being away at Dareport instead of being at church with us; and she said more than that, as how, now she thought over it, she saw as she hadn't done right by me and you all these years, and hoped to make a better wife what time she was left to us. I wasn't sure at church time as it wasn't a dream to see her sitting there beside me, and joining in the hymns, listening attentive to the parson as she has always been running down. She said on the way home she felt just as she did when she was a girl, five-and-twenty years ago, and used to come over here to church, afore she took up with the Methodies."

Ruth kissed her father.

"Then my fall has done good after all," she said. "It makes me happy to know it."

"I shall be happy when I see you quite yourself again, Ruth. Come back to us soon, dear."

"I will, father; in the spring I will come home again for good, I promise you," and so Ruth returned for a time to The Hold.

"I am glad you are back again, Ruth," Miss Carne, who had been down several times to see her, said. "I told you not to hurry yourself, and I would have done without you for another month, but you know I am really very glad to have you back again. Mary managed my hair very well, but I could not talk to her as I do to you."

Ruth had not been many hours in the house before she learnt from her fellow-servants that Mr. Gulston had been over two or three times since the shooting party, and that the servants in general had an opinion that he came over to see Miss Carne.

"It's easy to see that with half an eye," one of the girls said, "and I think Miss Margaret likes him too, and no wonder, for a properer-looking man is not to be seen; but I always thought she would have married her cousin. Every one has thought so for years."

"It's much better she should take the sailor gentleman," one of the elder women said. "I am not saying anything against Mr. Ronald, who is as nice a young gentleman as one would want to see, but he is her cousin, and I don't hold to marriages among cousins anyhow, and especially in a family like ours."

"I think it is better for us not to talk about it at all," Ruth said, quietly; "I don't think it right and proper, and it will be quite time enough to talk about Miss Margaret's affairs when we know she is engaged."

The others were silent for a minute after Ruth's remark, and then the under-housemaid, who had been an old playmate of Ruth's, said:

"You never have ideas like other people, Ruth Powlett. It is a funny thing that we can't say a word about people in the house without being snapped up."

"Ruth is right," the other said, "and your tongue runs too fast, Jane. As Ruth says, it will be quite time enough to talk when Miss Margaret is engaged; till then the least said the better."

In truth, Lieutenant Gulston had been several times at The Hold, and his friend the doctor, seeing his admonition had been altogether thrown away, avoided the subject, but from his gravity of manner showed that he had not forgotten it; and he shook his head sadly when one afternoon the lieutenant had obtained leave until the following day. "I wish I had never spoken. Had I not been an old fool I should have known well enough that he was fairly taken by her. We have sailed together for twelve years, and now there is an end to our friendship. I hope that will be all, and that he will not have reason to be sorry he did not take my advice and drop it in time. Of course she may have escaped and I think that she has done so; but it's a terrible risk—terrible. I would give a year's pay that it shouldn't have happened."

An hour before Lieutenant Gulston left his ship, Ronald Mervyn had started for The Hold. A word that had been said by a young officer of the flagship who was dining at mess had caught his ears. It was concerning his first-lieutenant.

"He's got quite a fishing mania at present, and twice a week he goes off for the day to some place twenty miles away—Carnesford, I think it is. He does not seem to have much luck; anyhow, he never brings any fish home. He is an awfully good fellow, Gulston; the best first-lieutenant I ever sailed with by a long way."

What Ronald Mervyn heard was not pleasant to him. He had noticed the attentions Gulston had paid to Margaret Carne at the ball, and had been by no means pleased at meeting him, installed at The Hold with the shooting party, and the thought that he had been twice a week over in that neighbourhood caused an angry surprise. The next morning, therefore, he telegraphed home for a horse to meet him at the station, and started as soon as lunch was over. He stayed half an hour at home, for his house lay on the road between the station and Carne's Hold. The answer he received from his sister to a question he put did not add to his good temper.

Oh, yes. Mr. Gulston had called a day or two after he had been to the shooting party, and they had heard he had been at The Hold several times since.

When he arrived there, Ronald found that Margaret and her brother were both in the drawing-room, and he stood chatting with them there for some time, or rather chatting with Margaret, for Reginald was dull and moody. At last the latter sauntered away.

"What's the matter with you, sir?" Margaret said to her cousin. "You don't seem to be quite yourself; is it the weather? Reginald is duller and more silent than usual, he has hardly spoken a word to-day."

"No, it's not the weather," he replied, sharply. "I want to ask you a question, Margaret."

"Well, if you ask it civilly," the girl replied, "I will answer it, but certainly not otherwise."

"I hear that that sailor fellow has been coming here several times. What does it mean?"

Margaret Carne threw back her head haughtily. "What do you mean, Ronald, by speaking in that tone; are you out of your mind?"

"Not more than the family in general," he replied, grimly; "but you have not answered my question."

"I have not asked Lieutenant Gulston what he comes here for," she said, coldly; "and, besides, I do not recognise your right to ask me such a question."

"Not recognise my right?" he repeated, passionately. "I should have thought that a man had every right to ask such a question of the woman he is going to marry."

"Going to marry?" she repeated, scornfully. "At any rate this is the first I have heard of it."

"It has always been a settled thing," he said, "and you know it as well as I do. You promised me ten years ago that you would be my wife some day."

"Ten years ago I was a child. Ronald, how can you talk like this! You know we have always been as brother and sister together. I have never thought of anything else of late. You have been home four or five months, anyhow, and you have had plenty of time to speak if you wanted to. You never said a word to lead me to believe that you thought of me in any other way than as a cousin."

"I thought we understood each other, Margaret."

"I thought so too," the girl replied, "but not in the same way. Oh, Ronald, don't say this; we have always been such friends, and perhaps years ago I might have thought it would be something more; but since then I have grown up and grown wiser, and even if I had loved you in the way you speak of, I would not have married you, because I am sure it would be bad for us both. We have both that terrible curse in our blood, and if there was not another man in the world I would not marry you."

"I don't believe you would have said so a month ago," Ronald Mervyn said, looking darkly at her. "This Gulston has come between us, that's what it is, and you cannot deny it."

"You are not behaving like a gentleman, Ronald," the girl said, quietly. "You have no right to say such things."

"I have a right to say anything," he burst out. "You have fooled me and spoilt my life, but you shall regret it. You think after all these years I am to be thrown by like an old glove. No, by Heaven; you may throw me over, but I swear you shall never marry this sailor or any one else, whatever I do to prevent it. You say I have the curse of the Carnes in my blood. You are right, and you shall have cause to regret it."

He leapt from the window, which Margaret had thrown open a short time before, for the fire had overheated the room, ran down to the stables, leapt on his horse, and rode off at a furious pace. Neither he nor Margaret had noticed that a moment before a man passed along the walk close under the window. It was Lieutenant Gulston. He paused for a moment as he heard his name uttered in angry tones, opened the hall door without ceremony, and hurried towards that of the drawing-room. Reginald Carne was standing close to it, and it flashed across Gulston's mind that he had been listening. He turned his head at the sailor's quick step. "Don't go in there just at present, Gulston, I fancy Margaret is having a quarrel with her cousin. They are quiet now, we had best leave them alone."

"He was using very strong language," the sailor said, hotly. "I caught a word or two as I passed the windows."

"It's a family failing. I fancy he has gone now. I will go in and see. I think it were best for you to walk off for a few minutes, and then come back again. People may quarrel with their relatives, you know, but they don't often care for other people to be behind the scenes."

"No, you are quite right," Gulston answered; "the fact is, for the moment I was fairly frightened by the violence of his tone, and really feared that he was going to do something violent. It was foolish, of course, and I really beg your pardon. Yes, what you say is quite right. If you will allow me I will have the horse put in the trap again. I got out at the gate and walked across the garden, telling the man to take the horse straight round to the stables; but I think I had better go and come again another day. After such a scene as she has gone through Miss Carne will not care about having a stranger here."

"No, I don't think that would be best," Reginald Carne said. "She would wonder why you did not come, and would, likely enough, hear from her maid that you had been and gone away again, and might guess you had heard something of the talking in there. No, I think you had better do as I said—go away, and come again in a few minutes."

The lieutenant accordingly went out and walked about the shrubbery for a short time, and then returned. Miss Carne did not appear at dinner, but sent down a message to say that she had so bad a headache she would not be able to appear downstairs that evening.

Reginald Carne did not play the part of host so well as usual. At times he was gloomy and abstracted, and then he roused himself and talked rapidly. Lieutenant Gulston thought that he was seriously discomposed at the quarrel between his sister and his cousin; and he determined at any rate not to take the present occasion to carry out the intention he had formed of telling Reginald Carne that he was in love with his sister, and hoped he would have no objection to his telling her so, as he had a good income besides his pay as first-lieutenant. When the men had been sitting silently for some time after wine was put on the table, he said:

"I think, Carne, I will not stop here to-night. Your sister is evidently quite upset with this affair, and no wonder. I shall feel myself horribly *de trop*, and would rather come again some other time if you will let me. If you will let your man put a horse in the trap I shall catch the ten o'clock train comfortably."

"Perhaps that would be best, Gulston. I am not a very lively companion at the best of times, and family quarrels are unpleasant enough for a stranger."

A few minutes later Lieutenant Gulston was on his way to the station. He had much to think about on his way home. In one respect he had every reason to be well satisfied with what he had heard, as it had left no doubt whatever in his mind that Margaret Carne had refused the offer of her cousin, and that the latter had believed that he had been refused because she loved him—Charlie Gulston. Of course she had not said so; still she could not have denied it, or her cousin's wrath would not have been turned against him.

Then he was sorry that such a quarrel had taken place, as it would probably lead to a breach between the two families. He knew Margaret was very fond of her aunt and the girls. Then the violence with which Ronald Mervyn had spoken caused him a deal of uneasiness. Was it possible that a sane man would have gone on like that? Was it possible that the curse of the Carnes was still working? This was an unpleasant thought; but that which followed was still more anxious.

Certainly, from the tone of his voice, he had believed that Ronald Mervyn was on the point of using violence to Margaret, and if the man was really not altogether right in his head there was no saying what he might do. As for himself, he laughed at the threats that had been uttered against him. Mad or sane, he had not the slightest fear of Ronald Mervyn. But if, as was likely enough, this mad-brained fellow tried to fix a quarrel upon him in some public way, it might be horribly unpleasant—so unpleasant that he did not care to think of it. He consoled himself by hoping that when Mervyn's first burst of passion had calmed down, he might look at the matter in a more reasonable light, and see that at any rate he could not bring about a public quarrel without Margaret's name being in some way drawn into it; that her cousin could not wish, however angry he might be with her.

It was an unpleasant business. If Margaret accepted him, he would take her away from all these associations. It was marvellous that she was so bright and cheerful, knowing this horrible story about that Spanish woman, and that there was a taint in the blood. That brother of hers, too, was enough to keep the story always in her mind. The doctor was certainly right about him. Of course he wasn't mad, but there was something strange about him, and at times you caught him looking at you in an unpleasant sort of way.

"He is always very civil," the lieutenant muttered to himself; "in fact, wonderfully civil and hospitable, and all that. Still I never feel quite at my ease with him. If I had been a rich man, and they had been hard up, I should have certainly suspected there was a design in his invitations, and that he wanted me to marry Margaret; but, of course, that is absurd. He can't tell that I have a penny beyond my pay; and a girl like Margaret might marry any one she liked, at any rate out of Devonshire. Perhaps he may not have liked the idea of her marrying this cousin of hers; and no doubt he is right there, and seeing, as I daresay he did see, that I was taken with Margaret, he thought it better to give me a chance than to let her marry Mervyn.

"I don't care a snap whether all her relations are mad or not. I know that she is as free from the taint as I am; but it can't be wholesome for a girl to live in such an atmosphere, and the next time I go over I will put the question I meant to put this evening, and if she says yes, I will very soon get her out of it all." And then the lieutenant indulged in visions of pretty houses, with bright gardens looking over the sea, and finally concluded that a little place near Ryde or Cowes would be in every way best and most convenient, as being handy to Portsmouth, and far removed from Devonshire and its associations. "I hope to get my step in about a year; then I will go on half-pay. I have capital interest, and I daresay my cousin in the Admiralty will be able to get me a dockyard appointment of some sort at Portsmouth; if not, I shall, of course, give it up. I am not going to knock about the world after I am married."

This train of thought occupied him until almost mechanically he left the train, walked down to the water, hailed a boat, and was taken alongside his ship.

CHAPTER IV.

A TERRIBLE DISCOVERY.

Margaret Carne's message as to her inability to come down to dinner was scarcely a veracious one. She was not given to headaches, and had not, so far as she could remember, been once laid up with them, but after what had been said, she did not feel equal to going downstairs and facing Charlie Gulston. She had never quite admitted to herself that she loved the young sailor who had for the last few weeks been so much at the house, and of whose reason for so coming she had but little doubt; but now, as she sat alone in the room, she knew well enough the answer she should give to his question, when it came.

At present, however, the discovery of her own feelings caused alarm rather than pleasure. There had been no signs of fear in her face when her cousin raged and threatened, but she did not believe that the threats were empty ones; he had often frightened her when she was a child by furious bursts of passion, and although it was many years now since she had seen him thus, she felt sure that he would do as he had threatened, and was likely enough to take any violent step that might occur to him in his passion, to carry out his threat.

Although she had put a bold front on it, Margaret felt at heart that his reproach was not altogether unjustified. There had been a boy and girl understanding between them, and although it had not been formally ratified of late years, its existence was tacitly recognised in both families, and until a few months before she herself had considered that in the natural course of events she should some day be Ronald Mervyn's wife.

Had he reproached her gently, she would have frankly admitted this, and would have asked him to forgive her for changing her mind now that years had wrought a change in her feelings; but the harshness and suddenness of his attack had roused her pride, and driven her to take up the ground that there was no formal engagement between them, and that as he had not renewed the subject for years she was at perfect liberty to consider herself free. She had spoken but the truth in saying that their near relationship was in her eyes a bar to their marriage. Of late years she had thought much more than she had when a girl over the history of the family and the curse of the Carnes, and although she had tried her best to prevent herself from brooding over the idea, she could not disguise from herself that her brother was at times strange and unlike other men, and her recollections of Ronald's outbursts of temper, as a boy, induced the suspicion that he, too, had not altogether escaped the fatal taint. Still, had not Charlie Gulston come across her path, it was probable that she would have drifted on as before, and would, when the time came have accepted Ronald Mervyn as her husband.

The next morning, when Ruth Powlett went as usual to call her mistress, she started with surprise as she opened the door, for the blind was already up and the window open. Closing the door behind her, she went in and placed the jug of hot water she carried by the washstand, and then turned round to arouse her mistress. As she did so a low cry burst from her lips, and she grasped a chair for support. The white linen was stained with blood, and Margaret lay there, white and still, with her eyes wide open and fixed in death. The clothes were drawn a short way down in order that the murderer might strike at her heart. Scarce had she taken this in, when Ruth felt the room swim round, her feet failed her, and she fell insensible on the ground.

In a few minutes the cold air streaming in through the open window aroused her. Feebly she recovered her feet, and, supporting herself against the wall, staggered towards the door. As she did so her eye fell on an object lying by the side of the bed. She stopped at once with another gasping cry, pressed her hand on her forehead, and stood as if fascinated, with her eyes fixed upon it. Then slowly and reluctantly, as if forced to act against her will, she moved towards the bed, stooped and picked up the object she had seen.

She had recognised it at once. It was a large knife with a spring blade, and a silver plate let into the buckhorn handle, with a name, G. Forester, engraved upon it. It was a knife she herself had given to her lover a year before. It was open and stained with blood. For a minute or two she stood gazing at it in blank horror. What should she do, what should she do? She thought of the boy who had been her playmate, of the man she had loved, and whom, though she had cast him off, she had never quite ceased to love. She thought of his father, the old man who had always been kind to her. If she left this silent witness where she had found it there would be no doubt what would come of it. For some minutes she stood irresolute.

"God forgive me," she said at last. "I cannot do it." She closed the knife, put it into her dress, and then turned round again. She dared not look at the bed now, for she felt herself in some way an accomplice in her mistress's murder, and she made her way to the door, opened it, and then hurried downstairs into the kitchen, where the servants, who were just sitting down to breakfast, rose with a cry as she entered.

"What is it, Ruth? What's the matter? Have you seen anything?"

Ruth's lips moved but no sound came from them, her face was ghastly white, and her eyes full of horror.

"What is it, child?" the old cook said, advancing and touching her, while the others shrank back, frightened at her aspect.

"Miss Margaret is dead," came at last slowly from her lips. "She has been murdered in the night," and she reeled and would have fallen again had not the old servant caught her in her arms and placed her in a chair. A cry of horror and surprise had broken from the servants, then came a hubbub of talk.

"It can't be true." "It is impossible." "Ruth must have fancied it." "It never could be," and then they looked in each other's face as if seeking a confirmation of their words.

"I must go up and see," the cook said. "Susan and Harriet, you come along with me; the others see to Ruth. Sprinkle some water on her face. She must have been dreaming."

Affecting a confidence which she did not feel, the cook, followed timidly by the two frightened girls, went upstairs. She stood for a moment hesitating before she opened the door; then she entered the room, the two girls not daring to follow her. She went a step into the room, then gave a little cry and clasped her hands.

"It is true," she cried; "Miss Margaret has been murdered!"

Then the pent-up fears of the girls found vent in loud screams, which were echoed from the group of servants who had clustered at the foot of the stairs in expectation of what was to come.

A moment later the door of Reginald Carne's room opened, and he came out partly dressed.

"What is the matter? What is all this hubbub about?"

"Miss Margaret is murdered, sir," the two girls burst out, pausing for an instant in their outcry.

"Murdered!" he repeated, in low tones. "You are mad; impossible!" and pushing past them he ran into Margaret's room.

"Ah!" he exclaimed, in a long, low note of pain and horror. "Good God, who can have done this?" and he leaned against the wall and covered his face with his hands. The old servant had advanced to the bed, and laid a hand on the dead girl. She now touched her master.

"You had better go away now, Mr. Reginald, for you can do nothing. She is cold, and must have been dead hours. We must lock the door up till the police come."

So saying, she gently led him from the room, closed the door and locked it. Reginald Carne staggered back to his room.

"Poor master," the old servant said, looking after him, "this will be a terrible blow for him; he and Miss Margery have always been together. There's no saying what may come of it," and she shook her head gravely; then she roused herself, and turned sharply on the girls.

"Hold your noise, you foolish things; what good will that do? Get downstairs at once."

Driving them before her, she went down to the kitchen, and out of the door leading to the yard, where one of the maids was at the moment telling the grooms what had happened.

"Joe, get on a horse and ride off and fetch Dr. Arrowsmith. He can't be of any good, but he ought to come. Send up Job Harpur, the constable, and then ride on to Mr. Volkes; he is the nearest magistrate, and will know what to do."

Then she went back into the kitchen.

"She has come to, Mrs. Wilson; but she don't seem to know what she is doing."

"No wonder," the cook said, "after such a shock as she has had; and she only just getting well after her illness. Two of you run upstairs and get a mattress off her bed and two pillows, and lay them down in the servants' hall; then take her in there and put her on them. Jane, get some brandy out of the cellaret and bring it here; a spoonful of that will do her good."

A little brandy and water was mixed, and the cook poured it between Ruth's lips, for she did not seem to know what was said to her, and remained still and impassive, with short sobs bursting at times from her lips. Then two servants half lifted her, and took her into the servants' hall, and laid her down on the mattress. All were sobbing and crying, for Margaret Carne had been greatly loved by those around her.

In half an hour the doctor arrived.

"Is it possible the news is true?" he asked as he leapt from his gig; the faces of those around were sufficient answer. "Good Heavens, what a terrible business! Tell Mr. Carne I am here."

Reginald Carne soon came down. He was evidently terribly shaken. He held out his hand in silence to the doctor.

"What does it all mean?" the latter said, huskily. "It seems too horrible to be true. Can it be that your sister, whom I have known since she was a child, is dead? Murdered, too! It seems impossible."

"It does seem impossible, doctor; but it is true. I have seen her myself," and he shuddered. "She has been stabbed to the heart."

The doctor wiped his eyes.

"Well, I must go up and see her," he said. "Poor child, poor child. No, you need not ring. I will go up by myself."

Dr. Arrowsmith had attended the family for many years, and knew perfectly well which was Margaret's room. The old cook was standing outside the door of the drawing-room.

"Here is the key, sir. I thought it better to lock the door till you came."

"Quite right," the doctor replied. "Don't let any one up till Mr. Volkes comes. The servant said he was going for him. Ah, here is Harpur. That is right, Harpur; you had better come up with me, but I shouldn't touch anything if I were you till Mr. Volkes comes; besides, we shall be having the Chief Constable over here presently, and it is better to leave everything as it is." They entered the room together.

"Dear, dear, to think of it now," the constable murmured, standing awe-struck at the door, for the course of his duty was for the most part simple, and he had never before been face to face with a tragedy like this.

The doctor moved silently to the bed, and leant over the dead girl.

"Stabbed to the heart," he murmured; "death must have been instantaneous." Then he touched her arm and tried to lift it.

"She has been dead hours," he said to the constable, "six or seven hours, I should say. Let us look round. The window is open, you see. Can the murderer have entered there?" He looked out. The wall was covered with ivy, and a massive stem grew close to the window. "Yes," he went on, "an active man could have climbed that. See, there are some leaves on the ground. I think, Harpur, your best plan will be to go down and take your station there and see no one comes along or disturbs anything. See, this jewel-box on the table has been broken open and the contents are gone, and I do not see her watch anywhere. Well, that is enough to do at present; we will lock this room up again until Mr. Volkes comes."

When they came downstairs, the cook again came out.

"Please, sir, will you come in here? Ruth Powlett, Miss Margaret's maid, seems very bad; it was she who first found it out, and it's naturally given her a terrible shock. She came down looking like a mad woman, then she fainted off, and she doesn't seem to have any sort of consciousness yet."

"Ruth Powlett! why, I have been attending her for the last three weeks. Yes, such a shock may be very serious in her case," and the doctor went in.

"Have you any sal volatile in the house?" he asked, after he had felt her pulse.

"There's some in the medicine chest, I think, sir, but I will soon see."

She went out and presently returned with a bottle. The doctor poured a teaspoonful into a glass and added a little water. Then he lifted Ruth's head, and forced it between her lips. She gasped once or twice, and then slightly opened her eyes.

"That is right, Ruth," the doctor said, cheeringly, "try and rouse yourself, child. You remember me, don't you?" Ruth opened her eyes and looked up.

"That's right, child, I mustn't have you on my hands again, you know." Ruth looked round with a puzzled air, then a sharp look of pain crossed her face.

"I know, Ruth," said the doctor, soothingly; "it is terrible for every one, but least terrible for your poor young mistress; she passed away painlessly, and went at once from life into death. Every one loved her, you know; it may be that God has spared her much unhappiness."

Ruth burst into a paroxysm of crying; the doctor nodded to the old servant.

"That's what I wanted," he whispered, "she will be better after this. Get a cup of hot tea for her, or beef-tea will be better still if you have any, make her drink it and then leave her for a time. I will see her again presently."

Immediately the doctor left him, Reginald Carne wrote a telegram to the Chief Constable of the county, and despatched a servant with orders to gallop as fast as he could to the station and send it off.

Mr. Volkes, the magistrate, arrived half an hour later, terribly shocked by the news he had heard. He at once set about making inquiries, and heard what the doctor and constable had to say. No one else had been in the room except the old cook, Mr. Carne, and the poor girl's own maid.

"It would be useless for you to question the girl to-day, Volkes. She is utterly prostrate with the shock, but I have no doubt she will be able to give her evidence at the inquest. So far as I can see there does not seem to be the slightest clue. Apparently some villain who knows something about the house has climbed through the window, stabbed her, and made off with her jewellery."

"It is a hideous business," the magistrate said; "there has not been such a startling crime committed in the county in all my experience. And to think that Margaret Carne should be the victim, a girl every one liked; it is terrible, terrible. What's your opinion, doctor? Some wandering tramp, I suppose?"

"I suppose so. Certainly it can be none of the neighbours. In the first place, as you say, every one liked her and in the second, a crime of that sort is quite out

44

of the way of our quiet Devonshire people. It must have been some stranger, that's evident. Yet on the other hand it is singular that the man should have got into her room. I don't suppose there has been a window fastened or a door locked on the ground floor for years; the idea of a burglary never occurs to any one here. By the way, the coroner ought to be informed at once. I will speak to Carne about it; if we do it this morning he will have time to send over this evening and summon a jury for to-morrow; the sooner it is over the better. Directly the Chief Constable arrives he will no doubt send round orders everywhere for tramps and suspicious persons to be arrested. Plymouth is the place where they are most likely to get some clue; in the first place it's the largest town in this part, and in the second there are sure to be low shops where a man could dispose of valuables."

In the afternoon, Captain Hendricks, the Chief Constable, arrived, and took the matter in hand. In the first place he had a long private conversation with Job Harpur, who had been steadily keeping watch in the garden beneath the window, leaving him with strict orders to let no one approach the spot.

He then, with a sergeant who had arrived with him, made a thorough search of the bedroom. After this he examined every one who knew anything about the matter, with the exception of Ruth Powlett, for whom the doctor said absolute quiet was necessary, as to all they knew about it. Then he obtained a minute description of the missing watch and jewels, and telegraphed it to Plymouth and Exeter. Having done this he went out into the garden again, and there a close search was made on the grass and borders for the marks of footsteps. When all this was done he had a long private conversation with Reginald Carne.

The news of Margaret Carne's murder created an excitement in Carnesford, such as had never been equalled since the day when Lady Carne murdered her child and the curse of Carne's Hold began its work. There was not a soul in the valley but knew her personally, for Margaret had taken great interest in village matters, had seen that soups and jellies were sent down from The Hold to those who were sick, had begged many a man off his rent when laid up or out of work, and had many pensioners who received weekly gifts of money, tea, or other little luxuries. She gave prizes in the school; helped the parson with his choir; and scarcely a day passed without her figure being seen in the streets of Carnesford. That she could be murdered seemed incredible, and when the news first arrived it was received with absolute unbelief. When such confirmation was received that doubt was no longer possible, all work in Carnesford was suspended. Women stood at their doors and talked to their neighbours and wept freely. Men gathered in knots and talked it over and uttered threats of what they would do if they could but lay hands on the murderer. Boys and girls walked up the hill and stood at the edge of the wood, talking in whispers and gazing on the house as if it presented some new and mysterious attraction. Later in the day two or three constables arrived, and asked many questions as to whether any one had heard any one passing through the street between one and three in the morning; but Carnesford had slept soundly, and no one was found who had been awake between those hours.

The little conclave in the sanctum at the "Carne's Arms" met half an hour earlier than usual. They found on their arrival there a stranger chatting with the landlord, who introduced him to them as Mr. Rentford, a detective officer from Plymouth.

"A sad affair, gentlemen, a sad affair," Mr. Rentford said, when they had taken their seats and lit their churchwardens. "As sad an affair, I should say, as ever I was engaged in."

"It is that," Jacob Carey said. "Here's Mr. Claphurst here, who has been here, man and boy, for nigh eighty years. He will tell you that such an affair as this has never happened in this part in his time."

"I suppose, now," the detective said, "there's none in the village has any theory about it; I mean," he went on, as none of his hearers answered, "no one thinks it can be any one but some tramp or stranger to the district?"

"It can't be no one else," Jacob Carey said, "as I can see. What do you say, Hiram Powlett? I should say no one could make a nearer guess than you can, seeing as they say it was your Ruth as first found it out."

"I haven't seen Ruth," Hiram said; "the doctor told me, as he came down, as she was quite upset with the sight, and that it would be no good my going up to see her, as she would have to keep still all day. So I can't see farther into it than another; but surely it must be some stranger."

"There was no one about here so far as you have heard, Mr. Powlett, who had any sort of grudge against this poor lady?"

"Not a soul, as far as I know," Hiram replied. "She could speak up sharp, as I have heard, could Miss Carne, to a slatternly housewife or a drunken husband; but I never heard as she made an enemy by it, though, if she had, he would have kept his tongue to himself, for there were not many here in Carnesford who would have heard a word said against Miss Carne and sat quiet over it."

"No, indeed," Jacob Carey affirmed, bringing down his fist with a heavy thump on his knee. "The Squire and his sister were both well liked, and I for one would have helped duck any one that spoke against them in the Dare. She

46

was the most liked, perhaps, because of her bright face and her kind words and being so much down here among us; but the Squire is well liked, too; he is not one to laugh and talk as she was, but he is a good landlord, and will always give a quarter's rent to a man as gets behindhand for no fault of his own, and if there is a complaint about a leaky roof or any repairs that want doing, the thing is done at once and no more talk about it. No, they have got no enemies about here as I know of, except maybe it's the poachers down at Dareport, for though the Squire don't shoot himself, he preserves strictly, and if a poacher's caught he gets sent to the quarter sessions as sure as eggs is eggs."

"Besides," the old clerk put in, "they say as Miss Carne's watch and things has been stolen; that don't look as if it was done out of revenge, do it?"

"Well, no," the detective said, slowly; "but that's not always to be taken as a sign, because you see if any one did a thing like that, out of revenge, they would naturally take away anything that lay handy, so as to make it look as if it was done for theft."

The idea was a new one to his listeners, and they smoked over it silently for some minutes.

"Lord, what evil ways there are in the world," Reuben Claphurst said at last. "Wickedness without end. Now what do you make out of this, mister? Of course these things come natural to you."

The detective shook his head. "It's too early to form an opinion yet, Mr. Claphurst—much too early. I dare say we shall put two and two together and make four presently, but at present you see we have got to learn all the facts, and you who live close ought to know more than we do, and to be able to put us on the track to begin with. You point me out a clue, and I will follow it, but the best dogs can't hunt until they take up the scent."

"That's true enough," the blacksmith said, approvingly.

"Have there been any strangers stopping in the village lately?" the detective asked.

"There have been a few stopping off and on here, or taking rooms in the village," the landlord answered; "but I don't think there has been any one fishing on the stream for the last few days."

"I don't mean that class; I mean tramps."

"That I can't tell you," the landlord replied; "we don't take tramps in here; they in general go to Wilding's beershop at the other end of the village. He can put up four or five for the night, and in summer he is often full, for we are just about a long day's tramp out from Plymouth, and they often make this their first stopping-place out, or their last stopping-place in, but it's getting late for them now, not many come along after the harvest is well over. Still, you know, there may have been one there yesterday, for aught I know."

"I will go round presently and ask. Any one who was here the night before might well have lain in the woods yesterday, and gone up and done it."

"I don't believe as you will ever find anything about it. There's a curse on Carne's Hold, as every one knows, and curses will work themselves out. If I were the Squire, I would pull the place down, every stick and stone of it, and I would build a fresh one a bit away. I wouldn't use so much as a brick or a rafter of the old place, for the curse might stick to it. I would have everything new from top to bottom."

"Yes, I have heard of the curse on Carne's Hold," the detective said. "A man who works with me, and comes from this part of the country, told me all about it as we came over to-day. However, that has nothing to do with this case."

"It's partly the curse as that heathen woman, as Sir Edgar brought home as his wife, laid on the place," the old clerk said, positively; "and it will go on working as long as Carne's Hold stands. That's what I says, and I don't think as any one else here will gainsay me."

"That's right enough," the blacksmith agreed, "I think we are all with you there, Mr. Claphurst. It ought to have been pulled down long ago after what has happened there. Why, if Mr. Carne was to say to me, 'Have the house and the garden and all rent free, Jacob Carey, as long as you like,' I should say, 'Thank you, Squire, but I wouldn't move into it, not if you give me enough beside to keep it up.' I call it just flying in the face of Providence. Only look at Hiram Powlett there; he sends his daughter up to be Miss Carne's maid at The Hold, and what comes of it? Why, she tumbles down the hill a-going up, and there she lies three weeks, with the doctor coming to see her every day. That was a clear warning if ever there was one. Who ever heard of a girl falling down and hurting herself like that? No one. And it would not have happened if it hadn't been for the curse of Carne's Hold."

"I shouldn't go so far as that," Hiram Powlett said. "What happened to my lass had nothing to do with The Hold; she might have been walking up the hill at any time, and she might have slipped down at any time. A girl may put her foot on a loose stone and fall without it having anything to say to The Hold one way or the other. Besides, I have never heard it said as the curse had aught to do except with the family."

"I don't know about that," the smith replied. "That servant that was killed by the Spanish woman's son; how about him? It seems to me as the curse worked on him a bit, too."

"So it did, so it did," Hiram agreed. "I can't gainsay you there, Jacob Carey; now you put it so, I see there is something in it, though never before have I heard of there being anything in the curse except in the family."

"Why, didn't Miles Jefferies, father of one of the boys as is in the stables, get his brains kicked out by one of the old Squire's horses?"

"So he did, Jacob, so he did; still grooms does get their brains kicked out at other places besides The Hold. But there is something in what you say, and if I had thought of it before, I would never have let my Ruth go up there to service. I thought it was all for the best at the time, and you knows right enough why I sent her up there, to be away from that George Forester; still, I might have sent her somewhere else, and I would have done if I had thought of what you are saying now. Sure enough no good has come of it. I can't hold that that fall of hers had aught to do with the curse of the Carnes, but this last affair, which seems to me worse for her than the first, sure enough comes from the curse."

"Who is this George Forester, if you don't mind my asking the question?" the detective said. "You see it's my business to find out about people."

"Oh, George hadn't nothing to do with this business," Hiram replied. "He's the son of a farmer near here, and has always been wild and a trouble to the old man, but he's gone away weeks ago. He got into a poaching scrape, and one of the keepers was hurt, and I suppose he thought he had best be out of it for a time; anyhow, he has gone. But he weren't that sort of a chap. No, there was no harm in George Forester, not in that way; he was lazy and fonder of a glass than was good for him, and he got into bad company down at Dareport, and that's what led him to this poaching business, I expect, because there was no call for him to go poaching. His father's got a tidy farm, and he wanted for nothing. If he had been there he couldn't have wanted to steal Miss Carne's jewellery. He was passionate enough, I know, and many a quarrel has he had with his father, but nothing would have made me believe, even if he had been here, that old Jim Forester's son had a hand in a black business like this; so don't you go to take such a notion as that into your head."

"He would not be likely to have any quarrel with Miss Carne?" the detective asked.

"Quarrel? No," Hiram replied sharply, for he resented the idea that any possible suspicion of Margaret Carne's murder should be attached to a man with whom Ruth's name had been connected. "I don't suppose Miss Carne ever spoke a word to him in her life. What should she speak to him for? Why, he had left the Sunday school years before she took to seeing after it. 'Tain't as if he had been one of the boys of the village."

As Jacob Carey, Reuben Claphurst, and the landlord, each gave an assenting murmur to Hiram's words, the detective did not think it worth while to pursue the point further, for there really seemed nothing to connect this George Forester in any way with Margaret Carne's death.

"Well," he said, taking up his hat, "I will go round to this beershop you speak of, and make inquiries as to whether any tramps have been staying there. It is quite certain this young lady didn't put an end to herself. What we have got to find out is: Who was the man that did it?"

CHAPTER V.

THE INQUEST.

It was six o'clock, and already quite dark, when, as Lieutenant Gulston was writing in his cabin, his servant told him that Dr. Mackenzie had just come off from the shore, and would be glad if he could spare him a few minutes' conversation.

"Tell him I will be on the quarter-deck in a minute." He added a few lines to the letter he was writing, put it in an envelope, and, taking his cap, went out, dropping the letter into the post-bag that hung near his cabin, and then went on to the quarter-deck. He was rather pleased with the doctor's summons, for he highly esteemed him, and regretted the slight estrangement which had arisen between them.

"Well, doctor," he asked, cheerily, "have some of the men been getting into mischief ashore?"

"No, lad, no," the doctor replied, and the first-lieutenant felt that something more serious was the matter, for since he had obtained his rank of first-lieutenant the doctor had dropped his former habit of calling him lad. "No, I have heard some news ashore that will affect you seriously. I am sorry, dear lad, very sorry. I may have thought that you were foolish, but that will make no difference now."

"What is it, doctor?" Lieutenant Gulston asked, with a vague alarm at the gravity of the doctor's manner of treating him.

"The evening papers came out with an early edition, Gulston, and the boys are shouting out the news of a terrible affair, a most terrible affair at your friends the Carnes'. Be steady, lad, be steady. It's a heavy blow for a man to have to bear. Miss Carne is dead."

"Dead! Margaret dead!" the lieutenant repeated, incredulously. "What are you saying, doctor? There must be some mistake. She was well yesterday, for I was over there in the evening and did not leave until nine o'clock. It can't be true."

"It is true, lad, unhappily; there is no mistake. She was found dead in her bed this morning."

The lieutenant was almost stunned by the blow.

"Good God!" he murmured. "It seems impossible."

The doctor walked away and left him for a minute or two to himself. "I have not told you all as yet, lad," he went on, when he returned; "it makes no difference to her, poor girl—none. She passed out of life, it seems, painlessly and instantly, but it is worse for those who are left."

He paused a moment. "She was found stabbed to the heart by a midnight robber."

An exclamation of horror broke from the sailor. "Murdered? Good Heavens!"

"Ay, lad, it is true. It seems to have been done in her sleep, and death was instantaneous. There, I will leave you for a while, now. I will put the paper in your cabin, so that when you feel equal to reading the details you can do so. Try and think it is all for the best, lad. No one knows what trouble might have darkened her life and yours had this thing not happened. I know you will not be able to think so now, but you will feel it so some day."

An hour later Lieutenant Gulston entered the doctor's cabin. There was a look of anger as well as of grief on his face that the doctor did not understand.

"Doctor, I believe this is no murder by a wandering tramp, as the paper says. I believe it was done from revenge, and that the things were stolen simply to throw people off the scent. I will tell you what took place yesterday. I drove up as far as the gate in the garden; there one road sweeps round in front of the house, the other goes straight to the stables; so I got down, and told the man he might as well drive straight in, while I walked up to the house. The road follows close under the drawing-room windows, and, one of these being open, as I passed I heard a man's voice raised loud in anger, so loudly and so passionately, indeed, that I involuntarily stopped. His words were, as nearly as I can recollect, 'You have fooled me and spoilt my life, but you shall regret it. You think after all these years I am to be thrown off like an old glove. No, by Heaven; you may throw me over, but I swear you shall never marry this sailor or anybody else, whatever I may have to do to prevent it. You say I have the curse of the Carnes in my blood! You are right, and you shall have cause to regret it.' The voice was so loud and passionate that I believed the speaker was about to do some injury to Margaret, for I did not doubt that it was to her he was speaking, and I ran round through the hall-door to the door of the room; but I found Carne himself standing there. He, too, I suppose, when he had been about to enter, had heard the words. He said, 'Don't go in just at present, Margaret and her cousin are having a quarrel, but I think it's over now.' Seeing that he was there at hand I went away for a bit, and found afterwards that Mervyn had jumped from the window, gone to the stable and ridden straight off. Margaret didn't come down to dinner, making an excuse that she was unwell. Now, what do you think of that, doctor? You know that Mervyn's mother was a Carne, and that he has this mad blood that you warned me against in his veins. There is his threat, given in what was an almost mad outburst of passion. She is found dead this morning; what do you think of it?"

"I don't know what to think of it, Gulston; I know but little of Mervyn myself, but I have heard men in his regiment say that he was a queer fellow, and though generally a most cheery and pleasant companion, he has at times fits of silence and moroseness similar, I should say, to those of his cousin, Reginald Carne. It is possible, lad, though I don't like to think so. When there is madness in the blood no one can say when it may blaze out, or what course it can take. The idea is a terrible one, and yet it is possible; it may indeed be so, for the madness in the family has twice before led to murder. The presumption is certainly a grave one, for although his messmates may consider Mervyn to be, as they say, a queer fellow, I do not think you would find any of them to say he was mad, or anything like it. Remember, Gulston, this would be a terrible accusation to bring against any man, even if he can prove—as probably he can prove—that he was at home, or here in Plymouth, at the time of the murder. The charge that he is mad, and the notoriety such a charge would obtain, is enough to ruin a man for life."

"I can't help that," the lieutenant said, gloomily. "I heard him threaten Margaret, and I shall say so at the coroner's inquest to-morrow. If a man is such a coward as to threaten a woman he must put up with any consequences that may happen to befall him."

The coroner and jury met in the dining-room at The Hold; they were all Carnesford men. Hiram Powlett, Jacob Carey, and the landlord of the "Carne's Arms" were upon it, for the summoning officer had been careful to choose on such an important occasion the leading men of the village. After having gone upstairs to view the body, the coroner opened the proceedings. The room was crowded. Many of the gentry of the neighbourhood were present. Lieutenant Gulston, with a hard set look upon his face, stood in a corner of the room with the doctor beside him. Ronald Mervyn, looking, as some of the Carnesford people remarked in a whisper, ten years older than he did when he drove through the village a few days before, stood on the other side of the table talking in low tones to some of his neighbours.

"We shall first, gentlemen," the coroner said, "hear evidence as to the finding of the body. Ruth Powlett, the maid of the deceased lady, is the first witness."

A minute later there was a stir at the door, and Ruth was led in by a constable. She was evidently so weak and unhinged that the coroner told her to take a chair.

"Now, Miss Powlett, tell us what you saw when you entered your mistress's room."

"Upon opening the door," Ruth said, in a calmer and more steady voice than was expected from her appearance, "I saw that the window was open and the blind up. I was surprised at this, for Miss Carne did not sleep with her window open in winter, and the blind was always down. I walked straight to the washstand and placed the can of hot water there; then I turned round to wake Miss Carne, and I saw her lying there with a great patch of blood on her nightdress, and I knew by her face that she was dead. Then I fainted. I do not know how long I lay there. When I came to myself I got up and went to the door, and went downstairs to the kitchen and gave the alarm."

"You did not notice that any of Miss Carne's things had been taken from the table?" the coroner asked.

"No, sir."

"Were there any signs of a struggle having taken place?"

"No, sir, I did not see any. Miss Carne lay as if she was sleeping quietly. She was lying on her side."

"The bedclothes were not disarranged?"

"No, sir, except that the clothes were turned down a short distance."

"You were greatly attached to your mistress, Miss Powlett?"

"Yes, sir."

"She was generally liked—was she not?"

"Yes, sir. Every one who knew Miss Carne was fond of her."

"Have any of you any further questions to ask?" the coroner asked the jury.

There was no reply.

"Thank you, Miss Powlett. I will not trouble you further at present."

The cook then gave her testimony, and Dr. Arrowsmith was next called. He testified to the effect that upon his arrival he found that the room had not been disturbed in any way; no one had entered it with the exception, as he understood, of Miss Carne's maid, the cook, and Mr. Carne. The door was locked. When he went in, he found the deceased was dead, and it was his opinion, from the coldness and rigidity of the body, that she must have been dead seven or eight hours. It was just nine o'clock when he arrived. He should think, therefore, that death had taken place between one and half-past two in the morning. Death had been caused by a stab given either with a knife or dagger. The blow was exactly over the heart, and extended down into the substance of the heart itself. Death must have been absolutely instantaneous. Deceased lay in a natural position, as if asleep. The clothes had been turned down about a foot, just low enough to uncover the region of the heart.

After making an examination of the body, he examined the room with the constable, and found that a jewel-box on the table was open and its contents gone. The watch and chain of the deceased had also disappeared. He looked out of the window, and saw that it could be entered by an active man by climbing up a thick stem of ivy that grew close by. He observed several leaves lying on the ground, and was of the opinion that the assassin entered there.

"From what you say, Dr. Arrowsmith, it is your opinion that no struggle took place?"

"I am sure that there was no struggle," the doctor replied. "I have no question that Miss Carne was murdered in her sleep. I should say that the bedclothes were drawn down so lightly that she was not disturbed."

"Does it not appear an extraordinary thing to you, Dr. Arrowsmith, that if, as it seems, Miss Carne did not awake, the murderer should have taken her life?"

"Very extraordinary," the doctor said, emphatically. "I am wholly unable to account for it. I can understand that had she woke and sat up, a burglar might have killed her to secure his own safety, but that he should have quietly and deliberately set himself to murder her in her sleep is to me most extraordinary."

"You will note this circumstance, gentlemen," the coroner said to the jury. "It is quite contrary to one's usual experiences in these cases. As a rule, thieves are not murderers. To secure their own safety they may take life, but as a rule they avoid running the risk of capital punishment, and their object is to effect robbery without rousing the inmates of the house. At present the evidence certainly points to premeditated murder rather than to murder arising out of robbery. It is true that robbery has taken place, but this might be merely a blind."

"You know of no one, Dr. Arrowsmith, who would have been likely to entertain any feeling of hostility against Miss Carne?"

"Certainly not, sir. She was, I should say, universally popular, and certainly among the people of Carnesford she was regarded with great affection, for she was continually doing good among them."

"I am prepared to give evidence on that point," a voice said from the corner of the room, and there was a general movement of surprise as every one turned round to look at the speaker.

"Then perhaps, sir, we may as well hear your evidence next," the coroner said, "because it may throw some light upon the matter and enable us to ask questions to the point of further witnesses."

The lieutenant moved forward to the table: "My name is Charles Gulston. I am first-lieutenant of the *Tenebreuse*, the flagship at Plymouth. I had the honour of the acquaintance of Mr. and Miss Carne, and have spent a day or two here on several occasions. I may say that I was deeply attached to Miss Carne, and had hoped some day to make her my wife. The day before yesterday I came over here upon Mr. Carne's invitation to dine and spend the night. His dogcart met me at the station. As we drove up to the last gate—that leading into the garden—I alighted from the trap and told the man to drive it straight to the stable, while I walked across the lawn to the house. The drawing-room window was open, and as I passed I heard the voice of a man raised in tones of extreme passion, so much so that I stopped involuntarily. His words were:

"'You have fooled me and spoilt my life, but you shall regret it. You think that after all these years I am to be thrown off like an old glove. No, by Heaven! You may throw me over, but I vow that you shall never marry this sailor, or any one else, whatever I may have to do to prevent it. You say I have the curse of the Carnes in my blood. You are right, and you shall have cause to regret it.'

"The words were so loud and the tone so threatening that I ran round into the house and to the door, and should have entered it had not Mr. Carne, who was standing there, having apparently just come up, begged me not to do so, saying that his sister and cousin were having a quarrel, but that it was over now. As he was there I went away for a few minutes, and when I returned I found that Miss Carne had gone upstairs, and that her cousin had left, having, as Mr. Carne told me, left by the open window."

While Lieutenant Gulston was speaking a deep silence reigned in the room, and as he mentioned what Reginald Carne had said, every eye turned towards Ronald Mervyn, who stood with face as white as death, and one arm with clenched hand across his breast, glaring at the speaker.

"Do you mean, sir——?" he burst out as the lieutenant ceased; but the coroner at once intervened.

"I must pray you to keep silent for the present, Captain Mervyn. You will have every opportunity of speaking presently.

"As to these words that you overheard, Mr. Gulston, did you recognise the speaker of them before you heard from Mr. Carne who was with his sister in the drawing-room?"

"Certainly. I recognised the voice at once as that of Captain Mervyn, whom I have met on several occasions."

"Were you impressed with his words, or did they strike you as a mere outburst of temper?"

"I was so impressed with the tone in which they were spoken that I ran round to the drawing-room to protect Miss Carne from violence."

"Was it your impression, upon thinking of them afterwards, that the words were meant as a menace to Miss Carne?"

"No, sir. The impression left upon my mind was that Captain Mervyn intended to fix some quarrel on me, as I had no doubt whatever that it was to me he alluded in his threats. The matter dwelt in my mind all the evening, for naturally nothing could have been more unpleasant than a public quarrel with a near relative of a lady to whom one is attached."

There was a long silence. Then the coroner asked the usual question of the jurymen.

None of them had a question to ask; indeed, all were so confounded by this new light thrown upon the matter that they had no power of framing a question.

Job Harpur was then called. He testified to entering the bedroom of the deceased with Dr. Arrowsmith, and to the examination he had made of it. There he had found the jewel-box opened, its contents abstracted, and the watch gone. He could find nothing else disarranged in the room, or any trace whatever that would give a clue as to the identity of the murderer. He then looked out of the window with Dr. Arrowsmith, and saw by a few leaves lying on the ground, and by marks upon the bark of the ivy, that some one had got up or down.

Dr. Arrowsmith had suggested that he should take up his post there, and not allow any one to approach, as a careful search might show footsteps or other marks that would be obliterated were people allowed to approach the window. When Captain Hendricks came they examined the ground together. They could find no signs of footsteps, but at a distance of some ten yards, at the foot of the wall, they found a torn glove, and this he produced.

"You have no reason in connecting this with the case in any way, I suppose, constable?" the coroner asked as the glove was laid on the table before him. "It might have been lying there for some time, I suppose."

"It might, sir."

It was a dog-skin glove stitched with red, with three lines of black and red stitching down the back. While the glove was produced and examined by the jury, Ronald Mervyn was talking in whispers to some friends standing round him.

"I wish to draw your attention," Lieutenant Gulston said in a low tone to Captain Hendricks, "that Captain Mervyn is at this moment holding in his hand a glove that in point of colour exactly matches that on the table; they are both a brighter yellow than usual." The Chief Constable glanced at the gloves and then whispered to the coroner. The latter started, and then said, "Captain Mervyn, would you kindly hand me the glove you have in your hand. It is suggested to me that its colour closely resembles that of the glove on the table." Mervyn, who had not been listening to the last part of the constable's evidence, turned round upon being spoken to.

"My glove, yes, here it is. What do you want it for?" The coroner took the glove and laid it by the other. Colour and stitching matched exactly; there could be no doubt but that they were a pair. A smothered exclamation broke from almost every man in the room.

"What is it?" Ronald Mervyn asked.

"The constable has just testified, Captain Mervyn, that he found this glove a few feet from the window of the deceased. No doubt you can account for its being there, but until the matter is explained it has, of course, a somewhat serious aspect, coupled with the evidence of Lieutenant Gulston."

Again Ronald Mervyn whitened to the hair.

"Do I understand, sir," he said in a low voice, "that I am accused of the murder of my cousin?"

"No one is at present accused," the coroner said, quietly. "We are only taking the evidence of all who know anything about this matter. I have no doubt whatever that you will be able to explain the matter perfectly, and to prove that it was physically impossible that you could have had any connection whatever with it."

Ronald Mervyn passed his hand across his forehead.

"Perhaps," the coroner continued, "if you have the fellow of the glove now handed to me in your pocket, you will kindly produce it, as that will, of course, put an end to this part of the subject."

"I cannot," Ronald Mervyn answered. "I found as I was starting to come out this morning that one of my gloves was missing, and I may say at once that I have no doubt that the other glove is the one I lost; though how it can have got near the place where it was found I cannot explain."

The men standing near fell back a little. The evidence given by Mr. Gulston had surprised them, but had scarcely affected their opinion of their neighbour, but this strong piece of confirmatory evidence gave a terrible shock to their confidence in him.

Mr. Carne was next called. He testified to being summoned while dressing by the cries of the servants, and to having found his sister lying dead.

"Now, Mr. Carne," the coroner said, "you have heard the evidence of Lieutenant Gulston as to a quarrel that appears to have taken place on the afternoon of this sad event, between your sister and Captain Mervyn. It seems from what he said that you also overheard a portion of it."

"I beg to state that I attach no importance to this," Reginald Carne said, "and I absolutely refuse to give any credence to the supposition that my cousin, Captain Mervyn, was in any way instrumental in the death of my sister."

"We all think that, Mr. Carne, but at the same time I must beg you to say what you know about the matter."

"I know very little about it," Reginald Carne said, quietly. "I was about to enter the drawing-room, where I knew my cousin and my sister were, and I certainly heard his voice raised loudly. I opened the door quietly, as is my way, and was about to enter, when I heard words that showed me that the quarrel was somewhat serious. I felt that I had better leave them alone, and therefore quietly closed the door again. A few seconds later Lieutenant Gulston rushed in from the front door, and was about to enter when I stopped him. Seeing that it was a mere family wrangle, it was better that no third person should interfere in it, especially as I myself was at hand, ready to do so if necessary, which I was sure it was not."

"But what were the words that you overheard, Mr. Carne?"

Reginald Carne hesitated. "I do not think they were of any consequence" he said. "I am sure they were spoken on the heat of the moment, and meant nothing."

"That is for us to judge, Mr. Carne. I must thank you to give them us as nearly as you can recollect."

"He said then," Reginald Carne said, reluctantly, "'I swear you shall never marry this sailor or any one else, whatever I may have to do to prevent it.' That was all I heard."

"Do you suppose the allusion was to Lieutenant Gulston?"

"I thought so at the time, and that was one of the reasons why I did not wish him to enter. I thought by my cousin's tone that did Lieutenant Gulston enter at that moment an assault might take place."

"What happened after the lieutenant, in compliance with your request, left you?"

"I waited a minute or two and then went in. My sister was alone. She was naturally much vexed at what had taken place."

"Will you tell me exactly what she said?"

Again Reginald Carne hesitated.

"I really don't think," he said after a pause, "that my sister meant what she said. She was indignant and excited, and I don't think that her words could be taken as evidence."

"The jury will make all allowances, Mr. Carne. I have to ask you to tell them the words."

"I cannot tell you the precise words," he said, "for she spoke for some little time. She began by saying that she had been grossly insulted by her cousin, and that she must insist that he did not enter the house again, for if he did she would certainly leave it. She said he was mad with passion; that he was in such a state that she did not feel her life was safe with him. I am sure, gentlemen, she did not at all mean what she said, but she was in a passion herself and would, I am sure, when she was cool, have spoken very differently."

There was a deep silence in the room. At last the coroner said:

"Just two more questions, Mr. Carne, and then we have done. Captain Mervyn, you say, had left the room when you entered it. Is there any other door to the drawing-room than that at which you were standing?"

"No, sir, there is no other door; the window was wide open, and as it is only three feet from the ground I have no doubt he went out that way. I heard him gallop off a minute or two later, so that he must have run straight round to the stables."

"In going from the drawing-room window to the stables, would he pass under the window of your sister's room?"

"No," Reginald replied. "That is quite the other side of the house."

"Then, in fact, the glove that was found there could not have been accidentally dropped on his way from the drawing-room to the stable?"

"It could not," Reginald Carne admitted, reluctantly.

"Thank you; if none of the jury wish to ask you any question, that is all we shall require at present."

The jury shook their heads. They were altogether too horrified at the turn matters were taking to think of any questions to the point. The Chief Constable then called the gardener, who testified that he had swept the lawn on the afternoon of the day the murder was committed, and that had a glove been lying at that time on the spot where it was discovered he must have noticed it.

When the man had done, Captain Hendricks intimated that that was all the evidence that he had at present to call.

"Now, Captain Mervyn," the coroner said, "you will have an opportunity of explaining this matter, and, no doubt, will be able to tell us where you were at the time Miss Carne met her death, and to produce witnesses who will at once set this mysterious affair, as far as you are concerned, at rest."

Ronald Mervyn made a step forward. He was still very pale, but the look of anger with which he had first heard the evidence against him had passed, and his face was grave and quiet.

"I admit, sir," he began in a steady voice, "the whole facts that have been testified. I acknowledge that on that afternoon I had a serious quarrel with my cousin, Margaret Carne. The subject is a painful one to touch upon, but I am compelled to do so. I had almost from boyhood regarded her as my future wife. There was a boy and girl understanding between us to that effect, and although no formal engagement had taken place, she had never said anything to lead me to believe that she had changed her mind on the subject; and I think I may say that in both of our families it was considered probable that at some time or other we should be married.

"On that afternoon I spoke sharply to her—I admit that—as to her receiving the attentions of another man; and upon her denying altogether my right to speak to her on such a subject, and repudiating the idea of any engagement between us, I certainly, I admit it with the greatest grief, lost my temper. Unfortunately I have been from a child given to occasional fits of passion. It is long since I have done so, but upon this occasion the suddenness of the shock, and the bitterness of my disappointment, carried me beyond myself, and I admit that I used the words that Lieutenant Gulston has repeated to you. But I declare that I had no idea whatever, even at that moment, of making any personal threat against her. What was in my mind was to endeavour in some way or other to prevent her marrying another man."

Here he paused for a minute. So far the effect of his words had been most favourable, and as he stopped, his friends breathed more easily, and the jury furtively nodded to each other with an air of relief.

"As to the glove," Ronald Mervyn went on, deliberately, "I cannot account for its being in the place where it was found. I certainly had both gloves on when I rode over here; how I lost it, or where I lost it, I am wholly unable to say. I may also add that I admit that I went direct from the drawing-room to the stable, and did not pass round the side of the house where the glove was found." He again paused. "As to where I was between one o'clock and half-past two the next morning, I can give you no evidence whatever." A gasp of dismay broke from almost every one in the room.

"It was becoming dark when I mounted my horse," he said, "and I rode straight away; it is my custom, as my fellow-officers will tell you, when I am out of spirits, or anything has upset me, to ride away for hours until the fit has left me, and I have sometimes been out all night. It was so on this occasion. I mounted and rode away. I cannot say which road I took, for when I ride upon such occasions, I am absorbed in my thoughts and my horse goes where he will. Of myself, I do not know exactly at what hour I got home, but I asked the stableman, who took my horse, next morning, and he said the clock over the stable-gate had just struck half-past three when I rode in. I do not know that I have anything more to say."

The silence was almost oppressive for a minute or two after he had finished, and then the coroner said: "The room will now be cleared of all except the jury."

The public trooped out in silence. Each man looked in his neighbour's face to see what he thought, but no one ventured upon a word until they had gone through the hall and out into the garden. Then they broke up in little knots, and began in low tones to discuss the scene in the dining-room. The shock given by the news of the murder of Miss Carne was scarcely greater than that which had now been caused by the proceedings before the coroner. A greater part of those present at the inquest were personal friends of the Carnes, together with three or four farmers having large holdings under them. Very few of the villagers were present, it being felt that although, no doubt, every one had a right to admission to the inquest, it was not for folks at Carnesford to thrust themselves into the affairs of the family at The Hold.

Ronald Mervyn had, like the rest, left the room when it was cleared. As he went out into the garden, two or three of his friends were about to speak to him, but he turned off with a wave of the hand, and paced up and down the front of the house, walking slowly, with his head bent.

"This is a horribly awkward business for Mervyn," one of the young men, who would have spoken to him, said. "Of course Mervyn is innocent; still it is most unfortunate that he can't prove where he was."

"Most unfortunate," another repeated. "Then there's that affair of the glove and the quarrel. Things look very awkward, I must say. Of course, I don't believe for a moment Mervyn did it, because we know him, but I don't know what view a jury of strangers might take of it."

Two or three of the others were silent. There was present in their minds the story of The Hold, and the admitted fact of insanity in the family of Ronald Mervyn, which was in close connection with the Carnes. Had it been any one else they, too, would have disbelieved the possibility of Ronald Mervyn having murdered Margaret Carne. As it was, they doubted: there had been other murders in the history of the Carnes. But no one gave utterance to these thoughts, they were all friends or acquaintances of the Mervyn family. Ronald might yet be able to clear himself completely. At any rate, at present no one was inclined to admit that there could be any doubt of his innocence.

"Well, what do you think, doctor, now?" Lieutenant Gulston asked his friend, as separated from the rest they strolled across the garden.

"I don't quite know what to think," Dr. Mackenzie said, after a pause.

"No?" Gulston said in surprise. "Why it seems to me as clear as the sun at noon-day. What I heard seemed pretty conclusive. Now there is the confirmation of the finding of the glove, and this cock and bull story of his riding about for hours and not knowing where he was."

"Yes, I give due weight to these things," the doctor said, after another pause, "and admit that they constitute formidable circumstantial evidence. I can't account for the glove being found there. I admit that is certainly an awkward fact to get over. The ride I regard as unfortunate rather than damnatory, especially if, as he says, his fellow officers can prove that at times, when upset, he was in the habit of going off for hours on horseback."

"But who else could have done it, Mackenzie? You see the evidence of the doctor went to show that she was murdered when asleep; no common burglar would have taken life needlessly, and have run the risk of hanging; the whole thing points to the fact that it was done out of revenge or out of ill-feeling of some sort, and has it not been shown that there is not a soul in the world except Mervyn who had a shadow of ill-feeling against her?"

"No, that has not been shown," the doctor said, quietly. "No one was her enemy, so far as the witnesses who were asked knew; but that is a very different thing; it's a very difficult thing to prove that any one in the world has no enemies. Miss Carne may have had some; some servant may have been discharged upon her complaint, she may have given deep offence to some one or other. There is never any saying."

"Of course that is possible," said the lieutenant again, "but the evidence all goes against one man, who is known to have an enmity against her, and who has, to say the least of it, a taint of insanity in his blood. What are the grounds on which you doubt?"

"Principally on his own statement, Gulston. I watched him narrowly from the time that you gave your evidence, and I own that my impression is that he is innocent. I give every weight to your evidence and that afforded by the glove, and to his being unable to prove where he was; and yet, alike from his face, his manner, and the tone of his voice, I do not think that he is capable of murder."

No other words were spoken for some time, then the lieutenant asked:

"Do you think that an insane person could commit a crime of this kind and have no memory of it in their saner moments?"

"That is a difficult question, Gulston. I do believe that a person in a sudden paroxysm of madness might commit a murder, and upon his recovery be perfectly unconscious of it; but I do not for a moment believe that a madman sufficiently sane to act with the cunning here shown in the mode of obtaining access, by the quiet stealthiness in which the victim was killed whilst in her sleep, and by the attempt to divert suspicion by the abstraction of the trinkets, would lose all memory of his actions afterwards. If Captain Mervyn did this thing, I am sure he would be conscious of it, and I am convinced, as I said, that he is not conscious."

"What will the jury think?" the lieutenant asked after a long pause.

"I think they are sure to return a verdict against him. A coroner's jury are not supposed to go to the bottom of a matter; they are simply to declare whether there is *primâ facie* evidence connecting any one with a crime; such evidence as is sufficient to justify them in coming to a conclusion that it should at any rate be further examined into. It's a very different thing with a jury at a trial; they have the whole of the evidence that can be obtained before them. They have all the light that can be thrown on the question by the counsel on both sides, and the assistance of the summing-up of the judge, and have then to decide if the guilt of the man is absolutely proven. A coroner's jury is not supposed to go into the whole merits of the case, and their finding means no more than the decision of a magistrate to commit a prisoner for trial. I think the coroner will tell the jury that in this case such evidence as there is before them points to the fact that Captain Mervyn committed this murder, and that it will be their duty to find such a verdict as will ensure the case being further gone into."

"Most of the jury are tenants of the Carnes," Gulston said; "two or three of them I know are, for I met them at the inn when I was over here fishing. They will scarcely like to find against a relation of the family."

"I don't suppose they will," the doctor argued, "but at the same time the coroner will not improbably point out to them that their verdict will simply lead to further investigation of the case, and that even for Captain Mervyn's own sake it is desirable that this should take place, for that the matter could not possibly rest here. Were they to acquit him, I imagine the Chief Constable would at once arrest him and bring him before a magistrate, who, upon hearing a repetition of the evidence given to-day, would have no choice but to commit him for trial."

"I suppose he would do that, anyhow?" Lieutenant Gulston said.

"Not necessarily. I fancy a man can be tried upon the finding of a coroner's jury as well as upon that of a magistrate. Perhaps, however, if the coroner's jury finds against him he may be formally brought up before the magistrates, and a portion of the evidence heard, sufficient to justify them in committing him for trial. See, people are going into the house again. Probably they have thrown the door open, and the jury are going to give their finding. I don't think we need go in."

CHAPTER VI.

RUTH POWLETT.

Lieutenant Gulston and his companion had not long to wait to learn the verdict, for in a few minutes the people began to pour out of the house, and a constable came out, and, after looking round, walked up to the lieutenant.

"Mr. Gulston," he said, "your presence will be required to-morrow at eleven o'clock at Mr. Volkes's. Captain Mervyn will be brought up there at eleven o'clock to-morrow."

"Very well," Mr. Gulston replied. "What verdict have the coroners jury found?"

"They have found Captain Mervyn guilty of wilful murder," the man replied.

The next morning the inquiry was heard before Mr. Volkes and two other magistrates, and the doctor's evidence, that of Mr. Gulston, the gardener, the cook, and the constable who found the glove, was considered sufficient. Mr. Carne was not summoned, and although Ruth Powlett's name was called, she did not answer to it, Dr. Arrowsmith explaining to the bench that she was too ill to be present. Captain Mervyn was asked if he had any questions to ask the witnesses, or any statement to make; but he simply said that he should reserve his defence, and the case was then adjourned for a week to see if any further evidence would be forthcoming, the magistrates intimating that unless some altogether new light was thrown upon the subject they should commit the prisoner for trial.

Very gravely and silently the men who composed the coroner's jury walked down to Carnesford; scarce a word was spoken on the way, and a stranger, meeting them, might have supposed, not unnaturally, that they were returning from a funeral. The news had arrived before them, having been carried down at full speed by one of the few villagers who had been present. It had at first been received with absolute incredulity. The idea that Captain Mervyn should kill Margaret Carne seemed so wild a proposition that the first person to arrive with it was wholly disbelieved, and even the confirmation of those who followed him was also doubted. People, however, moved towards the foot of the hill to meet the jury, and a small crowd had collected by the time they had come down. The jury, upon being questioned, admitted that they had found Ronald Mervyn guilty, and when the fact was grasped, a sort of awed silence fell upon their hearers.

"Why, whatever were you all thinking of?" one of the men said. "Why, you must have been downright mad. You find that Captain Mervyn was the murderer of his own cousin, and Mr. Carne your own landlord, too! I never heard tell of such a thing."

The jury, indeed, were regarded almost as culprits; even to themselves now, their verdict seemed monstrous, though at the time the evidence had appeared so strong that they had felt themselves unable to resist the coroner's expressed opinion that, upon the evidence before them, they had no course open but to return a verdict of wilful murder against Ronald Mervyn.

"You will hear about it presently, lads," Hiram Powlett said. "If you had been in our place, and had heard what we have heard, you would have said the same. I should have no more believed it myself this morning, if any one had told me that Captain Mervyn had murdered his cousin, than I should if they had told me that the mill stream was running the wrong way; but now I sees otherwise. There ain't one of us here as wouldn't have given another verdict if we could have done so, but having heard what we heard there weren't no other verdict to be given. I would have given a hundred pounds myself to have found any other way, but I couldn't go against my conscience; and besides, the coroner told us that if Captain Mervyn is innocent, he will have full opportunity of proving it at the trial. And now I must be off home, for I hear Mr. Carne sent down Ruth, as soon as she had given her evidence, in one of his carriages."

Ruth had so far recovered that she was sitting on a chair by the fire when her father entered. She had heard nothing of what had taken place at the inquest beyond her own evidence, and she looked anxiously at her father as he slowly took off his coat and hat and hung them up, and came over to the fire beside her.

"How are you feeling now, Ruth? You were looking sadly when you were in the court."

"I believe you will kill the child between you," Mrs. Powlett said, testily, as she entered with the dinner. "Any one can see with half an eye that she ain't fit to be going before a court and giving evidence after the shock as she 'as had. She ought to have been left quiet. If you had half the feeling of a man in you, Hiram Powlett, you wouldn't have let them do it. If I had been there I should have got up and said: 'Your worship can see for yourself as my daughter is more fit to be in bed than to be worried and questioned here. She ain't got nothing to tell you more than you knows yourself. She just came in and found her mistress dead, and that's all she knows about it.'"

"And what verdict did you find, father?" Ruth asked, as soon as her mother had finished.

"'What verdict did you find, father?' Ruth asked."

"Verdict! What verdict should they find," Mrs. Powlett said, angrily, "but that they just knew nothing at all about it?"

"That wasn't the verdict, Hesba," Hiram Powlett said, as he seated himself at the table; "I wish to God it had been. There was things came out at the trial as altogether altered the case. We found as one had been quarrelling with Miss Carne, and threatening what he would do to her. We found as something belonging to him had been found close at hand, where it could only have been put somewhere about the time of the murder. We found as the person couldn't tell us where he had been at the time; and though it were sorely against us to do it, and seemed the most unnatural thing in the world, we had to find a verdict of wilful murder against Captain Mervyn."

Ruth had risen from her seat as her father was speaking; her face had grown whiter and whiter as he went on, and one hand had gone to her heart, while the other clutched at the back of the chair. As he finished she gave a sudden start, and burst into a scream of hysterical laughter, so startling Hiram Powlett and his wife, neither of whom was looking at her, that the former upset his chair as he started to his feet, while the latter dropped the plate she was in the act of setting before him.

For some minutes the wild laughter rang through the house. Hesba had at once taken the girl in her arms, and seated her in the chair again, and after trying for a minute or two vainly to soothe her, turned to Hiram.

"Don't stand staring there, Hiram; run for the doctor. Look what you have done, with your stories about your courts and your verdicts. You have just scared her out of her mind."

Fortunately as Hiram ran up into the village street he saw Dr. Arrowsmith— who had waited at The Hold, talking over the matter to some of his neighbours—driving down the hill, and at once fetched him in to Ruth.

"The girl is in violent hysterics, Hiram," the doctor said, as soon as he had entered. "Carry her upstairs, and lay her down on the bed; it's no use trying to get her to drink that now"—for Mrs. Powlett was trying in vain to get Ruth to take some brandy—"she cannot swallow. Now I will help you upstairs with her. The great thing is to get her to lie down."

It seemed hours to Hiram Powlett, as he listened to the wild screaming and laughter overhead, but in reality it was not many minutes before the doctor came down again.

"I am going to drive home and get some chloroform," he said, "I shan't be two minutes gone;" and before Hiram could ask a question he hurried out, jumped into his dogcart, and drove off.

There was no change until his return, except that once or twice there was a moment's cessation in the screaming. Hiram could not remain in the house, but went out and walked up and down until the doctor returned.

"No change, I hear," the latter remarked, as he jumped down from the dogcart, for Ruth's cries could be heard down at the gate of the garden.

Then he hurried on into the house and upstairs, poured some chloroform into a handkerchief, and waved it in Ruth's face. Gradually the screams abated, and in two or three minutes the girl was lying quiet and still.

"Now, lift her head, Mrs. Powlett, while I pour a few drops of this narcotic between her lips."

"Can she swallow, sir?"

"Not consciously, but it will find its way down her throat. I don't like doing it, but we must send her to sleep. Weak as she is, and shaken by all she has gone through, she will kill herself if she goes on with these hysterics."

As soon as Ruth showed signs of returning consciousness, the doctor again placed the handkerchief near her face, keeping his fingers carefully on her pulse as he did so.

This was repeated again and again, and then the opiate began to take effect.

"I think she will do now," he said, at last; "it's a hazardous experiment, but it was necessary. Now you can go down to your husband for a few minutes, and tell him how she is. I shall remain here for a time."

"She is off now," Mrs. Powlett said, as she came downstairs.

"Asleep?" Hiram asked.

"Well, it's sleep, or chloroform, or laudanum, or a little of each of them," Mrs. Powlett said. "Anyhow, she is lying quiet, and looks as if she were asleep. Dear, dear, what things girls are. And to think that all these years we have never had a day's sickness with her, and now it all comes one on the top of the other; but, of course, when one's got a husband who comes and blurts things out before a girl that's that delicate that the wind would blow her over, what can you expect?"

"I didn't mean——" Hiram began, but Hesba cut him short.

"That's the way with men; they never do mean; they never use the little sense they have got. I don't expect that there's a man, woman, or child in Carnesford that wouldn't have known better. Here you had her down here for well nigh a month as bad as she could be; then she gets that terrible shock and goes off fainting all day; then she has to go into court, and as if that wasn't enough for her, you comes and blurts out before her that you found as Captain Mervyn murdered his cousin. I wouldn't call myself a man if I was you, Hiram Powlett. I had a better idea of you before."

"What could I have said?" urged Hiram, feebly.

"Said?" Hesba repeated, scornfully. "In the first place you need not have said anything; then if you couldn't hold your tongue, you might have said that, of course, you had found a verdict of wilful murder against some one or other, which would be quite true; but even if it hadn't been you need not have minded that when it comes to saving your own daughter's life. There, sit down and have some food, and go out to your mill."

Hiram Powlett had no appetite whatever, but he meekly sat down, ate a few mouthfuls of food, and then, when Hesba left the room for a moment, took his cap from the peg and went out. Mrs. Powlett ate her meal standing; she had no more appetite for it than her husband, but she knew she should not have an opportunity of coming downstairs again when once the doctor had left, so she conscientiously forced herself to eat as much as usual, and then, after clearing away the things, and warning the little servant that she must not make the slightest sound, she went into the parlour and sat down until the doctor came downstairs.

"She is quiet now. I will come back again when I have had my dinner. Sit close by her, and if you see any signs of change, sprinkle a little water on her face and send for me; and you may pour a few drops of brandy down her throat. If her breathing continues regular, and as slow as it is at present, do nothing until I return."

For a fortnight Ruth Powlett lay between life and death, then she turned the corner, and very slowly and gradually began to recover. Six weeks had passed by, and she was about again, a mere shadow of her former self. No further evidence of any kind had been obtained with reference to the murder at The Hold. Mrs. Mervyn had a detective down from London, and he had spent days in calling at all the villages within twenty miles in the endeavour to find some one who had heard a horseman pass between the hours of twelve and three. This, however, he failed to do; he had tracked the course of Ronald Mervyn up to ten o'clock, but after that hour he could gather no information. Even a reward of fifty pounds failed to bring any tidings of a horseman after that hour. Ronald Mervyn had followed a circuitous route, apparently going quite at random, but when heard of at ten o'clock he was but thirteen miles distant, which would have left an ample margin of time for him to have ridden to The Hold and carried out his designs.

The description of Margaret Carne's watch and jewellery had been circulated by the police throughout England, but so far none of it appeared to have been offered for sale at any jeweller's or pawnbroker's in the country. In South Devonshire, people were divided into two parties on the subject of Ronald Mervyn's guilt or innocence. No one remained neutral on the subject. Some were absolutely convinced that, in spite of appearances, he was innocent. Others were equally positive that he was guilty. The former insisted that the original hypothesis as to the murder was the correct one, and that it had been committed by some tramp. As to the impossibility of this man having killed Margaret Carne in her sleep, they declared that there was nothing in it. Every one knew that tramps were rough subjects, and this man might be an especially atrocious one. Anyhow, it was a thousand times more probable that this was how it came about than that Ronald Mervyn should have murdered his cousin.

The other party were ready to admit that it was improbable that a man should murder his cousin, but they fell back upon the evidence that showed he and no one else had done it, and also upon the well-known curse upon Carne's Hold, and the fact that Mervyn on his mother's side had the Carne blood in his veins. Every one knew, they argued, that mad people murder their husbands, wives, or children; why, then, not a cousin?

There was a similar difference of opinion on the subject among the little conclave in the snuggery at the "Carne's Arms."

Jacob Carey and the old clerk were both of opinion that Ronald Mervyn was guilty, the former basing his opinion solely upon the evidence, and the latter upon the curse of the Carnes. The landlord maintained a diplomatic reserve. It was not for him to offend either section of his customers by taking a decided side. He therefore contented himself by saying, "There's a great deal in what you say," to every argument brought forward in the coffee-room, the tap-room, or snuggery.

The "Carne's Arms" was doing a larger trade than it had ever done before. There were two detectives staying in the house, and every day coaches brought loads of visitors from Plymouth; while on Saturday and Monday hundreds of people tramped over from the railway station, coming from Plymouth and Exeter to have a view of the house where the tragedy had taken place. The pressure of business was indeed so great that the landlord had been obliged to take on two extra hands in the kitchen, and to hire three girls from the village to attend to the customers in the coffee-room and tap-room.

Hiram Powlett was Captain Mervyn's champion in the snuggery. It was true he had few arguments to adduce in favour of his belief, and he allowed the smith and Reuben Claphurst to do the greater part of the talking, while he smoked his pipe silently, always winding up the discussion by saying: "Well, neighbours, I can't do much in the way of arguing, and I allow that what you say is right enough, but for all that I believe Captain Mervyn to be innocent. My daughter Ruth won't hear a word said as to his being guilty, and I think with her."

Hiram Powlett and his wife had indeed both done their best to carry out the doctor's orders that nothing should be said in Ruth's hearing of the murder. But the girl, as soon as she was sufficiently recovered to talk, was always asking questions as to whether any further clue had been discovered as to the murderer, and she was indeed so anxious and urgent on the matter that the doctor had felt it better to withdraw his interdict, and to allow her father to tell her any little scraps of gossip he had picked up.

"The idea has evidently got possession of her mind, Hiram," the doctor said.

"She was very attached to her mistress, and is no doubt most anxious that her murderer shall be brought to justice. I have changed my opinion, and think now that you had better not shirk the subject. She has been a good deal more feverish again the last day or two. Of course she must stay here now until after the trial, which will come off in a fortnight. When that is over, I should strongly recommend you to send her away from here for a time; it doesn't matter where she goes to, so that she is away from here. If you have any friends or relations you can send her to, let her go to them; if not, I will see about some home for convalescent patients where she would be taken in. There are several of them about; one at the Isle of Wight, I believe. That would suit her very well, as the climate is mild. Anyhow, she must not stop here. I shall be heartily glad myself when the trial is over. Go where I will I hear nothing else talked about. No one attends to his own business, and the amount of drunkenness in the place has trebled. If I had my way, I would have a regulation inflicting a heavy fine upon every one who after the conclusion of the trial ventured to make any allusion, however slight, to it. It's disgusting to see the number of people who come here every day and go up the hill to have a look at the house."

As the day for the trial approached, Ruth Powlett became more and more anxious and nervous about it. It kept her awake at nights, and she brooded on it during the day. For hours she would sit with her eyes fixed upon the fire without opening her lips, and the doctor became seriously anxious lest she should be again laid up before it became necessary to give her evidence.

There was indeed a terrible fight going on in Ruth's mind. She knew that Captain Mervyn was innocent; she knew that George Forester was guilty, and yet the memory of her past life was still so strong in her that she could not bring herself to denounce him, unless it became absolutely necessary to do so to save Ronald Mervyn's life. Ronald had insulted and threatened her mistress, and had not George Forester been beforehand with him, he might have done her some grievous harm, or he might perhaps have murdered Lieutenant Gulston, for whom Ruth felt a strong attraction because she had discerned that Margaret loved him.

It was right, then, that Ronald Mervyn should suffer, but it was not right that he should be hung. If he could clear himself without her being obliged to denounce George Forester, let him do so; but if not, if he were found guilty, then she had no other course open to her. She must come forward and produce the knife and describe how she had found it, and confess why she had so long concealed it. All this would be very terrible. She pictured to herself the amazement of the court, the disapproval with which her conduct would be received, the way in which she would be blamed by all who knew her, the need there would be for going away from home afterwards and living somewhere where no one would know her story; but not for this did she ever waver in her determination. Ronald Mervyn must be saved from hanging, for she would be as bad as a murderess if she kept silent and suffered him to be executed for a crime she knew that he had not committed.

Still she would not do it until the last thing; not till everything else failed would she denounce George Forester as a murderer. She loved him no longer; she knew that had he not been interrupted he would perhaps have killed her. It was partly the thought of their boy-and-girl life, and of the hours they had spent together by the side of the Dare, that softened her heart; this and the thought of the misery of the kind old man, his father.

"I don't understand Ruth," the doctor said one day to Mrs. Powlett. "She ought to get better faster than she does. Of course she has had a terrible shock, and I quite understand its affecting her as it did, just as she was recovering from her former illness; but she does not mend as she ought to do. She has lost strength instead of gaining it during the past week. She is flushed and feverish, and has a hunted look about her eyes. If I had known nothing of the circumstances of the case I should have said that she has something on her mind."

"There is nothing she can have on her mind," Hesba Powlett replied. "You know we had trouble with her about that good-for-nothing George Forester?" The doctor nodded. It was pretty well known throughout the village how matters stood.

"She gave him up weeks and weeks ago, just at the time he went away, when he was wanted for the share he had in that poaching business up in the Carne Woods. She told her father that she saw we had been right, and would have nothing more to say to him. That was a week or more before she had that fall on the hill, and I have never heard her mention his name since. I feel sure that she is not fretting about him. Ruth has always been a sensible girl, and once she has made up her mind she wasn't likely to turn back again."

"No, I should not say that she was fretting on his account, Mrs. Powlett. Fretting in young women shows itself in lowness of spirits and general depression and want of tone. In her case it appears to me to be rather some sort of anxiety, though about what I cannot guess. If it had been any other girl in the village, I should have had my suspicion that she had taken a fancy in some way to Ronald Mervyn, and was anxious about the trial; but of course that is out of the question in Ruth's case. No doubt she is anxious about the trial, and has a nervous dread of being obliged to stand up and describe the scene again in a crowded court, and perhaps be questioned and cross-questioned. It's a trying thing for any one; still more so, of course, for a girl whose nerves have been shattered, and who is in a weak and debilitated state of health. Well, I shall be heartily glad when it's all over, and we settle down into our ordinary ways."

"What do you think will be the verdict, sir? Do you think they will find Captain Mervyn guilty?"

"I do not like to give an opinion, Mrs. Powlett. It depends so much on the jury, and on the way the counsel and judge put it, but I hardly think that the evidence is sufficient to hang a man. There are, of course, grave grounds for suspicion, but I should doubt whether any jury would find Mervyn guilty upon them. It would be amply sufficient if it were merely a case of robbery, but men don't like to find a verdict when there is a possibility of their finding out too late to save a man's life that they have been mistaken. At any rate, Mrs. Powlett, do your best to keep Ruth's thoughts from dwelling on the subject. I wish it was summer weather, and that she could sit out in the garden. Of course she is not strong enough to be able to walk, except for a hundred yards or so, but I would get her to take a little turn, if it's only once round the garden now and then."

"I don't think she would walk if she could, sir. When I was speaking the other day about her getting well enough to go out for walks, she turned white and shivered, and said she didn't want to go outside the door again, not for ever so long. That fall she got seems to have changed her altogether."

"Well, well, we must get her away, as I said, Mrs. Powlett. She wants more bracing air than you have got here, and to have the wind either coming straight off the sea or else to be in some hilly, breezy place."

"I am sure I don't know how it's to be managed. She can't go by herself, and I don't see how I am to leave Hiram."

"You will have to leave Hiram for a day or two, and take her wherever we fix upon as the best place and settle her there. Hiram will get on very well without you for a day or two. She is no more fit to travel alone than a baby. However, I must be off. Keep up her spirits as well as you can, and don't let her brood over this business."

At last the day when Ronald Mervyn was to be tried for murder arrived. The Assizes were at Exeter, and never in the memory of man had there been such numerous applications to the sheriff and other officials for seats in the court. The interest in the case had extended far beyond the limits of Devonshire. The rank in life of the victim and the accused, the cold-blooded nature of the murder, and the nature of the evidence rendered the affair a *cause célèbre*, and the *pros* and *cons* of the case were discussed far and wide.

The story of the curse of Carne's Hold had been given at full length by the reporters of the local papers and copied by all the journals of the kingdom, and the fact that madness was hereditary in the family went for much in the arguments of those who held that Captain Mervyn was guilty. Had it not been for this, the tide of public feeling would have been distinctly in favour of the accused.

By itself, the rest of the evidence was inconclusive. Men who have been jilted not unfrequently use strong language, and even threats, without anything coming of it. The fact of the glove having been found where it was was certainly suspicious, but, after all, that in itself did not count for much; the glove might have been blown to where it was found, or a dog might have picked it up and carried it there. A dozen explanations, all possible even if not probable, could be given for its presence, and before a man could be found guilty of murder upon circumstantial evidence, there must be no room whatever left for doubt. Therefore, the quarrel, the finding of the glove, and even the fact that Captain Mervyn was unable to prove an *alibi*, would scarcely have caused public opinion to decide against him had it not been for the fact of that taint of insanity in his blood. Call a dog mad and you hang him. Call a man mad and the public will easily credit him with the commission of the most desperate crimes; therefore, the feeling of the majority of those who assembled at the Court House at Exeter, was unfavourable to Ronald Mervyn.

The attitude of the prisoner did much to dispel this impression; he was grave, as one might well be with such a charge hanging over him, but there was nothing moody or sombre, still less wild, in his expression; he looked calmly round the court, acknowledged the encouraging nods given him by some of his fellow officers, who had come over to bear witness on the point of character, and who to a man believed him to be innocent. Certainly there was nothing to suggest in the slightest degree the suspicion of madness in his appearance; and many of those who had before been impressed by the story of the family taint, now veered round and whispered to their friends that the story of insanity was all nonsense, and that Ronald Mervyn looked wholly incapable of such a crime as that of which he was accused.

Dr. Arrowsmith had brought Ruth over under his personal charge. As she came out, when he called in his trap to take her to the station, he was surprised at the change which had taken place since he saw her the evening before. The anxious and nervous expression of her face was gone, and she looked calm and composed. There was indeed a certain determined expression in her face that led the doctor to believe that she had by a great effort conquered her fear of the ordeal to which she was to be exposed, and

76

had nerved herself to go through it unflinchingly. As they journeyed in the train she asked him:

"Shall we be in the court all the time, doctor?"

"No, Ruth, I do not think you will be in court. I fancy the witnesses remain in a room together until they are wanted. I myself shall be in court, as the solicitor for the defence is a personal friend of mine, and will give me a place at his table."

"Do you think, sir, that after I have given my evidence they would let me stand there until it is done?"

"I should hardly think so, Ruth, and I am sure it would be a very bad thing for you."

"I have a particular reason for wanting to be there, Dr. Arrowsmith, and to hear it to the end. A most particular reason. I can't tell you what it is, but I must be there."

The doctor looked at her in surprise.

"You think you will not feel the suspense as much if you are in the court as you would outside Ruth? Is that what you mean?"

"That's it, partly, sir. Anyhow, I feel that I must be there."

"Very well, Ruth, if you see it in that way, I will do what I can for you. I will ask Captain Hendricks to speak to the policemen in the court, and tell them to let you remain there after you have given your evidence. There will be a great crowd, you know, and it will be very close, and altogether I think it is foolish and wrong of you."

"I am sorry you think so, sir; but I do want to be there, whatever happens to me afterwards."

"Of course you can do as you like, Ruth; but the probability is that you will faint before you have been there five minutes."

"I will try not to, sir, and I don't think I shall. It is only when I get a sudden shock that I faint, and I don't think I can get one there."

CHAPTER VII.

THE VERDICT.

The trial of Ronald Mervyn for the murder of Margaret Carne was marked by none of the unexpected turns or sudden surprises that not unfrequently give such a dramatic interest to the proceedings. All the efforts of the police had failed in unearthing any facts that could throw a new light upon the subject, and the evidence brought forward was almost identical with that given at the coroner's inquest; the counsel asked a great many questions, but elicited no new facts of importance; the only witnesses called for the defence were those as to character, and one after another the officers of Mervyn's regiment came forward to testify that he was eminently popular, and that they had never observed in him any signs of madness.

They said that at times he got out of spirits, and was in the habit of withdrawing himself from their society, and that on these occasions he not infrequently went for long rides, and was absent many hours; he was, perhaps, what might be called a little queer, but certainly not in the slightest degree mad. Old servants of the family and many neighbours gave testimony to the same effect, and Dr. Arrowsmith testified that he had attended him from childhood, and that he had never seen any signs of insanity in his words or actions.

Ruth had escaped the one question which she dreaded, whether she had seen anything in the room that would afford a clue to the discovery of the perpetrator of the crime. She had thought this question over a hundred times, and she had pondered over the answer she should give. She was firmly resolved not to tell an actual lie, but either to evade the question by replying that when she recovered her senses she made straight to the door without looking round; or, if forced to reply directly, to refuse to answer, whatever the consequences might be. It was then with a sigh of deep relief that she left the witness-box, and took up her station at the point to which the policeman made way for her. As she did so, however, he whispered:

"I think you had better go out, my girl. I don't think this is a fit place for you. You look like to drop now;" but she shook her head silently, and took up her station in the corner, grasping in one hand something done up in many folds of paper in her pocket.

The same question had been asked other witnesses by the counsel for the defence, and he had made a considerable point of the fact that the constable and Dr. Arrowsmith both testified that the candles were standing one on each side of the looking-glass, and although the room had been carefully searched, no half-burnt match had been discovered. In his address for the defence he had animadverted strongly upon this point.

"It was a dark night, gentlemen. A dark night in November. You will remember we had the evidence that whoever committed this murder must have moved about the room noiselessly; the evidence shows that the murderer drew down the clothes so gently and softly that he did not awaken the sleeper. Now, as intelligent men, you cannot but agree with me that no man could have made his way about this absolutely dark room with its tables and its furniture, and carried out this murder in the way stated, without making some noise; it would be an utter impossibility. What is the conclusion? He was either provided with a light, or he was forced to strike a match and light a candle.

"In the latter case he must have been provided with silent matches, or the noise would have awakened the sleeper. Of one thing you may be sure, Captain Mervyn had not provided himself with silent matches; but even had not the sound of an ordinary match being struck awakened the sleeper, surely the sudden light would have done so. I ask you from your own experience whether, however soundly you might be sleeping, the effect of a candle being lit in your room would not awaken you; therefore I think it safe to assume that in the first place, because no match was found, and in the second place, because had a candle been lit it would assuredly have awakened the sleeper, and we know that she was not awakened, that no candle was lighted in the room.

"How then did the assassin manage after entering the room to avoid the dressing-table, the chairs, and other furniture, and to see to manipulate the bedclothes so gently that the sleeper was not awakened? Why, gentlemen, by means of the implement carried by every professional burglar, I mean, of course, a dark lantern. Opening the shade slightly, and carefully abstaining from throwing the light towards the bed, the burglar would make his way towards it, showing sufficient light to carry out his diabolical purpose, and then opening it freely to examine the room, open the trinket-box, and carry away the valuables.

"The counsel for the prosecution, gentlemen, has not even ventured to suggest that the prisoner, Captain Mervyn, was possessed of such an article. His course has been traced through every village that he rode, up to ten o'clock at night, by which time every shop had long been closed, and had he stopped anywhere to buy such an article we should surely have heard of it. Therefore, gentlemen, I maintain that even if this fact stood alone, it ought to convince you of the innocence of the prisoner.

"In his reply, the counsel for the prosecution had admitted that some weight must be attached to this point, but that it was quite possible that whoever entered the window might have felt on the table until he found a candlestick, and lit it, stooping down behind the table, or at the bottom of the bed, and so shading it with his coat that its light would not fall on the face of the sleeper. As for the point made that no match had been found, no great weight could be attached to it; the prisoner might have put it in his pocket or thrown it out of the window."

When the defence was concluded, and the counsel for the prosecution rose to speak, the feeling in the court was still against the prisoner.

In all that had been said the evidence pointed against him, and him only, as the author of the crime; no hint of suspicion had been dropped against any other person; and the manner in which the crime had been committed indicated strongly that it was the act of a person actuated by jealousy, or animosity rather than that of a mere burglar. This view of the case was strongly brought out by the counsel for the prosecution.

"The theory of the prosecution is," he said, "not that this unfortunate gentleman, while in the full possession of his senses, slew this lady, to whom he was nearly related, and for whom he had long cherished a sincere affection —the character you have heard given him by so many witnesses would certainly seem to show him to be a man incapable of such a crime. Our theory is that the latent taint of insanity in his blood—that insanity which, as you have heard from Dr. Arrowsmith and other witnesses, is hereditary in his ancestors on his mother's side, and has, before now, caused calamities, almost if not quite as serious as this—suddenly flamed out. We believe that, as has been shown by witnesses, he galloped away many miles over the country, but we believe that at last, wrought up to the highest pitch of frenzy, he returned, scaled the wall, opened the window, and murdered Miss Carne. You have heard that he was subject to moody fits, when he shunned all society; these fits, these wild rides you have heard of, are symptoms of a disordered mind. Perhaps had all gone happily with him, the malady would not have shown itself in a more serious form.

"Unfortunately, as we know, there was sharp and sudden unhappiness—such unhappiness as tries the fibre even of the sanest men, and might well have struck a fatal blow to his mind. It is not because you see him now, calm and self-possessed, that you are to conclude that this theory is a mistaken one. Many, even the most dangerous madmen, have long intervals when, apparently, their sanity is as perfect as that of other people. Then suddenly, sometimes altogether without warning, a change takes place, and the quiet and self-possessed man becomes a dangerous lunatic—perhaps a murderer.

"Such, gentlemen, is the theory of the prosecution. You will, of course, weigh it carefully in your minds, and it will be your duty, if you agree with it, to give expression to your opinion in your verdict."

The judge summed up the case with great care. After going through the evidence piecemeal, he told the jury that while the counsel for the defence had insisted upon the uncertainty of circumstantial evidence, and the numerous instances of error that had resulted from it, it was his duty to tell them that in the majority of cases of murder there could be, from the nature of things, only circumstantial evidence to go upon, for that men did not commit murder in the open streets in sight of other people. At the same time, when circumstantial evidence alone was forthcoming, it was necessary that it should be of the most conclusive character, and that juries should, before finding a verdict of guilty, be convinced that the facts showed that it was the prisoner, and he only, who could have done the deed.

"It is for you, gentlemen, to decide whether the evidence that has been submitted to you does prove, absolutely and conclusively to your minds, that the prisoner must have been the man who murdered Miss Carne. Counsel on both sides have alluded to the unquestioned fact that madness is hereditary in the family of the prisoner; whether or not it is inherited by him, is also for you to decide in considering your verdict. You will have to conclude first whether the prisoner did or did not commit this murder. If you believe that he did so, and that while he did so he was insane, and incapable of governing his actions, your duty will be to find him not guilty upon the ground of insanity."

The general tenor of the summing-up certainly showed that in the opinion of the judge the evidence, although strong, could not be considered as absolutely conclusive. Still, the bias was not strongly expressed, and when the jury retired, opinions in court were nearly equally divided as to what the verdict would be.

When he left the witness-box, Dr. Arrowsmith made his way to the corner in which one of the policemen had placed Ruth after giving her evidence. She had done this with a steadiness and composure that had surprised the doctor; she had fortunately escaped much questioning, for the counsel saw how fragile and weak she looked, and as she had but entered the room, seen her mistress dead, fainted and left again, there was but little to ask her. The questions put were: "Was the jewellery safe in the box when she left the room the night before? Did she remember whether the window was fastened or not?" To this her reply was negative. Miss Carne had shut it herself when she went up in the afternoon, and she had not noticed whether it was fastened. "Was the blind a Venetian or an ordinary roller blind?"

"A roller blind."

"Then, if the window opened, it could be pushed aside without noise. Did you notice whether the candlesticks were standing where you had left them?"

"I noticed that they were on the table and in about the same place where they were standing the night before, but I could not say exactly."

"I want you to go out, Ruth," Dr. Arrowsmith said, when he reached her after the jury had retired. "They may be an hour or more before they make up their minds. You are as white as death, child. Let me lead you out."

Ruth shook her head, and murmured, "I must stay." The doctor shrugged his shoulders and returned to his seat. It was an hour and a half before the door opened and the foreman of the jury entered. As he was unaccompanied, it was evident he wanted to ask a question.

"My lord," he said, "we are unanimous as to one part of the verdict, but we can't agree about the other."

"How do you mean, sir?" the judge asked. "I don't want to know what you are unanimous about, but I don't understand what you mean about being unanimous about one part of the verdict and not unanimous on the other."

The foreman hesitated. Then, to the astonishment of the court, the prisoner broke in in a clear steady voice:

"I will not accept acquittal, sir, on the ground of insanity. I am not mad; if I had been the events of the last two months would have driven me so. I demand that your verdict be guilty or not guilty."

The judge was too surprised to attempt to check the prisoner when he first began to speak, and although he attempted to do so before he had finished, the interruption was ineffectual.

"Go back, sir," the judge then said to the foreman. "You must be unanimous as to the whole of your verdict."

The interruption of the prisoner had enlightened those in court as to the nature of the foreman's question. Undoubtedly he had divined rightly. The jury were in favour of the verdict not guilty, but some of them would have added on the ground of insanity. The interruption, although irregular, if not unprecedented, had a favourable effect upon his hearers. The quickness with which the accused had seized the point, and the steady, resolute voice in which he had spoken, told in his favour, and many who before, had they been in the jury-box, would have returned the verdict of not guilty on the ground of insanity, now doubted whether they would add the concluding words.

A quarter of an hour later the jury returned.

"We are now unanimous, my lord. We say that the prisoner at the bar is not guilty."

A sound like a sigh of relief went through the court. Then every one got up, and there was a movement to the doors. The policeman lifted the bar, and Ronald Mervyn stepped out a free man, and in a moment was surrounded by a number of his fellow officers, while some of his neighbours also pressed forward to shake him by the hand.

"I will shake hands with no man," he said, drawing back; "I will greet no man so long as this cloud hangs over me—so long as it is unproved who murdered Margaret Carne."

"You don't mean it, Mervyn; you will think better of it in a few days," one of his fellow officers said, as they emerged into the open air. "What you have gone through has been an awful trial, but now that you are proved to be innocent you will get over it."

"I am not proved to be innocent, though I am not proved to be guilty. They have given me the benefit of the doubt; but to the end of my life half the world will believe I did it. Do you think I would go through life to be pointed at as the man who murdered his cousin? I would rather blow out my brains to-night. No, you will never see me again till the verdict of guilty has been passed on the wretch who murdered my cousin. Good-bye. I know that you believe me innocent, but I will not take your hands now. When you think it over, you will see as well as I do that you couldn't have a man in the regiment against whom men as he passed would whisper 'murderer.' God bless you all." And Ronald Mervyn turned and walked rapidly away. One or two of the officers would have followed him, but the colonel stopped them.

"Leave him alone, lads, leave him alone. We should feel as he does were we in his place. Good Heavens! how he must have suffered. Still, he's right, and however much we pity him, we cannot think otherwise. At the present moment it is clear that he could not remain in the regiment."

As soon as the crowd had turned away, Dr. Arrowsmith made his way to the point where Ruth had been standing. Somewhat to his surprise he found her still on her feet. She was leaning back in the corner with her eyes closed, and the tears streaming down her cheeks.

"Come, my dear," he said, putting his arm under hers, "let us be moving. Thank God it has all ended right."

"Thank God, indeed, doctor," she murmured. "I had hardly hoped it, and yet I have prayed so much that it might be so."

The doctor found that though able to stand while supported by the wall, Ruth was unable to walk. With the aid of a policeman he supported her from the court, placed her in a vehicle, and took her to an hotel.

"There, my dear," he said, when Ruth had been assisted up to a bedroom by two of the maids, "now you go to bed, and lie there till to-morrow morning. I will have a basin of strong broth sent you up presently. It's quite out of the question your thinking of going home to-night. I have several friends in the town, and am glad of the excuse to stay over the night. I will call for you at ten o'clock in the morning; the train goes at half-past ten; I will have your breakfast sent up here. I will go down to the station now. There are lots of people over here from Carnesford, and I will send a messenger back to your mother, saying that you have got through it better than I expected, but I wanted you to have a night's rest, and you will be home in the morning."

"Thank you, doctor; that is kind of you," Ruth murmured.

"Help her into bed, girls. She has been ill, and has had a very trying day. Don't ask her any questions, but just get her into bed as soon as you can."

Then the doctor went downstairs, ordered the broth and a glass of sherry for Ruth, and a bedroom for himself, and then went off to see his friends. In the morning he was surprised, when Ruth came downstairs, to see how much better she looked.

"My prescription has done you good, Ruth. I am glad to see you look wonderfully better and brighter."

"I feel so, sir. I went to sleep directly I had taken the broth and wine you sent me up, and I did not wake till they called me at half-past eight. I have not slept for an hour together for weeks. I feel as if there was such a load taken off my mind."

"Why, Ruth, you didn't know Captain Mervyn to speak to, did you, that you should feel such an interest in him?" the doctor said, looking at her sharply.

"No, sir, I have never once spoken to him that I know of."

"Then why do you care so much about his being acquitted?"

"It would have been dreadful if he had been found guilty when he was innocent all the time."

"But then no one knew he was innocent for certain," the doctor said.

"I felt sure he was innocent," Ruth replied.

"But why did you feel sure, Ruth?"

"I can't exactly say, sir, but I did feel that he was innocent."

The doctor looked puzzled, but at this moment the cab arrived at the station, and the subject was not renewed, but the doctor afterwards wondered to himself more than once whether Ruth could have any particular reason for her assurance of Ronald Mervyn's innocence.

For another ten days the Mervyn trial was the great topic of conversation throughout the country, and the verdict was canvassed with almost as much keenness and heat as the crime had been before the trial. Now that Ronald Mervyn was no longer in hazard of his life, the feeling of pity which had before told so strongly in his favour was wanting. If a man so far forgets himself as to use threats to a woman, he must not be surprised if he gets into trouble. Of course, now the jury had given a verdict of "Not guilty," there was no more to be said. There was no doubt he was a very lucky fellow, and the jury had given him the benefit of the doubt. Still, if he hadn't done it, who had killed Margaret Carne?

Such was the general opinion, and although Ronald had still some staunch adherents in his own neighbourhood, the tide of feeling ran against him.

Two months after the trial, Mrs. Mervyn died, broken down by grief, and while this naturally caused a renewal of the talk, it heightened rather than otherwise the feeling against her son. The general verdict was that it was his doing; whether he killed Margaret Carne or not, there was no doubt that he had killed his mother. All this was doubtless unfair, but it was not unnatural; and only those who believed thoroughly in Ronald's innocence felt how hard this additional pain must be for him.

Immediately the funeral was over, the two girls moved away to London, and the house was advertised to let, but the odour of the recent tragedy hung over it. No one cared to take a house with which such a story was connected. A month or two later there was a sale of the furniture; the house was then shut up and lost to the county. Ten days after the trial it was announced in *The Gazette* that Ronald Mervyn had retired from the service upon sale of his commission. No one had seen him after he had left the court a free man. His horses were sold a week later, and his other belongings forwarded from the regiment to an address he gave in London. His mother and sister had a few days later gone up for a day to town, and had met him there. He had already written to them that he intended to go abroad, and they did not seek to combat his resolution.

"I can never come back, mother, unless this is cleared up. You must feel as well as I do, that I cannot show my face anywhere. I am surprised that I have got off myself, and indeed if it were not that I am sure I never got off my horse that night, I should sometimes suspect that I must for a time have been really mad and have done what they accuse me of. I have already sent down a detective to the village. There must be some clue to all this if one could only hit upon it, but I own that at present I do not see where it is to be looked for. I do not believe that it was done by some passing tramp. I agree with every word that was said at my trial in that respect.

"Everything points to the fact that she was deliberately murdered, though who, except myself, could have entertained a feeling of animosity against Margaret, God only knows. There is one comfort, mother, and only one," he said with a hard laugh. "I can set our minds at ease on one point, which I have never felt sure about before, that is, that I have not inherited the curse of the Carnes. Had I done so, the last two months would have made a raving lunatic of me, whereas I have never felt my head cooler and my reason clearer than I have since the day I was arrested. But you mustn't grieve for me more than you can help, mother; now that it is over, I feel more for you and the girls than I do for myself. I have a sort of conviction that somehow, though I don't see how, the thing will be cleared up some day. Anyhow I mean to go and lead a rough life somewhere, to keep myself from brooding over it. The weight will really fall upon you, far more than upon me, and I should strongly advise you to shut up the house, let it if you can, and either come up here or settle in some place—either Brighton or Hastings—where this story will be soon forgotten and no one will associate your names with this terrible business."

About that time a stranger arrived at Carnesford. He announced that he was a carpenter from the North, and that he suffered from weak lungs, and had been recommended to live down South. After staying for a week at the "Carne's Arms," he stated that he liked the village so much that he should settle there if he saw a chance of making a livelihood, and as it happened that there was no carpenter in the village, the idea was received with favour, and a week later he was established in a cottage that happened to be vacant. As he was a man who seemed to have travelled about England a good deal, and was well spoken and informed, he soon took a good position in the place, and was even admitted to form one of the party in the snuggery, where he would talk well upon occasions, but was specially popular as an excellent listener.

When spring came there was a fresh sensation. The gardener at The Hold, in digging up some ground at the edge of the shrubbery, to plant some rhododendrons there, turned up the missing watch and jewellery of Margaret Carne. It was all buried together a few inches below the soil, without any wrapper or covering of any kind. Captain Hendricks arrived at Carnesford as soon as the news of the discovery reached him. Reginald Carne was himself away, having been absent ever since the trial took place. Most of the servants had left at once; the old cook and a niece of hers alone remaining in charge, and two stablemen from the garden also staying in the house.

Nothing came of the discovery; but it, of course, renewed the interest in the mystery of Margaret Carne's death, and the general opinion was that it was fortunate indeed for Ronald Mervyn that the discovery had not been made before his trial, for it completely demolished the theory that the murder was the work of a burglar. It was possible, of course, that such a man, knowing the active hue and cry that would be set on foot, and that it would be dangerous to offer the jewellery for sale, and still more dangerous to keep it about him, had at once buried it, intending to go back some day to recover it, for, as Reginald stated at the trial, the missing jewels were worth fifteen hundred pounds.

But had they been so hidden they would assuredly have been put in a box or some sort of cover that would protect them from the damp, and not have been merely thrust into the ground. Altogether the discovery greatly heightened, instead of diminishing, the impression that the murder was an act of revenge and not the outcome of robbery; and the cloud over Ronald Mervyn became heavier rather than lighter in consequence.

Ruth Powlett had gained health and strength rapidly after the verdict "Not guilty" had been returned against Ronald Mervyn. She was still grave and quiet, and as she went about her work at home, Hesba would sometimes tell her that she looked more like a woman of fifty than a girl of nineteen; but her mind had been lightened from the burden of her terrible secret, and she felt comparatively happy. She spent much of her time over at the Foresters', for the old man and his wife were both ailing, and they knew that there was little chance of their ever seeing their son again, for the gamekeeper who had been injured in the poaching affray had since died, and as the evidence given at the inquest all pointed to the fact that it was George Forester who had struck the blow that had eventually proved fatal, a verdict of "Wilful murder" had been returned against him.

Ruth's conscience was not altogether free as to her conduct in the matter, and at the time of Mrs. Mervyn's death she suffered much. As for Ronald Mervyn himself, she had little compassion for him. She would not have permitted him to be hung; but the disgrace that had fallen upon him, and the fact that he had been obliged to leave the country, affected her but little. She had been greatly attached to her mistress, who had treated her rather as a friend than as a servant; and that he should have insulted and threatened Margaret was in her eyes an offence so serious that she considered it richly deserved the punishment that had befallen him.

Until she heard of Mrs. Mervyn's death, she had scarcely considered that the innocent must suffer with the guilty, and after that she felt far more than she had done before, that she had acted wrongly in keeping the secret, the more so since the verdict returned against George Forester in the other case had rendered the concealment to some extent futile. But, indeed, Forester and his wife did not suffer anything like the pain and shame from this verdict that they would have done had their son been proved to have been the murderer of Miss Carne. Public opinion, indeed, ran against poaching as against drunkenness, or enlisting in the army, or other wild conduct; but it was not considered as an absolute crime, nor was the result of a fight, in which a keeper might be killed by a blow struck in self-defence, regarded as a murder, in whatever point of view the law might take it. Still Ruth suffered, and at times told herself bitterly that although she meant to act for the best, she had done wrongly and wickedly in keeping George Forester's secret.

Three months later, to the regret of all Carnesford, the carpenter, who, although not a first-rate hand, had been able to do the work of the village and neighbourhood, suddenly left. He had, he said, received a letter telling him he had come into a little property up in the North, and must return to see after it. So two days later the cottage again stood vacant, and Carnesford, when it wanted a carpenter's job done, was obliged to send over to the next village for a man to do it.

CHAPTER VIII.

ENLISTED.

It was in August, 1850. Some newly-arrived emigrants had just landed from their ship, and were walking through the streets of Cape Town, watching with great amusement the novel sights, the picturesque groups of swarthy Malays in huge beehive-shaped hats, with red-and-yellow bandanas round their necks, and their women in dresses of the most gorgeous colours. Settlers from inland farms rode at a reckless pace through the streets, and huge waggons drawn by eight or ten bullocks came creaking along, often at a trot. One of the party stopped before a placard.

"Active young men wanted for the Cape Mounted Rifles. For full particulars as to service and pay, inquire of the Adjutant at the Barracks of the Corps."

"I thought they were recruited in England," he muttered to himself. "I will go round presently and see about it, but I will look at the papers first. If there is any trouble on with the natives it would suit me well, but I certainly will not enlist merely to dawdle about in the towns. I would rather carry out my idea of buying a farm and going in for stock-raising." He went into a liquor shop, called for some of the native wine, and took up a newspaper. It contained numerous letters from settlers on the frontier, all saying that the attitude of the natives had changed greatly within the last few weeks, and that all sorts of alarming rumours were current, and it was feared that in spite of the solemn treaties they had made two years before, the natives were again going to take up arms.

"I think that's good enough," he said to himself. "There are likely to be stirring times again here. Nothing would suit my case better than an active life, hard work, and plenty of excitement."

Having finished his wine, he inquired the way to the barracks of the detachment of the corps stationed at Cape Town, and being directed to it, entered the gates. He smiled to himself at his momentary feeling of surprise at the sentry at the gate neglecting to salute him, and then inquiring for the orderly room, he went across the little barrack-yard and entered. The adjutant looked up from the table at which he was writing.

"I see a notice that you want men, sir," the new-comer said.

"Yes, we are raising two fresh troops. What age are you?"

"Twenty-eight."

"You have served before, have you not?" the adjutant said, looking at the well-knit figure standing before him.

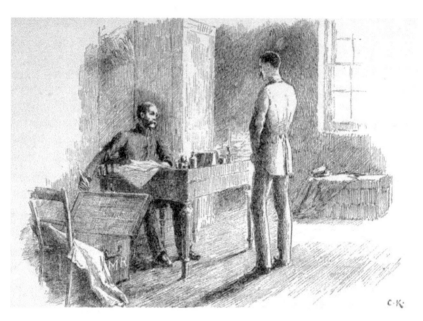

"'You have served before, have you not?' the Adjutant said."

"Yes, I have served before."

"Infantry or cavalry?"

"The infantry; but I can ride."

"Have you your papers of discharge?"

"No."

"Have you any one to speak to your character?"

"No one here. I only landed this morning by the *Thalia*, which came in from England last night."

"That is awkward," the officer said. "You know that as a rule we only enlist in

England, and only take applicants of good character."

"I am aware of that, sir; but as just at present you are likely to want men who can fight, character is not of so much importance."

The adjutant smiled, and again scrutinised the applicant closely.

"The man has been an officer," he said to himself. "Well, that is nothing to me; he has the cut of a soldier all over."

"Do you know the conditions of service? You provide your own horse and uniform. Government provides arms. In the event of your not being able to find your horse and uniform, Government will—as it is anxious to fill up the ranks as soon as possible—provide them, and stop the money from your pay."

"I can provide horse and uniform."

"Very well, then, I will take you," the officer said.

"I enlist as Harry Blunt. I may say, sir, that I should feel very greatly obliged if, as I know my duty, you would post me to a troop already up the country instead of to one of those you are raising, and who will have to learn their drill and how to sit a horse before they can be sent up on active duty."

"I can do that," the officer said; "it is only yesterday that we called for recruits, and we have only had two or three applications at present; there is a draft going on to Port Elizabeth next week, and if I find that you are, as you say, up in your drill, I will send you up with them."

"Thank you, sir, I am very much obliged to you."

"The major will be here at four o'clock," the adjutant said; "come in at that time, and you can be attested and sworn in."

"After all," Ronald Mervyn said to himself, as he strode away, "there's nothing like soldiering. I know I should have fretted for the old work if I had settled down on a farm, or even if I had gone in, as I half thought of doing, for shooting for a year or so before settling down. If these natives really mean to make trouble, we shall have an exciting time of it, for the men I have talked with who fought in the last war here say that they have any amount of pluck, and are enemies not to be despised. Now I will be off and look for a horse. I'd better not order my uniform until I am sworn in; the major may, perhaps, refuse me on the ground of want of character." He went up to two or three young farmers who were standing talking in the street.

"I am a stranger, gentlemen, and have just landed. I want to buy a good horse; can you tell me what is the best way to set about it?"

"You will have no difficulty about that," one of them replied, "for there's been a notice up that Government wants to buy horses, and at two o'clock this afternoon, those who have animals to dispose of fit for cavalry service are to bring them into the parade ground in front of the infantry barracks. Government has only asked for fifty horses, and there will probably be two or three times that number brought in. We have each brought in a horse or two, but they are rather expensive animals. I believe the horses are intended for mounts for staff-officers. They want more bone and strength than is general in the horses here."

"I don't much mind what I pay," Ronald said, carelessly. "However, gentlemen, I may see you down there, and if Government does not take your horses, perhaps I may make a deal with one of you."

At the appointed hour Ronald strolled down to the parade. There were a good many officers assembled there, and a large number of young Boer farmers, each with one or more horses, led by natives. The major and adjutant of the Cape Mounted Rifles were examining the horses, which were ridden up and down before them by their owners, the adjutant himself sometimes mounting and taking them a turn. Presently his eyes fell upon Ronald, who was closely scrutinising the horses.

"That is the young fellow I was speaking to you about, major, the man in the tweed suit examining that horse's mouth."

"Yes, I have no doubt you are right, Lawson; he has the cut of a military man all over, and beyond all question a gentleman. Out-ran the constable at home, I suppose. Well, we will take him anyhow; for rough work men of that stamp make the very best soldiers. I fancy we have more than one in our ranks now. No, you need not bring that horse up," he broke off, addressing the young farmer, whose horse Ronald had just been examining. "He's got some vice about him, or you would not be offering him at our prices."

"He's as good a horse as there is in the colony," the young Dutchman said; "but I am not offering him at your price. I thought that some young officer might be inclined to buy him, and I have brought him down to show. There is no vice about him that I know of, but he has only been mounted twice, and as he has never been off the farm before he is a bit fidgety."

"What do you want for him?" the major asked, examining the horse closely.

"I want a hundred and twenty pounds for him."

"A hundred and twenty fiddlesticks," the major said. "Why, man, there are not ten horses in the colony worth a hundred and twenty pounds."

"Perhaps not," the young Dutchman said, coolly, "but this is one of the ten."

Several of the other officers now came up and examined the horse, and they were unanimous in their approval of him.

"He would be worth three hundred as a hunter at home," one of them remarked, "but nobody's going to give such a price as that out here, when you can get a decent runner for twenty; but he is certainly the handsomest horse I have seen since I have been in the colony, and I have seen some good ones, too."

The farmer moved off with the horse. As he left the ground, Ronald again walked up to him.

"I like your horse," he said, "and if you will take a hundred pounds for him, I will give it you."

"Very well," the Dutchman said, "I will take it, but I wouldn't take a penny under. Have you the money here?"

"I have not got it in my pocket," Ronald replied, "but I have letters of credit on the bank. Walk round with me there, and I will give you the cash."

In ten minutes the money was obtained and handed to the farmer, who gave Ronald a receipt for it. Ronald took the halter from the hands of the native, and at once led the horse to the stable of the hotel at which he had already left his luggage. Then he ordered one of the cases to be opened, and took out a saddle and bridle which he had brought out with him in view of rough colonial work.

"I did not expect to be suited so soon," he said to himself, "and certainly did not expect to find such a mount here. I like him better than either of my old hunters, and will back him, after a couple of months' good handling, to win any military steeplechase. That's money well laid out; when a man may have to ride for his life, money in horseflesh is a good investment."

He went down at four o'clock, and was attested and sworn in.

"I saw you down on the parade ground, Blunt," the adjutant said. "We have bought a score of horses for the use of recruits. You can have one of them at the Government price if you choose."

"I am much obliged to you, sir," Ronald replied, "but I picked one up myself."

"He will have to pass inspection, you know, Blunt?"

"I think he's good enough to pass, sir," Ronald said, quietly. "I am considered a pretty good judge of a horse."

"There is the address of a tailor," the adjutant said, handing him a card; "he has got a supply of the right cloth, and has contracted to supply uniforms at a very reasonable price. You need not come into barracks until to-morrow, unless you choose."

"I thank you, sir. I have a few things to get, and I would rather not report myself until to-morrow afternoon, if you will give me leave."

"Very well, then, I will not ration you to-morrow. Report yourself to Sergeant Menzies any time before nine o'clock in the evening."

Ronald gave the military salute, turned on his heel, and went out of the barracks. He went straight to the tailor whose card had been given to him. "I want to be measured for a uniform for the Mounted Rifles," he said. "How much do you charge?"

"We supply tunic, jacket, and two pairs of breeches, and cap, for nine pounds."

"When can you let me have them?"

"In three days."

"I must have them by to-morrow afternoon, by six o'clock, and I will pay you two pounds extra to get them done by then. But mind, I want good-fitting clothes. Do you understand?"

"You will pay eleven pounds for them if I get them ready by six o'clock. Very well, then, I will try and do them."

"Of course you can do them, if you choose," Ronald said. "If you get them cut out and stitched together, I will come in at nine o'clock in the morning to try them on. Now where can I get jack-boots?"

"The last shop down the end of this street. Moens is the name. He always keeps a lot by him, and the Mounted Rifles here mostly deal with him."

Ronald was fortunate enough to obtain a pair of boots that fitted him well, and he now strolled back to his hotel. The next morning, after trying on his uniform, which was of dark green, he went to the stables and saddled his new purchase. The horse was fidgety and nervous from its new surroundings, and refused for some time to let him mount; but he patted and soothed it, and then putting one hand on the saddle, sprang into it at a bound. He rode at a walk through the streets, and when he got beyond the limits of the town touched the horse with his spurs. The animal reared up, lashed out behind once or twice, and then went off at a gallop. Ronald kept along the road until he was beyond the patches of land cultivated by the natives. When once in the open country, he left the road, and allowed the horse to gallop across country until its speed abated, by which time he was nearly ten miles from Cape Town; then he turned its head, and at a quiet pace rode back to the town.

"A month's schooling," he said, "and it will be an almost perfect horse; its pace is very easy, and there's no doubt about its strength and wind. You are a beauty, old boy," he went on, as he patted the animal's neck, "we shall soon be capital friends."

The uniform was delivered punctually, and after saying good-bye to his fellow-passengers who were staying at the hotel, Ronald put on his uniform, filled the valise, he had that afternoon purchased, with a useful kit, took out an excellent sporting rifle that would carry Government ammunition, and a brace of revolvers, and, packing up his other clothes and ordering all the baggage to be put away in a store until required, he mounted and rode into barracks.

"Where shall I find Sergeant Menzies?" he asked one of the men at the guardroom.

"His quarters are over there, the last door in that corner."

Ronald rode over to the point indicated, and then dismounted. He entered the passage. The sergeant's name was written on a piece of paper fastened on the first door. He came out when Ronald knocked. "I was ordered by the adjutant to report myself to you, sergeant," Ronald said, saluting.

"He told me that a recruit was coming, but how did you get your uniform? Why, you only enlisted yesterday."

"I hurried them up a bit," Ronald said. "Where shall I put my horse?"

The sergeant went into his quarters and came out with a lantern. He held it up and examined the horse.

"Well, lad, you have got a bonny beast, a downright beauty. You will have to get the regulation bridle, and then you will be complete. Let me look at you." He held up the lantern. "You will do, lad," he said, "if you make as good a soldier as you look. You only want the sword and belt to be complete. You will have them served you out in the morning. Now, come along and I will show you the stable." He made his way to the stable, where there was a vacant stall, and stood by while Ronald removed the saddle and bridle and put on the head-stall. "You can take an armful of hay from that rack yonder. I can't get him a ration of grain to-night, it's too late."

"He's just had a good feed," Ronald said, "and will not want any more, but I may as well give him the hay to amuse himself with. It will accustom him to his new quarters. What shall I do with my rifle and pistols?"

"Bring them with you, lad; but there was no occasion for you to have brought them. Government finds arms."

"I happened to have them with me," Ronald said, "and as the rifle carries Government ammunition, I thought they would let me use it."

"If it's about the right length I have no doubt they will be glad to do so, for we have no very great store of arms, and we are not quite so particular about having everything exactly uniform as they are in a crack corps at home. As for the pistols, there is no doubt about them, as being in the holsters they don't show. Several of the men have got them, and most of the officers. Now, I will take you up to your quarters." The room to which he led Ronald contained about a dozen men. Some had already gone to bed, others were rubbing up bits and accoutrements; one or two were reading. "Here's a new comrade, lads," the sergeant said; "Blunt's his name. He is a new arrival from home, and you won't find him a greenhorn, for he has served already."

Ronald had the knack of making himself at home, and was, before he turned in an hour later, on terms of good fellowship with his comrades.

In the morning, after grooming his horse, he went into the barrack-yard, when the troop formed up for dismounted drill.

"Will you take your place at once in the ranks?" Sergeant Menzies asked. "Do you feel equal to it?"

"Yes; I have not grown rusty," Ronald replied, as he fell in.

An hour's work sufficed to show Sergeant Menzies, who was drilling the troop, that the new recruit needed no instructions on that score, and that he was as perfect in his drill as any one in the troop.

"Are you as well up in your cavalry drill as in the infantry?" he asked Ronald as the troop fell out.

"No," Ronald said, "but when one knows one, he soon gets well at home in the other. At any rate, for simple work the system is exactly the same, and I think with two or three drills I shall be able to keep my place."

After breakfast the troop formed up again in their saddles, and the officers took their places in the ranks. As the sergeant handed to the adjutant some returns he had been compiling, the latter asked:

"By the way, sergeant, did the recruit Blunt join last night?"

"Yes, sir, and he is in his place now in the rear rank. He was in his uniform when he came, and I found this morning that he is thoroughly well up in his drill. A smart soldier all over, I should say. I don't know that he will do so well mounted, but I don't think you will see him make many blunders. He is evidently a sharp fellow."

"He ought not to have taken his place until I had passed his horse, sergeant. Still I can do that after parade drill is over."

The adjutant then proceeded to put the troop through a number of easy movements, such as forming from line to column, and back into line, and wheeling. There was no room for anything else in the barrack-yard, which was a small one, as the barracks would only hold a single troop. Before the movements were completed, the major came out. When the troop was dismissed Sergeant Menzies brought Ronald up to the two officers. He had in the morning furnished him with the regulation bridle, belt, and sword. Ronald drew up his horse at a short distance from the two officers and saluted.

"There's no doubt about his horse," the major said, "that is if he is sound. What a good-looking beast!"

"That it is, major. By Jove, I believe it's the very animal that young Boer asked us one hundred and twenty pounds for yesterday; 'pon my word, I believe it's the same."

"I believe it is," the major agreed. "What a soldierly-looking young fellow he is! I thought he was the right stamp yesterday, but I hardly expected to see him turn out so well at first."

The two officers walked up to Ronald, examined his horse, saddle, and uniform.

"That's not a regulation rifle you have got there," the major said.

"No, sir, it is one I brought from England with me. I have been accustomed to its use, and as it is the regulation bore, I thought perhaps I might carry it."

"It's a trifle long, isn't it?" the adjutant asked.

"Yes, sir, it's just two inches too long, but I can have that cut off by a gunsmith."

"Very well; if you do that you can carry it," the major said. "Of course it's much better finished than the regulation one, but not much different in appearance. Very well, we pass the horse." Ronald saluted and rode off to the stables.

"He hasn't come out penniless, anyhow," the major laughed.

"No, that's quite evident," the adjutant agreed. "I dare say his friends gave him a hundred or two to start on a farm, and when he decided to join us he thought he might as well spend it, and have a final piece of extravagance."

"I dare say that's it," the major agreed; "anyhow I think we have got hold of a good recruit this time."

"I wish they were all like him," the adjutant sighed, thinking of the trouble he often had with newly-joined recruits.

"By the way," the major said, "I have got word this morning that the draft is to be embarked to-morrow instead of next week. They took up a ship for them yesterday; it seems our men there are worked off their legs, for the Kaffirs are stealing cattle and horses in all directions, and the colonists have sent in such a strong letter of complaint to the Governor that even he thinks the police force on the frontier ought to be strengthened. Not, of course, that he admits in the slightest that there is any ground for alarm, or believes for a moment that the Kaffirs have any evil intentions whatever; still, to reassure the minds of the settlers, he thinks the troops may as well go forward at once."

"I wish to goodness," the adjutant said, bitterly, "that Sir Harry Smith would take a cottage for two or three months close to the frontier; it would not be long before his eyes were opened a little as to the character and intentions of the Kaffirs."

"It would be a good thing," the major agreed, "but I doubt if even that would do it till he heard the Kaffirs breaking in his doors; then the enlightenment would come too late to be of any service to the colony. By-the-bye, the colonel told me yesterday he should send me forward next week to see after things. He says that of course if there is any serious trouble he shall go forward himself."

The following morning the draft of Cape Mounted Rifles embarked on board a steamer and were taken down to Algoa Bay, and landed at Port Elizabeth, drenched to the skin by the passage through the tremendous surf that beats upon the coast, and were marched to some tents which had been erected for them on a bare sandhill behind the town.

Ronald Mervyn was amused at the variety of the crowd in the straggling streets of Port Elizabeth. Boer farmers, Hottentots, Malays, and Fingoes, with complexions varying through every shade of yellow and brown up to black; some gaily dressed in light cottons, some wrapped in a simple cowhide or a dirty blanket, many with but little clothing beyond their brass and copper ornaments.

The country round was most monotonous. As far as the eye could see it was nothing but a succession of bare, sandy flats, and, beyond these, hills sprinkled with bush and occasional clumps of aloes and elephant trees. Upon the following morning the troop marched, followed by a waggon containing their baggage and provisions, drawn by ten oxen. A little naked boy marched at the head of the oxen as their guide, and they were driven by a Hottentot, armed with a tremendous whip of immense length, made of plaited hide fastened to the top of a bamboo pole. After a fourteen miles' march the troop reached the Zwart Kop river, and, crossing the ford, encamped among the scattered mimosas and numerous wait-a-bit thorns. The horses were then knee-haltered, and they and the oxen were turned out to feed till night. The next day's march was a very long one, and for the most part across a sandy desert, to the Sunday River, a sluggish stream in which, as soon as the tents were pitched, the whole party enjoyed a bath.

"To-morrow we shall reach the Addoo Bush, Blunt," one of his comrades, who knew the country well, remarked. "This is near the boundary of what you may call the Kaffir country, although I don't think they have their kraals as far south as this, though there was fighting here in the last war, and may be again."

"But I thought our territory extended as far as the Kei River?"

"So it does nominally," the other said. "All the country as far as that was declared to be forfeited; but in point of fact the Kaffirs remained in possession of their lands on condition that they declared their allegiance to the Crown, and that each chief was made responsible for any cattle or other robberies, the spoor of which could be traced to his kraal. Of course they agreed to this, as, in fact, they would agree to anything, resolving, naturally, to break the conditions as soon as it suited them. Local magistrates and commissioners are scattered about among them, and there have been a lot of schools and missionary stations started. They say that they are having great success. Well, we shall see about that. In the last war the so-called Christian natives were among the first to turn against us, and I expect it will be the same here, for it's just the laziest and worst of the natives who pretend to become Christians. They get patches of land given them, and help in building their huts, and all sorts of privileges. By about half-a-day's work each week they can raise enough food to live upon, and all that is really required of them is to attend services on a Sunday. The business exactly suits them, but as a rule there are a great many more Hottentots than Kaffirs among the converts. I can give you a specimen of the sort of men they are. Not long since a gentleman was coming down with a waggon and a lot of bullocks from King Williamstown. The drivers all took it into their head to desert one day—it's a way these fellows have, one of them thinks he will go, and then the whole lot go, and a settler wakes up in the morning and finds that there isn't a single hand left on his place, and he has perhaps four or five hundred cows to be milked, and twice as many oxen and horses to look after. Well, this happened within a mile or so of the missionary station, so the gentleman rode over there and asked if some of the men would go with him down to Beaufort, a couple of days' march. Nobody would go; he raised his offers, and at last offered five times the usual

99

rate of pay, but not one of the lazy brutes would move, and he had at last to drive the whole lot down himself, with the aid of a native or two he picked up on the way. However, there has been pretty good order along the frontier for the last two years, partly due to the chiefs having to pay for all cattle traced to their kraals, partly to the fact that we have got four hundred Kaffir police—and an uncommon smart lot of fellows they are—scattered all along the frontier, instead of being, like us, kept principally in towns. You see, we are considered more as a military body. Of course, we have a much easier time of it than if we were knocking about in small parties among the border settlements; but there is a lot more excitement in that sort of life, and I hope that if there is trouble they will send us out to protect the settlements."

"I hope so," Ronald said, cordially. "Barrack life at a dull little town is the slowest thing in the world. I would never have enlisted for that sort of thing."

"Well, if what the settlers say turns out right, you will have plenty of excitement, I can tell you. I was in the last war, and I don't know that I want to go through another, for these beggars fight a great deal too well for it to be pleasant, I can tell you. The job of carrying despatches or escorting waggons through a bush where these fellows are known to be lurking, is about as nasty a one as a man can wish. At any moment, without the least notice, you may have half-a-dozen assegais stuck in your body. And they can shoot straight, too; their guns are long and clumsy, but they carry long distances—quite as far as our rifles, while, as for the line muskets, they haven't a chance with them."

Two more days' marching and the troop arrived at Grahamstown. Here they encamped near Fort England, where a wing of the 91st Regiment was quartered, and the next fortnight was spent in constant drills. The rifles were then ordered forward to King Williamstown, where two days later they were joined by the infantry.

Before starting, the adjutant had specially called the attention of Captain Twentyman, who commanded the troop, to his last joined recruit.

"You will find that man Blunt, who joined us yesterday, a good soldier, Twentyman. It may be he has been an officer, and has got into some row at home and been obliged to leave the service. Of course you noticed his horse on parade this morning; we have nothing like it in the Corps. The farmer who owned it offered it to us yesterday afternoon, and wanted a hundred and twenty pounds for it. He said that both his sire and dam were English hunters, the sire he had bought from an English officer, and the grandsire was a thoroughbred horse. The man has a large farm, about twenty-five miles from Cape Town, and goes in for horse-breeding; but I have seen nothing before of his as good as that. I expect the young fellow has spent his last penny in buying it. Of course I don't know what he will turn out in the way of conduct; but you will find, if he is all right in that respect, that he will make a first-rate non-commissioned officer, and mounted as he is, will, at any rate, be a most useful man for carrying despatches and that sort of thing. I confess I am very much taken with him. He has a steady, resolute sort of face; looks pleasant and good-tempered, too. Keep your eye upon him."

Captain Twentyman had done so during the voyage and on the line of march, and Ronald's quickness, alacrity, and acquaintance with his duty convinced him that the adjutant's supposition was a correct one.

"By Jove, Twentyman," an officer of the 91st said as he was standing beside him when Ronald rode up and delivered a message, "that fellow of yours is wonderfully well mounted. He's a fine soldierly-looking fellow, too, and I don't know why, but his face seems quite familiar to me."

"I fancy he has been an officer," Captain Twentyman replied, "we have several in the corps—men who have been obliged for some reason or other to sell out, and who, finding nothing else to do, have enlisted with us. You see the pay is a good deal higher than it is in the regular cavalry, and the men as a whole are a superior class, for you see they find their own horses and uniforms, so the life is altogether more pleasant than the regular service for a man of that kind. Almost all the men are of respectable family."

"I certainly seem to know his face," said the officer, thoughtfully, "although where I saw it I have not the least idea. What is his name?"

"He enlisted as Harry Blunt, but no doubt that's not his real name. Very few men of his kind, who enlist in the army, do so under their own names."

"I don't know any one of that name," the officer said, "but I certainly fancy I have seen your man before; however, I don't suppose in any case he would like being recognised; men who are under a cloud don't care about meeting former acquaintances."

A week later, to Ronald's great satisfaction, a party of twenty men, of whom he was one, under Troop-Lieutenant Daniels, were ordered to march the next morning to the Kabousie River, whence the settlers had written praying that a force might be sent for their protection, as the Kaffirs in the neighbourhood were becoming more and more insolent in their manner. Many of their cattle had been driven off, and they were in daily expectation of an attack. No waggons accompanied the party, as they would erect huts if they remained in one place, and would have no difficulty in obtaining provisions from the farmers. The men chosen for the service were all in high glee at the prospect of a change from the dulness of the life at King Williamstown, and were the objects of envy to their comrades.

The start was made at daybreak, and after two days' long marching they reached their destination. The country was a fertile one, the farmhouses were frequent, most of them embedded in orchards and vineyards, showing signs of comfort and prosperity.

"This is the first place that I have seen since I reached the colony," Ronald said to the trooper riding next to him, "where I should care about settling."

"There are a good many similar spots in this part of the country," the man said, "and I believe the folks here are everywhere doing well, and would do better if it were not for these native troubles. They suffered a lot in the last war, and will, of course, bear the brunt of it if the natives break out again. There are a good many English and Scotch settlers in this part. There are, of course, some Dutch, but as a rule they go in more for cattle-farming on a big scale. Besides, they do not care about English neighbours; they are an unsociable set of brutes, the Dutch, and keep themselves to themselves as much as possible."

CHAPTER IX.

THE OUTBREAK.

As it was possible that the detachment might remain for some time in their present quarters, Lieutenant Daniels at once set them to work to erect a couple of huts, each capable of holding ten men. Several of the farmers sent two or three of their native labourers to assist in cutting and bringing to the spot timber for the framework and supplying straw for thatching the roofs. The operation was not a long one. The walls were made with wattle plastered with mud, and the work was accomplished in a couple of days. The men were glad of the shelter, for, although the heat was very great during the day, the nights were cold and sharp. The horses were picketed behind the huts; the officer took up his quarters at a farmhouse a hundred yards away. Once housed, the men had little to do, for, in the daytime, there was no fear of the Kaffirs coming down on their plundering expeditions, such attempts being only made at night. When evening fell, the saddles were placed on the horses, and the men lay down in their clothes, simply taking off their jackets and jack-boots, so as to be in readiness to turn out at a moment's alarm. Sometimes they rode out in small parties patrolling the whole country, not with any idea of finding cattle-thieves, but merely to give confidence to settlers, whose Kaffir servants were sure to give intelligence to their friends in the bush of the presence of the Mounted Rifles in the neighbourhood.

When they had been there a fortnight they heard that the Governor had come to King Williamstown, and had summoned the various chiefs to assemble there. They had all come with the exception of the paramount Chief Sandilli, had assured the Governor of their fidelity, sworn allegiance anew, and ratified it by kissing the stick of peace. The Governor was so satisfied with their assurances that he issued a reply to the petitions of the colonists, saying that reports throughout British Kaffraria were most satisfactory, that the chiefs were astonished at the sudden arrival of the troops, and that he hoped to arrest some of the Kaffirs who had spread the alarming reports. The Governor gave his solemn assurance to those of the settlers who had left their farms that there was no occasion for alarm.

A commission, however, appointed by him to investigate the numerous complaints of the settlers, speedily forwarded to him such alarming accounts of the critical state of affairs, that he again left for the frontier, taking with him from Cape Town the 73rd Regiment and a detachment of artillery. A proclamation was at once issued for the establishment of a police force, the enrolment of new levies and of a corps of volunteers for self-defence, so as to leave the whole of the military at liberty for operations.

One day, towards the end of November, Ronald and a comrade had ridden some twelve miles out of the station, when they saw a young lady on horseback riding towards them. She drew rein when she reached them.

"We have had fifty cattle driven off in the night," she said, "and some of the neighbours have followed the trail. I am riding over to report the fact to your officer."

"We can report it," Ronald said, "and save you the trouble of riding further; but if you like we will ride back with you first, and see if we can be of any service."

"I am afraid it will be no use," the girl said; "they will be in the woods before they can be overtaken, and then, you know, there will be nothing to do but to report where their trail ended and wait for the chance of getting compensation from the chief."

By this time they were galloping back with her. The tale was similar to scores of others they had heard since their arrival in the valley, and they knew that there was but slight chance of recovering the trail, the order being stringent that they were on no account to enter the bush. The cattle, therefore, were as good as lost, for all were well aware that in the present state of things there was but little prospect of receiving compensation from the chief. The party found, indeed, upon their arrival at the farmhouse, which was a large and comfortable one, and furnished in English style, that the neighbours had returned, having traced the spoor of the stolen cattle up to the edge of the bush.

The farmer came out to the door as his daughter rode up.

"Come in," he said to the troopers, "and have some refreshment. The rascals have got away again. I expect that they are some of my old servants, for they knew the trick of the fastenings I have had put to the gate of the cattle-kraal, which would certainly have puzzled any of the Kaffirs. Now sit down and make yourselves at home."

The other settlers were already seated at the table that the Hottentots or, as they were always called, "tottie" servants, had laid with a profusion of food. The young lady, still in her blue riding-habit, did not sit down to the table, but moved about, seeing that the "tottie" girls attended to the wants of the guests. She was, Ronald thought, about eighteen years old, and had the graceful, active figure so common among girls who spend much of their time on horseback. She was strikingly pretty, and her expression of delicacy and refinement was unusual among the daughters of the colonial farmers. This he was not surprised at, when he glanced at her father, who was a fine-looking man, with a gray moustache.

"I am always glad to see the uniform again," he said, presently, to Ronald. "I served myself when I was a young man, and was an ensign in the Rifles at Waterloo, but I got tired of soldiering in the times of peace, and came out to the Cape thirty years ago, so you can well understand that I am fond of a sight of the uniform again, especially that of your corps, which is nearly the colour of my own. Well, I have had pretty nearly enough of the Cape, and intend in another year or two to go back home. I have moved a good many times, as you may imagine, since I came out, but I don't like running away, and, besides, just at present I should get nothing for my farm."

"I can imagine that farms are rather a drug in the market just now," Ronald replied, "especially those at the edge of the frontier. However, we must hope that this trouble will blow over, and now that the Governor is, as I hear, coming round with the 73rd, the Kaffirs may think better of it."

"I think they have made up their mind to give us a little trouble," the settler said. "Their witch-doctor, Umlanjeni, has been stirring them up with all sorts of predictions, and Sandilli, who no doubt set him to work, has, we know, been intriguing with the other chiefs. The sudden disappearance of the Kaffir servants from all the farms of this part of the country was, of course, in obedience to orders, and is certainly ominous. They say that there are altogether three thousand muskets, six million rounds of ball cartridge, and half-a-million assegais in the hands of the natives. It has been a suicidal business allowing trade in firearms and ammunition to be carried on with them. I wish that the talkative fools at Cape Town who manage our affairs were all located down on the frontier; they might learn some sense then as to the way of dealing with the natives. But the worst sign of all is that, as I have heard to-day from some of my Hottentots, the order has been given by Umlanjeni to slay and eat."

"To slay and eat!" Ronald repeated in surprise. "What does that mean, sir?"

"Ah, that question shows you have not been long in the colony," the settler said. "You know, the Kaffirs live at ordinary times entirely upon a vegetable diet, but it is their custom upon the approach of war to eat meat, believing that flesh gives them courage and ferocity. However, as it was only three weeks ago that the chiefs all swore to be peaceable and faithful, I hardly think that there's any danger of an outbreak for some time to come, perhaps not for some months. You see, it is just midsummer now, and my crops are nearly fit for cutting. I sent most of my cattle away a fortnight since, and when I have got my crops in I shall shut up the house and move into Grahamstown. We have many friends there, and shall stop there until we see what comes of this business, and when it is all over I shall dispose of my farm. I do not think there is any real danger here. We have always been on excellent terms with the natives, and Anta, who is chief of the tribe in this part, often comes down here and begs a bottle of Cape smoke or a pound of tobacco. He has smoked many a pipe in this room, and treacherous as the people are, I cannot think that he would allow his men to do us any harm. He generally addresses me as his white brother."

An active conversation was at the same time going on between the other guests, who were discussing the farm at which it would be best for neighbours to assemble in case of attack. The settler, whose name was Armstrong, had placed Ronald next himself, while his comrade was at the other end of the table, these being the only seats vacant at the table when they entered. Ronald and the settler chatted quietly together for some time. Mary Armstrong, who had taken her place leaning on the back of her father's chair, when she had seen the guests attended to, occasionally joined in.

Mr. Armstrong was pleased with his guest.

"I hope next time when you ride over in this direction you will call in again," he said. "I can assure you that we shall be heartily glad to see you, and, if you can get leave off duty for a night, to put you up. It is a real pleasure to me to have a chat with some one fresh from England, and to hear how things look after all these years. Why, I shall hardly know the country again, cut up as it seems to be with these railways."

After the meal was over, Ronald and his friend rode back to their quarters.

"That's a nice-looking little girl," the trooper said, as they rode away from the house; "they say her father is the richest man in these parts, and that he owns a lot of property at the Cape. If I were him I should live there instead of in this out-of-the-way place."

"I suppose he is fond of a country life," Ronald replied, ignoring the first part of the remark; "I should think that society in Cape Town is not very interesting."

"I don't know that," the other replied. "I know that if I had money enough to settle down there you wouldn't find me many hours knocking about here as a trooper."

"It's all a matter of taste," Ronald replied. "When I was at home I lived in the country and prefer it to town, and like an active life in the open air better than anything Cape Town could give me."

"That's a nice young fellow, Mary—that man in the Cape Rifles," Mr. Armstrong said to his daughter the same evening. "I should say he is altogether above his position, don't you think so?"

"I do not know that I thought much about it, father. Yes, I suppose he wasn't like an ordinary soldier."

"Not at all, Mary, not at all. I fancy from what I have heard that there are a good many young men of decent family serving in the corps. It's a thousand times better for a young fellow who's got neither money nor interest to come out here than to stay at home breaking his heart in trying to get something to do. Yes. I should say from his talk, and especially from the tone of his voice, that he has seen better days. It's a pity the colony can't afford to keep on foot four or five regiments of these Mounted Rifles. We should not hear much of native troubles if they did. The natives are much more afraid of them than of the soldiers; and no wonder. In the first place they are more accustomed to the country, and in the second place they are armed with weapons that will kill at a considerable distance, while Brown Bess is of no use at over a hundred yards. Well, I hope that young fellow will drop in again; I should like another chat with him. It's a pleasant change to meet any one who is willing to talk on some subject other than natives, and crops, and cattle."

A week later, Ronald was sent with a despatch to King Williamstown.

"There will be no answer, Blunt," Lieutenant Daniels said, as he handed it to him; "at least, no answer of any consequence. So you can stay a day in the town if you like."

"Thank you, sir; but as I do not care for towns, I will, if you will allow me, stop on my way back at Mr. Armstrong's. That is where the cattle were stolen the other day, and it will not be far out of my way from King Williamstown. He invited me to stay there for a day if I could get leave."

"Certainly, you can do so," the lieutenant said. "You can hear if there is any news of the Kaffirs stirring in that neighbourhood; they seem to have been a bit more quiet for the last week or so."

Two days later Ronald drew rein in front of Mr. Armstrong's house, late in the afternoon.

"I have taken you at your word, Mr. Armstrong," he said, as the farmer came to the door.

"I am glad to see you," the other said, cordially. "It is not a mere flying visit, I hope; but you will be able to stay with us till to-morrow?"

"Thank you, yes. I am not due at the station till to-morrow evening, and am my own master till then. I have been carrying a despatch to Williamstown."

"We have had some of the Kaffir police here to-day," the farmer said to him while they were at supper. "What do you think of them?"

"They seem smart fellows, and well up to their duty. So far as I can see they are just the sort of men for border police work."

"Yes," Mr. Armstrong agreed, "on any other border but this. To my mind they are much too closely related to the fellows in the bush to be trustworthy. They are all well enough for following up a trail or arresting a stray thief, and would, I dare say, be quite reliable if opposed to any tribe to which they were not akin, but I doubt whether they will stand to us if there is trouble with Sandilli, Macomo, and the rest of them. You see how powerful the influence of these chiefs is. When the order came, pretty nearly every Kaffir in this colony left instantly, many of them leaving considerable arrears of wages behind. If the tribal tie is so strong that men entirely beyond the reach of their chief come home the instant they are summoned, how can it be expected that the Kaffirs in this police force will fight against their own kindred?"

"It does not seem reasonable to expect such a thing, certainly," Ronald agreed. "I cannot think myself why they did not raise the force among the Fingoes. They are just as fine a race as the Kaffirs, and speak the same language, and yet they are bitterly hostile to them."

"Yes, it would have been better," Mr. Armstrong said. "I think that there was a prejudice against the Fingoes in the first place. They were not a powerful people like the Gaikas and Galegas and Basutos. A good many of them had escaped from the chiefs who held them in subjection, and came in and loafed about the colony. As all Kaffirs are given to thieving and drunkenness whenever they get the chance, the colonists looked down upon them more than upon the other natives. Not that there is any reason for their doing so, except that they saw more of them, for all the Kaffirs are the same in that respect."

"Do you think it is safe stopping here, Mr. Armstrong?" Ronald asked. They had been talking of the various cattle-stealing raids that had taken place at various points of the frontier.

"I still think so for the present. By New Year's Day I shall have got my crops in, and then I will go into town, as I told you I would; but in the meantime five or six of our nearest neighbours have agreed to move in here; I have the largest farm hereabout, and we could stand a stout siege."

"I am glad to hear that, Mr. Armstrong; the same thing has been done in a good many places and in that way you should be quite safe. I quite think the Kaffirs capable of coming down in small parties and attacking isolated houses, and murdering their occupants; but after their late protestations of fidelity, I cannot believe that the chiefs would permit anything like large parties to sally out to make war."

"That is my idea. But they are treacherous hounds, and there is never any trusting them."

"If you can manage to send one of your Fingoes off with news to us, you may be sure we shall be with you in the shortest possible time, and we will soon make mincemeat of them."

"Do not be too sure of that. I don't say in the open they would stand against a force of cavalry anywhere approaching their own numbers, but I can tell you that in the bush I consider they are fully a match for our troops man to man. What chance has a soldier with his clothes and fifty or sixty pounds weight on his back, who goes crashing along through the bushes and snapping the twigs with his heavy boots, against a native who can crawl along stark naked without making the slightest noise, and who gives the first intimation of his presence by a shot from behind a tree, or a stab with his spear? When I came out here I had naturally the same ideas as you have, and scoffed at the notion of naked savages standing up against a regular soldier, but I can tell you I have changed my opinion, and if the tribes under Sandilli are really in earnest, I promise you that you will want five times as many troops as we have got in the colony to tackle them."

Two days later a message arrived with orders to Lieutenant Daniels to rejoin with his detachment at once. On the 16th of December the whole of the troops in Albany and British Kaffraria were assembled and moved under the Commander-in-Chief towards the Amatolas, the object being to overawe the Gaikas without resorting to force, which was to be carefully avoided. The troops consisted of the 6th, 73rd, and 93rd Regiments and the Cape Mounted Rifles, altogether about 1,500 strong, with two divisions of the Kaffir police. The force moved in three columns. The Governor, who was with the central column, was met by a great number of the Gaikas chiefs, with about 3,000 of their men, at Fort Cox. They again expressed their desire for peace, but their bearing and attitude was not satisfactory. Sandilli and his half-brother, Anta, were declared by the Governor to be outlawed, and a reward issued for their apprehension.

A few days passed without further movement. On the evening of the 23rd, Sergeant Menzies said to Ronald, whom he met just as he had come out from Captain Twentyman's, "I have two pieces of news for you, Blunt. In the first place, as you know, Corporal Hodges has lost his stripes and has been sent back to the ranks for getting drunk. Captain Twentyman asked me who I could recommend for the stripes, and I told him I thought there was no one in the troop who would make a better non-commissioned officer than you would. He said that you were the man he had his eye upon. At ordinary times he should not have liked to give you your corporal's stripes after being such a short time in the corps, but that in the present state of things it was essential to have the best man who could be picked out, irrespective of his length of service: besides, as you have served before it makes it altogether a different thing."

"I am much obliged to you, sergeant," Ronald answered. "If it hadn't been for this trouble I should have preferred remaining in the ranks. I like a trooper's life and do not care about the extra pay one way or the other. Besides, as a non-commissioned officer one has more responsibility and less freedom. However, as it is I shall be glad of the step, for doubtless if there is fighting there will be a lot of scouting and escort work with very small detachments, and I confess I would prefer being in command of five or six men on such work as that, to being under the orders of a man who perhaps wouldn't know as well as I do what ought to be done. And now what is your next news?"

"The next is that our troop and B troop are to form part of a column, five hundred strong, that is to march to-morrow to a place where Sandilli is supposed to be concealed."

"Well, we shall see then," Roland said, "whether these fellows mean business or not."

"I was talking to the headquarter mess-sergeant. He tells me that the Governor's cock-sure there will be no fighting, but that Sandilli will either surrender at once or bolt before we get there."

"From all I can hear, sergeant, the Governor's opinions are usually wrong. However, we shall see about it to-morrow, and, at any rate, it's a good thing to have the question solved one way or the other. Nothing can be worse for the colonists and every one else than this state of suspense. The fellows will have to make up their mind one way or the other now."

In the morning the detachment, five hundred and eighty strong, under Colonel Mackinnon, marched from Fort Cox. The Kaffir police led the way, and were followed by the Cape Mounted Rifles, the infantry forming the rear. There were a good many natives about, but these shouted friendly greetings as the column passed, and it proceeded quietly until it reached the narrow rocky gorge of the Keiskamma, which could only be traversed in single file. Ronald Mervyn had been placed in orders the previous evening as corporal, and he was pleased to find by the remarks of the men that they did not grudge him his promotion, for soldiers are quick to recognise steadiness and ability, and they had long since concluded that Harry Blunt, although he never spoke about his military experiences, had served for some time, thoroughly knew his work, and had been a non-commissioned officer, if not an officer.

"I don't like the look of this place at all," he said to Sergeant Menzies as they halted at the mouth of the gorge. "If I were in command of the force moving among a population who might any moment show themselves hostile, I would not advance through this gorge till I had sent a company of infantry on ahead to skirmish among the bushes, and find out whether there is any one hidden there. On horseback as we are we should be almost at their mercy."

"The Kaffir policemen ahead ought to have done that work," the sergeant said. "Why, bless you, if there was as much as a fox lurking among the bushes they could find him."

"Yes, I have no doubt they could if they wanted to," Ronald agreed, "but the question is, do they want to? I have no faith whatever in those Kaffir police. I have been watching them for the last day or two talking to the Gaikas, and if the natives really mean mischief I would wager the police join them."

It was now their turn to enter the gorge, and as they moved along in single file, Ronald opened one of his holsters and held a revolver ready in hand, while he narrowly scanned the bushes that came down to the narrow path along which they were making their way. He drew a deep breath of relief when he emerged from the pass. As the troop reached the open ground they formed up and were about to move forward when they heard a sudden outburst of musketry—at first the deep roar of the long, heavy guns carried by the natives, and then quickly afterwards the continuous rattle of the soldiers' muskets.

A cry of rage broke from the troopers. Captain Twentyman, who was in command of the squadron, saw that cavalry could be of no use in the gorge, and that they would only add to the confusion did they try to go back to assist the infantry. He therefore spread them out in the shape of a fan in front of the entrance to the gorge, to protect it against any body of natives who might be approaching. Rifles in hand, and with eyes straining into the forest ahead of them, the cavalry sat their horses, anxiously listening to the din behind them. Presently the infantry began to emerge, and at last the whole of the force was reunited. It was found that the assistant surgeon and eleven men had been killed, and two officers and seven privates wounded. They had, however, beaten off the enemy with considerable loss.

As it was clear that, now the Kaffirs had broken into open war, it would be unsafe in the extreme with the force under him to endeavour to penetrate further, Colonel Mackinnon ordered the column to retire. The gorge was thoroughly searched by infantry before the movement began, and it was not until they had found it was completely deserted by the enemy that the column moved back. They reached camp in the evening, and the Governor, upon hearing what had taken place, immediately proclaimed martial law, and ordered a strict inquiry to be made into the conduct of the Kaffir police. In the morning, however, the encampment of the corps was found deserted, three hundred and eighty-five men, taking with them their wives, cattle, and equipments, having deserted to the enemy during the night. Two strong patrols were sent out to carry the news to the commanders of the other two columns, and to examine the state of the country. They came upon a sight that enraged the troops, even more than the attack upon themselves. A party of the 45th Regiment, consisting of a sergeant and fourteen privates, escorting waggons from Fort White to King Williamstown, had been suddenly attacked by the Kaffirs, who had murdered the whole party.

Ronald Mervyn did not hear of this unprovoked atrocity at the time.

At daybreak, six detachments—drawn from the Cape Mounted Rifles, and each composed of six men and a non-commissioned officer—were ordered to start at once to various settlements on the border, to warn the colonists of the outbreak of war. Ronald was placed in the command of one of these detachments, and was chosen to lead that which was to warn the settlers on the Kabousie River, as he was acquainted with the country there. It was hoped that these detachments would arrive in time, for it was supposed that the attack on the column had been an isolated affair, the work of the tribe in the immediate neighbourhood. Circumstances proved, however, that that action was only a part of a preconcerted plan, for on the following day, which happened to be Christmas, a simultaneous attack was made upon almost all the border settlements.

Some of these were military villages, Government having at the conclusion of the previous war given grants of land and assistance to start in their farms to a number of discharged soldiers, upon the condition of their turning out at any time for the defence of the country. A number of prosperous little villages had thus sprung up, and the settlers lived on most friendly terms with the neighbouring Kaffirs, constantly entertaining them as their guests and employing many of them on their farms. In a few cases the news of the fight at Keiskamma arrived in time for the settlers to prepare for defence, but in the great majority of cases they were taken by surprise and massacred, often by the very men who had just been sharing their Christmas dinner. Many of the villages were entirely destroyed, and in some cases not a single man escaped to tell the tale.

It needed no orders for the messengers to use speed. Ronald and his men went at a gallop, only breaking into a slower pace at times to enable the men to breathe their horses. They had a long ride before them, and anxious as he was to get on, it was necessary to spare the horses as much as possible. He arrived at the station his detachment had before occupied at about one o'clock. The inhabitants were just sitting down to dinner. A good many Kaffirs were scattered about through the village. These looked surprised at the arrival of a detachment of cavalry, and gradually disappeared, supposing that Ronald's party was but the advance guard of a larger body. As soon as the news spread, the inhabitants hurried from their houses, men, women, and children, loaded with such articles they could snatch up in their haste, and all hastened to the building which they had before decided should be used as a citadel in case of need. Boys galloped out to the fields to drive the cattle into the kraal that had been constructed within easy range of the guns of the defenders of the Fort. Men were placed on sentry, while others brought in from the houses food, bedding, and clothes, and in a short time the village was prepared for a defence.

Ronald made a stay of a few minutes only. A mouthful of food was given to the horses, as he watched the settlers collecting for defence, and then, satisfied that they were prepared against surprise here, he rode on with his men. At the isolated farmhouses he passed, horses were put into light carts as soon as his news was told. In these women and children were stowed. A bundle or two of clothes were thrown in, the men then mounted, and the whole made off at the top of their speed towards the nearest town. A few of the younger men, and those unencumbered by women and children, mounted their horses, and taking their arms, joined Ronald's party. The next village was five miles from the first, and as they approached they heard piercing screams mingled with yells. Putting spurs to their horses the little party dashed on. Round each of the five or six houses in the village were groups of Kaffirs, who were dragging the inhabitants from the houses and massacring them. One or two shots were heard as they rode up, showing that some of the men were selling their lives dearly. With a shout, the little party of horsemen, counting fifteen men, dashed in upon the Kaffirs. Taken wholly by surprise, the latter did not see their foes until they were just upon them, and it was too late to throw their assegais with effect. Pouring in a volley from their rifles the troop rode in among them, hewing right and left with their sabres, the sharp cracks of their pistols following in rapid succession. With yells of dismay the Kaffirs, although numbering upwards of a hundred, at once fled, making for the forest. The infuriated troopers and settlers followed them, cutting down or shooting numbers before they reached the shelter of the trees. In their rage they would have followed them had not Ronald called them off.

"It would only be throwing away your lives to enter the wood," he said. "We should have to dismount, and they could spear us as they chose. Besides, we have other work to do."

They rode straight back to the village. More than half of the inhabitants had been murdered, and the rest were gathered round their dead friends in attitudes of despair, many of them streaming with blood from several wounds.

"Friends," Ronald said, as he rode up, "you must be up and doing. You must either gather in one house for mutual defence—for we have to ride on and the natives will return as soon as we leave—or as will be much wiser, put your horses into light carts, take the bodies of your friends, some of them may be only stunned by the knobkerries, and drive for your lives to the town. We will stop another ten minutes. The natives will not venture out of the woods until we go on."

Ronald's words roused the unfortunate settlers from their stupor. The men, aided by the troopers, harnessed the horses to the carts, lifted the wounded and dead into them, and taking with them a few of their valuables, drove away, and Ronald rode on with his party. At one or two houses the attack had not begun, and the settlers at once harnessed up and drove off. In others the party arrived too late to save, although they were able to avenge by surprising and cutting up the treacherous servants who, aided by the Gaikas from the hills, had murdered their masters, and were engaged in the work of plunder when the troop rode up. In each case they found that the Fingo servants had shared the fate of their employers, showing that they had been kept in the dark as to the deadly intentions of the Kaffirs.

As he neared the house occupied by his friends, the Armstrongs, Ronald Mervyn's anxiety heightened. Each scene of massacre had added to his fears, and he chafed at the comparatively slow rate of speed at which it was now necessary to go in order to spare the tired horses. Presently he heard the sound of distant firing in the direction in which he knew the Armstrong's house was situated. It was a welcome sound, for although it showed that the party were attacked, it gave hopes that they had not been entirely taken by surprise, and were still defending themselves.

"Jones," he said, turning to one of the troopers, "you can't go faster than you are going, but my horse has plenty in hand. I will ride on with the burghers at full speed; you keep well together and follow as fast as you can. If they make a fight of it with us, your coming up suddenly may cow them and decide the matter."

CHAPTER X.

A SUCCESSFUL DEFENCE.

The sounds of firing still continued as Ronald Mervyn, with his party of burghers, rode at the top of their speed towards Mr. Armstrong's house. As they neared it a number of Kaffirs were seen gathered round it. As these perceived the approach of the horsemen there was a movement of flight, but a chief who was with them, seeing the smallness of the force approaching, called upon them to stand, and they at once gathered to meet the advancing horsemen.

"Halt," Ronald shouted as he pulled up his horse a hundred and fifty yards from the house, "there are a couple of hundred of them; we shall be riddled with spears if we charge them, and shall throw away our lives without being of any assistance to our friends. Dismount, lads, and tie your horses up to the trees. Don't tie them too firmly, for if they make a rush we must ride off and then return again. Now each get behind a tree and open a steady fire upon them. Let each pick out his man and don't throw away a shot. Don't all fire together. Let the man on the right fire first, and then the one next to him, and so on, so that two or three of the right hand men can be loaded again before the last on the left has emptied his rifle."

A second or two later the first rifle spoke out and a native fell. Shot after shot was fired and every bullet told. The two chiefs were among the first who fell, and their loss to some extent paralysed the advance of the natives. Some of them ran back to the shelter under the house, but forty or fifty of them with loud shouting rushed forward.

"Give them one volley," Ronald shouted, "and then to your horses."

Every loaded gun was discharged; the men unhitched their horses, sprang into their saddles, and dashed off. All were accustomed to load on horseback, and as soon as the cartridges were down and the caps on, Ronald led them back again. The natives were this time holding the orchard. Ronald took a sweep as if to cut them off from the house, and, afraid of being separated, they ran back to rejoin their comrades. A volley was poured in, and then a charge was made upon them, sword and pistol in hand.

For a minute or two there was a sharp fight. Many of the natives were shot or cut down, while several of the burghers received assegai wounds.

A large body of natives were running up to the assistance of their comrades, when the six men of the Mounted Rifles rode up. The advancing natives paused at the sight of the soldiers, and before they could make up their minds to advance, the greater portion of those who had occupied the orchard were killed.

"Draw off fifty yards," Ronald said, "and reload rifles and pistols."

This was done, and several steady volleys poured into the Kaffirs.

"That will do," Ronald said; "they are beginning to slip off. Now we will charge straight down upon them; I and my troopers will cut our way through and enter the house. There is fighting going on in there still. Do you, gentlemen, take our horses as we dismount, and ride off, and then open fire again on the rascals from a distance. We shall be able to hold the house if we can once enter."

The plan was carried out. With a desperate charge they burst through the natives round the door. Ronald and the troopers sprang to the ground, and threw the reins of their horses to the colonists who caught them and rode off again.

"Close the door behind you," Ronald said, as he sprang forward into the passage, which was crowded with natives. The troopers followed him, closing and barring the door behind them. There was a sharp fight in the passage, but Ronald's two revolvers and the rifles of his men were more than a match for the natives, and in two or three minutes the last of them fell.

"Close and bar all the shutters," Ronald shouted, as he rushed into the dining-room, over the bodies of eight or ten natives lying inside.

His appearance was greeted with a hearty cheer, and Mr. Armstrong and three or four others ran in through the door of an inner room.

"Thank God we are in time," Ronald said, grasping Mr. Armstrong's hand.

"Thank God, indeed," the farmer replied. "We have had a hot time for the last hour."

"Miss Armstrong is not hurt, I hope?"

"No, she has escaped without a scratch, and I think that that's more than any of the rest of us can say."

"I must see about my men now," Ronald said; "will you get all the shutters downstairs fastened and barred?"

Ronald ran out and found that his men had just succeeded in clearing the house. They had found several Kaffirs upstairs engaged in the work of plundering. Some of them had been cut down, whilst others had jumped from the open windows. As soon as the shutters had been fastened, Ronald and his men took their places at the upper windows and opened fire upon the natives, who were already drawing off. The fire of the defenders of the house was aided by that of the burghers, and the retreat of the natives soon became a flight, many dropping before they were out of range of the rifles. As soon as the natives were fairly in retreat Ronald again went downstairs, where he found Mr. Armstrong and the other defenders of the house engaged attending upon the wounded. Ronald looked round the room.

"My daughter is in there," Mr. Armstrong said, pointing to the inner room. "She has behaved splendidly through it all, but she broke down when she found that the danger was over. I think you had better leave her alone for a few minutes."

"No wonder!" Ronald said, as he looked round the room. Seven or eight natives lay dead close to the doorway, three or four others in other parts of the room, three white men and two women also lay dead; and on the ground lay a table-cloth, broken plates and dishes, and the remains of a feast. Mr. Armstrong and four other farmers were now engaged in attending to each other's wounds, and binding them up with bandages made out of strips of the table-cloth.

"I was never so pleased in my life," Mr. Armstrong said, "as when I heard the first sound of your guns. Who you were I could not of course make out, but I supposed it must be a party from one of the villages which had got news of the attack on us here."

"It is partly so, sir," Ronald said. "We have six of our men besides myself, and fourteen or fifteen burghers joined us as we came along. I hear them riding up to the door now. I am sorry to say that no more were to be obtained, for the attack has been general, and I fear that three parts of the villages along the frontier have been destroyed, and their inhabitants massacred. Fortunately we arrived in time to save the place where we were before encamped, and to rescue a few of those at the next village. But at fully half the farmhouses we passed the work of massacre had already been carried out."

The front door was now opened, and the burghers entered. Ronald found that two of the party had been killed in the charge up to the house, and that most of them had received more or less serious wounds in the fight, while three of the Rifles had also been pierced with the assegais. He himself had been struck by a spear that had glanced off his ribs, inflicting a nasty flesh wound, while another assegai had laid open his cheek. Mary Armstrong and two other women now came out from the inner room and assisted in dressing the wounds, while the men who were unhurt carried the bodies of the Kaffirs who had fallen in the house some distance away, while those of the white men and women were placed side by side in another room. They then got buckets of water and soon removed the pools of blood from the floor.

"Now, Mary," Mr. Armstrong said, "will you and your friends get a fresh table-cloth out, and bring in some cold meat and bread and anything else that you can lay your hands on, for our brave friends? The rascals can't have had time to find out our cellar, and though I don't think any of our party want anything to eat, a draught of spirits and water will be acceptable all round."

"Not for those who are wounded, father; tea will be better for them, I am sure."

"Perhaps it will, my dear."

The women were glad of something to do. One of them was the wife of one of the farmers who had fallen, but she, too, in a dull mechanical manner, aided Mary Armstrong and the other, and as soon as the place was made quite tidy, six or seven children, of different ages, were called out from the inner room.

Ronald and the troopers did justice to the food, for they had ridden upwards of sixty miles, and had had nothing to eat save a piece of hard biscuit before starting.

"Now," Mr. Armstrong said, when their appetites were appeased, "tell us by what miracle you arrived here just in time to save us. I thought all the troops in the colony were somewhere near Fort Cox, at least that was the news that came to us yesterday."

"So we were, sir," Ronald said. "A column advanced from there yesterday morning, and were attacked by the Kaffirs in the gorge of the Keiskamma and some twenty or thirty killed and wounded. It occurred through the treachery of the Kaffir police, all of whom deserted last night. Some parties were sent off the first thing this morning to warn the border settlements, but I am afraid that very few of them arrived in time. We shall have terrible tidings, I fear, of this day's work everywhere."

"You are in command of this party?"

"Yes; I got my corporal's stripes the day before yesterday, and I was lucky enough to be chosen to command this detachment, as I knew the country; and now, sir, how did this business begin here?"

"We were at dinner," Mr. Armstrong said, "when without the least notice, just as we had finished, there was a rush through the door. All my friends had brought their rifles with them, and the instant the Kaffirs entered we knew what was up. Those who could caught their rifles, others snatched up table-knives, and the fight began. As you saw, several of our party were killed at once, but the rest of us made such a good fight with our clubbed rifles and knives that for the moment we cleared the room, then two of us held the door while the rest fell back into the inner room, where, fortunately, all the children were at the time, for the table was not large enough to hold us all, and they had had their meal first.

"Directly those who got in there recapped their rifles—for we found that our rascally Hottentot servants had removed the caps while we were at dinner—Thompson and I, who were at the door, fell back. Then, you see, matters were easy enough. Two of us were posted at the door of the inner room, and the moment a native showed himself inside the door of this room he was shot down. Of course we had shut the shutters of the inner room directly we entered, and one of us kept guard there. I don't think the Kaffirs would ever have forced their way in; but no doubt, as soon as they had stripped the house of everything valuable to them, they would have set it on fire, and then we should have had the choice of being burnt out here or being speared outside.

"I need not say that we had all agreed that it was a thousand times better to die here than to trust ourselves to those fiends, who always put their prisoners to death with atrocious tortures. Anyhow, my friends, we owe our lives to you, for sooner or later the end must have come to us. Now what are you going to do? You do not think of pushing on any further, I hope."

"No, I think that would be useless," Ronald said. "The massacre is apparently universal, and evidently began at the same time all along the line. We should be too late to warn any one now. Still," he said, rising suddenly from his seat, "we might not be too late to rescue them. There may be other parties holding out. I hadn't thought of that, and we had better push on further."

"I doubt if our horses can go any further," one of the men said. "Mine could scarcely carry me for the last five miles."

"Yes, that is so," Ronald said. "I think my horse is good for another twenty miles, and the horses of our friends the burghers are quite fresh, so I will leave you here and ride on with them. You will, of course, keep a sharp look-out; but I do not think it likely that they will renew the attack. They must have lost between fifty and sixty men. I will ride on with the burghers to the last settlement along this line. It is not, I think, more than twenty miles further. We will sleep there and return the first thing in the morning. By that time, Mr. Armstrong, you will, I suppose, be ready to move into town."

"Yes, I shall be ready by that time," the farmer said. "I sent off four loads of wheat yesterday morning, and the waggons will be back to-night. I will pack everything I want to take, and we shall be ready to start by the time you return. Of course, I shall drive the cattle with us—that is, if there are any cattle left to drive."

"I saw them in the kraal behind the house as we rode up," Ronald said. "I suppose the Kaffirs thought they might as well finish with you first, and they could then divide the cattle among them at their leisure."

"Well, that's good news," the settler said. "I made sure they were all gone. But don't you think you have done enough for to-day?"

"Yes; don't go any further," Mary Armstrong added.

"I feel that it is my duty to go, Miss Armstrong. I would much rather stay, I can assure you, but it's possible some of the garrisons may be holding out."

"Yes, we are wrong to ask you to stay," Mr. Armstrong said; "but just wait a minute, my horses are kraaled with the cattle. I will bring one round and change the saddles; it will be a pity to founder that splendid horse of yours. You see he has got a lot of English blood in him, and can't go on for ever like our Cape horses."

Five minutes later, mounted on a fresh horse, Ronald started with the burghers. Every farm they visited exhibited a spectacle of desolation; many had been forsaken some time previously, but they had been broken into, and, in many cases, fired. In others, the bodies of the occupants were beneath the embers of their homes; in a few the settlers had not been taken unawares, and stains of blood round the buildings showed that they had sold their lives dearly, and inflicted considerable loss on the Kaffirs before they had succeeded in bursting open the doors. In one little cluster of three or four houses, the bodies of men, women, and children lay scattered about; but one stoutly-built farmhouse, inhabited by a Boer farmer and six sons, had resisted all the attacks of the Kaffirs. The natives had drawn off before the arrival of the troops. The Boer stated that he intended to see it out.

"Two of my sons," he said, "have already driven off the cattle and horses. I have got a couple of cows in milk in the shed adjoining the house, and I shall bring them inside at night. The Kaffirs will never beat down my shutters or door, and one of us will watch by turns, so that we will give it them hot if they do venture to come on; but I think they have had pretty nearly enough of us."

This was the only house where a successful resistance was made, and on getting to the last station the party bivouacked near the ruins of the house, and, placing two men on guard, were soon asleep. They were undisturbed till morning, and mounting as soon as it was daylight, rode back to Mr. Armstrong's station. Three waggons had arrived late the night before, and with the assistance of the troopers were already loaded with furniture and other effects.

Two of the burghers offered to assist Mr. Armstrong in driving his cattle and horses to King Williamstown. The party was accompanied by the other settlers and their families, several of whom had saved their waggons and animals, as the Kaffirs had made their first attack upon Mr. Armstrong, knowing from the Hottentot servants that the settlers from three or four of the adjoining farms would be gathered there. Their defeat, therefore, had saved not only Mr. Armstrong's, but the other farms from pillage. Very warm were the thanks that the settlers, before starting, bestowed upon Ronald and the troopers, and Ronald, as soon as the caravan had started, rode somewhat thoughtfully off with his men to the first place he had visited.

Here they found that the Kaffirs, after they had left, had made a determined attack upon the place, but had been beaten off with much loss after several hours' fighting. The settlers were now, however, occupied in preparing to leave their farms, as the attack might at any moment be renewed, and perhaps with overwhelming numbers. The party of mounted police remained in the village until the following morning, as their horses, after their heavy work on the previous day, were not fit to take the long journey back to the camp. On the following morning they saw the settlers fairly on their way, and then galloped off to rejoin their corps at Fort Cox.

As they ascended a piece of rising ground within a mile of the Fort, and obtained a fair view of it, they reined in their horses simultaneously. The Fort itself appeared silent and deserted, but at a distance of a few hundred yards from it they could see a large number of men moving about.

"Those are not soldiers," Ronald exclaimed, "they must be Kaffirs. By Jove, the place is absolutely besieged. Look at the puffs of smoke. Yes, there can be no doubt about it. I expect the column has gone out again, and the Kaffirs are trying to take it before they return. Well, lads, it's too late in the afternoon now for us to do anything. We had better ride back two or three miles and then camp for the night. In the morning we must try and find out what has taken place, and where the troop have got to."

All agreed that this was the best plan, and they accordingly rode quietly back, as for aught they could tell keen eyes might be upon them. They did not attempt to halt until it was quite dark, when they turned off at right angles to their former course, and after riding for about a mile, encamped in a clump of bushes. They had plenty of cold meat with them, for the settlers had, before starting, filled their haversacks. There was, therefore, no occasion to light a fire, which, indeed, they would in no case have done, as, should a Kaffir catch sight of a light, he would assuredly bring an overpowering force down upon them.

"We will have two out on sentry, and relieve guard every hour," Ronald said, "but we can eat our meal in comfort first. There is no fear of their coming down upon us at present, at any rate."

The manner in which he had led them in the attack on the Kaffirs had greatly impressed the men, and they yielded as ready and willing obedience, as if their corporal had been an officer. After the meal was over, Ronald placed a sentry on each side of the bush.

"I will relieve you at the end of an hour," he said. "Keep your ears open. I shall go out for a bit and reconnoitre, and mind you don't shoot me as I come back. I will give a low whistle, like this, when I get near you. If you hear any one approaching, and he doesn't whistle, challenge, but don't shout too loud, or you might be heard by any Kaffirs who may be in search of us. If he don't answer, challenge again, and then step into the bushes. If he comes on, and you are sure it is a man, fire; but don't fire if you have the slightest doubt, for it might be a stray animal, and your rifle might bring the Kaffirs down on us."

During the greater part of the night, Ronald moved about, keeping about a hundred yards from the clump, and returning every hour to see the sentries changed. Towards morning, having heard nothing to lead him to suppose that there were any Kaffirs in the neighbourhood, he returned to the bushes, and threw himself down for a couple of hours' sleep. At daybreak, they were in the saddle again, and approaching as near as they dared to the Fort, they concealed themselves, and presently succeeded in capturing a Kaffir woman who was out collecting sticks. One of the troop knew a little of the language, and from her they learnt that the greater part of the soldiers had marched away on the previous morning, and also gathered the direction they had taken. Keeping up a vigilant look-out, they rode in that direction, and presently met a detachment of the 91st and their own troop of the Rifles marching back to Fort Cox.

The force was under the command of Colonel Somerset, the colonel of the Cape Mounted Rifles. Captain Twentyman, to whom Ronald reported himself, rode forward at once to the colonel with the news that Fort Cox was invested by the enemy. Ronald was sent for, and questioned as to the strength of the Kaffirs. He said that owing to the position from which he had seen them, he only commanded a view of a portion of the ground. There appeared to him to be seven or eight hundred men so far as he could see, but, of course, there might have been double that force on the other side.

"Well, I think we ought to push forward at once," the colonel said to the officer commanding the infantry. "The Governor is in the Fort, and the force for its defence is a very small one. At any rate we must try to relieve him."

The troops were halted for half an hour, and as the news soon spread that the

Kaffirs were beleaguering Fort Cox, and that they would probably have to fight their way through, they formed up with alacrity as soon as the order was given. The Cape Mounted Rifles went out in skirmishing order, ahead of the infantry, keeping a vigilant look-out for lurking foes. The men had learned from Ronald's party of the massacre at the border settlements, and were burning with impatience to get at the enemy.

After marching two miles, the column came to a spot where a broad belt of wood extended across the country. As the mounted men approached this, several assegais were hurled from the bushes. The cavalry replied with their rifles, and then fell back upon the infantry, who advanced with a cheer against the wood. Half the cavalry were dismounted, and, handing their horses to their comrades, advanced on foot. Ronald was one of those who remained behind. Keeping up a heavy fire at their invisible foe, the 91st advanced into the wood. The troopers with the horses listened anxiously to the sound of the fray—the rattle of musketry, the loud reports of the Kaffir rifles, and their shrill yells, amid which a British cheer could be occasionally heard.

"It's hot work in there, corporal," Lieutenant Daniels said. "Too hot to be pleasant, I should say. Judging by the yelling, the wood must be full of Kaffirs."

"I should think so too, sir," Ronald agreed. "I fancy each Kaffir is capable of doing an immense amount of yelling; but still, as you say, the wood must be full of them to make such a terrific noise as that."

A quarter of an hour passed, and then the rifles emerged from the wood. Those with the horses at once galloped forward to meet them, and soon all were in the saddle. Ronald heard Captain Twentyman, who had led the dismounted party, say to the lieutenant:

"There are too many of them, Daniels; the wood is crowded with them. Take half the troop and draw off to the right, and I will take the other half to the left. The 91st will fall back directly. As they come out, prepare to charge the Kaffirs in flank if they pursue them."

Now the redcoats began to appear at the edge of the wood. They were in pairs, and every two men were carrying a wounded comrade. Presently the main body came out in regular order with their faces to the enemy. With yells of triumph the Kaffirs poured out from the wood. The rifles fidgeted in their saddles for the order to charge, but Lieutenant Daniels had his eye upon the other wing of the troop, and Captain Twentyman did not give the order to advance until he saw that the Kaffirs were so far out upon the plain that they could not get back to the wood before he would be upon them. Then he gave the order to charge, and as his men got into motion, Lieutenant Daniels gave the same order. As he saw the cavalry sweeping down, Colonel Somerset gave the word, and the 91st poured a tremendous volley into the Kaffirs, and a moment later the two bodies of cavalry swept down on their flank. With a yell of fear the Kaffirs ran for the wood, but numbers of them were cut down before they could gain shelter. Then the cavalry fell back and joined the infantry. It was found there had been a desperate hand-to-hand struggle, bayonets against assegais. Two officers and twenty privates had been killed, and a great many of the men wounded. They afterwards learned that the Kaffir loss in killed had exceeded two hundred.

The party then fell back and rejoined Colonel Mackinnon. There was now an anxious consultation, when it was decided that as Fort Cox could probably resist all attacks of the enemy, it would be better not to attempt an advance to its relief until a junction had been effected with the other columns, which were now at a considerable distance away. On the 31st, the news reached them that that morning the Governor, with a small body of Cape Mounted Rifles, had made a dash right through the enemy, and had ridden to King Williamstown, twelve miles away, where he had at once issued a proclamation calling upon the colonists to rise *en masse* to assist the troops to expel the Gaikas from the Amatolas, while a force of Fingoes was at once ordered to be raised.

In the meantime, the Kaffirs were plundering and destroying all over the country. The settlers entirely abandoned their farms; and the roads to Williamstown, Grahamstown, and Beaufort were blocked with the great herds of cattle driven in. The news came that the Gaikas had been joined by the T'Slambies and Tambookies, numbering not less than 15,000 men; and it was reported that an influential chief—Kairie—who could put 10,000 men in the field, was preparing to make common cause with the rebels. The Hottentots of the London missionary station at Cat River, who had for years been fed and clothed by the Government, and put into free possession of a beautiful and fertile district, joined the Kaffirs, and took a leading part in their attacks on the settlers. Their example was speedily followed by the so-called Christian Hottentots at the missionary settlements of Shiloh and Theopolis.

Against such overpowering forces as were now leagued against him, the Governor could do nothing with the small body of troops at his disposal, and was forced to remain inactive at Williamstown until reinforcements could arrive. He contented himself, therefore, with throwing supplies into Forts Cox, White, and Hare, this being accomplished only after severe contests with the natives. Bodies of Kaffirs had now completely overrun the colony, rendering even communication between the towns dangerous in the extreme, unless sent by messengers escorted by considerable bodies of troops.

On arriving at King Williamstown, Ronald Mervyn was greatly disappointed to find that the Armstrongs had gone on to Grahamstown. He found a letter awaiting him from Mr. Armstrong, saying that he was very sorry to leave without another opportunity of thanking him for the immense services he had rendered him, "but," he said, "my daughter, now that it is all over, is terribly shaken by all she has gone through, and I think it necessary to get her to a place a little further removed from all this trouble. I shall probably leave for England before long. I hope to see you before we go, but, if not, I will write to you, giving you our address in England, and we shall both be very glad to see you if you return, as I hope you will, and that before long. We shall never forget how much we owe you."

"Perhaps it is better so," Ronald said, as he finished the letter. "It would only have made it harder for me if I had seen her again. For if there is one thing more certain than another, it is that I can never ask any woman to be my wife."

The Cape Town Rifles were before long joined by two troops from Cape Town and Elizabeth Town, and were continually employed in escorting convoys and carrying despatches. A batch of twenty recruits also came up to fill the vacancies that had already been made by the war, and to bring the troops engaged up to their full force. One of the four men who joined Captain Twentyman's troop gave a slight start of surprise as his eyes fell upon Ronald Mervyn. He looked at him several times, and a slight smile stole across his face.

"Who is that corporal?" he asked one of the troopers.

"Corporal Blunt," the man said; "and a fine fellow he is, too. He led a small detachment of our men splendidly in an affair down by the Kabousie River. Why do you ask? Have you ever seen him before?"

"No," the man said, carelessly; "but he reminded me of some one I knew at home."

"He is a first-rate soldier," the man said, "and I expect he will get the first vacancy among the sergeants. We all think he has been an officer, though he never talks about it. He's the best-tempered fellow possible, but you can never get him to talk about the past. However, that makes no difference to us."

"Not a bit," the recruit agreed. "I dare say he isn't the only one with a queer history in the regiment."

"I didn't say he had a queer history," the man replied, angrily. "He is as good a comrade, and as good a fellow as one wants to meet; there's not a man in the troop grudges his being pushed on."

"I meant no offence," the recruit said. "The man he reminded me of had a queer history, and I suppose that is what put it into my head."

"Well, if you don't want your head punched, you had better say nothing against Blunt," the trooper grumbled, "either in my hearing or out of it."

The recruit turned away and occupied himself in grooming his horse.

"This is a rum start," he said to himself. "Who would have thought of meeting Captain Mervyn out here? I saw in one of the papers, soon after I came out, the account of his trial. I wonder how I should have felt if I had been standing in his place? So he has changed his name. I suppose he arrived at the Cape when I was up the country, and must have enlisted at once, for it's nearly three months since I joined the depôt, and a draft had only sailed the day before. At any rate it's not likely he will know me; not that he could do me any harm if he did, still it's always useful to know a man and to know something against him, especially when he doesn't know you. If I ever get into a row I can put the screw on nicely."

As the recruit, who had enlisted in the name of Jim Smith, had expected would be the case, Ronald Mervyn's eye showed no signs of recognition as it fell upon his face. He thought the new recruit was a strapping fellow, and would be a good man to have beside one in a hand-to-hand fight with the Kaffirs; but beyond this he gave him no further thought.

A considerable number of the Fingo allies had now arrived at King Williamstown. They had no idea whatever of discipline, and looked every bit as wild as their Kaffir foes. But there was no doubt they were ready to fight, for they were eager to be led against the Kaffirs, who had so long kept them in slavery. They had been armed with muskets, and each carried a heavy knobkerrie. At present they had nothing to do but to sleep and eat, to dance war dances, and to get drunk whenever they could obtain sufficient money to indulge in that luxury.

They were accompanied by their wives, who not only waited upon and cooked for them, but earned money by going out into the woods and bringing in bundles of faggots. Numbers of Hottentot women were engaged upon the same work, while the men of the same tribe looked after the great herds of cattle, furnished drivers for the waggons, helped in the commissariat stores, and, so far as their lazy nature permitted, made themselves useful.

"If I were the General," Ronald said one day to Sergeant Menzies, "I wouldn't have a Hottentot about the place. I believe that they are all in league with the enemy. Look how they all went over from the missionary stations, and the farmers tell me they left in the majority of cases on the day before the massacre. It's quite evident that the Kaffirs somehow always get information of our movements. How could they have laid that ambush for us at Keiskamma River if they had not known the column was going that way? How was it they were ready to attack the detachments that went with provisions to the Forts? It could not have been from their own people, for not a Kaffir has been near us since the troubles began. I believe it's these hateful little Hottentots."

"They are hateful," the sergeant said, "whether they are traitors or not. Except the Bushmen, I do believe that they are the most disgusting race on the face of the earth, with their stunted bodies and their yellow faces, and their filthy and disgusting ways. I don't know that I should turn them out of the camp if I were the General, but I should certainly order them to be washed. If you get half-a-dozen of them on the windy side of you, it's enough to make you sick."

"I wonder the Kaffirs didn't exterminate the little brutes," Ronald Mervyn said. "I suppose they would have done if it had not been for the Dutch first and us afterwards. The missionaries made pets of them, and nice pets they have turned out. It is just the same thing in India. It's the very dregs of the people the missionaries always pick up with."

CHAPTER XI.

ATTACK ON A WAGGON-TRAIN.

"Sergeant Blunt, you will take a detachment of fourteen men, ride down to Port Elizabeth, and escort some waggons back here. There will be a party of native levies to come back with you, so that they, with your party, will make a pretty strong force. The dangerous point is, of course, the Addoo Bush. It is, I hear, full of these Kaffir villains. Going down you will pass through it by daylight; and, travelling fast, there is no fear of their interfering with a party like yours. Coming back the Fingoes will let you know of any danger, and I should hardly think that the natives will venture to attack so strong a party; still, as the waggons will be laden with ammunition, and these fellows always seem in some way or other to know exactly what is going on, you cannot be too careful."

"Very well, sir. I will do my best in the matter."

An hour later Ronald started with the detachment. They travelled rapidly, and reached Port Elizabeth on the third day after starting, without any adventure whatever. The waggons were not ready to start, for a heavy sea was setting in, and the boats could not continue the work of unloading the ship that had arrived with the ammunition two days before. Ronald, after seeing that the horses were well cared for, the rations served out, and the cooking commenced, strolled down to the beach to watch the heavy surf breaking on the shore.

The encampment of the native levies was on the shore, and a white officer was inspecting their arms when Ronald arrived. He stood for some time watching the motley group of Fingoes; some of them were in blankets, others in karosses of cow skin, many with feathers stuck in their hair, all grinning and highly amused at the efforts of their officer to get them to stand in regular line, and to hold their muskets at an even slope on their shoulders. Some of their wives were looking on and laughing; others were squatting about by the shelters they had erected, cooking mealies for dinner. The officer, who was quite a young man, seeing Ronald looking on, said, ruefully:

"I don't think there is any making soldiers out of these fellows, sergeant."

"I don't think they would be any the better for it if you could, sir," Ronald said. "The fellows will fight after their own fashion, and I do not think any amount of drill would improve them in the slightest; in fact, it would only puzzle and confuse them to try to teach them our discipline. They must skirmish with the Kaffirs in Kaffir fashion. When it comes to regular fighting, it must be done by the troops. All you can expect of the native levies is that they shall act as our scouts, find out where the enemy are hiding, prevent surprises, and pursue them when we have defeated them."

"Do they not try to drill them up at the front?"

"Not at all, sir. It would be quite useless to attempt it. So that they attend on parade in the right number—and their own head man looks after that—nothing more is expected of them. They march in a straggling body anyhow, and when it comes to fighting, they fight in their own way, and a very useful way it is."

"Well, I am very glad to hear you say so, sergeant. I have been doing the best I can to give them some idea of drill; but I have, as you see, failed altogether. I had no orders except to take command of these fellows, but I supposed I was expected to drill them to some extent; still, if you say they have given it up as hopeless in the front, I need not bother myself about it."

"I don't think you need, sir. I can assure you that no attempt is made to drill them in that way at the front."

The young officer, with an air of relief, at once dismissed the natives from parade.

"I am in charge of the party of Rifles going up with you to-morrow, sir, or at least as soon as the waggons are ready for you."

"Oh, is it you, sergeant? I heard that a detachment of your corps were to accompany us. I suppose you have just arrived from King Williamstown?"

"I came in about an hour ago, sir, and have just been seeing that the men were comfortable."

"Did you meet with any Kaffirs on the way down?"

"We saw no sign of them. We came through the Addoo Bush, which is the most dangerous point, at a trot. Not that there was much chance of their attacking us. The natives seldom attack unless there is something to be got by it; but we shall have to be careful as we go back. We shall be a fairly strong party, but others as strong have been attacked; and the fact of our having ammunition—the thing of all others they want—is, of course, against us."

"But how will they know that we are carrying ammunition?"

"From the Hottentots, who keep them informed of everything," Ronald said. "At least, we have no doubt whatever that it is the Hottentots. Of course, the General doesn't think so. If he did, I suppose he would keep them out of camp; but there is only one opinion in the ranks about it."

The conversation was interrupted by yells and screams from the natives, and a general rush down to the beach.

"There is something the matter," the young officer exclaimed; and he and Ronald ran down to the edge of the water.

They soon saw what was the occasion of the alarm among the natives. Some of the women and boys had been down at the edge of the surf, collecting bits of wood, as they were thrown up, for their fires. A boy of some fourteen years of age had seen a larger piece than usual approaching the shore, and just as a wave had borne it in, he made a dash into the water, eager to be the first to capture the prize. Ignorant, however, of the force of the water, he had been instantly swept off his feet by the back rush of the wave. The next roller had carried him some little distance up, and then borne him out again, and he was now in the midst of the surf. He could swim a little, but was helpless in the midst of such a sea as this. The natives on the beach were in a state of the wildest excitement; the women filled the air with their shrill screams, the men shouted and gesticulated.

"Nothing can save him," the officer said, shaking his head. Ronald looked round; there was no rope lying anywhere on the shore.

"There's just a chance, I think," he said, throwing off his belt, tunic, and boots. "Make these fellows join hand in hand, sir; I will swim out to him— he's nearly gone now—and bring him in. We shall be rolled over and over, but if the line of men can grab us and prevent the under-current from carrying us out again, it will be all right."

The officer was about to remonstrate, but Ronald, seizing the moment when a wave had just swept back, rushed in, sprang head foremost into the great wall of approaching water, and in half a minute later appeared some distance out. A few vigorous strokes took him to the side of the drowning boy, whom he seized by his shoulders; then he looked towards the shore. The young officer, unable to obtain a hearing from the excited Fingoes, was using his cane vigorously on their shoulders, and presently succeeded in getting them to form a line, holding each other by the hands. He took his place at their head, and then waved his hand to Ronald as a sign that he was ready.

Good swimmer as he was, the latter could not have kept much longer afloat in such a sea; and was obliged to continue to swim from shore to prevent himself from being cast up by each wave which swept under him like a racehorse, covering him and his now insensible burden. The moment he saw that the line was formed he pulled the boy to him and grasped him tightly; then he laid himself broadside to the sea, and the next roller swept him along with resistless force on to the beach. He was rolled over and over like a straw, and just as he felt that the impetus had abated, and he was again beginning to move seaward, an arm seized him.

For a few seconds the strain was tremendous, and he thought he would be torn from the friendly grasp; then the pressure of the water diminished and he felt himself dragged along, and a few seconds later was beyond the reach of the water. He was soon up on his feet, feeling bruised, shaken, and giddy; the natives, who had yelled with joy as they dragged him from the water, now burst into wailings as they saw that the boy was, as they thought, dead.

"Carry him straight up to the fires," Ronald said as soon as he recovered his shaken faculties.

The order was at once obeyed. As soon as he was laid down, Ronald seized the blanket from one of the men's shoulders, and set the natives to rub the boy's limbs and body vigorously; then he rolled him in two or three other blankets, and telling the men to keep on rubbing the feet, began to carry out the established method for restoring respiration, by drawing the boy's arms above his head, and then bringing them down and pressing them against his ribs. In a few minutes there was a faint sigh, a little later on an attempt to cough, and then the boy got rid of a quantity of sea water.

"He will do now," Ronald said. "Keep on rubbing him, and he will be all right in a quarter of an hour." As Ronald rose to his feet a woman threw herself down on her knees beside him, and seizing his hand pressed it to her forehead, pouring out a torrent of words wholly beyond his comprehension, for although he had by this time acquired some slight acquaintance with the language, he was unable to follow it when spoken so volubly. He had no doubt whatever that the woman was the boy's mother, and that she was thanking him for having preserved his life. Not less excited was a native who stood beside him.

"This is their head man," the officer interpreted; "he is the boy's father, and says that his life is now yours, and that he is ready to give it at any time. This is a very gallant business, sergeant, and I wish I had the pluck to have done it myself. I shall, of course, send in a report about your conduct. Now come to my tent. I can let you have a shirt and pair of trousers while yours are being dried."

"Thank you, sir; they will dry of themselves in a very few minutes. I feel cooler and more comfortable than I have done for a long time; ten minutes under this blazing sun will dry them thoroughly."

It was another two days before the sea subsided sufficiently for the surf-boats to bring the ammunition to shore, and during that time the chief's wife came several times up to the barracks, each time bringing a fowl as a present to

Ronald.

"What does that woman mean, sergeant?" one of the men asked on the occasion of her second visit. "Has she fallen in love with you? She takes a practical way of showing her affection. I shouldn't mind if two or three of them were to fall in love with me on the same terms."

Ronald laughed.

"No, her son got into the water yesterday, and I picked him out, and this is her way of showing her gratitude."

"I wonder where she got the fowls from," the trooper said. "I haven't seen one for sale in the town anywhere."

"She stole them, of course," another trooper put in, "or at least if she didn't steal them herself she got some of the others to do it for her. The natives are all thieves, man, woman, and child; they are regularly trained to it. Sometimes fathers will lay wagers with each other as to the cleverness of their children; each one backs his boy to steal something out of the other's hut first, and in spite of the sharp watch you may be sure they keep up, it is very seldom the youngsters fail in carrying off something unobserved. It's a disgrace in a native's eyes to be caught thieving; but there's no disgrace whatever, rather the contrary, in the act itself. There's only one thing that they are as clever at as thieving, and that is lying. The calmness with which a native will tell a good circumstantial lie is enough to take one's breath away."

Ronald knew enough of the natives to feel that it was probable enough that the fowls were stolen; but his sense of morality was not sufficiently keen for him to hurt the woman's feelings by rejecting her offerings.

"The Kaffirs have proved themselves such an ungrateful set of scoundrels," he argued to himself, "that it is refreshing to see an exception for once."

As soon as the ammunition was on shore it was loaded into three waggons, and on the following morning the party started. It was slow work, after the rapid pace at which Ronald and his men had come down from King Williamstown, and the halting-places were the same as those at which the troop had encamped on its march up the country five months before.

The greatest caution was observed in their passage through the great Addoo Bush, for although this was so far from the main stronghold of the natives, it was known that there were numbers of Kaffirs hiding there, and several mail carriers had been murdered and waggons attacked. The party, however, were too strong to be molested, and passed through without adventure. The same vigilance was observed when crossing over the sandy flats, and when they passed through Assegai Bush. Once through this, the road was clear to

Grahamstown. Here they halted for a day, and then started on the road leading through Peddie to King Williamstown. After a march of fifteen miles they halted at the edge of a wide-spreading bush. They had heard at Grahamstown that a large body of Kaffirs were reported to be lying there, and as it was late in the afternoon when they approached it, Ronald advised the young officer in command of the Fingoes to camp outside and pass through it by daylight.

"The greatest caution was observed in their passage through the great Addoo Bush."

"There is no making a rush," he said; "we must move slowly on account of the waggons, and there will be no evading the Kaffirs. I do not think there is much chance of their attacking such a strong party as we are; but if we are attacked, we can beat them off a great deal better in the daylight than at night; in the darkness we lose all the advantage of our better weapons. Besides, these fellows can see a great deal better than we can in the dark."

They started as soon as it was light. The Fingoes, who were a hundred strong, were to skirmish along the road ahead and in the wood on each flank of the waggons, round which the detachment of Rifles were to keep in a close body, the Fingo women and children walking just ahead of the bullocks. Scarcely a word was spoken after they entered the forest. The waggons creaked and groaned, and the sound of the sharp cracks of the drivers' whips alone broke the silence. The Rifles rode with their arms in readiness for instant use, while the Fingoes flitted in and out among the trees like dark shadows. Their blankets and karosses had been handed to the women to carry, and they had oiled their bodies until they shone again, a step always taken by the natives when engaged in expeditions in the bush, with the view of giving more suppleness to the limbs, and also of enabling them to glide through the thorny thickets without being severely scratched.

They had got about half-way through the bush without anything being seen of the lurking enemy, when a sudden outburst of firing, mingled with yells and shouts, was heard about a quarter of a mile ahead.

"The scoundrels are attacking a convoy coming down," Ronald exclaimed.

"Shall we push on to their aid, sergeant?" the young officer, who was riding next to Ronald, asked.

"I cannot leave the waggons," Ronald said; "but if you would take your men on, sir, we will be up as soon as we can."

The officer shouted to his Fingoes, and at a run the natives dashed forward to the scene of the conflict, while Ronald urged the drivers, and his men pricked the bullocks with their swords until they broke into a lumbering trot.

In a few minutes they arrived on the scene of action. A number of waggons were standing in the road, and round them a fight was going on between the Fingoes and greatly superior numbers of Kaffirs. Ronald gave the word, and his men charged down into the middle of the fight. The Kaffirs did not await their onslaught, but glided away among the trees, the Fingoes following in hot pursuit until recalled by their officer, who feared that their foes might turn upon them when beyond the reach of the rifles of the troopers.

Ronald saw at once as he rode up that although the Fingoes had arrived in time to save the waggons, they had come too late to be of service to the majority of the defenders. Some half-dozen men, gathered in a body, were still on their feet, but a score of others lay dead or desperately wounded by the side of the waggons. As soon as the Fingoes returned and reported the Kaffirs in full flight, Ronald and the troops dismounted to see what aid they could render. He went up to the group of white men, most of whom were wounded.

"This is a bad job," one of them said; "but we thought that as there were about thirty of us, the Kaffirs wouldn't venture to attack us. We were all on the alert, but they sprang so suddenly out of the bushes that half of us were speared before we had time to draw a trigger.

"What had we better do, sir—go on or go back?" This question was addressed to the young officer.

"I should think that now you have got so far you had better go on," he said. "The Kaffirs are not likely to return for some little time. I will give you half my Fingoes to escort you on through the wood. Don't you think that will be the best plan, sergeant?"

"I think so, sir. I will let you have half my men to go back with them. The rest of us had better stay here until they return. But, first of all, we will see to these poor fellows. They may not be all dead."

Most of them, however, were found to be so, the Kaffirs having sprung upon them and cut their throats as soon as they had fallen. Two of them who had fallen near the group which had maintained the resistance were, however, found to be still living, and these were lifted into the waggons. Just as the party were going to move on towards the coast, a groan was heard among the bushes by the side of the road. Ronald and two of the troopers at once proceeded to the spot.

"Good Heavens!" the former exclaimed, as he leaned over the man who was lying there, "it is Mr. Armstrong."

He was lifted up and carried into the road. An assegai had passed through both legs, and another had transfixed his body near the right shoulder. The point projected some inches through the back, the shaft having broken off as he fell. Ronald seized the stump of the spear, and with the greatest difficulty drew it out from the wound.

"Cut his things off," he said to the troopers, "and tear up something and lightly bandage the wound. I am afraid it is a fatal one." Then he hurried off to the men.

"Were there not some women in the waggons?" he asked.

"Yes, there were three of them," the man said; "a girl and two women. The women were the wives of two of the men who have been killed. The girl was the daughter of another. I suppose the natives must have carried them off, for I see no signs of them."

Ronald uttered an exclamation of horror; he knew the terrible fate of women who fell into the hands of the Kaffirs. He returned to the officer.

"What is it, sergeant?" he asked. "Any fresh misfortune?"

"A young lady, sir, daughter of that poor fellow we have just picked up, and two other women, have been carried off by the natives."

"Good Heavens!" the young man said, "this is dreadful; they had a thousand times better have been shot with their friends. What's to be done, sergeant?"

"I don't know," Ronald said, "I can't think yet. At any rate, instead of waiting till the party with these waggons come back, I will push straight on out of the wood, and will then send the rest of my men back at full gallop to meet you, then you can all come on together. I think you said you would take command of the party going back with the waggons."

The two trains were at once set in motion. Ronald's party met with no further interruption until they were clear of the bush. As soon as he was well away from it, he sent back the Rifles to join the other party, and return with them through the forest. He went on for half a mile further, then halted the waggons and dismounted.

Mr. Armstrong had been placed in one of the waggons going up the country, as they were nearer to a town that way than to Port Elizabeth; besides, Ronald knew that if he recovered consciousness, he would for many reasons prefer being up the country. Ronald walked up and down, restless and excited, meditating what step he had best take, for he was determined that in some way or other he would attempt to rescue Mary Armstrong from the hands of the natives. Presently the head man of the Fingoes came up to him, and said, in a mixture of English and his own tongue:

"My white friend is troubled; can Kreta help him?"

"I am troubled, terribly troubled, Kreta. One of the white ladies who has been carried off by the Kaffirs is a friend of mine. I must get her out of their hands."

Kreta looked grave.

"Hard thing that, sir. If go into bush get chopped to pieces."

"I must risk that," Ronald said; "I am going to try and save her, whether it costs me my life or not."

"Kreta will go with his white friend," the chief said; "white man no good by himself."

"Would you, Kreta?" Ronald asked, eagerly. "But no, I have no right to take you into such danger as that. You have a wife and child; I have no one to depend upon me."

"Kreta would not have a child if it had not been for his white friend," Kreta said; "if he goes, Kreta will go with him, and will take some of his men."

"You are a good fellow, Kreta," Ronald said, shaking the chief heartily by the hand. "Now, what's the best way of setting about it?"

The Fingo thought for some little time, and then asked:

"Is the white woman young and pretty?"

"Yes," Ronald replied, rather surprised at the question.

"Then I think she's safe for a little while. If she old and ugly they torture her and kill her quick; if she pretty and young, most likely they send her as present to their big chief; perhaps Macomo, or Sandilli, or Kreli, or one of the other great chiefs, whichever tribe they belong to. Can't do nothing to-day; might crawl into the wood; but if find her how can get her out? That's not possible. The best thing will be this: I will send two of my young men into the bush to try and find out what they do with her, and where they are going to take her. Then at night we try to cut them off as they go across the country. If we no meet them we go straight to Amatolas to find out the kraal to which they take her, and then see how to get her off."

"How many men will you take, Kreta?"

"Five men," the chief said, holding up one hand; "five enough to creep and crawl. No use to try force; too many Kaffirs. Five men might do; five hundred no good."

"I think you are right, chief. It must be done by craft if at all."

"Then I will send off my two young men at once," the chief said. "They go a long way round, and enter bush on the other side; then creep through the bush and hear Kaffir talk. If Kaffir sees them they think they their own people; but mustn't talk; if they do, Kaffirs notice difference of tongue. One, two words no noticed, but if talk much find out directly."

"Then there's nothing for me to do to-night," Ronald said.

The chief shook his head. "No good till quite dark."

"In that case I will go on with the convoy as far as Bushman's River, where we halt to-night."

"Very well," the chief said. "We go on with you there, and then come back here and meet the young men, who will tell us what they have found out."

The chief went away, and Ronald saw him speaking to some of his men. Then two young fellows of about twenty years old laid aside their blankets, put them and their guns into one of the waggons, and then, after five minutes' conversation with their chief, who was evidently giving them minute instructions, went off at a slinging trot across the country.

In less than an hour the party that was escorting the settlers' waggons through the bush, and the mounted men who had gone to meet them, returned together, having seen no sign of the enemy. The waggons were set in motion, and the march continued. Ronald Mervyn rode up to the officer of the native levy.

"I am going, sir, to make what may seem a most extraordinary request, and indeed it is one that is, I think, out of your power to grant; but, if you give your approval, it will to some extent lessen my responsibility."

"What is it, sergeant?" the young officer asked, in some surprise.

"I want when we arrive at the halting-place to hand over the command of my detachment to the corporal, and for you to let me go away on my own affairs. I want you also to allow your head man, Kreta, and five of his men, leave of absence."

The young officer was astonished. "Of course I am in command of the convoy, and so have authority over you so long as you are with me; but as you received orders direct from your own officers to take your detachment down to the coast, and return with the waggons, I am sure that I have no power to grant you leave to go away."

"No, sir, that's just what I thought; but at the same time, if you report that, although you were unable to grant me leave, you approved of my absence, it will make it much easier for me. Not that it makes any difference, sir, because I admit frankly that I should go in any case. It is probable that I may be reduced to the ranks; but I don't think that, under the circumstances, they will punish me any more severely than that."

"But what are the circumstances, sergeant? I can scarcely imagine any circumstance that could make me approve of your intention to leave your command on a march like this."

"I was just going to tell you them, sir, but I may say that I do not think it at all probable that there will be any further attack on the convoy. There is no more large bush to pass between this and Williamstown, and so far as we have heard, no attempt has been made further on the road to stop convoys. That poor fellow who is lying wounded in the waggon is a Mr. Armstrong. He was an officer in the service when he was a young man, and fought, he told me, at Waterloo. His place is near the spot where I was quartered for two months just before the outbreak, and he showed me great kindness, and treated me as a friend. Well, sir, one of the three women who were, as you heard, carried off in the waggons, was Mr. Armstrong's daughter. Now, sir, you know what her fate will be in the hands of those savages: dishonour, torture, and death. I am going to save her if I can. I don't know whether I shall succeed; most likely I shall not. My life is of no great consequence to me, and has so far been a failure; but I want to try and rescue her whether it costs me my life or not. Kreta has offered to accompany me with five of his men. Alone, I should certainly fail, but with his aid there is a chance of my succeeding."

"By Jove, you are a brave fellow, sergeant," the young officer said, "and I honour you for the determination you have formed," and waiving military etiquette, he shook Ronald warmly by the hand. "Assuredly I will, so far as is in my power, give you leave to go, and will take good care that in case you fail, your conduct in thus risking your life shall be appreciated. How do you mean to set about it?"

Ronald gave him a sketch of the plan that had been determined upon by himself and Kreta.

"Well, I think you have a chance at any rate," the officer said, when he concluded. "Of course the risk of detection in the midst of the Kaffirs will be tremendous, but still there seems just a chance of your escape. In any case no one can possibly disapprove of your endeavour to save this young lady from the awful fate that will certainly be hers unless you can rescue her. Poor girl! Even though I don't know her, it makes my blood run cold to think of an English lady in the hands of those savages. If I were not in command of the convoy, I would gladly go with you and take my chance."

As soon as the encampment was reached, Kreta came up to Ronald.

"Must change clothes," he said, "and go as Kaffir." Ronald nodded his head, as he had already decided that this step was absolutely necessary.

"Must paint black," the chief went on; "how do that?"

"The only way I can see is to powder some burnt wood and mix it with a little oil."

"Yes, that do," the chief said.

"I will be with you in five minutes. I must hand over the command to the corporal."

"Corporal James," he said, when he went up to him, "I hand over the command of this detachment to you. You are, of course, to keep by the waggons and protect them to King Williamstown."

"But where are you going, sergeant?" the corporal asked, in surprise.

"I have arranged with Mr. Nolan to go away on detached duty for two or three days. I am going to try to get the unfortunate women who were carried off this morning out of the hands of the Kaffirs." The corporal looked at him as if he had doubts as to his sanity.

"I may not succeed," Ronald went on, "but I am going to try. At any rate, I hand over the command to you. I quite understand that Mr. Nolan cannot give me leave, and that I run the risk of punishment for leaving the convoy; but I have made up my mind to risk that."

"Well, of course you know best, sergeant; but it seems to me that, punishment or no punishment, there is not much chance of your rejoining the corps; it is just throwing away your life going among them savages."

"I don't think it is as bad as that," Ronald said, "although of course there is a risk of it. At any rate, corporal, you can take the convoy safely into King Williamstown. That's your part of the business."

Ronald then returned to the encampment of the native levies. A number of sticks were charred and then scraped. There was no oil to be found, but as a substitute the charcoal was mixed with a little cart-grease. Ronald then stripped, and was smeared all over with the ointment, which was then rubbed into him. Some more powdered charcoal was then sprinkled over him, and this also rubbed until he was a shiny black, the operation affording great amusement to the Fingoes. Then a sort of petticoat, consisting of strips of hide reaching half-way down to the knee and sewn to a leathern belt, was put round his waist, and his toilet was complete.

Nothing could be done as to his hair, which was already cut quite short to prevent its forming a receptacle for dust. The Kaffirs have, as a rule, scarcely any hair on their heads, and nothing could have made Ronald's head resemble theirs. As, however, the disguise was only meant to pass at night, this did not matter. When all was done, the Fingoes applauded by clapping their hands and performing a wild dance round Ronald, while the women, who now crowded up, shrieked with laughter.

The chief walked gravely round him two or three times, and then pronounced that he would pass muster. A bandolier for cartridges, of native make, was slung over his shoulder, and with a rifle in one hand and a spear in the other, and two or three necklaces of brass beads round his neck, Ronald would, at a short distance, pass muster as a Kaffir warrior. In order to test his appearance, he strolled across to where Mr. Nolan was inspecting the serving out of rations.

"What do you want?" the officer asked. "The allowance for all the men has been served out already; if you haven't got yours you must speak to Kreta about it. I can't go into the question with each of you."

"Then you think I shall do very well, Mr. Nolan?"

The officer started.

"Good Heavens, sergeant, is it you? I had not the slightest conception of it. You are certainly admirably disguised, and, except for your hair, you might walk through the streets of Cape Town without any one suspecting you; but you will never be able to get through the woods barefooted."

"I have been thinking of that myself," Ronald said, "and the only thing I can see is to get them to make me a sort of sandal. Of course it wouldn't do in the daytime, but at night it would not be observed, unless I were to go close to a fire or light of some sort."

"Yes, that would be the best plan," the officer agreed. "I dare say the women can manufacture you something in that way. There is the hide of that bullock we killed yesterday, in the front waggon; it was a black one."

Ronald cut off a portion of the hide, and went across to the natives and explained to them what he wanted. Putting his foot on the hide, a piece was cut off large enough to form the sole of the foot and come up about an inch all round; holes were made in this, and it was laced on to the foot with thin strips of hide. The hair was, of course, outside, and Ronald found it by no means uncomfortable.

"You ride horse," the chief said, "back to bush. I take one fellow with me to bring him back."

Ronald was pleased at the suggestion, for he was by no means sure how he should feel after a walk of ten miles in his new foot-gear.

CHAPTER XII.

IN THE AMATOLAS.

The corporal had already spread the news among the men of Ronald's intended enterprise, and they gave him a hearty cheer as he rode off. Mr. Nolan had advised him to keep the native who was going to fetch his horse back.

"You won't want to walk into King Williamstown in that guise," he said; "therefore you had best put your uniform into the valise, and tell the man to meet you at any point you like—I should say the nearer to the bush the better; for if you succeed in getting the young lady out of these rascals' clutches you may be pursued, and, if your horse is handy, may succeed in getting her away, when you would otherwise be soon overtaken."

Ronald thankfully accepted the suggestion, for he saw that it might indeed be of vital importance to him to have his horse ready at hand.

With a last wave of his hand he rode off, the chief and his six companions trotting alongside.

The sun had set an hour when they reached the spot at which the chief had directed his two followers to meet him. They had not yet arrived.

"Do you think they will be sure to be able to find the place?" Ronald asked the chief.

"A Fingo never loses his way," the chief replied. "Find his way in dark, all same as day."

In spite of the chief's assurance, Ronald was fidgety and anxious. He wrapped a blanket round him, and walked restlessly up and down. It was nearly an hour before the chief, who, with his companions, had thrown himself down and lighted a pipe, which passed from hand to hand, said suddenly:

"One man come!"

Ronald listened intently, but could hear nothing. A moment later a dark figure came up.

Kreta at once questioned him, and a long conversation took place between them.

"What is he saying, chief? What is he saying?" Ronald broke in impatiently several times; but it was not until the man had finished that the chief translated.

"White girl alive, incos, the other two women alive, but not live long, torture them bad. Going to take girl to Macomo."

"Thank God for that," Ronald exclaimed, fervently, for he had all day been tormented with the fear that Mary Armstrong might have met with her fate directly she was carried away.

"Where are they going to take her?"

"A lot of them go off to-night; go straight to Amatolas; take her with them."

"How many, Kreta; will there be any chance of attacking them on the way?"

The chief asked a question of his messenger.

"Heaps of them," he said to Ronald, for the natives are incapable of counting beyond very low figures. "Too many; no chance to attack them; must follow behind. They show us the way."

"But how do we know whereabouts they will come out of the wood, Kreta? It's miles long; while we are watching at one place, they may be off in another."

"That's so, incos; no use to watch the wood. We must go on to the Great Fish River. Only two places where they can ford it—Double Drift and Cornetjies Drift, one hour's walk apart. Put half one place, half the other; then when they pass, follow after and send messengers to fetch up others."

"That will do very well, chief; that's a capital idea of yours. You are sure that there's no other way they can go?"

"Heaps of ways," the chief said, "but those shortest ways—sure to go short ways, so as to pass over ground quickly."

"What are they going back for?"

"No bullock in bush, incos, eaten up all the things round, want to go home to kraals; besides hear that many white soldiers come over sea to go to Amatolas to fight."

"How far is it to these fords?"

"Three hours' march. We start now. Kaffirs set out soon. Get on horse again."

Ronald was not sorry to do so, for he felt that in the dark he should run a considerable risk of laming himself against stones or stumps, and in any case he would scratch himself very severely with the thorns.

"Tell me, chief," he said, when they had started, "how did your messenger learn this, and what has become of your other man?"

"Not know about other man," the chief said. "Perhaps they caught him and killed him; perhaps he is hiding among them and dare not venture out. This man tell he go into forest and creep and crawl for a long time, then at last he saw some Kaffirs come along; he followed them, and at last they came to place in the bush where there was a heap of their fellows. They were all gathered round something, and he heard women crying very loud. Presently some of the men went away and he could see what it was—two white women tied to trees. The Kaffirs had stripped them and cut their flesh in many places. They die very soon, perhaps to-night or to-morrow morning. Then he crawl up and lay in the bushes, very close, and listen to talk. He heard that to-night heap party go away to Amatolas and take white woman as present for Macomo; then other Kaffirs come and lie down all about, and he did not dare move out till the light go away. Then he crawl through the bushes a good piece; then he got up and ran to bring the news."

"He has done very well," Ronald said; "tell him he shall be well rewarded. Now I think he might as well go to the camp and tell the officer there from me that two of the white women have been killed; but that the other has been taken away, as I hoped she would be, and that I am going after her."

"Message no use," the chief said, after a moment's thought; "better take him with us, may be useful by-and-by; may want to send to settlement."

"Perhaps it would be as well," Ronald agreed; "and the message is of no real importance."

After three hours' fast travelling—the natives going at a run, in spite of the darkness of the night, and Ronald leaving the reins loose, and trusting to his horse to feel his way—they came to the river; after making a narrow examination of the bank, the chief pronounced the ford to be a quarter of a mile lower down, and in a few minutes they came upon the spot where a road crossed the river.

"I think this way they are most likely to take," the chief said, when they had crossed the stream. "Country more broken this way, and further from towns, not so much chance of meeting soldiers. You and I and four men will stay here; three men go on to other ford, then if they cross there, send one man to tell us; the other two follow them, and see which way they go."

"Do you know the Amatolas at all, chief?"

"Not know him, incos; never been there; travel all about these parts in last war, but never go up to Amatolas."

"Then, of course, you do not know at all where Macomo's kraal is?"

"Not know him at all. We follow men, sure enough we get there."

The three men had not started above five minutes, when the chief said in a low tone:

"They are coming," and gave an order to one of his men, who at once set off at the top of his speed to overtake the others and bring them back.

It was nearly ten minutes before Ronald could hear the slightest sound, then he became conscious of a low murmur of voices in the air, and a minute or two later there was a splashing of water at the ford, fifty yards from the spot where they had lain down under a bush. One of the natives had, at Kreta's orders, taken the horse away, the chief telling him to go half a mile off, as were it to paw the ground suddenly, or make any noise, the attention of the Kaffirs, if within hearing, would be instantly drawn to it.

Dark as the night was, the figures of those crossing the water could be dimly made out, and Ronald judged there must be fully three hundred of them. After the first few had passed they came along in such a close body that he was unable to make out whether there was a female among them. The numbers of the Kaffirs sufficed to show him there was no chance whatever of effecting a rescue of Mary Armstrong while surrounded by so large a body.

As soon as all had crossed, two of the Fingoes followed close upon their traces, five minutes afterwards another started, and scarcely had he gone when the three men who had been sent to the other ford returned with the messenger who had recalled them. They left at short intervals after each other, and then Ronald mounted his horse, which had now been fetched up, and followed with Kreta.

"There is no fear of our missing them, chief?"

"No fear of that, incos; that star over there shines over the Amatolas, they go straight for it; besides, the two men behind them can hear them talking. If they turn off one come back to tell us."

But they did not turn off, but kept on for hours in a straight undeviating line, travelling at a fast walk. Roland Mervyn kept wondering how Mary Armstrong was bearing up. She was a strong active girl, accustomed to plenty of exercise, and at ordinary times could doubtless have walked a long distance; but the events of the day, the sudden attack upon the waggons, her capture by the Kaffirs, her uncertainty as to the fate of her father, the harrowing tortures of her companions, which she had probably been compelled to witness, and the hopelessness of her own fate, might well have broken her down. He was sure that the Kaffirs would compel her to walk as long as she could drag her limbs along, but as she was destined as a present to their chief, they might, when she could go no further, carry her.

He groaned at his helplessness to aid her, and had he not had a perfect faith in the cunning of his companions, and in their ability to follow her up wherever she was taken, he would have been inclined to take the mad step of charging right in among the Kaffirs, upon the one chance of snatching her up and carrying her off from among them.

Roland Mervyn, of the Cape Rifles, was a very different man from Captain Mervyn, of the Borderers. The terrible event that had caused him to throw up his commission and leave the country had in other respects been of great advantage. He had for years been haunted by the fear of madness, and whenever he felt low and out of spirits this fear of insanity had almost overpowered him. The trial had cured him of this; he had convinced himself that had he inherited the slightest taint of the curse of the Carnes, he would have gone mad while he was awaiting his trial; that he had kept his head perfect under such circumstances seemed to him an absolute proof that he was as sane as other men, and henceforth he banished the fear that had so long haunted him.

It was in truth that fear which had held him back so long from entering into a formal engagement with his cousin Margaret. He looked upon it as an absolutely settled thing that they would be married some day, but had almost unconsciously shrunk from making that day a definite one; and although for the moment he had burst into a fit of wild anger at being as he considered thrown aside, he had since acknowledged to himself that Margaret's decision had been a wise one, and that it was better that they two should not have wedded.

He had always been blessed with good spirits, except at the times when the fit of depression seized him; but since he had been at the Cape, and been on active duty, these had entirely passed away, and his unvarying good temper under all circumstances had often been the subject of remark among his comrades.

As he rode along that night he acknowledged, what he had never before admitted to himself, that he loved Mary Armstrong. The admission was a bitter rather than a pleasant one.

"I shall never marry now," he had said to his mother, at his last interview with her. "No wife or child of mine shall ever hear it whispered that her husband or father was a murderer. Unless this cloud is some day lifted—and how it can be, Heaven only knows—I must go through the world alone," and so he thought still. It might be that as Harry Blunt he might settle down in the Colony and never be recognised; but he would always have the fear that at any moment some officer he had known, some man of his regiment, some emigrant from his own county, might recognise him, and that the news would be passed round that Harry Blunt was the Captain Mervyn who escaped, only from want of legal proof, from being hung as the murderer of his cousin.

"I didn't think I was such a fool," he muttered to himself, "as to be caught by a pretty face. However, it will make no difference. She will never know it. If her father recovers, which is doubtful, she will go back with him to the old country. If not, she will go back alone, for without friends or relatives she cannot stay here, and she will never dream that the sergeant of the Cape Rifles, who had the luck twice to save her life—that is, if I do save it—was fool enough to fall in love with her."

An hour before morning one of the Fingoes came back from the front with the news that the Kaffirs had turned off into a kloof, and were going to halt there. The party soon collected, and retired to a clump of trees a mile back. One of them was ordered to act as sentry near the kloof, and bring back word at once should any movement take place. The rest of the party, upon reaching the shelter of the trees, threw themselves upon the ground, and were soon fast asleep; even Ronald, anxious as he was, remaining awake but a few minutes after the others.

The sun was high before they awoke. As they were eating their breakfast the sentry returned, and another was despatched to take his place. The man reported that he had seen nothing of the main body of Kaffirs, but that four of them were placed on the watch near the kloof. Kreta led Ronald to the edge of the wood, and pointing to a jagged range of hills in the distance said, "Amatolas."

"How far are they away, Kreta?"

"Six hours' fast walking," the chief said. "They get to foot of hills to-night. If Macomo's kraal anywhere this side, they may get there. If not, they wait and rest a bit, and then go on. No need travel fast when get to hills; they know very well no white soldier there."

"What had we better do, do you think?"

"They have plenty of men always on look-out, sure to be some on hills. I will send two men after these fellows, and they creep and crawl through the bushes, find out the way and bring news to me; then when they come back we will start."

"But we must be there in the evening," Ronald said; "we must be there, chief; do you hear?"

"Yes, incos, but it seems to me that it do no good to throw our lives away. If you say go, Kreta will go too, but if we killed, girl will be killed too, and no good that, that Kreta can see; if we go in daytime we killed, sure enough. Not possible to get into Amatolas without being seen; all grass and smooth land at foot of hill. On hill some places trees, there we manage very well; some open spaces, there they see us."

"I don't wish to throw our lives away, chief; if I wanted to throw my own away, I have no right to sacrifice yours and your men's; but scouts on the look out would surely take us at a distance for a party of their own men returning from some plundering expedition, probably as part of the party ahead, who had hung back for some purpose on the road."

"Great many kraals, great many people in Amatolas," the chief said; "sure to meet some one. They begin to ask questions, and see very soon we not Kaffirs, see directly you not Kaffir; might pass at night very well, but no pass in day. But perhaps we have time, incos. Chiefs wander about, hold council and meet each other; perhaps Macomo not at home, very likely he away when they get there."

"Pray God it may be so," Ronald said, despairingly. "It seems the only hope we have. Well, Kreta, I put myself in your hands. You know much more about it than I do. As you say, we shall do no good to Miss Armstrong by throwing away our lives, therefore, I put aside my own plans and trust to you."

"I no say we can save her, incos, but if we can we will. You make sure of that."

The next night took them to the foot of the hills, and when the Kaffirs halted, the chief ordered two of his men to make a circuit, climb the hill, and conceal themselves in the bush before morning broke, so that when the Kaffirs moved on they could at once follow them without having to cross in daylight the grassy slopes of the foot hills. Minute instructions were given to both to follow close behind the Kaffir party, the order being that if either of them could pounce upon a solitary native, he was to stun him with his knobkerry, and force him when he recovered to give information as to the distance, direction, and road to Macomo's kraal, and that he was then to be assegaid at once. Feeling that Ronald might not altogether approve of this last item, for he was aware that the white men had what he considered a silly objection to unnecessary bloodshed, Kreta, whilst telling Ronald the rest of the instructions he had given to the spies, did not think it necessary to detail this portion of them.

"Where shall we stay till morning?" Ronald inquired of him; "the country seems perfectly flat and unbroken, their look-out will see us a long way off."

"Yes, incos, we lie down in little bush behind there. We send horse back to first wood and tell man to bring him every night to bottom of the hill, or if he sees us from a distance coming down the hill with Kaffirs after us, to come to meet us. We lie down till morning. Then when they go on, we go on too, little time afterwards, as you said, and follow as far as first wood; look-out think we belong to big party; then we hide there till one of my men come back. I told them we should be somewhere in wood, and he is to make signals as he walks along. We will push on as far as we can, so that we don't come upon kraals."

"That will do very well indeed," Ronald said, "for every inch that we can get nearer to Macomo's kraal is so much gained."

He removed the pistols from his holsters, and fastened them to his belt, putting them so far back that they were completely hidden by the blanket he wore over his shoulders, and then went with the party some little distance back, and lay down till morning. Almost as soon as it was daybreak, the Fingo who was on the watch announced that the Kaffirs were moving, and the little party at once followed. The Kaffirs had disappeared among the woods, high up on the hill side, when they began to ascend the grassy slope. They had no doubt that they were observed by the Kaffir watchmen, but they proceeded boldly, feeling sure it would be supposed that they belonged to the party ahead of them.

The path through the forest was a narrow one, and they moved along in single file. One of the party went fifty yards ahead, walking cautiously, and listening intently for suspicious sounds; the rest proceeded noiselessly, prepared to bound into the forest directly the man ahead gave the signal that any one was approaching. For upwards of a mile they kept their way, the ground rising continually; then they reached a spot where a deep valley fell away at their feet. It divided into several branches, and wreaths of smoke could be seen curling up through the trees at a number of points. Similar indications of kraals could be seen everywhere upon the hill side, and Kreta shook his head and said:

"No can go further. Heaps of Kaffir all about. Must wait now."

Even Ronald, anxious as he was to go on, felt that it would be risking too much to proceed. The kraals were so numerous that as soon as they got into the valley they would be sure to run into one, and, moreover, the path would fork into many branches, and it would be impossible for them to say which of these the party ahead had taken.

They turned aside into the wood for some little distance and lay down, one being left on the watch in the bush close to the path. The hours passed slowly while they waited the return of one of the scouts, who had been ordered to follow close upon the footsteps of the Kaffirs to Macomo's kraal. It was three o'clock before the look-out by the path returned, accompanied by one of them.

He said a few words to the chief, and although Ronald could not understand him he saw by the expression of Kreta's face that the news was satisfactory.

"Girl got to Macomo's kraal," the chief said. "Macomo not there. Gone to Sandilli. May come back to-night. Most likely get drunk and not come back till to-morrow. Macomo drink very much."

"All the better," Ronald said. "Thank God we have got a few hours before us."

The man gave a narration of his proceedings to Kreta, who translated them to Ronald.

Directly the Kaffirs had passed the point where he and his comrade were hidden, they came out of the bush and followed closely behind them, sometimes dropping behind a little so as to be quite out of sight if any of them should look round, and then going on faster until they could get a glimpse of them, so as to be sure that they were going in the right direction. They had passed through several kraals. Before they came to each of these the men had waited a little, and had then gone on at a run, as if anxious to catch up the main body. They had thus avoided questioning.

Three hours' walking took them to Macomo's kraal, and they had hung about there until they found out that Macomo was away, having gone off early to pay a visit to Sandilli. Kreta did not translate his followers' description of the manner in which this information had been obtained, and Ronald, supposing they had gathered it from listening to the Kaffirs, asked no questions. As soon as they had learned what they wanted to know, one of them had remained in hiding near the village, and the other had returned with the news. He had been nearly twice as long coming back as he was going, as this time he had been obliged to make a circuit so as to pass round each of the kraals, and so to avoid being questioned.

"Did he see the young lady?" Ronald asked; "and how was she looking?"

Yes, he had seen her as they passed his ambush the first thing in the morning. She looked very white and tired, but she was walking. She was not bound in any way. That was all he could tell him.

"How soon can we go on, chief?" Ronald asked, impatiently. "You see, it is three hours' marching even if we go straight through."

"Can go now," the chief said. "Now we know where Macomo's kraal is we can go straight through the bush."

They went back to the path. The Fingo pointed to the exact position among the hills where Macomo's kraal was. There were two intermediate ridges to be crossed, but Ronald did not doubt the Fingo's power to follow a nearly direct line to the spot.

"Now," the chief said, "you follow close behind me. Keep your eyes always on ground. Do not look at trees or rocks, or anything, but tread in my footsteps. Remember if you tread on a twig, or make the least sound, perhaps some one notice it. We may be noticed anyhow. Fellows upon the watch may see us moving through the trees overhead, but must risk that; but only don't make noise."

Ronald promised to obey the chief's instructions, and the party, again leaving the path, took their way through the trees straight down into the valley. At times they came to such precipitous places that they were forced to make detours to get down them. One of the men now went ahead, the rest following at such a distance that they could just keep him in sight through the trees. From time to time he changed his course, as he heard noises or the sound of voices that told him he was approaching a kraal. At times they came across patches of open ground. When it was impossible to avoid these they made no attempt to cross them rapidly, as they knew that the sharp eyes of the sentries on the hill top could look down upon them. They, therefore, walked at a quiet pace, talking and gesticulating to each other as they went, so that they might be taken for a party going from one kraal to another.

It was eight o'clock in the evening, and the sun had set some time, when they approached the kraal of Macomo.

It was a good-sized village, and differed little from the ordinary Kaffir kraals except that two or three of the huts were large and beehive-shaped. There was a good deal of noise going on in the village; great fires were burning, and round these numbers of the Kaffirs were dancing, representing by their action the conflict in which they had been engaged, and the slaughter of their enemies. The women were standing round, keeping up a monotonous song, to the rhythm of which the men were dancing.

As they approached within a hundred yards of the edge of the clearing round the village, a sharp hiss was heard among the bushes. Kreta at once left the path, the others following him. They were at once joined by the other scouts.

"What is the news?"

"The white woman is still in the woman's hut next to that of Macomo."

"Are there any guards at the door?" Ronald asked. The chief put the question.

"No, no guards have been placed there. There are many women in the hut. There was no fear of her escape. Besides, if she got out, where could she go to?"

"Well, now, incos, what are we to do?" the chief asked. "We have brought you here, and now we are ready to die if you tell us. What you think we do next?"

"Wait a bit, Kreta, I must think it over."

Indeed, Ronald had been thinking all day. He had considered it probable that Mary Armstrong would be placed in the hut of one of the chief's wives. The first question was how to communicate with her. It was almost certain that either some of the women would sit up all night, or that sentries would be placed at the door. Probably the former. The Kaffirs had made a long journey, and had now doubtless been gorging themselves with meat. They would be disinclined to watch, and would consider their responsibility at an end when they had handed her over to the women. It was almost certain that Mary herself would be asleep after her fatigue of the last three days; even the prospect of the terrible fate before her would scarce suffice to keep her awake.

"Do you think two women will sit up with her all night?"

"Two or three of them, sure," Kreta replied.

"My plan is this, Kreta; it may not succeed, but I can think of no other. In the first place, I will go into the kraal. I will wait until there is no one near the door, then I will stoop and say in a loud voice, so that she may hear, that she is to keep awake at night. Macomo's women are none of them likely to understand English, and before they run out to see what it is, I shall be gone. If they tell the men they have heard a strange voice speaking unknown words, they will be laughed at, or at most a search will be made through the kraal, and of course nothing will be found. Then, to-night, chief, when everything is still, I propose that three of you shall crawl with me into the kraal. When we get to the door of the hut, you will draw aside the hide that will be hanging over it and peep in. If only two women are sitting by the fire in the centre, two of you will crawl in as noiselessly as possible. I know that you can crawl so that the sharpest ear cannot hear you. Of course, if there are three, three of you will go in; if two, two only. You will crawl up behind the women, suddenly seize them by the throat and gag and bind them. Then you will beckon to the young lady to follow you. She will know from my warning that you are friends. If she has a light dress on, throw a dark blanket round her, for many of the Kaffirs will go on feasting all night, and might see her in the light of the fire. Then I will hurry her away, and your men follow us so as to stop the Kaffirs a moment and give us time to get into the bushes if we are seen."

"Kreta will go himself," the chief said, "with two of his young men. Do you not think, incos, that there is danger in your calling out?"

"Not much danger, I think, Kreta. They will not dream of a white man being here, in the heart of the Amatolas. I think there is less danger in it than that the girl might cry out if she was roused from her sleep by men whom she did not know. She might think that it was Macomo come home."

Kreta agreed in this opinion.

"I will go down at once," Ronald said; "they're making such a noise that it is unlikely any one outside the hut would hear me, however loud I spoke, while if I waited until it got quieter, I might be heard. Take my rifle, Kreta, and one of the pistols; I want to carry nothing extra with me, in case I have to make a sudden bolt for it."

Mary Armstrong was lying apparently unnoticed by the wall of the hut, while a dozen women were chattering round the fire in the centre. Suddenly she started; for from the door, which was but three feet high, there came a loud, clear voice, "Mary Armstrong, do not sleep to-night. Rescue is at hand."

The women started to their feet with a cry of alarm at these mysterious sounds, and stood gazing at the entrance; then there was a clamour of tongues, and presently one of them, older than the rest, walked to the entrance and looked out.

"There is no one here," she said, looking round, and the greater part of the women at once rushed out. Their conduct convinced Mary Armstrong that she was not in a dream, as she at first thought, but had really heard the words. Who could have spoken them, or what rescue could reach her? This she could not imagine; but she had sufficient self-possession to resume her reclining position, from which she had half risen, and to close her eyes as if sound asleep. A minute later, one of the women appeared with a blazing brand, and held it close to her eyes.

"The girl is asleep," she said in Kaffir, which Mary understood perfectly; "what can have been the words we heard?"

"It must have been an evil spirit," another woman said; "who else can have spoken in an unknown tongue to us?"

There was a good deal of hubbub in the kraal when the women told their story; some of the men took up their weapons and searched the village and the surrounding bushes, but the greater portion altogether disbelieved the story. Whoever heard of a spirit talking in an unknown tongue to a lot of women? If he had wanted to say anything to them, he would have spoken so that they could understand. It must have been some man who had drunk too much, and who bellowed in at the door to startle them; and so gradually the din subsided, the men returned to the dance, and the women to their huts.

Had Mary Armstrong been in spirits to enjoy it, she would have been amused at the various propositions started by the women to account for the voice they had heard; not one of them approached the truth, for it did not occur to them as even possible that a white man should have penetrated the Amatolas to Macomo's kraal.

CHAPTER XIII.

THE RESCUE.

Ronald, with Kreta and two of his men, now crept down to the very edge of the bushes at a spot where they could command a view of the entrance to the hut. For a long time female figures came in and out, and it was not until long past midnight that they saw the last female figure disappear inside and the skin drawn across the entrance.

"How long shall we give them, Kreta?"

"In an hour Kreta will go see," the chief said; "but better give two hours for all to be fast asleep."

In about an hour Ronald, who had been half lying on the ground with his head on his hands, looked round and found that the chief had stolen away. He sat up and watched the hut intently. The fires were burning low now, although many of the Kaffirs were sitting round them; but there was still light enough for him, looking intently, to see a figure moving along. Once or twice he fancied he saw a dark shadow on the ground close to the hut, but he was not sure, and was still gazing intently when there was a touch on his shoulder, and, looking round, he saw the chief beside him.

"Two women watch," he said, "others all quiet. Give a little time longer, to make sure that all are asleep, then we go on."

It seemed to Ronald fully two hours, although it was less than one, before Kreta again touched him.

"Time to go, incos," he said. "You go down with me to the hut, but not quite close. Kreta bring girl to you. You better not go. Kreta walk more quietly than white man. Noise spoil everything, get all of us killed."

Ronald gave his consent, though reluctantly, but he felt it was right that the Fingo, who was risking his life for his sake, should carry out his plans in his own way. Kreta ordered one of his men to rejoin his companions, and with the other advanced towards the village.

When within forty yards of the hut, he touched Ronald and whispered to him to remain there. Then he and his companion lay down on the ground, and, without the slightest sound that Ronald could detect, disappeared in the darkness, while Ronald stood with his revolver in his hand, ready at any moment to spring forward and throw himself upon the Kaffirs.

Mary Armstrong lay awake, with every faculty upon the stretch. Where the succour was to come from, or how, she could not imagine; but it was evident, at least, that some white man was here, and was working for her. She listened intently to every sound, with her eyes wide open, staring at the two women, who were cooking mealies in the fire, and keeping up a low, murmured talk. She had not even a hope that they would sleep. She knew that the natives constantly sit up talking and feasting until daylight is close at hand; and as they had extra motives for vigilance, she was sure that they would keep awake.

Suddenly, so suddenly that she scarcely knew what had happened, the two women disappeared from her sight. A hand had grasped each tightly by the throat, another hand seized the hair, and, with a sharp jerk, pulled the head on one side, breaking the neck in a moment—a common mode among the Kaffirs of putting any one to death. The whole thing did not occupy a moment, and as the women disappeared from her sight, two natives rose to their feet and looked round. Convinced that this was the succour promised her, she sat up. One of the natives put his finger upon his lips to indicate the necessity of silence, and beckoned for her to rise and come to him. When she did so he wrapped her in a dark blanket and led her to the door. He pushed aside the hanging and went out.

Mary followed close behind him. He now put the blanket over her head and lifted her in his arms. A momentary dread seized her lest this might be an emissary of some other chief, who had sent him to carry off Macomo's new captive, but the thought of the English words reassured her; and, at any rate, even if it were so, her position could not possibly be worse than on the return of Macomo the next morning. She was carried a short distance, then she heard her bearer say in English: "Come along; I take her a bit further. Too close to Kaffir still." She was carried on for some distance. Then there was a stop, and she was placed on her feet; the blanket was removed from her head, and a moment later a dark figure seized her hand.

"Thank God, we have got you out, Miss Armstrong."

The revulsion of feeling at hearing her own tongue was so great that she was not capable of speaking, and she would have fallen had she not been clasped in the arms of the person who addressed her. Her surprise at feeling that the arms that encircled her were bare, roused her.

"Who are you, sir?" she asked, trembling.

"I am Sergeant Blunt, Miss Armstrong. No wonder you did not know me. I am got up in native fashion. You can trust yourself with me, you know."

"Oh, yes, yes," the girl sobbed. "I know I can, you saved my life once before.

How did you come here? And, oh, can you tell me any news about my father?"

"He is hurt, Miss Armstrong, but I have every hope that he will recover. Now you must be strong, for we must be miles from here before morning. Can you walk?"

"Oh yes, I can walk any distance," the girl said. "Yesterday it seemed to me that I could not walk an inch further were it to save my life, and they had to carry me the last mile or two, but now I feel strong enough to walk miles."

"She can walk at present, chief," Ronald said, "let us go forward at once."

They were now on the pathway leading down to the kraal. The chief took the lead, telling Mary Armstrong to take hold of his blanket and follow close behind him, while Ronald followed on her heels, the other Fingoes keeping in the rear. The darkness beneath the trees was dense, and it was some time before Ronald could make out even the outline of the figures before him. Before approaching a kraal a halt was always made, and one of the Fingoes went on ahead to see if the fires were out and all natives inside their huts. Several times, although all the human beings were asleep, the scout returned, saying that they could not pass through the kraal, for the dogs had scented him and growled fiercely, and would set up such a barking when the party passed as to bring all the village out to see what was the matter.

Then long detours, that would have been difficult through the thick bush in daylight, but at night were almost impossible, had to be made. Each time that this had to be done, Kreta lifted Mary Armstrong and carried her, and she had now become so exhausted that she was unable even to protest. Ronald would have carried her himself, but he felt that it would be worse than useless to attempt to do so. Though unencumbered, he had the greatest difficulty in making his way through the bushes, which scratched and tore his flesh terribly; but the chief seemed to be possessed of the eyes of a bat, and glided through them, scarcely moving a twig as he passed. After going on for upwards of three hours, the chief stopped.

"It will be getting light soon. We must hide her now. Cannot get further until to-morrow night."

Although Ronald Mervyn, struggling along in the darkness, had not noticed it, the party had for the last hour turned off from the line they had before been following. They stopped by a little stream, running down the valley. Here a native refilled the gourds, and Mary Armstrong felt better after a drink of water.

"I think," Ronald said to her, "that if you were to bathe your face and hands it would refresh you. There is a rock here just at the edge of the stream, I am sure your feet must be sore and blistered. It will be half an hour before there is a gleam of light, and I should recommend you to take off your shoes and stockings and paddle your feet in the water."

"That would be refreshing," the girl said. "My feet are aching dreadfully. Now please tell me all that has happened, and how you came to be here."

Sitting beside her, Ronald told her what had been done from the time when his party arrived and beat off the natives attacking the waggons.

"How can I thank you enough?" she said, when he had finished. "To think that you have done all this for me."

"Never mind about thanks, Miss Armstrong; we are not out of the wood yet, our dangers are only half over, and if it were not that I trust to the cunning of our good friend Kreta and his Fingoes I should have very little hope of getting out of this mess. I think it is just beginning to get light, for I can make out the outlines of the trunks of the trees, which is more than I could do before. I will go and ask Kreta what he is going to do, and by the time I come back perhaps you had better get your shoes on again, and be ready for a start. I don't suppose we shall go far, but no doubt he will find some sort of hiding-place." Kreta, in fact, was just giving instructions to his men.

"We are going out to find some good place to hide away in to-day," he said. "In the morning they search all about the woods. We must get into shelter before it light enough for the men on hill tops to see down through trees. You stop here quiet. In half an hour we come back again. There is plenty time; they no find out yet that woman gone."

In a few minutes Mary Armstrong joined Ronald.

"How do you feel now?" he asked.

"All the fresher and better for the wash," she said; "but I really don't think I could walk very far, my feet are very much blistered. I don't see why they should be so bad; we have only gone about twenty-four miles each day, and I always considered that I could walk twenty miles without difficulty."

"It makes all the difference how you walk, Miss Armstrong. No doubt, if you had been in good spirits, and with a pleasant party, you could have walked fifty miles in two days, although that is certainly a long distance for a woman; but depressed and almost despairing, as you were, it told upon you generally, and doubtless you rather dragged your feet along than walked."

"I don't want to think about it," the girl said, with a shudder. "It seems to have been an awful dream. Some day I will tell you about it; but I cannot now."

"Here are some mealies and some cold meat. We each brought a week's supply with us when we left the waggons. I am sure that you will be all the better for eating something."

"I do feel very hungry, now I think of it," the girl assented; "I have hardly eaten a mouthful since that morning."

"I am hungry myself," Ronald said "I was too anxious yesterday to do justice to my food."

"I feel very much better now," the girl said when she had finished. "I believe I was faint from want of food before, although I did not think of it. I am sure I could go on walking now. It was not the pain that stopped me, but simply because I didn't feel as if I could lift my foot from the ground. And there is one thing I want to say: I wish you would not call me Miss Armstrong, it seems so formal and stiff, when you are running such terrible risks to save me. Please call me Mary, and I will call you Harry. I think I heard you tell my father your name was Harry Blunt."

"That is the name I enlisted under, it is not my own name; men very seldom enlist under their own names."

"Why not?" she asked in surprise.

"Partly, I suppose, because a good many of us get into scrapes before we enlist, and don't care for our friends to be able to trace us."

"I am sure you never got into a scrape," the girl said, looking up into Ronald's face.

"I got into a very bad scrape," Ronald answered, "a scrape that has spoilt my whole life; but we will not talk about that. But I would rather, if you don't mind, that you should call me by my own name now we are together. If we get out of this I shall be Sergeant Blunt again, but I should like you to call me Ronald now."

"Ronald," the girl said, "that sounds Scottish."

"I am not Scotch, nor so far as I know is there any Scotch blood in my veins, but the name has been in the family a good many years; how it got there I do not know."

"I almost wish it was dark again," the girl said, with a little laugh; "in the dark you seem to me the Sergeant Blunt who came just in time to save us that day the farm was attacked; but now I can see you I cannot recognise you at all; even your eyes look quite different in that black skin."

"I flatter myself that my get up is very good," Ronald laughed. "I have had some difficulty in keeping up the colour. Each day before starting we have gone to our fires and got fresh charcoal and mixed it with some grease we brought with us and rubbed it in afresh."

"Your hair is your weak point, Ronald; but, of course, no European could make his hair like a native's. Still, as it is cut so close, it would not be noticed a little way off."

Two or three of the Fingoes had by this time returned, and in a few minutes all had gathered at the spot. Kreta listened to the reports of each of his men, and they held a short consultation. Then he came up to Ronald.

"One of my men has found a place that will do well," he said. "It is time we were going."

One of the Fingoes now took the lead; the others followed. A quarter of an hour's walk up the hill, which grew steeper and steeper every step, brought them to a spot where some masses of rock had fallen from above. They were half covered with the thick growth of brushwood. The native pushed one of the bushes aside, and showed a sort of cave formed by a great slab of rock that had fallen over the others. Kreta uttered an expression of approval. Two of the natives crept in with their assegais in their hands. In two or three minutes one of them returned with the bodies of two puff adders they had killed. These were dropped in among some rocks.

"You can go in now," Kreta said. "There are no more of them."

Ronald crawled in first, and helped Mary Armstrong in after him; the natives followed. Kreta came in last, carefully examining the bush before he did so, to see that no twig was broken or disarranged. He managed as he entered to place two or three rocks over the entrance.

"Good place," he said, looking round as he joined the others. It was indeed of ample size to contain the party, and was some four feet in height. Light came in in several places between the rocks on which the upper slab rested.

"It could not be better, Kreta, even if it had been made on purpose. It was lucky indeed your fellow found it."

"We found two or three others," the chief said, "but this best."

"It is lucky those men came in first and found the snakes," Mary Armstrong said, "for we have not got here the stuff we always use in the colony as an antidote, and their bite is almost always fatal unless that can be used in time." Ronald was aware of this, and had, indeed, during the night's march, had snakes constantly in his mind, for he knew that they abounded in the hills.

One of the Fingoes had taken his station at the entrance, having moved one of the stones the chief had placed there, so that he could sit with his head out of the opening. Half an hour after they had entered the cave he turned round and spoke to the chief.

"The Kaffirs are hunting," Kreta said. Listening at the opening they could hear distant shouts. These were answered from many points, some of them comparatively close.

"The news is being passed from kraal to kraal," Ronald said; "they will be up like a swarm of bees now, but search as they will they are not likely to find us here. Do you think they will trace us at all, chief?"

"They will find where we stopped close to kraal," Kreta said; "the dead leaves were stirred by our feet; after that not find, too many people gone along path; ground very hard; may find, sometime, mark of the white woman's shoe; but we leave path many times, and after I carry no find at all. Mountains very big, much bush; never find here."

The chief now told his follower to replace the stone and join the others, and ordered all to be silent. Sitting with his ear at one of the openings he listened to the sounds in the woods; once or twice he whispered that Kaffirs were passing close, searching among the bushes; and one party came so near that their words could be plainly heard in the cave. They were discussing the manner in which the fugitive had escaped, and were unanimous in the belief that she had been carried off by the followers of some other chief, for that an enemy should have penetrated into the heart of the Amatolas did not strike them as possible.

The argument was only as to which of the other chiefs would have ventured to rob Macomo, and the opinion inclined to the fact that it must have been Sandilli himself, who would doubtless have heard, from the messenger sent over on the previous afternoon to inform Macomo, of the return of the band with a pretty young white woman as a captive. Macomo had of course been drunk, and Sandilli might have determined to have the prize carried off for himself.

Mary Armstrong shuddered as she listened to the talk, but when they had gone on Kreta said:

"Good thing the Kaffirs have that thought, not search so much here. Search in Sandilli's country. Perhaps make great quarrel between Macomo and Sandilli. Good thing that."

As the day went on the spirits of the Fingoes rose, and in low tones they expressed their delight at having outwitted the Kaffirs.

No footsteps had been heard in their neighbourhood for some time, and they felt sure that the search had been abandoned in that quarter. Towards sunset all ate a hearty meal, and as soon as it became dark the stones at the entrance were removed and the party crept out. Mary Armstrong had slept the greater part of the day, and Ronald and the Fingoes had also passed a portion of their time in sleep. They started, therefore, refreshed and strong.

It took them many hours of patient work before they arrived at the edge of the forest on the last swell of the Amatolas. They had been obliged to make many detours to avoid kraals, and to surmount the precipices that often barred their way. They had started about eight in the evening, and it was, as they knew from the stars, fully three o'clock in the morning when they emerged from the forest.

Mary Armstrong had kept on well with the rest; her feet were extremely painful, but she was now strong and hopeful, and no word of complaint escaped her. Ronald and the chief kept by her side, helping her up or down difficult places, and assisting her to pass through the thorny bushes, which caught her dress, and would have rendered it almost impossible for her to get through unaided. Once out of the bush, the party hurried down the grassy slope, and then kept on a mile further. The chief now gave a loud call. It was answered faintly from the distance; in five minutes the sound of a horse's hoofs were heard, and in a short time the Fingo who had been left in charge of it, galloped up with Ronald's horse. Mary Armstrong was sitting on the ground, for she was now so utterly exhausted she could no longer keep her feet, and had, since they left the bush, been supported and half carried by Ronald and Kreta. She made an effort to rise as the horse came up.

"Please wait a moment; I will not be above two minutes," Ronald said; "but I really cannot ride into Williamstown like this."

He unstrapped his valise, took the jack-boots that were hanging from the saddle, and moved away in the darkness. In two or three minutes he returned in his uniform.

"I feel a civilised being again," he said, laughing; "a handful of sand at the first stream we come to will get most of this black off my face. I have left my blanket as a legacy to any Kaffir who may light upon it. Now I will shift the saddle a few inches further back. I think you had better ride before me, for you are completely worn out, and I can hold you there better than you could hold yourself if you were to sit behind me." He strapped on his valise, shifted his saddle, lifted Mary up, and sprang up behind her.

"Are you comfortable?" he asked.

"Quite comfortable," she said, a little shyly, and then they started. The light was just beginning to break in the east as they rode out from the clump of trees. They were not out of danger yet, for parties of Kaffirs might be met with at any time until they arrived within musket shot of King Williamstown. The Fingoes ran at a pace that kept the horse at a sharp trot. It was very pleasant to Ronald Mervyn to feel Mary Armstrong in his arms, and to know, as he did, how safe and confident she felt there; but he did not press her more closely than was necessary to enable her to retain her seat, or permit himself to speak in a softer or tenderer tone than usual.

"If we should come across any of these scoundrels, Mary," he said, presently, "do you take the reins. Do you think you can sit steady without my holding you firmly?"

"Yes," the girl said, "if I put one foot on yours I could certainly hold on. I could twist one of my hands in the horse's mane."

"Can you use a pistol?"

"Of course I can," she replied. "I was as good a shot as my father."

"That is all right, then. I will give you one of my pistols; then I can hold you with my right arm, for the horse may plunge if a spear strikes him. I will use my pistol in my left hand. I will see that no one catches the bridle on that side; do you attend to the right. I hope it won't come to that, still there's never any saying, and we shall have one or two nasty places to pass through on our way down. We have the advantage that should there be any Kaffirs there they will not be keeping a watch this way, and we may hope to get pretty well through them before they see us."

"Will you promise me one thing, Ronald?" she asked. "Will you shoot me if you find that we cannot get past?"

Ronald nodded.

"I am not at all afraid of death," she said; "death would be nothing to that. I would rather die a thousand times than fall into the hands of the Kaffirs again."

"I promise you, Mary, my last shot but one shall be for you, my last for myself; but if I am struck off the horse by a bullet or assegai you must trust to your own pistol."

"I will do that, Ronald; I have been perfectly happy since you took me out of the hut, and have not seemed to feel any fear of being recaptured, for I felt that if they overtook us I could always escape so. On the way there, if I could have got hold of an assegai I should have stabbed myself."

"Thank God you didn't," said Ronald, earnestly, "though I could not have blamed you."

They paused at the entrance to each kloof through which they had to pass, and the Fingoes went cautiously ahead searching through the bushes. It was not until he heard their call on the other side that Ronald galloped after them.

"I begin to hope that we shall get through now," Ronald said, after emerging from one of these kloofs; "we have only one more bad place to pass, but, of course, the danger is greatest there, as from that the Kaffirs will probably be watching against any advance of the troops from the town."

The Fingoes were evidently of the same opinion, for as they approached it Kreta stopped to speak to Ronald.

"Kaffir sure to be here," he said, "but me and my men can creep through; but we must not call to you, incos; the Kaffirs would hear us and be on the watch. Safest plan for us to go through first, not go along paths, but through bush; then for you to gallop straight through; even if they close to path, you get past before they time to stop you. I think that best way."

"I think so too, Kreta. If they hear the horse's hoofs coming from behind they will suppose it is a mounted messenger from the hills. Anyhow, I think that a dash for it is our best chance."

"I think so, incos. I think you get through safe if go fast."

"How long will you be getting through, Kreta?"

"Quarter of an hour," the chief said; "must go slow. Your ride four, five minutes."

Kreta stood thoughtfully for a minute or two.

"Me don't like it, incos. Me tell you what we do. We keep over to left, and then when we get just through the bush we fire our guns. Then the Kaffirs very much surprised and all run that way, and you ride straight through."

"But they might overtake you, Kreta."

"They no overtake," the chief said, confidently. "We run fast and get good start. Williamstown only one hour's walk; run less than half hour. They no catch us."

When the Fingoes had been gone about ten minutes, Ronald, assured that the Kaffirs would be gathered at the far side of the kloof, went forward at a walk. Presently he heard six shots fired in rapid succession. This was followed by an outburst of yells and cries in front, and he set spurs to his horse and dashed forward at a gallop. He was nearly through the kloof when a body of Kaffirs, who were running through the wood from the right, burst suddenly from the bushes into the path. So astonished were they at seeing a white man within a few yards of them that for a moment they did not think of using their weapons, and Ronald dashed through them, scattering them to right and left. But others sprang from the bushes. Ronald shot down two men who sprang at the horse's bridle, and he heard Mary Armstrong's pistol on the other side. He had drawn his sword before setting off at a gallop. "Hold tight, Mary," he said, as he relaxed his hold of her and cut down a native who was springing upon him from the bushes. Another fell from a bullet from her pistol, and then he was through them. "Stoop down, Mary," he said, pressing her forward on the horse's neck and bending down over her. He felt his horse give a sudden spring, and knew that it was hit with an assegai; while almost at the same instant he felt a sensation as of a hot iron running from his belt to his shoulder, as a spear ripped up cloth and flesh and then glanced along over him.

A moment later and they were out of the kloof, and riding at full speed across the open. Looking over his shoulder he saw that the Kaffirs gave up pursuit after following for a hundred yards. Over on the left he heard dropping shots, and presently caught a glimpse in that direction of the Fingoes running in a close body, pursued at the distance of a hundred yards or so by a large number of Kaffirs. But others had heard the sound of firing, for in a minute or two he saw a body of horsemen riding at full speed from Williamstown in the direction of the firing. He at once checked the speed of his horse.

"We are safe now, Mary; that is a troop of our corps. Are you hit?"

"No, I am not touched. Are you hurt, Ronald? I thought I felt you start."

"I have got a bit of a scratch on the back, but it's nothing serious. I will get off in a moment, Mary; the horse has an assegai in his quarters, and I must get it out."

"Take me down, too, please; I feel giddy now it is all over."

Ronald lifted her down, and then pulled the assegai from the horse's back.

"I don't think much harm is done," he said; "a fortnight in the stable and he will be all right again."

"You are bleeding dreadfully," the girl exclaimed, as she caught sight of his back. "It's a terrible wound to look at."

"Then it looks worse than it is," he laughed. "The spear only glanced along on the ribs. It's lucky I was stooping so much. After going through what we have we may think ourselves well off indeed that we have escaped with such a scratch as this between us."

"It's not a scratch at all," the girl said, indignantly; "it's a very deep bad cut."

"Perhaps it is a bad cut," Ronald smiled, "but a cut is of no consequence one way or the other. Now let us join the others. Ah, here they come, with Kreta showing them the way."

The troopers had chased the Kaffirs back to the bush, and, led by the Fingo, were now coming up at a gallop to the spot where Ronald and Mary Armstrong were standing by the horse.

"Ah, it is you, sergeant," Lieutenant Daniels exclaimed, for it was a portion of Ronald's own troop that had ridden up. "I never expected to see you again, for we heard the day before yesterday from the officer who came in with the ammunition waggons that you had gone off to try to rescue three ladies who had been carried off by the Kaffirs. It was a mad business, but you have partly succeeded, I am glad to see," and he lifted his cap to Mary Armstrong.

"Partly, sir," Ronald said. "The wretches killed the other two the day they carried them off. This is Miss Armstrong. I think you stopped at her father's house one day when we were out on the Kabousie."

"Yes, of course," the lieutenant said, alighting. "Excuse me for not recognising you, Miss Armstrong; but, in fact——"

"In fact, I look very pale, and ragged, and tattered."

"I am not surprised at that, Miss Armstrong. You must have gone through a terrible time, and I heartily congratulate Sergeant Blunt on the success of his gallant attempt to rescue you."

"Have you heard from my father? How is he?"

"Your father, Miss Armstrong! I have heard nothing about him since I heard from Sergeant Blunt that you had all got safely away after that attack."

"He was in the waggon, sir," Ronald explained; "he was hurt in the fight with the Kaffirs, and Mr. Nolan brought him back in the waggons."

"Oh, I heard he had brought a wounded man with him; but I did not hear the name. Nolan said he had been badly wounded, but the surgeon told me he thought he might get round. I have no doubt that the sight of Miss Armstrong will do him good."

"Perhaps, sir," Ronald said, faintly, "you will let one of the troop ride on with Miss Armstrong at once. I think I must wait for a bit."

"Why, what is it, sergeant?" the lieutenant asked, catching him by the arm, for he saw that he was on the point of falling. "You are wounded, I see; and here am I talking about other things and not thinking of you."

Two of the troop leapt from their horses and laid Ronald down, for he had fainted, overcome partly by the pain and loss of blood, but more by the sudden termination of the heavy strain of the last four days.

"It is only a flesh wound, Miss Armstrong. There is no occasion for fear. He has fainted from loss of blood, and I have no doubt but he will soon be all right again. Johnson, hand your horse over to Miss Armstrong, and do you, Williams, ride over with her to the hospital. We will have Sergeant Blunt in the hospital half an hour after you get there, Miss Armstrong."

"It seems very unkind to leave him," the girl said, "after all he has done for me."

"He will understand it, my dear young lady, and you can see him in the hospital directly you get there."

Mary reluctantly allowed herself to be lifted into the saddle, and rode off with the trooper.

"Now take his jacket and shirt off," the lieutenant said, "it's a nasty rip that he has got. I suppose he was leaning forward in the saddle when the spear touched him. It's lucky it glanced up instead of going through him."

The soldiers removed Ronald's coat. There was no shirt underneath, for he had not waited to put one on when he mounted. The troopers had heard from their comrades, on the return of the escort, that the sergeant had, before starting, got himself up as a native; and they were not therefore surprised, as they otherwise would have been, at his black skin.

"Put your hand into the left holster of my saddle," the lieutenant said. "You will find two or three bandages and some lint there; they are things that come in handy for this work. Lay the lint in the gash. That's right. Press it down a little, and put some more in. Now lift him up a bit, while I pass these bandages round his body. There; I think he will do now; but there's no doubt it is a nasty wound. It has cut right through the muscles of the back. Now turn him over, and give me my flask from the holster."

Some brandy and water was poured between Ronald's lips, and he soon opened his eyes.

"Don't move, sergeant, or you will set your wound off bleeding again. We will soon get you comfortably into hospital. Ah, that is the very thing; good men," he broke off, as Kreta and the Fingoes brought up a litter which they had been busy in constructing. "Miss Armstrong has ridden on to the hospital to see her father. She wanted to stop, but I sent her on, so that we could bandage you comfortably."

"I think I can sit a horse now," Ronald said, trying to rise.

"I don't know whether you can or not, sergeant; but you are not going to try. Now, lads, lift him on to the litter."

Kreta and the two troopers lifted him carefully on to the litter; then four of the Fingoes raised it to their shoulders. Another took Ronald's horse, which now limped stiffly, and led it along behind the litter; and with the troop bringing up the rear, the party started for King Williamstown.

CHAPTER XIV.

RONALD IS OFFERED A COMMISSION.

As soon as Mary Armstrong reached the hospital, the trooper who had accompanied her took her to the surgeon's quarters. The officer, on hearing that a lady wished to speak to him, at once came out.

"I am Mary Armstrong," the girl said as she slipped down from the horse. "I think my father is here, wounded. He came up in the waggons the day before yesterday, I believe."

"Oh yes, he is here, Miss Armstrong. I had him put in one of the officers' wards that is otherwise empty at present."

"How is he, doctor?"

"Well, I am sorry to say that just at present he is very ill. The wounds are not, I hope, likely to prove fatal, though undoubtedly they are very serious; but he is in a state of high fever—in fact, he is delirious, principally, I think, owing to his anxiety about you, at least so I gathered from the officer who brought him in, for he was already delirious when he arrived here."

"I can go to him, I hope?"

"Certainly you can, Miss Armstrong. Your presence is likely to soothe him. The ward will be entirely at your disposal. I congratulate you most heartily upon getting out of the hands of the Kaffirs. Mr. Nolan told us of the gallant attempt which a sergeant of the Cape Mounted Rifles was going to make to rescue you; but I don't think that any one thought he had the shadow of a chance of success."

"He succeeded, doctor, as you see; but he was wounded to-day just as we were in sight of the town. They are bringing him here. Will you kindly let me know when he comes in and how he is?"

"I will let you know at once, Miss Armstrong; and now I will take you to your father."

One of the hospital orderlies was standing by the bedside of Mr. Armstrong as his daughter and the surgeon entered. The patient was talking loudly.

"I tell you I will go. They have carried off Mary. I saw them do it and could not help her, but I will go now."

Mary walked to the bedside and bent down and kissed her father.

"I am here, father, by your side. I have got away from them, and here I am to nurse you."

The patient ceased talking and a quieter expression came over his face. Mary took his hand in hers and quietly stroked it.

"That's right, Mary," he murmured; "are the bars of the cattle kraal up? See that all the shutters are closed, we cannot be too careful, you know."

"I will see to it all, father," she said, cheerfully; "now try to go to sleep."

A few more words passed from the wounded man's lips, and then he lay quiet with closed eyes.

"That is excellent, Miss Armstrong," the surgeon said; "the consciousness that you are with him has, you see, soothed him at once. If he moves, get him to drink a little of this lemonade, and I will send you in some medicine for him shortly."

"How are the wounds, doctor?"

"Oh, I think the wounds will do," the surgeon replied; "so far as I can tell, the assegai has just missed the top of the lung by a hair's breadth. Two inches lower and it would have been fatal. As for the wounds in the legs, I don't anticipate much trouble with them. They have missed both bones and arteries and are really nothing but flesh wounds, and after the active, healthy life your father has been living, I do not think we need be uneasy about them."

In half an hour the surgeon looked in again.

"Sergeant Blunt has arrived," he said. "You can set your mind at ease about him; it is a nasty gash, but of no real importance whatever. I have drawn the edges together and sewn them up; he is quite in good spirits, and laughed and said that a wound in the back could scarcely be called an honourable scar. I can assure you that in ten days or so he will be about again."

"Would you mind telling him," Mary asked, "that I would come to see him at once, but my father is holding my hand so tight that I could not draw it away without rousing him?"

"I will tell him," the surgeon said. "Oh, here is the orderly with your medicine as well as your father's."

The orderly brought in a tray with a bowl of beef tea and a glass of wine. "You will take both these, if you please, Miss Armstrong, and I will have the other bed placed by the side of your father, so that you can lie down with him holding your hand. You are looking terribly pale and tired, and I do not want you on my hands too."

The tray was placed upon the table within Mary's reach, and the surgeon stood by and saw that she drank the wine and beef tea. He and the orderly then moved the other couch to the side of Mr. Armstrong's bed, and arranged it so that Mary could lie down with her hand still in her father's.

"Now," he said, "I recommend you to go off to sleep soon. I am happy to say that your father is sleeping naturally, and it may be hours before he wakes. When he does so, he will be sure to move and wake you, and the sight of you will, if he is sensible, as I expect he will be, go a long way towards his cure."

Captain Twentyman, when he returned in the afternoon from a reconnaissance that he had been making with a portion of the troop, called at once to see Ronald, but was told that he was sound asleep, and so left word that he would come again in the morning.

The news of Sergeant Blunt's desperate attempt to rescue three white women who had been carried off by the Kaffirs had, when reported by Lieutenant Nolan, been the subject of much talk in the camp. Every one admitted that it was a breach of discipline thus to leave the party of which he was in command when upon special service, but no one seriously blamed him for this. Admiration for the daring action and regret for the loss of so brave a soldier, for none thought that there was the slightest chance of ever seeing him again, overpowered all other feelings. Mr. Nolan stated that the sergeant had told him that one of the three women was the daughter of the wounded man he had brought in with him, and that he had known her and her father before, and it was generally agreed that there must have been something more than mere acquaintance in the case to induce the sergeant to undertake such a desperate enterprise. Great interest was therefore excited when, upon the return of Lieutenant Daniels' party, it became known that he had fallen in with Sergeant Blunt and a young lady, and that the sergeant was severely wounded. All sorts of questions were asked the lieutenant.

"Ten to one she's pretty, Daniels," a young subaltern said.

"She is pretty, Mellor," another broke in; "I caught a glimpse of her, and she is as pretty a girl as I have seen in the colony, though, of course, she is looking utterly worn out."

"He is a gentleman," another officer, who had just come up, said. "I have been talking to Nolan, and he tells me that Sergeant Blunt spoke of her as a lady, and said that her father had served in the army and fought as a young ensign at Waterloo."

"Mr. Armstrong is a gentleman," Lieutenant Daniels said. "He had a farm on the Kabousie River, that is where Blunt got to know him. He had the reputation of being a wealthy man. Blunt was in command of a party who came up and saved them when they were attacked by the Kaffirs on Christmas Day. So this is the second time he has rescued the young lady."

"I hope Mr. Armstrong isn't going to be a stern father, and spoil the whole romance of the business," young Mellor laughed. "One of your troopers, Daniels, however brave a fellow, can hardly be considered as a good match for an heiress."

"Blunt is as much a gentleman as I am," Lieutenant Daniels said, quietly. "I know nothing whatever of his history or what his real name is, for I expect that Blunt is only a *nom-de-guerre*, but I do know that he is a gentleman, and I am sure he has served as an officer. More than that I do not want to know, unless he chooses to tell me himself. I suppose he got into some scrape or other at home; but I wouldn't mind making a heavy bet that, whatever it was, it was nothing dishonourable."

"But how did he get her away from the Kaffirs? It seems almost an impossibility. I asked the head man of the Fingoes, who was with him," another said, "but he had already got three parts drunk, so I did not get much out of him; but as far as I could make out, they carried her off from Macomo's kraal in the heart of the Amatolas."

"Oh, come now, that seems altogether absurd," two or three of the officers standing round laughed, and Mellor said, "Orpheus going down to fetch Eurydice back from Hades would have had an easy task of it in comparison."

"I am glad to see that you have not forgotten your classical learning, Mellor," one of the older officers said, "but certainly, of the two, I would rather undertake the task of Orpheus, who was pretty decently treated after all, than go to Macomo's kraal to fetch back a lady-love. Well, I suppose we shall hear about it to-morrow, but I can hardly believe this story to be true. The natives are such liars there's no believing what they say."

The next morning, after breakfast, Captain Twentyman and Lieutenant Daniels walked across to the hospital. They first saw the surgeon.

"Well, doctor, how is my sergeant?"

"On the high way to recovery," the surgeon said, cheerfully. "Of course, the wound will be a fortnight, perhaps three weeks, before it is healed up sufficiently for him to return to duty, but otherwise there is nothing the matter with him. A long night's rest has pulled him round completely. He is a little weak from loss of blood; but there is no harm in that. There is, I think, no fear whatever of fever or other complications. It is simply a question of the wound healing up."

"And the colonist—Armstrong his name is, I think, whose daughter was carried away—how is he going on?"

"Much better. His daughter's presence at once calmed his delirium, and this morning, when he woke after a good night's sleep, he was conscious, and will now, I think, do well. He is very weak, but that does not matter, and he is perfectly content, lying there holding his daughter's hand. He has asked no questions as to how she got back again, and, of course, I have told her not to allude to the subject, and to check him at once if he does so. The poor girl looks all the better for her night's rest. She was a wan-looking creature when she arrived yesterday morning, but is fifty per cent. better already, and with another day or two's rest, and the comfort of seeing her father going on well, she will soon get her colour and tone back again."

"I suppose we can go up and see Blunt, and hear about his adventures?"

"Oh, yes, talking will do him no harm. I will come with you, for I was too busy this morning, when I went my rounds, to have any conversation with him except as to his wound."

"My inquiries are partly personal and partly official," Captain Twentyman said. "Colonel Somerset asked me this morning to see Blunt, and gather any information as to the Kaffirs' positions that might be useful. I went yesterday evening to question the Fingo head man who went with him, but he and all his men were as drunk as pigs. I hear that when they first arrived they said they had carried the girl off from Macomo's kraal, but of course there must be some mistake; they never could have ventured into the heart of the Amatolas and come out alive."

The three officers proceeded together to the ward in which Ronald was lying.

"Well, sergeant, how do you feel yourself?" Captain Twentyman asked.

"Oh, I am all right, sir," Ronald answered cheerfully. "My back smarts a bit, of course, but that is nothing. I hope I shall be in the saddle again before long —at any rate before the advance is made."

"I hope so, Blunt. And now, if you feel up to telling it, I want to hear about your adventure. Colonel Somerset asked me to inquire, as it will throw some light on the numbers and position of the Kaffirs; besides, the whole camp is wanting to know how you succeeded in getting Miss Armstrong out of the hands of the Kaffirs. I can assure you that there is nothing else talked about."

"There is nothing much to talk about, as far as I am concerned, sir," Ronald said. "It was the Fingoes' doing altogether, and they could have managed as well, indeed better, without me."

"Except that they would not have done it, unless you had been with them."

175

"No, perhaps not," Ronald admitted. "I was lucky enough down at Port Elizabeth to fish out the son of Kreta, the head man of the party, who had been washed off his feet in the surf; and it was out of gratitude for that that he followed me."

"Yes, we heard about that business from Mr. Nolan, and although you speak lightly of it, it was, he tells us, a very gallant affair indeed. But now as to this other matter."

"In the first place, Captain Twentyman, I admit that going off as I did was a great breach of duty. I can only say that I shall be willing, cheerfully, to submit to any penalty the colonel may think fit to inflict. I had no right whatever to leave my detachment on what was really private business; but even if I had been certain that I should have been shot as a deserter on my return to the regiment, I should not have hesitated in acting as I did."

"We all understand your feelings, Blunt," Captain Twentyman said, kindly, "and you have no need to make yourself uneasy on that score. To punish a man for acting as you have done would be as bad as the sea story of the captain who flogged a seaman, who jumped overboard to save a comrade, for leaving the ship without orders. Now for your story: all we have heard is that your Fingo says you carried off the young lady from Macomo's kraal, but, of course, that is not believed."

"It is quite true, nevertheless," Ronald said. "Well, this is how it was, sir," and he gave a full account of the whole adventure.

"Well, I congratulate you most heartily," Captain Twentyman said when he finished; "it is really a wonderful adventure—a most gallant business indeed, and the whole corps, officers and men, will be proud of it."

"I should be glad, sir, if there could be some reward given to Kreta and his men; as you will have seen from my story, any credit that there is in the matter is certainly their due."

"I will see to that," the officer replied. "The Fingo desires are, happily, easily satisfied; a good rifle, a few cows, and a barrel of whisky make up his ideal of happiness. I think I can promise you they shall have all these."

In the afternoon, Mr. Armstrong again dropped off to a quiet sleep. This time he was not holding his daughter's hand, and as soon as she saw that he was fairly off she stole out of the room, and finding the surgeon, asked if he would take her up to the ward where Sergeant Blunt was lying.

"Yes, I shall be happy to take you up at once, Miss Armstrong. Everything is tidy just at present, for I have had a message from Colonel Somerset that he and the General are coming round the wards. I don't suppose they will be here for half an hour, so you can come up at once."

The sick men in the wards were surprised when the surgeon entered, accompanied by a young lady. She passed shyly along between the rows of beds until she reached that of Ronald. She put her hand in his, but for a moment was unable to speak. Ronald saw her agitation, and said cheerfully: "I am heartily glad, Miss Armstrong, to hear from the doctor such a good account of your father. As for me, I shall not be in his hands many days. I told you it was a mere scratch, and I believe that a good-sized piece of sticking-plaster was all that was wanted."

"You haven't thought me unkind for not coming to see you before, I hope," the girl said; "but I have not been able till now to leave my father's room for a moment."

"I quite understood that, Miss Armstrong, and indeed there was no occasion for you to come to me at all. It would have been quite time enough when I was up and about again. I only wish that it was likely that Mr. Armstrong would be on his feet as soon as I shall."

"Oh, he is going on very well," Mary said. "I consider that you have saved his life as well as mine. I feel sure it is only having me with him again that has made such a change in him as has taken place since yesterday. The doctor says so, too. I have not told him yet how it has all come about, but I hope ere very long he may be able to thank you for both of us."

"You thanked me more than enough yesterday, Miss Armstrong, and I am not going to listen to any more of it. As far as I can see, you could not have done me any greater service than by giving me the opportunity you have. Every one seems disposed to take quite a ridiculous view of the matter, and I may look forward to getting a troop-sergeantship when there is a vacancy."

The girl shook her head. She was too much in earnest even to pretend to take a light view of the matter. Just at that moment there was a trampling of horses outside, and the sharp sound of the sentries presenting arms.

"Here is the General," Ronald said, with a smile, "and although I don't wish to hurry you away, Miss Armstrong, I think you had better go back to your father. I don't know whether the Chief would approve of lady visitors in the hospital."

"Good-bye," the girl said, giving him her hand. "You won't let me thank you, but you know."

"I know," Ronald replied. "Good-bye"

She looked round for the surgeon, who had, after taking her up to Ronald, moved away for a short distance, but he was gone, having hurried off to meet the General below, and with a last nod to Ronald, she left the ward. She passed out through the door into the courtyard just as the group of officers were entering.

"That is Miss Armstrong," the surgeon said, as she passed out.

"What, the girl who was rescued?" Colonel Somerset said; "a very pretty, ladylike-looking young woman. I am not surprised, now that I see her, at this desperate exploit of my sergeant."

"No, indeed," the General said, smiling. "It's curious, colonel, what men will do for a pretty face. Those other two poor creatures who were carried off were both murdered, and I don't suppose their deaths have greatly distressed this young fellow one way or the other. No doubt he would have been glad to rescue them; but I imagine that their deaths have not in any way caused him to regard his mission as a failure. I suppose that it's human nature, colonel."

Colonel Somerset laughed.

"You and I would have seen the matter in the same light when we were youngsters, General."

The officers went through the wards, stopping several times to speak a few words to the patients.

"So this is the deserter," Colonel Somerset said, with some assumed sternness, as they stopped by Ronald's bedside. "Well, sir, we have had a good many of those black rascals desert from our ranks, but you are the first white soldier who has deserted since the war began. Of course, you expect a drumhead court-martial and shooting as soon as the doctor lets you out of his hands."

Ronald saw that the old colonel was not in earnest.

"It was very bad, colonel," he said, "and I can only throw myself on your mercy."

"You have done well, my lad—very well," the colonel said, laying his hand on his shoulder. "There are some occasions when even military laws give place to questions of humanity, and this was essentially one of them. You are a fine fellow, sir; and I am proud that you belong to my corps."

The General, who had stopped behind speaking to another patient, now came up.

"You have done a very gallant action, Sergeant Blunt," he said. "Captain Twentyman has reported the circumstances to me; but when you are out of hospital you must come to head-quarters and tell me your own story. Will you see to this, Colonel Somerset?"

"Certainly, sir. I will send him over, or rather bring him over to you, as soon as he's about, for I should like to hear the whole story also."

In ten days Ronald Mervyn was on his feet again, although not yet fit for duty; the wound had healed rapidly, but the surgeon said it would be at least another fortnight before he would be fit for active service. As soon as he was able to go out and sit on the benches in the hospital yard, many of his comrades came to see him, and there was a warmth and earnestness in their congratulations which showed that short as his time had been in the corps, he was thoroughly popular with them. Sergeant Menzies was particularly hearty in his greeting.

"I knew you were the right sort, Harry Blunt, as soon as I set eyes upon you," he said; "but I did not expect you were going to cut us all out so soon."

"How is my horse, sergeant?"

"Oh, he's none the worse for it, I think. He has been taking walking exercise, and his stiffness is wearing off fast. I think he misses you very much, and he wouldn't take his food the first day or two. He has got over it now, but I know he longs to hear your voice again."

Sometimes, too, Mary Armstrong would come out and sit for a time with Ronald. Her father was progressing favourably, and though still extremely weak, was in a fair way towards recovery.

"Will you come in to see father?" Mary said one morning; "he knows all about it now; but it was only when he came round just now that the doctor gave leave for him to see you."

"I shall be very glad to see him," Ronald said, rising. "I own that when I saw him last I entertained very slight hopes I should ever meet him alive again."

"He is still very weak," the girl said, "and the doctor says he is not to be allowed to talk much."

"I will only pay a short visit, but it will be a great pleasure to me to see him; I have always felt his kindness to me."

"Father is kind to every one," the girl said, simply. "In this instance his kindness has been returned a hundred-fold."

By this time they had reached the door of the ward.

"Here is Mr. Blunt come to see you, father. Now you know what the doctor said; you are not to excite yourself, and not to talk too much, and if you are not good, I shall take him away."

"I am glad to see you are better, Mr. Armstrong," Ronald said, as he went up to the bed, and took the thin hand in his own.

"God bless you, my boy," the wounded man replied; "it is to you I owe my recovery, for had you not brought Mary back to me, I should be a dead man now, and would have been glad of it."

"I am very glad, Mr. Armstrong, to have been able to be of service to your daughter and to you; but do not let us talk about it now; I am sure that you cannot do so without agitating yourself, and the great point at present with us all is for you to be up and about again. Do your wounds hurt you much?"

"Not much; and yours, Blunt?"

"Oh, mine is a mere nothing," Ronald said, cheerfully, "it's healing up fast, and except when I forget all about it, and move sharply, I scarcely feel it. I feel something like the proverbial man who swallowed the poker, and have to keep myself as stiff as if I were on inspection. This ward is nice and cool, much cooler than they are upstairs. Of course the verandah outside shades you. You will find it very pleasant there when you are strong enough to get up. I am afraid that by that time I shall be off, for the troops are all on their march up from the coast, and in another ten days we expect to begin operations in earnest."

"I don't think the doctor ought to let you go," Mary Armstrong said. "You have done quite your share, I am sure."

"I hope my share in finishing up with these scoundrels will be a good deal larger yet," Ronald laughed. "My share has principally been creeping and hiding, except just in that last brush, and there, if I mistake not, your share was as large as mine. I only fired three shots, and I think I heard your pistol go four times."

"Yes, it is dreadful to think of now," the girl said; "but somehow it didn't seem so at the time. I feel shocked now when I recall it."

"There's nothing to be shocked at, Miss Armstrong; it was our lives or theirs; and if your hand had not been steady, and your aim true, we should neither of us be here talking over the matter now. But I think my visit has been long enough. I will come in again, Mr. Armstrong, to-morrow, and I hope each day to find you more and more able to take your share in the talk."

In another ten days Ronald rejoined his troop, and the next day received an order to be ready at four o'clock to accompany Colonel Somerset to the General's.

"Now, sergeant, take a seat," the General said, "and tell me the full story of your adventures."

Ronald again repeated his story. When he had done, the General remarked:

"Your report more than bears out what I heard from Captain Twentyman. I have already talked the matter over with Colonel Somerset, and as we consider that such an action should be signally rewarded, Colonel Somerset will at once apply for a commission for you in your own corps, or if you would prefer it, I will apply for a commission for you in one of the line regiments. I may say that the application under such circumstances would certainly be acceded to."

"I am deeply obliged to you for your kindness, sir, and to you, Colonel Somerset; but I regret to say that, with all respect, I must decline both offers."

"Decline a commission!" the General said in surprise. "Why, I should have thought that it was just the thing that you would have liked—a dashing young fellow like you, and on the eve of serious operations. I can hardly understand you."

Ronald was silent for a moment.

"My reason for declining it, sir, is a purely personal one. Nothing would have given me greater pleasure than a commission so bestowed, but there are circumstances that absolutely prevent my mingling in the society of gentlemen. The name I go by is not my true one, and over my own name there is so terrible a shadow resting that so long as it is there—and I have little hope of its ever being cleared off—I must remain as I am."

Both officers remained silent a moment.

"You are sure you are not exaggerating the case, Blunt?" Colonel Somerset said after a pause. "I cannot believe that this cloud of which you speak can have arisen from any act of yours, and it would be a pity indeed were you to allow any family matter to weigh upon you thus."

Ronald shook his head. "It is a matter in which I am personally concerned, sir, and I do not in any way exaggerate it. I repeat, I must remain in my present position."

"If it must be so, it must," the General said, "though I am heartily sorry. At least you will have the satisfaction of seeing your name in General Orders this evening for an act of distinguished bravery."

"Thank you, sir," and Ronald, seeing the conversation was at an end, saluted to the two officers, went out, and rode back to his quarters.

The town was full of troops now, for the regiments that had been despatched from England had nearly all arrived upon the spot, and the operations against the Kaffirs in the Amatolas were to begin at once. Some of the troops, including two squadrons of the Rifles, were to march next morning.

Ronald went about his duties till evening, and then turned out to walk to the hospital. As he passed through the streets, he saw a group round one of the Rifles, who had just come out from a drinking shop, and was engaged in a fierce altercation with a Fingo. The man was evidently the worse for liquor, and Ronald went up to him and put his hand on his shoulder.

"You had better go off to the barracks at once," he said, sharply; "you will be getting into trouble if you stay here."

The man turned savagely round.

"Oh, it's you, Sergeant Blunt? Hadn't you better attend to your own business? I am not committing any crime here. I haven't been murdering women, or anything of that sort."

Ronald started back as if struck. The significance of the tone in which the man spoke showed him that these were no random words, but a shaft deliberately aimed. In a moment he was cool again.

"If you do not return to the barracks at once," he said, sternly, "I will fetch a corporal's guard and put you in the cells."

The man hesitated a moment, and then muttering to himself, reeled off towards the barracks. Had the blow come a month before, Ronald Mervyn would have felt it more, for absorbed in his active work, on horseback the greater portion of his time, the remembrance of the past had become blunted, and the present had occupied all his thoughts. It was only occasionally that he had looked back to the days when he was Captain Mervyn, of the Borderers. But from the hour he had brought Mary Armstrong safely back to her father, the past had been constantly in his mind because it clashed with the present.

Before, Ronald Mervyn and Harry Blunt had almost seemed to be two existences, unconnected with each other; now, the fact of their identity had been constantly in his thoughts. The question he had been asking himself over and over again was whether there could be a permanent separation between them, whether he could hope to get rid of his connection with Ronald Mervyn, and to continue to the end of the chapter as Harry Blunt. He had told himself long before that he could not do so, that sooner or later he should certainly be recognised; and although he had tried to believe that he could pass through life without meeting any one familiar with his face, he had been obliged to admit that this was next to impossible.

Had he been merely a country gentleman, known only to the people within a limited range of distance, it would have been different; but an officer who has served ten years in the army has innumerable acquaintances. Every move he makes brings him in contact with men of other regiments, and his circle goes on constantly widening until it embraces no small portion of the officers of the army. Then every soldier who had passed through his regiment while he had been in it would know his face; and, go where he would, he knew that he would be running constant risks of detection. More than one of the regiments that had now arrived at King Williamstown had been quartered with him at one station or another, and there were a score of men who would recognise him instantly did he come among them in the dress of an officer. This unexpected recognition, therefore, by a trooper in his own corps, did not come upon him with so sudden a shock as it would have done a month previously.

"I knew it must come," he said to himself bitterly "and that it might come at any moment. Still it is a shock. Who is this man, I wonder? It seemed to me, when he first came up, that I had some faint remembrance of his face, though where, I have not the least idea. It was not in the regiment, for he knows nothing of drill or military habits. Of course, if he had been a deserter, he would have pretended ignorance, but one can always tell by little things whether a man has served, and I am sure that this fellow has not. I suppose he comes from somewhere down home.

"Well, it can't be helped. Fortunately, I have won a good name before this discovery is made, and am likely to reap the benefit of what doubt there may be. When a man shows that he has a fair amount of pluck, his comrades are slow to credit him with bad qualities. On the whole, perhaps it is well that it should have come on this evening of all when I had quite made up my mind as to my course, for it strengthens me in my decision as to what I ought to do. It is hard to throw away happiness, but this shows how rightly I decided. Nothing will shake me now. Poor little girl! it is hard for her, harder by far than for me. However, it is best that she should know it now, than learn it when too late."

CHAPTER XV.

A PARTING.

The sun had already set an hour when Ronald Mervyn reached the hospital, but the moon had just risen, and the stars were shining brilliantly.

Mary Armstrong met him at the door.

"I saw you coming," she said, "and father advised me to come out for a little turn, it is such a beautiful evening."

"I am glad you have come out, Mary; I wanted to speak to you."

Mary Armstrong's colour heightened a little. It was the first time he had called her by her Christian name since that ride through the Kaffirs. She thought she knew what he wanted to speak to her about, and she well knew what she should say.

"Mary," Ronald went on, "you know the story of the poor wretch who was devoured by thirst, and yet could not reach the cup of water that was just beyond his grasp?"

"I know," Mary said.

"Well, I am just in that position. I am so placed by an inscrutable Fate, that I cannot stretch out my hand to grasp the cup of water."

The girl was silent for a time.

"I will not pretend that I do not understand you, Ronald. Why cannot you grasp the cup of water?"

"Because, as I said, dear, there is a fate against me; because I can never marry; because I must go through the world alone. I told you that the name I bear is not my own. I have been obliged to change it, because my own name is disgraced; because, were I to name it, there is not a man here of those who just at present are praising and making much of me, who would not shrink from my side."

"No, Ronald, no; it cannot be."

"It is true, dear; my name has been associated with the foulest of crimes. I have been tried for murdering a woman, and that woman a near relative. I was acquitted, it is true: but simply because the evidence did not amount to what the law required. But in the sight of the world I went out guilty."

"Oh, how could they think so?" Mary said, bursting into tears; "how could they have thought, Ronald, those who knew you, that you could do this?"

"Many did believe it," Ronald said, "and the evidence was so strong that I almost believed it myself. However, thus it is. I am a marked man and an outcast, and must remain alone for all my life, unless God in His mercy should clear this thing up."

"Not alone, Ronald, not alone," the girl cried "there, you make me say it."

"You mean you would stand by my side, Mary? Thank you, my love, but I could not accept the sacrifice. I can bear my own lot, but I could not see the woman I loved pointed at as the wife of a murderer."

"But no one would know," Mary began.

"They would know, dear. I refused a commission the General offered me to-day, because were I to appear as an officer there are a score of men in this expedition who would know me at once; but even under my present name and my present dress I cannot escape. Only this evening, as I came here, I was taunted by a drunken soldier, who must have known me, as a murderer of women. Good Heavens! do you think I would let any woman share that? Did I go to some out-of-the-way part of the world, I might escape for years; but at last the blow would come. Had it not been for the time we passed together when death might at any moment have come to us both, had it not been that I held you in my arms during that ride, I should never have told you this, Mary, for you would have gone away to England and lived your life unhurt; but after that I could not but speak. You must have felt that I loved you, and had I not spoken, what would you have thought of me?"

"I should have thought, Ronald," she said, quietly, "that you had a foolish idea that because my father had money, while you were but a trooper, you ought not to speak; and I think that I should have summoned up courage to speak first, for I knew you loved me, just as certainly as I know that I shall love you always."

"I hope not, Mary," Ronald said, gravely; "it would add to the pain of my life to know that I had spoilt yours."

"It will not spoil mine, Ronald; it is good to know that one is loved by a true man, and that one loves him, even if we can never come together. I would rather be single for your sake, dear, than marry any other man in the world. Won't you tell me about it all? I should like to know."

"You have a right to know, Mary, if you wish it;" and drawing her to a seat, Ronald told her the story of the Curse of the Carnes, of the wild blood that flowed in his veins, of his half-engagement to his cousin, and of the circumstances of her death. Only once she stopped him.

"Did you love her very much, Ronald?"

"No, dear; I can say so honestly now. No doubt I thought I loved her, though I had been involuntarily putting off becoming formally engaged to her; but I know now, indeed I knew long ago, that my passion when she threw me off was rather an outburst of disappointment, and perhaps of jealousy, that another should have stepped in when I thought myself so sure, than of real regret. I had cared for Margaret in a way, but now that I know what real love is, I know it was but as a cousin that I loved her."

Then he went on to tell her the proofs against himself; how that the words he had spoken had come up against him; how he had failed altogether to account for his doings at the hour at which she was murdered; how his glove had borne evidence against him.

"Is that all, Ronald?"

"Not quite all, dear. I saw in an English paper only a few days ago that the matter had come up again. Margaret's watch and jewels were found in the garden, just hidden in the ground, evidently not by a thief who intended to come again and fetch them, but simply concealed by some one who had taken them and did not want them. If those things had been found before my trial, Mary, I should assuredly have been hung, for they disposed of the only alternative that seemed possible, namely, that she had been murdered by a midnight burglar for the sake of her valuables."

Mary sat in silence for a few minutes, and then asked one or two questions with reference to the story.

"And you have no idea yourself, Ronald, not even the slightest suspicion, against any one?"

"Not the slightest," he said; "the whole thing is to me as profound a mystery as ever."

"Of course, from what you tell me, Ronald, the evidence against you was stronger than against any one else, and yet I cannot think how any one who knew you could have believed it."

"I hope that those who knew me best did not believe it, Mary. A few of my neighbours and many of my brother officers had faith in my innocence; but, you see, those in the county who knew the story of our family were naturally set against me. I had the mad blood of the Carnes in my veins; the Carnes had committed two murders in their frenzy, and it did not seem to them so strange that I should do the same. I may tell you, dear, that this trial through which I have passed has not been altogether without good. The family history had weighed on my mind from the time I was a child, and at times I used to wonder whether I had madness in my blood, and the fear grew upon me and embittered my life. Since that trial it has gone for ever. I know that if I had had the slightest touch of insanity in my veins I must have gone mad in that awful time; and much as I have suffered from the cloud that rested on me, I am sure I have been a far brighter and happier man since."

A pressure of the hand which he was holding in his expressed the sympathy that she did not speak.

"What time do you march to-morrow, Ronald?"

"At eight, dear."

"Could you come round first?"

"I could, Mary; but I would rather say good-bye now."

"You must say good-bye now, Ronald, and again in the morning. Why I ask you is because I want to tell my father. You don't mind that, do you? He must know there is something, because he spoke to-day as if he would wish it to be as I hoped, and I should like him to know how it is with us. You do not mind, do you?"

"Not at all," Ronald said. "I would rather that he did know."

"Then I will tell him now," the girl said. "I should like to talk it over with him," and she rose. Ronald rose too.

"Good-bye, Mary."

"Not like that, Ronald," and she threw her arms round his neck. "Good-bye, my dear, my dear. I will always be true to you to the end of my life. And hope always. I cannot believe that you would have saved me almost by a miracle, if it had not been meant we should one day be happy together. God bless you and keep you."

There was a long kiss, and then Mary Armstrong turned and ran back to the hospital.

Father and daughter talked together for hours after Mary's return. The disappointment to Mr. Armstrong was almost as keen as to Mary herself. He had from the first been greatly taken by Harry Blunt, and had encouraged his coming to the house. That he was a gentleman he was sure, and he thought he knew enough of character to be convinced that whatever scrape had driven him to enlist as a trooper, it was not a disgraceful one.

"If Mary fancies this young fellow, she shall have him," he had said to himself. "I have money enough for us both, and what good is it to me except to see her settled happily in life?"

After the attack upon his house, when he was rescued by the party led by Ronald, he thought still more of the matter, for some subtle change in his daughter's manner convinced him that her heart had been touched. He had fretted over the fact that after this Ronald's duty had kept him from seeing them, and when at last he started on his journey down to the coast he made up his mind, that if when they reached England he could ascertain for certain Mary's wishes on the subject, he would himself write a cautious letter to him, putting it that after the service he had rendered in saving his life and that of his daughter, he did not like the thought of his remaining as a trooper at the Cape, and that if he liked to come home he would start him in any sort of business he liked, adding, perhaps, that he had special reasons for wishing him to return.

After Ronald's rescue of his daughter, Mr. Armstrong regarded it as a certainty that his wish would be realised. He was a little surprised that the young sergeant had not spoken out, and it was with a view to give him an opportunity that he had suggested that Mary should go out for a stroll on the last evening. He had felt assured that they would come in hand in hand, and had anticipated with lively pleasure the prospect of paying his debt of gratitude to the young man. It was with surprise, disappointment, and regret that he listened to Mary's story.

"It is a monstrous thing," he said, when she had finished. "Most monstrous; but don't cry, my dear, it will all come right presently. These things always work round in time."

"But how is it to come right, father? He says that he himself has not the slightest suspicion who did it."

"Whether he has or not makes no difference," Mr. Armstrong said, decidedly. "It is quite certain, by what you say, this poor lady did not kill herself. In that case, who did it? We must make it our business to find out who it was. You don't suppose I am going to have your life spoiled in such a fashion as this. Talk about remaining single all your life, I won't have it; the thing must be set straight."

"It's very easy to say 'must,' father," Mary said, almost smiling at his earnestness, "but how is it to be set straight?"

"Why, by our finding out all about it, of course, Mary. Directly I get well enough to move—and the doctor said this morning that in a fortnight I can be taken down to the coast—we will follow out our original plan of going back to England. Then we will go down to this place you speak of—Carnesworth, or whatever it is, and take a place there or near there; there are always places to be had. It makes no difference to us where we go, for I don't suppose I shall find many people alive I knew in England. We will take some little place, and get to know the people and talk to them. Don't tell me about not finding out; of course we shall be able to find out if it has been done by any one down there; and as you say that the burglar or tramp theory is quite disproved by the finding of these trinkets, it must be somebody in the neighbourhood. I know what these dunderheaded police are. Not one in ten of them can put two and two together. The fellows at once jumped to the conclusion that Mervyn was guilty, and never inquired further."

"He says he had a detective down, father, for some weeks before the trial, and that one has been remaining there until quite lately."

"I don't think much of detectives," Mr. Armstrong said; "but of course, Mary, if you throw cold water on the scheme and don't fancy it, there's an end of it."

"No, no, father, you know I don't mean that, only I was frightened because you seemed to think it so certain we should succeed. There is nothing I should like better; it will matter nothing to me if we are years about it so that we can but clear him at last."

"I have no notion of spending years, my dear. Before now I have proved myself a pretty good hand at tracking the spoor of Kaffirs, and it's hard if I can't pick up this trail somehow."

"We will do it between us, father," Mary said, catching his confidence and enthusiasm, and kissing him as he sat propped up with pillows. "Oh, you have made me so happy. Everything seemed so dark and hopeless before, and now we shall be working for him."

"And for yourself too, Miss Mary; don't pretend you have no personal interest in the matter."

And so, just as the clock struck twelve, Mary Armstrong lay down on her bed in the little ante-room next to her father's, feeling infinitely happier and more hopeful than she could have thought possible when she parted from Ronald Mervyn three hours before. Ronald himself was surprised at the brightness with which she met him, when at six o'clock he alighted from his horse at the hospital. "Come in, Ronald," she said, "we were talking—father and I—for hours last night, and we have quite decided what we are going to do."

"So you have come to say good-bye, Mervyn—for, of course, you are Mervyn to us," Mr. Armstrong said, as he entered the room, "Well, my lad, it's a bad business that my little girl was telling me about last night, and has knocked over my castles very effectually, for I own to you that I have been building. I

189

knew you were fond of my girl; you never would have done for her what you did unless you had been, and I was quite sure that she was fond of you; how could she help it? And I had been fancying as soon as this war was over—for, of course, you could not leave now—you would be coming home, and I should be having you both with me in some snug little place there. However, lad, that's over for the present; but not for always, I hope. All this has not changed my opinion of the affair. The fact that you have suffered horribly and unjustly is nothing against you personally; and, indeed, you will make Mary a better husband for having gone through such a trial than you would have done had not this come upon you."

"I am sure I should," Ronald said, quietly; "I think I could make her happy, but I fear I shall never have a chance. She has told you what I said last night. I have been awake all the night thinking it over, and I am sure I have decided rightly. My disgrace is hard enough to bear alone; I will never share it with her."

"I think you are right, Mervyn—at least for the present. If, say in five years hence, you are both of the same mind towards each other, as I do not doubt you will be," he added, in reply to the look of perfect confidence that passed between his daughter and Ronald, "we will talk the matter over again. Five years is a long time, and old stories fade out of people's remembrance. In five years, then, one may discuss it again; but I don't mean Mary to wait five years if I can help it, and she has no inclination to wait five years either, have you, child?" Mary shook her head. "So I will tell you what we have resolved upon, for we have made up our minds about it. In the first place somebody murdered this cousin of yours; that's quite clear, isn't it?"

"That is quite clear," Ronald replied. "It is absolutely certain that it was not a suicide."

"In the next place, from what she says, it is quite clear also that this was not done by an ordinary burglar. The circumstances of her death, and the discovery that her watch and jewels were hastily thrust into the ground and left there to spoil, pretty well shows that."

"I think so," Ronald said. "I am convinced that whoever did it, the murder was a deliberate one, and not the work of thieves."

"Then it is evident that it was the work of some one in the neighbourhood, of some one who either had a personal hatred of your cousin, or who wished to injure you."

"To injure me," Ronald repeated in surprise. "I never thought of it in that way. Why to injure me?"

"I say to injure you, because it seems to me that there was a deliberate attempt to fix the guilt upon you. Some one must have put your glove where it was found, for it appears, from what you told Mary, that you certainly could not have dropped it there."

"It might seem so," Ronald said, thoughtfully, "and yet I cannot believe it; in fact, I had, so far as I know, no quarrel with any one in the neighbourhood. I had been away on service for years, and so had nothing to do with the working of the estate, indeed I never had an angry word with any man upon it."

"Never discharged any grooms, or any one of that sort?"

"Well, I did discharge the groom after I got back," Ronald replied, "and the coachman too, for I found, upon looking into the accounts, that they had been swindling my mother right and left; but that can surely have nothing to do with it. The glove alone would have been nothing, had it not been for my previous quarrel with my cousin—which no one outside the house can have known of—and that unfortunate ride of mine."

"Well, that may or may not be," Mr. Armstrong said; "anyhow, we have it that the murder must have been committed by some one in the neighbourhood, who had a grudge against your cousin or against yourself. Now, the detective you have had down there, my daughter tells me, has altogether failed in finding the clue; but, after all, that shows that he is a fool rather than that there is no clue to be found. Now, what Mary and I have settled upon is this: directly we get back we shall take a pretty little cottage, if we can get one, down at the village."

"What, at Carnesford?"

"Yes, Carnesford. We shall be two simple colonists, who have made enough money to live upon, and have fixed upon the place accidentally. Then we shall both set to work to get to the bottom of this affair. We know it is to be done if we can but get hold of the right way, and Mary and I flatter ourselves that between us we shall do it. Now that's our plan. It's no use your saying yes or no, because that's what we have fixed upon."

"It's very good of you, sir——" Mervyn began.

"It's not good at all," Mr. Armstrong interrupted. "Mary wants to get married, and I want her to get married, and so we have nothing to do but to set about the right way of bringing it about. And now, my boy, I know we must not keep you. God bless you, and bring you safely through this war, and I tell you it will be a more troublesome one than your people think. You will write often, and Mary will let you know regularly how we are getting on."

He held out his hand to Mervyn, who grasped it silently, held Mary to him in a close embrace for a minute, and then galloped away to take his place in the ranks of his corps.

The troop to which Ronald belonged was not, he found, intended to start at once to the front, but was to serve as an escort to Colonel Somerset, who had now been appointed as Brigadier-General in command of a column that was to start from Grahamstown. At eight o'clock they started, and arrived late in the afternoon at that place, where they found the 74th Highlanders, who had just marched up from Port Elizabeth. They had prepared for active service by laying aside their bonnets and plaids, adopting a short dark canvas blouse and fixing broad leather peaks to their forage caps. On the following morning the 74th, a troop of Colonial Horse, the Cape Rifles, and some native levies, marched to attack the Hottentots on the station of the London Missionary Society. Joined by a body of Kaffirs, these pampered converts had in cold blood murdered the Fingoes at the station, and were now holding it in force.

After a march of twenty miles across the plain, the troops reached the edge of the Kat River, where the main body halted for a couple of hours, the advance guard having in the course of the day had a skirmish with the natives and captured several waggons. One officer of the native levies had been killed, and two others wounded. A further march of five miles was made before morning, and then the troops halted in order to advance under cover of night against the position of the enemy, twelve miles distant. At half-past one in the morning the Infantry advanced, the Cavalry following two hours later. The road was a most difficult one, full of deep holes and innumerable ant-hills; and after passing through a narrow defile, thickly strewn with loose stones and large rocks, over which in the darkness men stumbled and fell continually, the Cavalry overtook the Infantry at the ford of the Kareiga River, and went on ahead. In the darkness several companies of the Infantry lost their way, and daylight was breaking before the force was collected and in readiness for the assault.

The huts occupied by the enemy stood on one side of a grassy plain, three-quarters of a mile in diameter, and surrounded by a deep belt of forest. The Fingo levies were sent round through the bush to the rear of the huts, and the Cavalry and Infantry then advanced to the attack. The enemy skirmished on the plain, but the Cavalry dashed down upon them and drove them into a wooded ravine, from which they kept up a fire for some time, until silenced by two or three volleys from the Infantry. The main body of the rebels was drawn up in front of their huts, and as soon as the troops approached, and the Cavalry charged them, they took to flight. A volley from the Fingoes in the bush killed several of them; the rest, however, succeeded in gaining the forest.

The village was then burnt, and 650 cattle and some horses and goats, all stolen from neighbouring settlers, were recovered.

The column then marched back to their bivouac of the night before, and the following day returned to Grahamstown. There was no halt here, for the next morning they marched to join the column from King Williamstown. The road led through the Ecca Pass, where constant attacks had been made by natives upon waggons and convoys going down the road; but without opposition they crossed the Koonap River, and at the end of two days' march encamped on a ridge where the Amatola range could be seen, and finally joined the column composed of the 91st Regiment and the rest of the Cape Mounted Rifles, encamped near Fort Hare.

Two days later, the whole force, amounting to 2,000 men, advanced to the base of the Amatolas and encamped on the plains at a short distance from the hills. The attack was made in two columns; the 74th, a portion of the native levies, and of the Mounted Rifles, were to attack a formidable position in front, while the 91st were to march round, and, driving the enemy before them, to effect a junction at the end of the day with the others. The Cavalry could take no part in the attack of the strong position held by the Kaffirs, which was a line of perpendicular cliffs, the only approach to which was up the smooth grassy incline that touched the summit of the cliff at one point only. The 74th moved directly to the attack, the native levies skirmishing on both flanks. The enemy, who could be seen in large numbers on the height, waited until the Highlanders were well within range before they opened fire.

The Cavalry below watched the progress of the troops with anxiety. They replied with steady volleys to the incessant firing of the enemy, advancing steadily up the slope, but occasionally leaving a wounded man behind them. Two companies went ahead in skirmishing order, and climbing from rock to rock, exchanged shots with the enemy as they went. They succeeded in winning a foothold at the top of the cliff and drove off the defenders, who took refuge in a thick forest a few hundred yards in the rear.

As soon as the rest of the regiment had got up, they advanced against the wood, from which the enemy kept up a constant fire, and pouring in steady volleys, entered the forest and drove the enemy before them foot by foot, until the Kaffirs retreated into a thick bush absolutely impenetrable to the soldiers. On emerging from the forest the troops were joined by the other column, which had driven the enemy from their position on the Victoria heights, and had burned two of their villages. While the fighting was going on between the first division and the enemy, the second division had been engaged in another portion of the hills, and had penetrated some distance. Skirmishing went on during the rest of the day, but at nightfall the troops returned to the camp that they had left in the morning. The Kaffirs had suffered considerable loss during the day, two of their leading chiefs being amongst the slain, and Sandilli himself narrowly escaped being taken prisoner.

The Cape Mounted Rifles attached to the 74th had taken no part in the affair, for the ground had been altogether impracticable for cavalry.

The troops, when they returned, were utterly exhausted with the fatigues that they had undergone, but were well satisfied with the events of the day.

"It is well enough for a beginning," Ronald said to Sergeant Menzies; "but what is it? These hills extend twenty or thirty miles either way, at the very least—twice as far, for anything I know. They contain scores of kraals—I don't suppose I am far out when I say hundreds. We have burnt three or four, have marched a mile or two into the woods, have killed, perhaps, a hundred Kaffirs at the outside, and have lost in killed and wounded about fifty of our own men. I suppose, altogether, there are fifteen or twenty thousand Kaffirs there. They have no end of places where our fellows can't possibly penetrate. There's no holding a position when we have taken it. The columns may toil on through the woods, skirmishing all the way, but they only hold the ground they stand on. Why, sergeant, it will take a dozen expeditions, each made with a force three or four times larger than we have now, before we can produce much effect on the Amatolas."

"I am afraid it will, Blunt," the sergeant said, "before we break down the rebellion. There is one thing—they say that the Kaffirs have got twenty or thirty thousand cattle among the hills. If we can drive them off, we shall do more good than by killing Kaffirs. The chiefs care but little how much their followers are shot down, but they do care mightily for the loss of their wealth. Cattle are the one valuable possession of the Kaffirs. Shooting men has very little effect on those who are not shot; as for driving them out of one part of the country, it makes no difference to them one way or another; they can put up their kraals anywhere. The one point on which you can hit them is their cattle. A chief's consequence depends on the number of bullocks he owns. A young Kaffir cannot marry unless he has cattle to buy a wife with. Putting aside their arms and their trumpery necklaces and bracelets, cattle are the sole valuables of the Kaffirs. You will see, if we can capture their cattle, we shall put an end to the war; but no amount of marching and fighting will make any great impression upon them."

The prognostications of the two soldiers proved correct; it was only after six invasions of the Amatolas by very much larger forces, after hard fighting, in which the troops did not always have the best of it, after very heavy losses, and after capturing some 14,000 cattle, that the conquest of the Amatolas was finally achieved.

So far, Ronald had heard nothing more as to the discovery of his identity by one of the men of his troop. He thought that the man could not have mentioned it to any one else, for he felt sure that had it become generally known he must have heard of it. He would have noticed some change in the manner of the men, and it would certainly have come to the ears of Menzies or one of the other non-commissioned officers, who would, of course, come to him to inquire whether there was any truth in the report; besides, the man must have known him from the time he joined the troop, and could have mentioned it before if he had wanted to do so. Ronald supposed, then, that he had kept silence either because he thought that by originating the report to the disadvantage of a popular man in the corps he might, though it proved to be true, be regarded with general hostility, or, that the man might intend to keep his secret, thinking that some day or other he might make it useful to him. No doubt he never would have said what he did had he not been excited by liquor.

Ronald hardly knew whether to be glad or sorry that the secret was still kept. It would, he felt sure, come out sooner or later, and in some respects he would rather have an end of the suspense, and face it at once. His position was a strong one, his officers were all markedly kind to him, and his expedition into the Amatolas had rendered him the most popular man in the corps among his comrades. The fact, too, as told by Colonel Somerset to his officers, and as picked up by the men from their talk, that he had refused a commission, added to his popularity; the men were glad to think that their comrade preferred being one of them to becoming an officer, and that the brave deed they were all proud of had not been done to win promotion, but simply to save women in distress.

There had been sly laughter among the men when their comrades told them how pretty was the girl Ronald had brought back; and there had been keen wagering in the regiment that there would be a wedding before they marched, or at any rate that they should hear there would be one on their return from the war. The one contingency had not occurred. The other it seemed was not to take place, for in answer to a question as to how the wounded colonist was going on, Ronald had said carelessly that he was mending fast, and would be well enough to be taken down to the coast in a fortnight, and that the doctor thought by the time he reached England he would be completely set up again. So the bets were paid, but the men wondered that their sergeant had not made a better use of his opportunities, for all agreed that a girl could hardly refuse a man who had done so much for her, even if her father were a wealthy colonist, and he only a trooper in the Mounted Rifles.

CHAPTER XVI.

SEARCHING FOR A CLUE.

The landlord of the "Carne's Arms" was somewhat puzzled by a stranger who had just been dropped at his door by the coach from Plymouth. He did not look like either a fisherman or an artist, or even a wandering tourist. His clothes were somewhat rough, and the landlord would have taken him for a farmer, but what could any strange farmer be stopping at Carnesford for? There were no farms vacant in the neighbourhood, nor any likely to be, so far as the landlord knew; besides, the few words his guest had spoken as he entered had no touch of the Devonshire dialect. While he was standing at the door, turning the matter over in his mind—for he rather prided himself upon his ability to decide upon the calling and object of his guests, and was annoyed by his failure to do so in the present instance—the man he was thinking of came out of the coffee-room and placed himself beside him.

"Well, landlord, this is a pretty village of yours; they told me in Plymouth it was as pretty a place as any about, and I see they were right."

"Yes, most folks think it's pretty," the landlord said, "although I am so accustomed to it myself I don't see a great deal in it."

"Yes, custom is everything. I have been accustomed for a great many years to see nothing much but plains, with clumps of bush here and there, and occasionally a herd of deer walking across it. I have been farming down at the Cape, and so, you see, a quiet, pretty place like this is very pleasant to me."

"I should think it is quiet enough farming there," the landlord said. "I have heard from folk who have been out in some of those parts that you often haven't a neighbour nearer than four miles away."

"That's true enough, landlord, but the life is not always quiet for all that. It's not quiet, for instance, when you hear the yell of a hundred or so savages outside your windows, or see a party driving half your cattle away into the bush."

"No, I shouldn't call that quiet; and that is what you have been doing?"

"Yes, I was in the disturbed part when the Kaffirs rose. Most of our neighbours were killed, and we had a hard time of it, but some mounted police came up just in time. I have had trouble three or four times before, and it's no use going on for years rearing cattle if they are to be all swept away by the natives, and you are running the risk of getting your throat cut in the bargain; so, after this last affair, I locked up my farmhouse, drove off what cattle I had got left, and sold them for what I could get for them, and here I am."

"Yes, here you are," repeated the landlord; "and what next?"

"The ship touched at Plymouth, and I thought I might as well get out there as anywhere else. Well, there is too much noise and bustle at Plymouth. I haven't been used to it, and so now I am just looking for a little place to suit me. I have been up to Tavistock, and then some one said that Carnesford was a pretty village. I said I would look at Carnesford, and so you see here I am."

"What sort of a place are you looking for?" the landlord asked, looking at his visitor closely, and mentally appraising his worth.

"Oh, quite a little place, I should say about twenty pounds a year. I suppose one could get a girl to help from the village, and could live for another eighty. That's about what I could afford."

"Oh, yes, I should say you could do that," said the landlord, thoughtfully, "but I don't know that there is any such place to let anywhere about here. There is a nice cottage at the other end of the village just empty. It's got a good garden, and is rather away from the rest of the houses; but the rent is only half-a-crown a week. That wouldn't do for you."

"Well, I wanted something better than that; but still I might have a look at it. Of course if I took it I should want to stay, and I might as well spend a little money in doing it up to my fancy as in paying higher rent. By the way, my name is Armstrong. Perhaps you wouldn't mind putting on your hat and showing me this place you speak of. We have been used to roughing it, and don't want anything fine."

The cottage was certainly large and roomy, and stood in a pretty garden. But its appearance was not prepossessing, for it differed from most of the other little houses in the village inasmuch as it was not, like them, half hidden by roses and creepers climbing over it.

"Yes, it's rough, decidedly rough," Mr. Armstrong said, "still there is a pretty view down the valley. Now I should save nearly fourteen pounds in rent by taking this instead of a twenty pound a year house; and if one were to put up a verandah round it, touch up the windows somehow, and put pretty paper on the walls, I should say that at the end of two years it would stand me in just the same. That and plenty of roses and things would make it a pretty little place. Who is the landlord?"

"The landlord is Mr. Carne, up at The Hold; that's the big house on the hill. But he is away at present. Mr. Kirkland, a lawyer at Plymouth, is his agent, and sees to the letting of his houses and that sort of thing. His clerk comes over once a month to collect the rents. I expect you would have to go to him even if Mr. Carne was at home. Squire was never much down in the village in the best of times, and we have hardly seen his face since his sister's death."

"Yes, they were telling us about that affair at Plymouth," the colonist said, quietly. "It was a bad business. Well, have you got some pretty sociable sort of fellows in the village? I like a chat as well as any man, and I should want some one to talk to."

"Well, I don't know that they would be your sort," the landlord said, doubtfully. "There's the clergyman—and the doctor——"

"Oh, no. I don't want to have to do with clergymen and doctors—we colonists are pretty rough and ready fellows, and it's no odds to us what a man is. A man stops at your door, and in he comes, and he is welcome—though he is only a shepherd on the look-out for work; sometimes one of the Kaffir chiefs with nothing on but a blanket and a leather apron, will stalk in and squat down and make himself at home. Oh, no. It's tradesmen I mean, and perhaps the small farmers round."

"Well, we are pretty well off for that, Mr. Armstrong. There is Hiram Powlett, the miller, and Jacob Carey, the blacksmith—they drop in pretty regular every evening and smoke a pipe with me, in what I call my snuggery; and there's old Reuben Claphurst—he was the clerk at one time, and is a wonderful chap for knowing the history of every family for miles round; and there's some of the farmers often come in for a glass—if you are not too proud for that sort of company."

"Proud! Bless your heart, what is there to be proud about; ain't I been working as a farmer for years and years with no one to talk to but my own hands?—I mean my own men. No, that's just the thing to suit me; anyhow, I think I will try the experiment. If at the end of a couple of years I don't like it, why, there is no harm done."

"Well, I am sure we shall be all glad to have you here, Mr. Armstrong; we like getting some one from outside, it freshens our ideas up a bit and does us good. We are cheerful enough in summer with the artists that come here sketching, and with the gentlemen who sometimes come to fish; but the rest of the year I don't often have a stranger at the 'Carne's Arms.'"

Two days later Mr. Armstrong returned to Carnesford with a builder from Plymouth. The following day, five or six workmen appeared, and in a fortnight a considerable transformation had been made in the cottage. A verandah was run round the front and two sides. Some rustic woodwork appeared round the windows, and the interior of the house was transformed with fresh paper and paint. Nothing could be done in the way of roses and creepers, as these could not be moved at that time of year, for it was now just midsummer.

The day after the workmen went out, a waggon load of furniture, simple and substantial, arrived, and on the following day the coach brought down the new tenants. A girl had already been engaged in the village to act as servant. Miss Armstrong was quietly and plainly dressed, and might, by her attire, be taken for the daughter of a small farmer, and the opinion in the village, as the newcomers walked through on their way to the cottage, was distinctly favourable. In a very short time Mr. Armstrong became quite a popular character in Carnesford, and soon was on speaking terms with most of the people. He won the mothers' hearts by patting the heads of the little girls, and praising their looks. He had a habit of carrying sweets in his pockets, and distributing them freely among the children, and he would lounge for hours at the smith's door, listening to the gossip that went on, for in Carnesford, as elsewhere, the forge was the recognised meeting-place of those who had nothing to do. He was considered a wonderful acquisition by the frequenters of the snuggery at the "Carne's Arms," and his stories of life at the Cape gave an added interest to their meetings. Hearing from Hiram Powlett that he had a wife and daughter, he asked him to get them, as a matter of kindness, to visit his daughter; and within a fortnight of his arrival, he and Mary went to tea to the Mill.

Several times the conversation in the snuggery turned upon the murder at The Hold. In no case did the new-comer lead up to it, but it cropped up as the subject which the people of Carnesford were never weary of discussing. He ventured no opinions and asked no questions upon the first few occasions when the subject was being discussed, but smoked his pipe in silence, listening to the conversation.

"It seems strange to me," he said at last, "that you in this village should never have had a suspicion of any one except this Captain Mervyn; I understand that you, Mr. Claphurst, and you, Mr. Carey, have never thought of any one else; but Mr. Powlett—he always says he is sure it isn't him. But if it wasn't him, Mr. Powlett, who do you think it was?"

"Ah, that is more than I can tell," Hiram replied. "I have thought, and I have thought, till my head went round, but I can't see who it can have been."

"Miss Carne seems to have had no enemies?"

"No, not one—not as I ever heard of. She was wonderful popular in the village, she was; and as for the Squire, except about poaching, he never quarrelled with any one."

"Had he trouble with poachers, then?"

"Well, not often; but last year, before that affair, there was a bad lot about. They were from Dareport—that's two miles away, down at the mouth of the river—with one or two chaps from this village, so it was said. About a fortnight—it may be three weeks—before Miss Carne was killed, there was a fight up in the woods between them and the gamekeepers. One of the keepers got stabbed, but he didn't die until some time afterwards; but the jury brought it in wilful murder all the same. It didn't matter much what verdict they brought in, 'cause the man as the evidence went against had left the country— at least, he hadn't been seen hereabouts."

"And a good job too, Hiram—a good job too," Jacob Carey put in.

"Yes," Hiram said, "I admit it; it was a good job as he was gone—a good job for us all. He would never have done any good here, anyway; and the best job as ever he did for himself, as I know of, was when he took himself off."

There was a general chorus of assent.

"What was the man's name?" Mr. Armstrong asked, carelessly.

"His name was George Forester," Jacob Carey said.

As they were going out from the snuggery that evening, the landlord made a sign to Mr. Armstrong that he wanted to speak to him. He accordingly lingered until the other men had left.

"Oh, I thought I would just tell you, Mr. Armstrong, seeing that your daughter and you have been to the Mill, it's just as well not to talk about the poaching and George Forester before Ruth Powlett. You see, it's rather a sore subject with her. She was engaged to that George Forester, and a lot of trouble it gave her father and mother. Well, I expect she must have seen now that she had a lucky escape. Still, a girl don't like a man as she has liked being spoken against, so I thought that I would say a word to you."

"Thank you; that's very friendly of you. Yes, you may be sure that I won't introduce the subject. I am very glad you told me, or I might have blundered upon it and hurt the girl's feelings. She doesn't look very strong, either. She has a nervous look about her, I think."

"She used to be very different, but she had a great shock. She was the first, you know, to go into Miss Carne's room and find her dead. She was her maid before that, and she was ill for weeks after. It came on the top of an illness, too. She fell down on the hill coming home from church, and they found her lying insensible there, and she was very bad—had the doctor there every day. Then came this other affair, and I dare say this business of George Forester's helped too. Anyhow, she was very bad, and the doctor thought at one time that she wouldn't get over it."

Mr. Armstrong walked home thoughtfully.

"Well, father, what is your news?" Mary Armstrong said, as he entered. "I can see you have heard something more than usual."

"Well, my dear, I don't know that it's anything, but at the same time it certainly is new, and gives us something to follow up. It seems that there was a fellow named George Forester living somewhere about here, and he was engaged to your friend, Ruth Powlett, but her father and mother disapproved of it highly. They say he was a bad lot; he got mixed up with a gang of poachers, and some little time before this murder, about three weeks before, they had a fight with Mr. Carne's keepers; one of the keepers was mortally wounded, it was said by this George Forester. The man lived for some time, but at last died of the wound, and the jury brought in a verdict of wilful murder against George Forester, who had been missing from the time of the fight."

"Yes, father, but that seems no great clue."

"Perhaps not, Mary, but it shows at least that there was one fellow about here who may be considered to have had a quarrel with the Carnes, and who was a thoroughly bad character, and who—and this is of importance—was engaged, with or without her parents' consent, to Miss Carne's own maid."

Mary gave a little gasp of excitement.

"Now it seems, further," her father went on, "that some time between this poaching affray and the murder—I could not inquire closely into dates—Ruth Powlett was found insensible on the road going up the hill, and was very ill for some days; she said she had had a fall, and of course she may have had, although it is not often young women fall down so heavily as to stun themselves. But it may of course have been something else."

"What else, father?"

"Well, it is possible she may have met this lover of hers, and that they may have had a quarrel. Probably she knew he had been engaged in this poaching affair, and may have told him that she would have nothing more to do with him, and he may have knocked her down. Of course, this is all mere supposition, but it is only by supposition that we can grope our way along. It seems she was well enough anyhow to go up to her place again at The Hold, for she was the first to discover the murder, and the shock was so great that she was ill for weeks, in fact in great danger; they say she has been greatly changed ever since. I don't know whether anything can be made of that, my dear."

"I don't know. I don't see what, father," Mary said, after thinking for some time, "unless she is fancying since that it was this man who did it. Of course, anyhow, it would be a fearful shock for a girl to find her mistress lying murdered, and perhaps it may be nothing more than that."

"No doubt, it may be nothing more than that, Mary; but it's the other side of the case we have to look at. Let us piece the things together. Here we have four or five facts, all of which may tell. Here is a bad character in the village; that is one point. This man had a poaching affray with Mr. Carne's keepers; he killed, or at any rate the coroner's jury found that he killed, one of the keepers. He is engaged to Miss Carne's own maid. This maid is just after this poaching business found insensible in the wood, and tells rather an improbable story as to how it came about. She is the first to enter her mistress's room, and then she has a serious illness. Of course, any girl would be shocked and frightened and upset, but it is not so often that a serious illness would be the result. And lastly, she has been changed ever since. She has, as you remarked to me the other day, an absent, preoccupied sort of way about her. Taken altogether, these things certainly do amount to something."

"I think so too, father; I think so too," Mary Armstrong said, walking up and down the little room in her excitement. "I do think there may be something in it; and you see, father, after this poaching business, the man wanted to get away, and he may have been in want of money, and so have thought of taking Miss Carne's watch and jewels to raise money to take him abroad."

"So he might, my dear. That is certainly a feasible explanation, but unfortunately, instead of taking them away, you see he buried them."

"Yes, father, but he only just pushed them into the ground, the report said; because on reading through the old files of the newspapers the other day I particularly noticed that. Well, father, you see, perhaps just as he was leaving the house a dog may have barked, or something may have given him a scare, and he may just have hidden them in the ground, intending to come for them next day; and then, what with the excitement and the police here, and the search that was being made, he could get no opportunity of getting them up again, and being afraid of being arrested himself for his share in the poaching affray, he dared not hang about here any longer, but probably went down to Plymouth and got on board ship there. Of course, all this is nothing more than supposition, still it really does not seem improbable, father. There is only one difficulty that I can see. Why should he have killed Miss Carne, because the doctors say that she was certainly asleep?"

"We cannot tell, dear. She may have moved a little. He may have thought that she would wake, and that he had better make sure. He was a desperate man, and there is no saying what a desperate man will do. Anyhow, Mary, this is a clue, and a distinct one, and we must follow it up. It may lead us wrong in the end, but we shall not be losing time by following it, for I shall keep my ears open, and may find some other and altogether different track."

"How had we better follow it?" Mary asked, after having sat silent for some minutes. "This Forester is gone, and we have no idea where. I think the only person likely to be able to help us is Ruth Powlett."

"Exactly so, my dear."

"And she would not be likely to speak. If she knows anything she would have said it at the trial had she not wished to shield this man, whom she may love in spite of his wickedness."

"Quite so, my dear; and besides," and he smiled, "young women in love are not disposed to believe in their lovers' guilt."

"How can you say so, father?" Mary said, indignantly; "you would not compare——"

"No, no, Mary; I would not compare the two men; but I think you will admit that even had the evidence against Ronald Mervyn been ten times as conclusive as it was, you would still have maintained his innocence against all the world."

"Of course I should, father."

"Quite so, my dear; that is what I am saying; however, if our supposition is correct in this case, the girl does believe him to be guilty, but she wishes to shield him, either because she loves him still or has loved him. It is astonishing how women will cling to men even when they know them to be villains. I think, dear, that the best way of proceeding will be for you to endeavour to find out from Ruth Powlett what she knows. Of course it will be a gradual matter, and you can only do it when she has got to know and like you thoroughly."

"But, father," Mary said, hesitating, "will it not be a treacherous thing for me to become friends with her for the purpose of gaining her secret?"

"It depends how you gain it, Mary. Certainly it would be so were you to get it surreptitiously. That is not the way I should propose. If this girl has really any proof or anything like strong evidence that the murder was committed by this man Forester, she is acting wrongly and cruelly to another to allow the guilt to fall upon him. In time, when you get intimate with her, intimate enough to introduce the subject, your course would be to impress this upon her so strongly as to induce her to make an open confession. Of course you would point out to her that this could now in no way injure the man who is her lover, as he has gone no one knows where, and will certainly never return to this country, as upon his appearance he would at once be arrested and tried on the charge of killing the gamekeeper. All this would be perfectly open and above-board. Then, Mary, you could, if you deemed it expedient, own your own strong interest in the matter. There would be nothing treacherous in this, dear. You simply urge her to do an act of justice. Of course it will be painful for her to do so, after concealing it so long. Still, I should think from the little I have seen of her that she is a conscientious girl, and is, I doubt not, already sorely troubled in her mind over the matter."

"Yes, father, I agree with you. There would be nothing treacherous in that. I have simply to try to get her to make a confession of anything she may know in the matter. I quite agree with you in all you have said about the man, but I do not see how Ruth Powlett can know anything for certain, whatever she may suspect; for if she was, as you say, dangerously ill for a long time after the murder, she cannot very well have seen the man, who would be sure to have quitted the country at once."

"I am afraid that that is so, Mary. Still, we must hope for the best, and if she cannot give us absolute evidence herself, what she says may at least put us in the right track for obtaining it. Even if no legal evidence can be obtained, we might get enough clues, with what we have already, to convince the world that whereas hitherto there seemed no alternative open as to Mervyn's guilt, there was in fact another against whom there is at any rate a certain amount of proof, and whose character is as bad as that of Captain Mervyn is good. This would in itself be a great step. Mervyn has been acquitted, but as no one else is shown to have been connected with it in any way, people are compelled, in spite of his previous character, in spite of his acquittal, in spite in fact even of probability, to consider him guilty. Once shown that there is at least reasonable ground for suspicion against another, and the opinion, at any rate of all who know Mervyn, would at once veer round."

"Very well, father; now you have done your part of the work by finding out the clue, I will do mine by following it up. Fortunately, Ruth Powlett is a very superior sort of girl to any one in the village, and I can make friends with her heartily and without pretence. I should have found it very hard if she had been a rough sort of girl, but she expresses herself just as well as I do, and seems very gentle and nice. One can see that even that sharp-voiced stepmother of hers is very fond of her, and she is the apple of the miller's eye. But you must not be impatient, father; two girls can't become great friends all at once."

"I think, on the whole, Miss Armstrong," her father said, "you are quite as likely to become impatient as I am, seeing that it is your business much more than mine."

"Well, you may be sure I shall not lose more time than I can help, father." Mary Armstrong laughed. "You don't know how joyous I feel to-night, I have always been hopeful, but it did seem so vague before. Now that we have got what we think to be a clue, and can set to work at once, I feel ever so much nearer to seeing Ronald again."

The consequence of this conversation was that Mary Armstrong went very frequently down to the mill, and induced Ruth Powlett, sometimes, to come up and sit with her.

"I am very glad, Mr. Armstrong," Hiram Powlett said, one evening, when they happened to be the first two to arrive in the snuggery, "that my Ruth seems to take to your daughter. It's a real comfort to Hesba and me. You would have thought that she would have taken to some of the girls she went to school with, but she hasn't. I suppose she is too quiet for them, and they are too noisy for her. Anyhow, until now, she has never had a friend, and I think it will do her a world of good. It's bad for a girl to be alone, and especially a girl like Ruth. I don't mind telling you, Mr. Armstrong, that Hesba and I have an idea that she has got something on her mind, she has been so changed altogether since Miss Carne's murder. I might have thought that she had fretted about that scamp Forester going away, for at one time the girl was very fond of him, but before it happened she told me that she had found out he would never make her a good husband, and would break it off altogether with him; so you see I don't think his going away had anything to do with it. Once or twice I thought she was going to say something particular to me, but she has never said it, and she sits there and broods and broods till it makes my heart ache to see her. Now she has got your daughter to be friends with, perhaps she may shake it off."

"I hope she may, Mr. Powlett. It's a bad thing for a girl to mope. I know Mary likes your daughter very much; perhaps, if she has anything on her mind, she will tell Mary one of these days. You see, when girls get to be friends, they open their hearts to each other as they won't do to any one else."

"I don't see what she can have on her mind," the miller said, shaking his head. "It may only be a fancy of mine. Hesba and I have talked it over a score of times."

"Very likely it's nothing, after all," Mr. Armstrong said. "Girls get strange fancies into their heads, and make mountains out of molehills. It may be nothing, after all; still, perhaps she would be all the better for the telling of it."

Hiram Powlett shook his head decidedly. "Ruth isn't a girl to have fancies. If she is fretting, she is fretting over something serious. I don't know why I am talking so to you, Mr. Armstrong, for I have never spoken to any one else about it; but your daughter seems to have taken so kindly to Ruth that it seems natural for me to speak to you."

"I am glad you have done so, Mr. Powlett, and I hope that good may come from our talk."

It was not until a fortnight after this chat that Mary had anything to communicate to her father, for she found that whenever she turned the conversation upon the topic of the murder of Miss Carne, Ruth evidently shrank so much from it that she was obliged to change the subject.

"To-day, father, I took the bull by the horns. Ruth had been sitting there for some time working without saying a word, when I asked her suddenly, as if it was what I had been thinking over while we were silent: 'What is your opinion, Ruth? Do you think that Captain Mervyn really murdered his cousin?' She turned pale. She has never much colour, you know, but she went as white as a sheet, and then said, 'I am quite sure that he did not do it, but I don't like talking about it.' 'No, of course not,' I said. 'I can quite understand that after the terrible shock you had. Still, it is awful to think that this Captain Mervyn should have been driven away from his home and made an outcast of if he is innocent.' 'It serves him right,' Ruth said, passionately. 'How dare he insult and threaten my dear Miss Margaret? Nothing is too bad for him.' 'I can't quite agree with you there,' I said. 'No doubt he deserved to be punished, and he must have been punished by being tried for his cousin's murder; but to think of a man spending all his life, branded unjustly with the crime of murder, is something too terrible to think of.' 'I dare say he is doing very well,' she said, after a pause. 'Doing well,' I said, 'doing well! What can you be thinking of, Ruth? What sort of doing well can there be for a man who knows that at any moment he may be recognised, that his story may be whispered about, and that his neighbours may shrink away from him; that his wife, if he ever marries, may come to believe that her husband is a murderer, that his children may bear the curse of Cain upon them? It is too terrible to think of. If Captain Mervyn is guilty, he ought to have been hung; if he is innocent, he is one of the most unfortunate men in the world.' Ruth didn't say anything, but she was so terribly white that I thought she was going to faint. She tried to get up, but I could see she couldn't, and I ran and got her a glass of water. Her hand shook so that she could hardly hold it to her lips. After she drank some she sat for a minute or two quiet, then she murmured something about a sudden faintness, and that she would go home. I persuaded her to stay a few minutes longer. At last she got up. 'I am subject to fainting fits,' she said; 'it is very silly, but I cannot help it. Yes, perhaps what you say about

Captain Mervyn is right, but I never quite saw it so before. Good-bye,' and then she went off, though I could see she was scarcely able to walk steadily. Oh, father, I feel quite sure that she knows something; that she can prove that Ronald is innocent if she chooses; and I think that sooner or later she will choose. First of all she was so decided in her assertion that Ronald was innocent; she did not say 'I think,' or 'I believe,' she said 'I am quite sure.' She would never have said that unless she knew something quite positive. Then the way that she burst out that it served him right, seems to me, and I have been thinking about it ever since she went away an hour ago, as if she had been trying to convince herself that it was right that he should suffer, and to soothe her own conscience for not saying what would prove him innocent."

"It looks like it, Mary; it certainly looks like it. We are on the right trail, my girl, I am sure. That was a very heavy blow you struck her to-day, and she evidently felt it so. Two or three more such blows, and the victory will be won. I have no doubt now that Ruth Powlett somehow holds the key of this strange mystery in her hand, and I think that what you have said to her to-day will go a long way towards inducing her to unlock it. Forester was the murderer of Miss Carne, I have not a shadow of doubt, though how she knows it for certain is more than I can even guess."

CHAPTER XVII.

RUTH POWLETT CONFESSES.

Upon the morning after the conversation with his daughter, Mr. Armstrong had just started on his way up the village when he met Hiram Powlett.

"I was just coming to see you, Mr. Armstrong, if you can spare a minute."

"I can spare an hour—I can spare the whole morning, Mr. Powlett. I have ceased to be a working bee, and my time is at your disposal."

"Well, I thought I would just step over and speak to you," Hiram began, in a slow, puzzled sort of a way. "You know what I was telling you the other day about my girl?"

"Yes; I remember very well."

"You don't know, Mr. Armstrong, whether she has said anything to your daughter?"

"No; at least not so far as I have heard of. Mary said that they were talking together, and something was said about Miss Carne's murder; that your daughter turned very pale, and that she thought she was going to faint."

"That's it; that's it," Hiram said, stroking his chin, thoughtfully, "that murder is at the bottom of it. Hesba thinks it must be that any talk about it brings the scene back to her; but it does not seem to me that that accounts for it at all, and I would give a lot to know what is on the girl's mind. She came in yesterday afternoon as white as a sheet, and fainted right off at the door. I shouldn't think so much of that, because she has often fainted since her illness, but that wasn't all. When her mother got her round she went upstairs to her room, and didn't come down again. There is not much in that, you would say; after a girl has fainted she likes to lie quiet a bit; but she didn't lie quiet. We could hear her walking up and down the room for hours, and Hesba stole up several times to her door and said she was sobbing enough to break her heart. She is going about the house again this morning, but that white and still that it is cruel to look at her. So I thought after breakfast that I would put on my hat and come and have a talk with you, seeing that you were good enough to be interested in her. You will say it's a rum thing for a father to come and talk about his daughter to a man he hasn't known more than two months. I feel that myself, but there is no one in the village I should like to open my mind to about Ruth, and seeing that you are father of a girl about the same age, and that I feel you are a true sort of a man, I come to you. It isn't as if I thought that my Ruth could have done anything wrong. If I did, I would cut my tongue out before I would speak a word. But I know my Ruth. She has always been a good girl: not one of your light sort, but earnest and steady. Whatever is wrong, it's not wrong with her. I believe she has got some secret or other that is just wearing her out, and if we can't get to the bottom of it I don't believe Ruth will see Christmas," and Hiram Powlett wiped his eyes violently.

"Believe me, I will do my best to find it out if there is such a secret, Mr. Powlett. I feel sure from what I have seen of your daughter, that if a wrong has been done of any kind it is not by her. I agree with you that she has a secret, and that that secret is wearing her out. I may say that my daughter is of the same opinion. I believe that there is a struggle going on in her mind on the subject, and that if she is to have peace, and as you say health, she must unburden her mind. However, Mr. Powlett, my advice in the matter is, leave her alone. Do not press her in any way. I think that what you said to me before is likely to be verified, and that if she unburdens herself it will be to Mary; and you may be sure whatever is the nature of the secret, my daughter will keep it inviolate, unless it is Ruth's own wish that it should be told to others."

"Thankee, Mr. Armstrong, thankee kindly; I feel more hopeful now. I have been worrying and fretting over this for months, till I can scarce look after my work, and often catch myself going on drawing at my pipe when it's gone out and got cold. But I think it's coming on; I think that crying last night meant something, one way or the other. Well, we shall see; we shall see. I will be off back again to my work now; I feel all the better for having had this talk with you. Hesba's a good woman, and she is fond of the child; but she is what she calls practical—she looks at things hard, and straight, and sensible, and naturally she don't quite enter into my feelings about Ruth, though she is fond of her too. Well, good morning, Mr. Armstrong; you have done me good, and I do hope it will turn out as you say, and that we shall get to know what is Ruth's trouble."

An hour later, Mary Armstrong went down to the mill to inquire after Ruth. She found her quiet and pale.

"I am glad you have come in, Miss Armstrong," Hesba said, "our Ruth wants cheering up a bit. She had a faint yesterday when she got back from your place, and she is never fit for anything after that except just to sit in her chair and look in the fire. I tell her she would be better if she would rouse herself."

"But one cannot always rouse oneself, Mrs. Powlett," Mary said; "and I am sure Ruth does not look equal to talking now. However, she shall sit still, and I will tell her a story. I have never told you yet that I was once carried off by the Kaffirs, and that worse than death would have befallen me, and that I should have been afterwards tortured and killed, if I had not been rescued by a brave man."

"Lawk-a-mussy, Miss Armstrong, why you make my flesh creep at the thought of such a thing? And you say it all happened to you? Why, now, to look at you, I should have thought you could hardly have known what trouble meant, you always seem so bright and happy; that's what Ruth has said, again and again."

"You shall judge for yourself, Mrs. Powlett, if you can find time to sit down and listen, as well as Ruth."

"I can find time for that," Hesba said, "though it isn't often as I sits down till the tea is cleared away and Hiram has lit his pipe."

Mary sat down facing the fire, with Ruth in an arm-chair on one side of her, and Mrs. Powlett stiff and upright on a hard settle on the other. Then she began to tell the story, first saying a few words to let her hearers know of the fate of women who fell into the hands of the Kaffirs. Then she began with the story of her journey down from King Williamstown, the sudden attack by natives, and how after seeing her father fall she was carried off. Then she told, what she had never told before, of the hideous tortures of the other two women, part of which she was compelled to witness, and how she was told that she was to be preserved as a present to Macomo. Then she described the dreary journey. "I had only one hope," she said, "and it was so faint that it could not be called a hope; but there was one man in the colony who somehow I felt sure would, if he knew of my danger, try to rescue me. He had once before come to our aid when our house was attacked by Kaffirs, and in a few minutes our fate would have been sealed had he not arrived. But for aught I knew he was a hundred miles away, and what could he do against the three hundred natives who were with me? Still, I had a little ray of hope, the faintest, tiniest ray, until we entered the Amatolas——they are strong steep hills covered with forest and bush, and are the stronghold of the Kaffirs, and I knew that there were about twenty thousand natives gathered there. Then I hoped no longer. I felt that my fate was sealed, and my only wish and my only longing was to obtain a knife or a spear, and to kill myself."

Then Mary described the journey through the forest to the kraal, the long hours she had sat waiting for her fate with every movement watched by the Kaffir women, and her sensations when she heard the message in English. Then she described her rescue from the kraal, her flight through the woods, her concealment in the cave, her escape from the Amatolas, the ride with the trooper holding her on his saddle, and the final dash through the Kaffirs.

Her hearers had thrown in many interjections of horror and pity, loud on the part of Hesba, mere murmurs on that of Ruth, who had taken Mary's hand in hers, but the sympathetic pressure told more than words.

"And you shot four of them, Miss Armstrong!" Hesba ejaculated, in wide-eyed astonishment. "To think that a young girl like you should have the death of four men on her hands! I don't say as it's unchristian, because Christians are not forbidden to fight for their lives, but it does seem downright awful!"

"It has never troubled me for a single moment," Mary said. "They tried to kill me, and I killed them. That is the light I saw it in, and so would you if you had been living in the colony."

"But you have not finished your story," Ruth said, earnestly. "Surely that is not the end of it!"

"No; my father recovered from his wound, and so did the soldier who saved me, and as soon as my father was able to travel, he and I went down to the coast and came home."

"That cannot be all," Ruth whispered; "there must be something more to tell, Mary."

"I will tell you another time, Ruth," Mary said, in equally low tones, and then rising, put on her hat again, said good-bye, and went out.

"Did you ever, Ruth?" Hesba Powlett exclaimed as the door closed. "I never did hear such a story in all my life. And to think of her shooting four men! It quite made my flesh creep; didn't it yours?"

"There were other parts of the story that made my flesh creep a great deal more, mother."

"Yes, it was terrible! And she didn't say a single word in praise of what the soldier had done for her. Now that seems to me downright ungrateful, and not at all what I should have thought of Miss Armstrong."

"I suppose she thought, mother, that there was no occasion to express her opinion of his bravery or to mention her gratitude. The whole story seemed to me a cry of praise and a hymn of gratitude."

"Lord, Ruth, what fancies you do take in your head, to be sure! I never did hear such expressions!"

Two days passed without Ruth going up to the Armstrongs'; on the third day Mary again went down.

"Well, Ruth, as you have not been to see me, I have come to see you again."

"I was coming up this afternoon. If you don't mind, I will go back with you now, instead of your staying here. We are quieter there, you know. Somehow, one cannot think or talk when people come in and out of the room every two or three minutes."

"I quite agree with you, Ruth, and, if you don't mind my saying so, I would very much rather have you all to myself."

The two girls accordingly went back to the cottage. Mary, who was rather an industrious needlewoman, brought out a basket of work. Ruth, who for a long time had scarcely taken up a needle, sat with her hands before her.

When two people intend to have a serious conversation with each other, they generally steer wide of the subject at first, and the present was no exception.

"I think it would be better for you, Ruth, to occupy yourself with work a little, as I do."

"I used to be fond of work," Ruth replied, "but I don't seem to be able to give my attention to it now. I begin, and before I have done twenty stitches, somehow or other my thoughts seem to go away, and by the end of the morning the first twenty stitches are all I have done."

"But you oughtn't to think so much, Ruth. It is bad for any one to be always thinking."

"Yes, but I can't help it. I have so much to think about, and it gets worse instead of better. Now, after what you said to me the other night, I don't know what to do. It seemed right before. I did not think I was doing much harm in keeping silence; now I see I have been, oh, so wrong!" and she twined her fingers in and out as if suffering bodily pain.

"My poor Ruth!" Mary said, coming over to her and kneeling down by her side. "I think I know what is troubling you."

The girl shook her head.

"Yes, dear, I am almost sure you have known something all along that would have proved Captain Mervyn was innocent, and you have not said it."

Ruth Powlett did not speak for a minute or two, then she said, slowly:

"I do not know how you have guessed it, Mary. No one else even seems to have thought of it. But, yes, that is it, and I do so want some one to advise me what to do. I see now I have been very wicked. For a long time I have been fighting against myself. I have tried so hard to persuade myself that I had not done much harm, because Captain Mervyn was acquitted. I have really known that I was wrong, but I never thought how wrong until you spoke to me."

"Wait, Ruth," Mary said; "before you tell me your secret I must tell you mine. It would not be fair for you to tell me without knowing that. You remember the story I was telling you about my being carried off?"

A fresh interest came into Ruth's face.

"Yes," she said, "and you promised you would tell me the rest another time. I thought you meant, of course, you would tell me that when this war out there is over, you would some day marry the soldier who has done so much for you."

"I was going to tell you, Ruth, why I am not going to marry him."

"Oh, I thought you would be sure to," Ruth said in a tone of deep disappointment. "It seemed to me that it was sure to be so. I thought a man would never have risked so much for a woman unless he loved her."

"He did love me, Ruth, and I loved him. I don't think I made any secret of it. Somehow it seemed to me that he had a right to me, and I was surprised when the time went on and he didn't ask me. When the last day came before he was to march away to fight again, I think that if he had not spoken I should have done so. Do not think me unmaidenly, Ruth, but he was only a sergeant and I was a rich girl, for my father is a great deal better off than he seems to be, and I thought that perhaps some foolish sort of pride held him back, for I was quite sure that he loved me. But he spoke first. He told me that he loved me, but could never ask me to be his wife; that he could never marry, but he must go through the world alone to the end of his life."

"Oh, Mary, how terrible!" Ruth said, pitifully, "how terrible! Was he married before, then?"

"No, Ruth, it was worse than that; there was a great shadow over his life; he had been tried for murder, and though he had been acquitted, the stigma was still upon him. Go where he would he might be recognised and pointed out as a murderer; therefore, unless the truth was some day known and his name cleared, no woman could ever be his wife."

Ruth had given a little gasp as Mary Armstrong began, then she sat rigid and immovable.

"It was Captain Mervyn," she said, at last, in a low whisper.

"Yes, Ruth. Sergeant Blunt was Captain Mervyn; he had changed his name, and gone out there to hide himself, but even there he had already been recognised; and, as he said—for I pleaded hard, Ruth, to be allowed to share his exile—go where he would, bury himself in what out-of-the-way corner he might, sooner or later some one would know him, and this story would rise up against him, and, much as he loved me—all the more, perhaps, because he loved me so much—he would never suffer me to be pointed at as the wife of a murderer."

"You shall not be," Ruth said, more firmly than she had before spoken. "You shall not be, Mary. I can clear him, and I will."

It was Mary Armstrong's turn to break down now. The goal had been reached, Ronald Mervyn would be cleared; and she threw her arms round Ruth and burst into a passion of tears. It was some time before the girls were sufficiently composed to renew the conversation.

"First of all, I must tell you, Mary," Ruth began, "that you may not think me more wicked than I am, that I would never have let Captain Mervyn suffer the penalty of another's crime. Against the wish, almost in the face of the orders of the doctor, I remained in court all through the trial, holding in my hand the proof of Captain Mervyn's innocence, and had the verdict been 'guilty' I was ready to rush forward and prove that he was innocent. I do not think that all that you suffered when you were in the hands of the Kaffirs was worse than I suffered then. I saw before me the uproar in court: the eyes that would be all fixed upon me; the way that the judge and the counsel would blame me for having so long kept silence; the reproach that I should meet with when I returned home; the shame of my dear old father; the way in which every soul in the village would turn against me; but I would have dared it all rather than that one man should suffer for the sin of another. And now, having told you this first, so that you should not think too hardly of me, I will tell you all."

Then Ruth told her of her girlish love for George Forester; how she had clung to him through evil report, and in spite of the wishes of her father and mother, but how at last the incident of the affray with the gamekeepers had opened her eyes to the fact that he was altogether reckless and wild, and that she could never trust her happiness to him. She told how Margaret Carne had spoken to her about it, and how she had promised she would give him up; then she told of that meeting on the road on the way to church; his passionate anger against herself; the threats he had uttered against Miss Carne for her interference, and the way in which he had assaulted her.

"I firmly believe," Ruth said, "he would have murdered me had he not heard people coming along the road." Then she told how she found the open knife stained with blood at Margaret Carne's bedside, and how she had hidden it. "I did not do it because I loved him still, Mary," she said. "My love seemed to have been killed. I had given him up before, and the attack he made upon me had shown me clearly how violent he was, and what an escape I had had; but I had loved him as a boy, and it was the remembrance of my girlish love, and not any love I then had, that sealed my lips; but even this would not have silenced me, I think, had it not been for the sake of his father. The old man had always been very, very kind to me, and the disgrace of his son being found guilty of this crime would have killed him. I can say, honestly, it was this that chiefly influenced me in deciding to shield him. As to Captain Mervyn, I was, as I told you, determined that though I would keep silent if he were acquitted, I would save him if he were found guilty. I never thought for a moment that acquittal would not clear him. It seemed to me that the trouble that had fallen on him was thoroughly deserved for the way in which he had spoken to Miss Carne; but I thought when he was acquitted he would take his place in his regiment again, and be none the worse for what had happened. It was only when I found that he had left the regiment, and when Mrs. Mervyn and her daughters shut up the house and went to live far away, that I began to trouble much. I saw now how wicked I had been, though I would never quite own it even to myself. I would have told then, but I did not know who to tell it to, or what good it could do if told. Mr. Forester was dead now, and the truth could not hurt him. George Forester had gone away, and would never come back; you know they found a verdict of wilful murder against him for killing the keeper. Somehow it seemed too late either to do good or harm. Every one had gone. Why should I say anything, and bring grief and trouble on my father and mother, and make the whole valley despise me? It has been dreadful," she said, wanly. "You cannot tell how dreadful. Ever since you came here and tried to make a friend of me, I have been fighting a battle with myself. It was not right that you should like me—it was not right that any one should like me—and I felt at last that I must tell you; you first, and then every one. Now after what you have told me it will not be so hard. Of course I shall suffer, and my father will suffer; but it will do good and make you and Captain Mervyn happy for the truth to be known, and so I shall be able to brave it all much better than I should otherwise have done. Who shall I go to first?"

"I cannot tell you, Ruth. I must speak to my father, and he will think it over, and perhaps he will write and ask Ronald how he would like it done. There is no great hurry, for he cannot come home anyhow till the war is finished, and it may last for months yet."

"Well, I am ready to go anywhere and to tell every one when you like," Ruth said. "Do not look so pitiful, Mary. I am sure I shall be much happier, whatever happens, even if they put me in prison, now that I have made up my mind to do what is right."

"There is no fear of that, I think, Ruth. They never asked you whether you had found anything; and though you certainly hid the truth, you did not absolutely give false evidence."

"It was all wrong and wicked," Ruth said, "and it will be quite right if they punish me; but that would be nothing to what I have suffered lately. I should feel happier in prison with this weight off my mind. But can you forgive me, Mary? Can you forgive me causing such misery to Captain Mervyn, and such unhappiness to you?"

"You need not be afraid about that," Mary said, laying her hand assuringly on Ruth's shoulder. "Why, child, you have been a benefactor to us both! If you had told all about it at first, Ronald would never have gone out to the Cape; father and I would have been killed in the first attack; and if we had not been, I should have been tortured to death in the Amatolas; and, last of all, we should never have seen and loved each other. Whatever troubles you may have to bear, do not reckon Ronald's displeasure and mine among them. I shall have cause to thank you all the days of my life, and I hope Ronald will have cause to do so too. Kiss me, Ruth; you have made me the happiest woman in the world, and I would give a great deal to be able to set this right without your having to put yourself forward in it."

Ruth was crying now, but they were not tears of unhappiness. They talked for some time longer, sitting hand in hand; and then, as Mr. Armstrong's step was heard coming up to the cottage, Ruth seized her hat and shawl.

"I dare not see him," she said; "he may not look at it as you do."

"Yes, he will," Mary said. "You don't know my father; he is one of the tenderest hearted of men." But Ruth darted out just as the door opened.

"What is it?" Mr. Armstrong asked in surprise. "Ruth Powlett nearly knocked me down in the passage, and rushed off without even the ordinary decency of apologising."

"Ruth has told me everything, father. We can clear Ronald Mervyn as soon as we like." And Mary Armstrong threw her arms round her father's neck.

"I thank God for that, Mary. I felt it would come sooner or later, but I had hardly hoped that it would come so soon. I am thankful, indeed, my child; how did it all come about?"

Mary repeated the story Ruth Powlett told her.

"Yes, there's no doubt about it this time," her father said. "As you say, there could be no mistake about the knife, because she had given it to him herself, and had had his initials engraved upon it at Plymouth. I don't think any reasonable man could have a doubt that the scoundrel did it; and now, my dear, what is to be done next?"

"Ah, that is for you to decide. I think Ronald ought to be consulted."

"Oh, you think that?" Mr. Armstrong said, quickly. "You think he knows a great deal better what ought to be done than I do?"

"No, I don't exactly mean that, father; but I think one would like to know how he would wish it to be done before we do anything. There is no particular hurry, you know, when he once knows that it is all going to be set right."

"No, beyond the fact that he would naturally like to get rid of this thing hanging over him as soon as he can. Now, my idea is that the girl ought to go at once to a magistrate and make an affidavit, and hand over this knife to him. I don't know how the matter is to be re-opened, because Ronald Mervyn has been acquitted, and the other man is goodness knows where."

"Well, father, there will be time enough to think over it, but I do think we had better tell Ronald first."

"Very well, my dear, as you generally have your own way, I suppose we shall finally settle on that, whether we agree now or three days hence. By the way, I have got a letter in my pocket for you from him. The Cape mail touched at Plymouth yesterday."

"Why did you not tell me of it before, father?" the girl said, reproachfully.

"Well, my dear, your news is so infinitely more important, that I own I forgot all about the letter. Besides, as this is the fourth that you have had since you have been here, it is not of such extreme importance."

But Mary was reading the letter and paid no attention to what her father was saying. Presently she gave a sudden exclamation.

"What is it, my dear; has he changed his mind and married a Kaffir woman? If so, we need not trouble any more about the affair."

"No, papa; it is serious—quite serious."

"Well, my dear, that would be serious; at least I should have thought you would consider it so."

"No, father; but really this is extraordinary. What do you think he says?"

"It is of no use my thinking about it, Mary," Mr. Armstrong said, resignedly, "especially as I suppose you are going to tell me. I have made one suggestion, and it seems that it is incorrect."

"This is what he says, father: 'You know that I told you a trooper in my company recognised me. I fancied I knew the man's face, but could not recall where I had seen it. The other day it suddenly flashed upon me; he is the son of a little farmer upon my cousin's estate, a man by the name of Forester. I often saw him when he was a young fellow, for I was fond of fishing, and I can remember him as a boy who was generally fishing down in the mill-stream. I fancy he rather went to grief afterwards, and have some idea he was mixed up in a poaching business in the Carne woods. So I think he must have left the country about that time. Curious, isn't it, his running against me here? However, it cannot be helped. I suppose it will all come out, sooner or later, for he has been in the guardroom several times for drunkenness, and one of these times he will be sure to blurt it out.'"

"Isn't that extraordinary, father?"

"It is certainly an extraordinary coincidence, Mary, that these two men—the murderer of Miss Carne and the man who has suffered for that murder should be out there together. This complicates matters a good deal."

"It does, father. There can be no doubt of what is to be done now."

"Well, now I quite come round on your side, Mary; nothing should be done until Mervyn knows all about it, and can let us know what his views are. I should not think that he could have this man arrested out there merely on his unsupported accusation, and I should imagine that he will want an official copy of Ruth Powlett's affidavit, and perhaps a warrant sent out from England, before he can get him arrested. Anyhow, we must go cautiously to work. When Ruth Powlett speaks, it will make a great stir here, and this Forester may have some correspondent here who would write and tell him what has happened, and then he might make a bolt of it before Ronald can get the law at work and lay hold of him."

"I should rather hope, for Ruth's sake, that he would do so, father. She is ready to make her confession and to bear all the talk it will make and the blame that will fall upon her; but it would be a great trial to her to have the man she once loved brought over and hung upon her evidence."

"So it would, Mary, so it would; but, on the other hand, it can be only by his trial and execution that Mervyn's innocence can be absolutely proved to the satisfaction of every one. It is a grave question altogether, Mary, and at any rate we will wait. Tell Mervyn he has all the facts before him, and must decide what is to be done. Besides, my dear, I think it will be only fair that Ruth should know that we are in a position to lay hands on this Forester before she makes the confession."

"I think so too, father. Yes, she certainly ought to be told; but I am sure that now she has made up her mind to confess she will not draw back. Still, of course, it would be very painful for her. We need not tell her at present; I will write a long letter to Ronald and tell him all the ins and outs of it, and then we can wait quietly until we hear from him."

"You need not have said that you will write a long letter, Mary," Mr. Armstrong said, drily, "considering that each time the mail has gone out I have seen nothing of you for twenty-four hours previously, and that I have reason to believe that an extra mail cart has had each time to be put on to carry the correspondence."

"It's all very well to laugh, father," Mary said, a little indignantly, "but you know that he is having fights almost every day with the Kaffirs, and only has our letters to look forward to, telling him how we are getting on and——and ——"

"And how we love him, Mary, and how we dream of him, etc., etc."

Mary laughed.

"Never mind what I put in my letters, father, as long as he is satisfied with them."

"I don't, my dear. My only fear is that he will come back wearing spectacles, for I should say that it would ruin any human eyes to have to wade through the reams of feminine handwriting you send to him. If he is the sensible fellow I give him credit for, he only reads the first three words, which are, I suppose, 'my darling Ronald' and the last four, which I also suppose are 'your ever loving Mary.'"

The colour flooded Mary Armstrong's cheeks.

"You have no right even to guess at my letters, father, and I have no doubt that whether they are long or short, he reads them through a dozen times."

"Poor fellow, poor fellow!" Mr. Armstrong said, pityingly. "Nevertheless, my dear, important as all these matters are, I do not know why I should be compelled to fast. I came in an hour ago, expecting to find tea ready, and there are no signs of it visible. I shall have to follow the example of the villagers when their wives fail to get their meals ready, and go down to the 'Carne's Arms' for it."

"You shall have it in five minutes, father," Mary Armstrong said, running out. "Men are so dreadfully material that whatever happens their appetite must be attended to just as usual."

And so three days afterwards a full account of all that Ruth Powlett had said, and of the circumstances of the case, was despatched to "Sergeant Blunt, Cape Mounted Rifles, Kaffirland."

CHAPTER XVIII.

GEORGE FORESTER'S DEATH.

Ronald Mervyn led so active a life for some months after the departure of Mr. Armstrong and his daughter, that he had little time to spend in thought, and it was only by seizing odd minutes between intervals of work that he could manage to send home a budget at all proportionate in size to that which he regularly received. When the courier came up with the English mails there had been stern fighting, for although the British force was raised by the arrival of reinforcements from India and England to over 5,000 men, with several batteries of artillery, it was with the greatest difficulty that it gradually won its way into the Kaffir stronghold. Several times the troops were so hardly pressed by the enemy that they could scarcely claim a victory, and a large number of officers and men fell. The Cape Mounted Rifles formed part of every expedition into the Amatolas, and had their full share of fighting. Ronald had several times distinguished himself, especially in the fight in the Water Kloof Valley, when Colonel Fordyce, of the 74th, and Carey and Gordon, two officers of the same regiment, were killed, together with several of their men, while attacking the enemy in the bush. He was aware now that his secret was known to the men. He had fancied that searching and inquisitive glances were directed towards him, and that there was a change in the demeanour of certain men of his troop, these being without exception the idlest and worst soldiers. It was Sergeant Menzies who first spoke to him on the subject. It was after a hard day's march when, having picketed their horses and eaten their hastily cooked rations, the two non-commissioned officers lit their pipes and sat down together at a short distance from the fire.

"I have been wanting to speak to you, lad, for the last day or two. There is a story gaining ground through the troop that, whether it is true or whether it is false, you ought to know."

"I guessed as much, Menzies," Ronald said. "I think I know what the story is, and who is the man who has spread it. It is that I bore another name in England."

"Yes, that's partly it, lad. I hear that you are rightly Captain Mervyn."

"Yes, that's it, Menzies, and that I was tried and acquitted for murder in England."

"That's the story, my lad. Of course, it makes no difference to us who you are, or what they say you have done. We who know you would not believe you to have committed a murder, much less the murder of a woman, if all the juries in the world had said you had. Still I thought I would let you know that the story is going about, so that you might not be taken aback if you heard it suddenly. Of course, it's no disgrace to be tried for murder if you are found innocent; it only shows that some fools have made a mistake, and been proved to be wrong. Still, as it has been talked about, you ought to know it. There is a lot of feeling in the regiment about it now, and the fellow who told the story has had a rough time of it, and there's many a one would put a bullet into him if he had the chance. What they say is, whether you are Captain Mervyn or not is nothing to anybody but yourself. If you were tried and acquitted for this affair it ought to have dropped and nothing more been said about it, and they hold that anyhow a man belonging to the corps ought to have held his tongue about anything he knew against another who is such a credit to us."

"The man might have held his tongue, perhaps," Ronald said, quietly; "but I never expected that he would do so. The fellow comes from my neighbourhood, and bore a bad character. A man who has shot a gamekeeper would be pretty sure to tell anything he knew to the disadvantage of any one of superior rank to himself. Well, sergeant, you can only tell any one who asks you about it that you have questioned me, and that I admitted at once that the story was true—that I was Captain Mervyn, and that I was tried for murder and acquitted. Some day I hope my innocence may be more thoroughly proved than it was on the day I was acquitted. I daresay he has told the whole of the facts, and I admit them freely."

"Well, lad, I am glad you have spoken. Of course it will make no difference, except perhaps to a few men who would be better out of the corps than in it; and they know too well what the temper of the men is to venture to show it. I can understand now why you didn't take a commission. I have often wondered over it, for it seemed to me that it was just the thing you would have liked. But I see that till this thing was cleared up you naturally wouldn't like it. Well, I am heartily sorry for the business, if you don't mind my saying so. I have always been sure you were an officer before you joined us, and wondered how it was that you left the army. You must have had a sore time of it. I am sorry for you from my heart."

Ronald sat quiet for some time thinking after Sergeant Menzies left him, then rose and walked towards the fire where the officers were sitting.

"Can I speak with you a few minutes, Captain Twentyman?" he said. The officer at once rose.

"Anything wrong in the troop, sergeant?"

"No, sir; there is nothing the matter with the troop, it is some business of my own. May I ask if you have heard anything about me, Captain Twentyman?"

"Heard anything! In what way do you mean, sergeant?"

"Well, sir, as to my private history."

"No," the officer said, somewhat puzzled.

"Well, sir, the thing has got about among the men. There is one of them knew me at home, and he has told the others. Now that it is known to the men, sooner or later it will be known to the officers, and therefore I thought it better to come and tell you myself, as captain of my troop."

"It can be nothing discreditable, I am quite sure, sergeant," the officer said, kindly.

"Well, sir, it is discreditable; that is to say, I lie under a heavy charge, from which I am unable to clear myself. I have been tried for it and found not guilty, but I am sure that if I had been before a Scotch jury the verdict would have been not proven, and I left the court acquitted indeed, but a disgraced and ruined man."

"What was the charge?"

"The charge was murder," Ronald said, quietly. Captain Twentyman started, but replied:

"Ridiculous. No one who knew you could have thought you guilty for a moment."

"I think that none who knew me intimately believed in my guilt, but I am sure that most people who did not so know me believed me guilty. I daresay you saw the case in the papers. My real name, Captain Twentyman, is Ronald Mervyn, and I was captain in the Borderers. I was tried for the murder of my cousin, Margaret Carne."

"Good Heavens! Is it possible?" Captain Twentyman exclaimed. "Of course I remember the case perfectly. We saw it in the English papers somewhere about a year ago, and it was a general matter of conversation, owing, of course, to your being in the army. I didn't know what to think of it then, but now I know you, the idea of your murdering a woman seems perfectly ridiculous. Well, is there anything you would wish me to do!"

"No, sir; I only thought you ought to be told. I leave it with you to mention it to others or not. Perhaps you will think it best to say nothing until the story gets about. Then you can say you are aware of it."

"Yes, I think that would be the best," Captain Twentyman said, after thinking it over. "I remember that I thought when I read the account of that trial that you were either one of the most lucky or one of the most unfortunate men in the world. I see now that it was the latter."

A few days later, an hour or two before the column was about to march, a flag hoisted at the post-office tent told the camp that the mail had arrived, and orderlies from each corps at once hurried there. As they brought the bags out they were emptied on the ground. Some of the sergeants set to work to sort the letters, while the officers stood round and picked out their own as they lay on the grass.

"Here, Blunt, here's one for you," Sergeant Menzies said, when Ronald came up.

Ronald took the letter, and sauntering away a short distance, threw himself on the ground and opened it. After reading the first line or two he leaped to his feet again, and took a few steps up and down, with his breath coming fast, and his hands twitching. Then he stood suddenly still, took off his cap, bent his head, put his hand over his eyes, and stood for a few minutes without moving. When he put his cap on again his face was wet with tears, his hands were trembling so that when he took the letter again he could scarce read it. A sudden exclamation broke from him as he came upon the name of Forester. The letter was so long that the trumpets were sounding by the time he had finished. He folded it and put it in his tunic, and then strode back with head erect to the spot where the men of his troop were saddling their horses. As he passed on among them a sudden impulse seized him, and he stopped before one of the men and touched him on the shoulder.

"You villain," he said, "you have been accusing me of murder. You are a murderer yourself."

The man's face paled suddenly.

"I know you, George Forester," Ronald went on, "and I know that you are guilty. You have to thank the woman who once loved you that I do not at once hand you over to the provost-marshal to be sent to England for trial, but for her sake I will let you escape. Make a confession and sign it, and then go your way where you will, and no search shall be made for you; if you do not, to-morrow you shall be in the hands of the police."

"There is no evidence against me more than against another," the man said, sullenly.

"No evidence, you villain?" Ronald said. "Your knife—the knife with your initials on it—covered with blood, was found by the body."

The man staggered as if struck.

"I knew I had lost it," he said, as if to himself, "but I didn't know I dropped it there."

At this moment the bugle sounded.

"I will give you until to-morrow morning to think about it," and Ronald ran off to mount his horse, which he had saddled before going for his letter.

Sergeant Menzies caught sight of his comrade's face as he sprang into the saddle.

"Eh, man," he said, "what's come to you? You have good news, haven't you, of some kind? Your face is transfigured, man!"

"The best," Ronald said, holding out his hand to his comrade. "I am proved to be innocent."

Menzies gave him a firm grip of the hand, and then each took his place in the ranks. There was desperate fighting that day with the Kaffirs. The Cape Mounted Rifles, while scouting ahead of the infantry in the bush, were suddenly attacked by an immense body of Kaffirs. Muskets cracked, and assegais flew in showers. Several of the men dropped, and discharging their rifles, the troopers fell back towards the infantry. As they retreated, Ronald looked back. One of the men of his troop, whose horse had been shot under him, had been overtaken by the enemy, and was surrounded by a score of Kaffirs. His cap was off, and Ronald caught sight of his face. He gave a shout, and in an instant had turned his horse and dashed towards the group.

"Come back, man, come back!" Captain Twentyman shouted. "It's madness!"

But Ronald did not hear him. The man whose confession could alone absolutely clear him was in the hands of the Kaffirs, and must be saved at any cost. A moment later he was in the midst of the natives, emptying his revolvers among them. Forester had sunk on one knee as Ronald, having emptied one of his revolvers, hurled it in the face of a Kaffir; leaning over, he caught Forester by the collar, and, with a mighty effort, lifted and threw him across the saddle in front of him, then bending over him, he spurred his horse through the natives. Just at this moment Captain Twentyman and a score of the men rode up at full speed, drove the Kaffirs back for an instant, and enabled Ronald to rejoin his lines. Three assegais had struck him, and he reeled in the saddle as, amidst the cheers of his companions, he rode up.

"One of you take the wounded man in front of you," Lieutenant Daniels said, "and carry him to the rear. Thompson, do you jump up behind Sergeant Blunt, and support him. There is no time to be lost. Quick, man, these fellows are coming on like furies."

The exchange was made in half a minute; one of the men took George Forester before him, another sprang up behind Ronald and held him in his saddle with one hand, while he took the reins in the other. Then they rode fast to the rear, just as the leading battalion of infantry came up at a run and opened fire on the Kaffirs, who, with wild yells, were pressing on the rear of the cavalry.

When Ronald recovered his senses he was lying in the ambulance waggon, and the surgeon was dressing his wounds.

"That's right, sergeant," he said, cheeringly, "I think you will do. You have three nasty wounds, but by good luck I don't think any of them are vital."

"How is Forester?" Ronald asked.

"Forester?" the surgeon repeated in surprise, "Whom do you mean, Blunt?"

"I mean Jim Smith, sir; his real name was Forester."

"There is nothing to be done for him," the surgeon said. "Nothing can save him; he is riddled with spears."

"Is he conscious?" Ronald asked.

"No, not at present."

"Will he become conscious before he dies, sir?"

"I don't know," the surgeon replied, somewhat puzzled at Ronald's question. "He may be, but I cannot say."

"It is everything to me, sir," Ronald said. "I have been accused of a great crime of which he is the author. He can clear me if he will. All my future life depends upon his speaking."

"Then I hope he may be able to speak, Blunt, but at present I can't say whether he will recover consciousness or not. He is in the waggon here, and I will let you know directly if there is any change."

Ronald lay quiet, listening to the firing that gradually became more distant, showing that the infantry were driving the Kaffirs back into the bush. Wounded men were brought in fast, and the surgeon and his assistant were fully occupied. The waggon was halted now, and at Ronald's request the stretchers upon which he and Forester were lying were taken out and laid on the grass under the shade of a tree.

Towards evening, the surgeon, having finished his pressing work, came to them. He felt George Forester's pulse.

"He is sinking fast," he said, in reply to Ronald's anxious look. "But I will see what I can do."

He poured some brandy between George Forester's lips, and held a bottle of ammonia to his nose. Presently there was a deep sigh, and then Forester opened his eyes. For a minute he looked round vaguely, and then his eye fell upon Ronald.

"So you got me out of the hands of the Kaffirs, Captain Mervyn," he said, in a faint voice. "I caught sight of you among them as I went down. I know they have done for me, but I would rather be buried whole than hacked into pieces."

"I did my best for you, Forester," Mervyn said. "I am sorry I was not up a minute sooner. Now, Forester, you see I have been hit pretty hard, too; will you do one thing for me? I want you to confess about what I was speaking to you: it will make all the difference to other people."

"I may as well tell the truth as not," Forester said; "though I don't see how it makes much difference."

"Doctor," Ronald said, "could you kindly send and ask Captain Twentyman and Lieutenant Daniels to come here at once? I want them to hear."

George Forester's eyes were closed, and he was breathing faintly when the two officers, who had ridden up a few minutes before with their corps, came up to the spot.

The surgeon again gave the wounded man some strong cordial.

"Will you write down what he says?" Ronald asked Captain Twentyman.

The latter took out a note-book and pencil.

"I make this confession," Forester said, faintly, "at the request of Captain Mervyn, who risked his life in getting me out from among the Kaffirs. My real name is George Forester, and at home I live near Carnesford, in Devonshire. I was one night poaching in Mr. Carne's woods, with some men from Dareport, when we came upon the keepers. There was a fight. One of the keepers knocked my gun out of my hand, and as he raised his stick to knock me on the head, I whipped out my knife, opened it, and stuck it into him. I didn't mean to kill him, it was just done in a moment; but he died from it. We ran away. Afterwards I found that I had lost my knife. I suppose I dropped it. That's all I have to say."

"Not all, Forester, not all," said Ronald, who had listened with impatience to the slowly-uttered words of the wounded man; "not all. It isn't that, but about the murder of Miss Carne I want you to tell."

"The murder of Miss Carne," George Forester repeated, slowly. "I know

227

nothing about that. She made Ruth break it off with me, and I nearly killed Ruth, and would have killed her if I had had the chance, but I never had. I was glad when I heard she was killed, but I don't know who did it."

"But your knife was found by her body," Ronald said. "You must have done it, Forester."

"Murdered Miss Carne!" the man said, half raising himself on his elbow in surprise. "Never. I swear I had nothing to do with it."

A rush of blood poured from his mouth, for one of the spears had pierced his lung, and a moment later George Forester fell back dead. The disappointment and revulsion of feeling were too great for Ronald Mervyn, and he fainted. When he recovered, the surgeon was leaning over him.

George Forester's death.

"You mustn't talk, lad; you must keep yourself quite quiet, or we shall have fever setting in, and all sorts of trouble."

Ronald closed his eyes, and lay back quietly. How could this be? He thought of Mary Armstrong's letter, of the chain of proofs that had accumulated against George Forester. They seemed absolutely convincing, and yet there was no doubting the ring of truth in the last words of the dying man. His surprise at the accusation was genuine; his assertion of his innocence absolutely convincing; he had no motive for lying; he was dying, and he knew it. Besides, the thing had come so suddenly upon him there could have been no time for him to frame a lie, even if he had been in a mental condition to do so. Whoever killed Margaret Carne, Ronald Mervyn was at once convinced that it was not George Forester. There he lay, thinking for hours over the disappointment that the news would be to Mary Armstrong, and how it seemed more unlikely than ever that the mystery would ever be cleared up now. Gradually his thoughts became more vague, until at last he fell asleep.

Upon the following day the wounded were sent down under an escort to King Williamstown, and there for a month Ronald Mervyn lay in hospital. He had written a few lines to Mary Armstrong, saying that he had been wounded, but not dangerously, and that she need not be anxious about him any more, for the Kaffirs were now almost driven from their last stronghold, and that the fighting would almost certainly be over before he was fit to mount his horse again. "George Forester is dead," he said. "He was mortally wounded when fighting bravely against the Kaffirs. I fear, dear, that your ideas about him were mistaken, and that he, like myself, has been the victim of circumstantial evidence; but I will tell you more about this when I write to you next."

While lying there, Ronald thought over the evidence that had been collected against George Forester, and debated with himself whether it should be published, as Mary had proposed. It would, doubtless, be accepted by the world as proof of Forester's guilt and of his own innocence; and even the fact that the man, when dying, had denied it, would weigh for very little with the public, for men proved indisputably to be guilty often go to the scaffold asserting their innocence to the last. But would it be right to throw this crime upon the dead man when he was sure that he was innocent? For Ronald did not doubt for a moment the truth of the denial. Had he a right, even for the sake of Mary's happiness and his own, to charge the memory of the dead man with the burden of this foul crime? Ronald felt that it could not be. The temptation was strong, but he fought long against it, and at last his mind was made up.

"No," he said at last, "I will not do it. George Forester was no doubt a bad man, but he was not so bad as this. It would be worse to charge his memory with it than to accuse him if he were alive. In the one case he might clear himself; in the other he cannot. I cannot clear my name by fouling that of a dead man."

And so Ronald at last sat down to write a long letter to Mary Armstrong, telling her the whole circumstances; the joy with which he received her news; his conversation with George Forester, which seemed wholly to confirm her views; the pang of agony he had felt when he saw the man who he believed could alone clear him, in the hands of the Kaffirs, and his desperate charge to rescue him; and then he gave the words of the confession, and expressed his absolute conviction that the dying man had spoken the truth, and that he was really innocent of Margaret Carne's murder.

He then discussed the question of still publishing Ruth Powlett's statement, giving first the cause of George Forester's enmity against Margaret Carne, and the threat he had uttered, and then the discovery of the knife.

"I fear you will be ashamed of me, Mary, when I tell you that, for a time, I almost yielded to the temptation of clearing myself at his expense. But you must make allowance for the strength of the temptation: on the one side was the thought of my honour restored, and of you won; on the other, the thought that, now George Forester was dead, this could not harm him. But, of course, I finally put the temptation aside; honour purchased at the expense of a dead man's reputation would be dishonour indeed. Now I can face disgrace, because I know I am innocent. I could not bear honour when I knew that I had done a dishonourable action; and I know that I should utterly forfeit your love and esteem did I do so. I can look you straight in the face now; I could never look you straight in the face then. Do not grieve too much over the disappointment. We are now only as we were when I said good-bye to you. I had no hope then that you would ever succeed in clearing me, and I have no hope now. I have not got up my strength again yet, and am therefore perhaps just at present a little more disposed to repine over the disappointment than I ought to do; but this will wear off when I get in the saddle again. There will, I think, be no more fighting—at any rate with the Sandilli Kaffirs—for we hear this morning that they have sent in to beg for peace, and I am certain we shall be glad enough to grant it, for we have not much to boast about in the campaign. Of course they will have to pay a very heavy fine in cattle, and will have to move across to the other side of the Kei. Equally of course there will be trouble again with them after a time, when the memory of their losses has somewhat abated. I fancy a portion of our force will march against the Basutos, whose attitude has lately been very hostile; but now that the Gaikas have given in, and we are free to use our whole force against them, it is scarcely probable they will venture to try conclusions with us. If they settle down peaceably I shall probably apply for my discharge, and perhaps go in for farming, or carry out my first idea of joining a party of traders going up the country, and getting some shooting among the big game.

"I know that, disappointed as you will be with the news contained in this letter, it will be a pleasure to you to tell the girl you have made your friend, that after all the man she once loved is innocent of this terrible crime. She must have suffered horribly while she was hiding what she thought was the most important part of the evidence; now she will see that she has really done no harm; and as you seem to be really fond of her, it will, I am sure, be a great pleasure to you to be able to restore her peace of mind in both these respects. I should think now that you and your father will not remain any longer at Carnesford, where neither of you has any fitting society of any sort, but will go and settle somewhere in your proper position. I would much rather that you did, for now it seems absolutely certain that nothing further is to be learned, it would trouble me to think of you wasting your lives at Carnesford.

"You said in your last letter that the discovery you had made had brought you four years nearer to happiness, but I have never said a word to admit that I should change my mind at the end of the five years that your father spoke of. Still, I don't know, Mary. I think my position is stronger by a great deal than it was six months ago. I told my captain who I was, and all the other officers now know. Most of them came up and spoke very kindly to me before I started on my way down here, and I am sure that when I leave the corps they will give me a testimonial, saying that they are convinced by my behaviour while in the corps that I could not have been guilty of this crime. I own that I myself am less sensitive on the subject than I was. One has no time to be morbid while leading such a life as I have been for the last nine months. Perhaps——but I will not say any more now. But I think somehow, that, at the end of the five years, I shall leave the decision in your hands. It has taken me two or three days to write this letter, for I am not strong enough to stick to it for more than half an hour at a time; but as the post goes out this afternoon I must close it now. We have been expecting a mail from England for some days. It is considerably overdue, and I need not say how I am longing for another letter from you. I hear the regiment will be back from the front to-night; men and horses want a few days' rest before starting on this long march to Basutoland. I shall be very glad to see them back again. Of course, the invalids who, like myself, are somewhat pulled down by their wounds, are disgusted at being kept here. The weather is frightfully hot, and even in our shirt sleeves we shall be hardly able to enjoy Christmas day."

The Cape Rifles arrived at King Williamstown an hour after the post had left, and in the evening the colonel and several of the officers paid a visit to the hospital to see how their wounded were getting on. Ronald, who was sitting reading by his bedside, and the other invalids who were strong enough to be on their feet, at once got up and stood at attention. Stopping and speaking a few words to each of the men of his own corps, the colonel came on. "Mervyn," he said, as he and the officers came up to Ronald, "I want to shake your hand. I have heard your story from Captain Twentyman, and I wish to tell you, in my own name and in that of the other officers of the regiment, that we are sure you have been the victim of some horrible mistake. All of us are absolutely convinced that a man who has shown such extreme gallantry as you have, and whose conduct has been so excellent from the day he joined, is wholly incapable of such a crime as that with which you were charged. You were, of course, acquitted, but at the same time I think that it cannot but be a satisfaction for you to know that you have won the esteem of your officers and your comrades, and that in their eyes you are free from the slightest taint of that black business. Give me your hand."

Ronald was unable to speak; the colonel and all the officers shook him by the hand, and the former said: "I must have another long talk with you when we get back from the Basuto business. I have mentioned you very strongly in regimental orders upon two occasions for extreme gallantry, and I cannot but think that it would do you some good in the eyes of the public were a letter signed by me to appear in the English papers, saying that the Sergeant Blunt of my regiment, who has so signally distinguished himself, is really Captain Mervyn, who in my opinion and that of my officers is a cruelly injured man. But we can talk over that when I see you again."

After the officer left the room, Ronald Mervyn sat for some time with his face buried in his hands. The colonel's words had greatly moved him. Surely such a letter as that which Colonel Somerset had proposed to write would do much to clear him. He should never think of taking his own name again or re-entering any society in which he would be likely to be recognised, but with such a testimonial as that in his favour he might hope in some quiet place to live down the past, and should he again be recognised, could still hold up his head with such an honourable record as this to produce in his favour. Then his thoughts went back to England. What would Mary and her father say when they read such a letter in the paper? It would be no proof of his innocence, yet he felt sure that Mary would insist upon regarding it as such, and would hold that he had no right to keep her waiting for another four years. Indeed he acknowledged to himself that if she did so he would have no right to refuse any longer to permit her to be mistress of her own fate.

CHAPTER XIX.

THE FIRE AT CARNE'S HOLD.

Things went on quietly with Mr. Armstrong and his daughter after the latter had despatched her letter, saying that Ruth Powlett was ready to confess the truth respecting George Forester. The excitement of following up the clue was over, and there was nothing to do until they heard from Ronald as to how he wished them to proceed. So one morning Mr. Armstrong came down and told Mary to pack up at once and start with him at twelve o'clock for London. "We are getting like two owls, and must wake ourselves up a bit." Mary ran down to the mill to say good-bye to Ruth, and tell her that she and her father had to go to London for a short time. They were ready by the time named, for there was little packing to do, and at twelve o'clock the trap from the "Carne's Arms" came up to the door, and took them to the station. A month was spent in London, sight-seeing. By the end of that time both had had enough of theatres and exhibitions, and returned to Carnesford.

"Well, what is the news, neighbours?" Mr. Armstrong asked, as he entered the snuggery on the evening of his return.

"There is not much news here," Jacob Carey said; "there never is much news to speak of in Carnesford; but they say things are not going on well up at The Hold."

"In what way, Mr. Carey?"

"Well, for some time there has been a talk that the Squire was getting strange in his ways. He was never bright and cheerful like Miss Margaret, but always seemed to be a-thinking, and as often as not when he rode through here, would take no more notice of you when he passed than if you hadn't been there. He was always wonderful fond of books they say, and when a man takes to books, I don't think he is much good for anything else; but ever since Miss Margaret's death, he has been queerer than before, and they said he had a way of walking about the house all hours of the night. So it went on until just lately. Now it seems he is worse than ever. They can hear him talking to himself, and laughing in a way as would make you creep. Folks say as the curse of the Carnes has fallen on him bad, and that he is as mad as his grandfather was. The women have all left except the old cook, who has got a girl to stay with her. They lock the door at night, and they have got the men from the stable to sleep in the house unknown to the master. One day last week, when Mr. Carne was out for the day, old Hester came down and saw the parson, and he sent for Dr. Arrowsmith, and they had a quiet talk over it. You see it is a mighty awkward thing to meddle with. Mr. Carne has got no relations so far as is known, except Mrs. Mervyn's daughters, who are away living, I hear, at Hastings, and Captain Mervyn, who is God knows where. Of course, he is the heir, if the Squire doesn't marry and have children, and if he were here it would be his business to interfere and have the Squire looked after or shut up if needs be; but there don't seem any one to take the matter up now. The doctor told Hester that he could do nothing without being called in and seeing for himself that Mr. Carne was out of his mind. The parson said the only thing she could do was to go to Mr. Volkes, the magistrate, and tell him she thought there was danger of murder if something wasn't done. Hester has got plenty of courage, and said she didn't think there was any danger to her, 'cause the Squire had known her from the time he had known anything."

"I don't know," Mr. Armstrong said. "Mad people are often more dangerous to those they care for than to strangers. Really, this is very serious, for from what you have told me, the madness of the Carnes is always of a dangerous kind. One thing is quite evident—Captain Mervyn ought to come back at once. There have been tragedies enough at Carne's Hold without another."

"Ay, and there will be," put in Reuben Claphurst, "as long as Carne's Hold stands; the curse of the Spanish woman rests upon it."

"What you say is right enough, Mr. Armstrong," Hiram Powlett agreed. "No doubt the Miss Mervyns know where their brother is, and could let him know; but would he come back again? I have always said as how we should never see Captain Mervyn back again in these parts until the matter of Miss Carne's death was cleared up."

Mr. Armstrong sat looking at the fire. "He must be got back," he said. "If what you say is true, and Mr. Carne's going off his head, he must be got back."

Hiram Powlett shook his head.

"He must come back," Mr. Armstrong repeated; "it's his duty, pleasant or unpleasant. It may be that he is on his way home now; but if not, it would hasten him. You look surprised, and no wonder; but I may now tell you, what I haven't thought it necessary to mention to you before—mind, you must promise to keep it to yourselves—I met Captain Mervyn out at the Cape, and made his acquaintance there. He was passing under another name, but we got to be friends, and he told me his story. I have written to him once or twice since, and I will write to him now and tell him that if he hasn't already started for home, it's his duty to do so. I suppose it was partly his talking to me about this place that made me come here to see it at first, and then I took to it."

The surprise of the others at finding that Mr. Armstrong knew Ronald was very great. "I wonder you didn't mention it before," Jacob Carey said, giving voice to the common feeling. "We have talked about him so often, and you never said a word to let us know you had met him."

"No, and never should have said a word but for this. You will understand that Captain Mervyn wouldn't want where he was living made a matter of talk; and though when he told me the story he did not know I was coming to Carnesford, and so didn't ask me not to mention it, I consider I was bound to him to say nothing about it. But now that I know he is urgently required here, I don't see there's occasion any longer to make a secret of the fact that he is out in South Africa."

"Yes, I understand, Mr. Armstrong," Hiram Powlett agreed. "Naturally, when he told you about himself, he did not ask it to be kept a secret, because he did not know you would meet any one that knowed him. But when you did meet such, you thought that it was right to say nothing about it, and I agree with you; but of course this matter of the Squire going queer in his mind makes all the difference, and I think, as you says, Captain Mervyn ought to be fetched home. When he has seen the Squire is properly taken care of, he can go away where he likes."

"That is so," Jacob Carey agreed. "Mervyn ought to know what is doing here, and if you can write and tell him that he is wanted you will be doing a good turn for the Squire as well as for him. And how was the captain looking, Mr. Armstrong?"

"He was looking very well when I first knew him," Mr. Armstrong replied; "but when I saw him last he had got hurt in a brush with the natives but it was nothing serious, and he was getting over it."

"The same set as attacked your farm, Mr. Armstrong, as you was telling us about?"

"I don't suppose it was the same party, because there were thousands of them scattered all over the colony, burning and plundering. Captain Mervyn had a narrow escape from them, and was lucky in getting out of it as well as he did."

"They said he was a good fighter," Jacob Carey put in. "The papers said as he had done some hard fighting with them Afghans, and got praised by his general."

"Yes, he's a fine fellow," Mr. Armstrong said, "and, I should say, as brave as a lion."

"No signs of the curse working in him?" Hiram Powlett asked, touching his forehead. "They made a lot of it at the trial about his being related to the Carnes, and about his being low in spirits sometimes; but I have seen him scores of times ride through the village when he was a young chap, and he always looked merry and good-tempered."

"No," Mr. Armstrong said, emphatically, "Ronald Mervyn's brain is as healthy and clear as that of any man in England. I am quite sure there is not the slightest touch of the family malady in him."

"Maybe not, maybe not," Reuben Claphurst said; "the curse is on The Hold, and he has nothing to do with The Hold yet. If anything happens to the Squire, and he comes to be its master, you will see it begin to work, if not in him, in his children."

"God forbid!" Mr. Armstrong said, so earnestly that his hearers were almost startled. "I don't much believe in curses, Mr. Claphurst, though, of course, I believe in insanity being in some instances hereditary; but, at the same time, if I were Ronald Mervyn and I inherited Carne's Hold, I would pull the place down stone by stone, and not leave a vestige of it standing. Why, to live in a house like that, in which so many tragedies have taken place, is enough in itself to turn a sane man into madness."

"That's just how I should feel," Hiram Powlett said. "Now a stranger who looked at The Hold would say what a pleasant, open-looking house it was; but when you took him inside, and told him what had happened there, it would be enough to give him the creeps. I believe it was being up there that was the beginning of my daughter's changing so. I never made a worse job of a thing than I did when I got her up there as Miss Carne's maid, and yet it was all for her good. And now, neighbours, it's my time to be off. It's a quarter to nine and that is five minutes later than usual."

Mr. Armstrong and Mary sat talking until nearly eleven about what he had heard about Mr. Carne. She had not been gone upstairs a minute when she ran down again from her bedroom, which was at the back of the house.

"Father, there is a light in the sky up at the top of the hill, just where Carne's Hold lies. I went to the window to draw down the blinds and it caught my eye at once."

Mr. Armstrong ran out into the road.

As Mary had said, there was a glare of light over the trees on the hill, rising and falling. "Sure enough it's a fire at The Hold," he said, as he ran in and caught up his hat. Then he hurried down the village, knocking at each door and shouting, "There is a fire at The Hold!"

Just as he reached the other end a man on horseback dashed down the hill, shouting "Fire!" It was one of the grooms at The Hold.

"Is it at the house?" Mr. Armstrong asked, as he drew up for a moment at the inn.

"Yes, it's bursting out from the lower windows; it has got a big hold. I am going to the station, to telegraph to Plymouth and Exeter for engines."

"How about those in the house?" Mr. Armstrong asked.

"Some of them got out by the back way, and we got some of them out by ladders. The others are seeing to that. They sent me off at once."

A minute or two later, men came clattering down the quiet street at a run, and some of them overtook Mr. Armstrong as he hurried up the hill.

"Is that you, Mr. Armstrong?" a voice asked behind him.

"Yes, it's me, Carey."

"I thought it was," the smith said. "I caught sight of your figure against the light up there in front. I couldn't help thinking, when you shouted at my door that there was a fire at The Hold, what we were talking about this evening, and your saying that if the place was yours you would pull it down stone by stone. But perhaps we may save it yet. We shall have a couple of score of men there in a few minutes."

"I fancy there is not much chance of that, Carey. I spoke to the groom as he rode through, and he tells me that the fire when he came away was bursting from several of the lower windows; so it has got a good hold, and they are not likely to have much water handy."

"No, that's true enough. There's a big well a hundred feet deep in the stable-yard, and a force pump, which takes two men to work. It supplied the house as well as the stables. That's the only water there will be, and that won't be much good," he added, as, on emerging from the wood, they suddenly caught sight of the house.

From the whole of the lower windows in front the flames were bursting out.

"It's travelled fast," the smith said. "The dining-room and drawing-room and library are all on fire."

"Yes, that's curious, too," Mr. Armstrong remarked. "One would have thought it would have mounted up to the next floor long before it travelled so far along on a level. Ah, it's going up to the floor above now."

As he spoke a spout of light flame suddenly appeared through the window over the front door.

"That's the staircase window, I suppose."

Two or three minutes' running took them up on to the lawn.

"I will go and lend a hand at those pumps," Jacob Carey said.

"It's not the slightest use," Mr. Armstrong replied. "You might as well try to blow out that fire with your breath as to put it out by throwing a few pails of water on it. Let us see that every one is out first; that's the main matter."

They joined a group of men and women, who were standing looking at the flames: they were the two women, the groom and gardener, and four or five men who had already come up from the village.

The gardener was speaking.

"It's no use to work at the pumps; there are only four or five pails. If it was only at one end we might prevent its spreading, but it's got hold all over."

"I can't make it out," the groom said. "One of the horses was sick, and I was down there giving him hot fomentations with my mate. I had been there perhaps an hour when I saw a light coming out of the drawing-room window, and I ran up shouting; and then I saw there was a light in the dining-room and library too. Then I ran round to the back of the house, and the housekeeper's room there was alight, too. I run in at the kitchen door and upstairs, and woke the gardeners and got them out. The place was so full of smoke, it was as much as we could do to get downstairs. Then we got a long ladder, and put it against Mrs. Wilson's window, and got her and the girl down. Then we came round this side, and I got up and broke a pane in Mr. Carne's window and shouted. I could not make him hear, so I broke another pane and unfastened the window and lifted it, and went in. I thought he must have been stifled in bed, for the smoke was as thick as possible, and I had to crawl to the bed. Well, master wasn't there. I felt about to see if he was on the floor, but I could find nothing of him; the door was open, and I expect he must have been woke up by the smoke, and went out to see what was the matter, and perhaps got choked by it. I know I was nearly choked myself by the time I got my head out of the window again."

"He may have got to the upper storey," Jacob Carey said. "We had best keep a look-out round the house, so as to be ready to put the ladder up at once if we see him. There is nothing else to do, is there, Mr. Armstrong? You are accustomed to all sorts of troubles, and may know best what we ought to do."

"I can't think of anything," Mr. Armstrong replied. "No, if he's not in his own room it seems hopeless to search for him. You see the flames have broken out from several windows of the first floor. My own idea is, from what you say as to the fire having spread into all the rooms on the ground floor when you

238

discovered it, that the poor gentleman must have set fire to the house himself in half-a-dozen places, and as likely as not may have been suffocated almost at once."

"I shouldn't wonder if that was it," the smith said. "It's not natural that the fire should have spread all over the lower part of the house in such a short time. You know what we were saying this evening. It's just the sort of trick for a madman to play."

The smith was interrupted by a sudden exclamation from those standing round, followed by a shout of "There he is!" A dormer window on the roof of the oldest part of the house opened, and a figure stepped out on to a low parapet that ran round the house.

"All right, sir, all right," Jacob Carey shouted out at the top of his voice; "we will have a ladder for you in no time," and he and a score of men ran to fetch the long ladder that was leaning against the side of the house.

It was soon lowered, brought round, and placed against the parapet close to where Reginald Carne was standing.

"Now then, sir," Jacob Carey shouted again, "it's all right. You can come down safe enough."

But Mr. Carne paid no attention to the shout; he was pacing up and down along the parapet and was tossing his arms about in a strange manner. Suddenly he turned, seized the ladder, and pushed it violently sideways along the parapet. Those below vainly tried to keep it steady.

"Look out!" the smith shouted, "leave go and clear out, or he will have it down on you."

The men holding the ladder dashed away from the foot, and the ladder fell with a crash upon the ground, while a peal of wild laughter broke out from above.

"The Squire has gone clean mad," Jacob Carey said to Mr. Armstrong, as he joined him; "either the fire has driven him mad, or, what is more likely, he went mad first and then lit the fire. However, we must save him if we can."

"Look there, Carey, if we lifted the ladder and put it up between that chimney and the window next to it, he can't slide it either one way or another, as he did before; and he certainly could not throw it backwards, if we plant the foot well away from the house."

"That's right enough," the smith agreed, "but if he won't come down, he won't."

"We must go up and make him, Carey. If you and I and a couple of strong men go up together, we ought to be able to master him. Of course, we must take up rope with us, and bind him and then lower him down the ladder."

"We might do that," the smith said; "but supposing the ladder catches fire?"

"The fire won't touch it at that point, Carey. You see, it will go up just between the rows of windows."

"So it will; anyhow, we might take up a long rope, if they have got one, so as to lower ourselves down if the ladder does catch fire."

He spoke to one of the grooms. "Have you got plenty of rope?"

"Plenty," the man said. "I will fetch you a couple of long coils from the stables. Here, one of you, come along with me."

"Now we will get the ladder up," Mr. Armstrong said.

With the aid of a dozen men—for the whole village was now upon the spot—the ladder was again lifted, and dropped so that the upper end fell between a chimney and a dormer window. Reginald Carne again attempted to cast it down, but a number of men hung on to the lower part of the ladder, and he was unable to lift it far enough to get it out of the niche into which it had fallen. Then he turned round and shook his fist at the crowd. Something flashed in the light of the flames, and half-a-dozen voices exclaimed: "He has got a knife." At this moment the clergyman and doctor arrived together on the scene.

"What is to be done, doctor?" Jacob Carey asked. "I don't mind going up, with some others to back me, to have a tussle with him on the roof; but he would knife us one by one as we got up to the parapet, and, though I don't think as I am a coward, I don't care about chucking away my life, which is of use to my wife and children, to save that of a madman whose life ain't of no use to hisself or any one else."

"No, I don't see why you should, Carey," the doctor said; "the best plan will be to keep away from the ladder for the present. Perhaps, when he thinks you are not going to make the attempt, he will move away, and then we can get up there before he sees us. I will go first because he knows me, and my influence may quiet him, but we had better arm ourselves with sticks so as to knock that knife out of his hand."

Reginald Carne stood guarding the ladder for a few minutes. By this time the whole of the first floor was in a blaze, the flames rushing out with fury from every window. Seeing that he did not move, the doctor said at last:

"Well, we must risk it. Give me a stick, Carey, and we will make a try, anyhow."

"You can't go now," Mr. Armstrong said, suddenly; "look, the ladder is alight."

This was indeed the case. The flames had not absolutely touched it, but the heat was so great that it had been slowly charring, and a light flame had now suddenly appeared, and in a moment ten or twelve feet of the ladder were on fire.

"It is of no use," the doctor said, dropping the stick that Jacob Carey had just cut for him in the shrubbery; "we can do nothing for him now."

There was scarcely a word spoken among the little crowd of spectators on the lawn. Every moment was adding to their number as Mr. Volkes, the magistrate, and several other gentlemen rode up on horseback, and men came up from all the farmhouses and cottages within a circle of a couple of miles. All sorts of suggestions were made, but only to be rejected.

"It is one thing to save a man who wants to be saved," the doctor said, "but quite another thing to save one who is determined not to be saved." This was in answer to a proposal to fasten a stone on to a light line and throw it up on to the roof. "The man is evidently as mad as a March hare."

There could be no doubt of that. Reginald Carne, seeing that his assailants, as he considered them, could not get at him, was making gestures of triumph and derision at them. Now from the second floor windows, the flames began to spurt out, the glass clattering down on to the gravel below.

"Oh, father, what a pitiful sight!"

Mr. Armstrong turned. "What on earth brings you here, Mary? Run away, child. This is a dreadful business, and it will be haunting you."

"I have seen more shocking things, father," she said, quietly. "Why did you not bring me up with you at first? I ran upstairs to get my hat and shawl, and when I came back you were gone. Of course, I came up at once, just as every one else in the village has done, only I would not come and bother you when I thought you were going to do something. But there's nothing to be done now but wait. This must surely be the end of the curse of Carne's Hold, father?"

"It ought to be, my dear. Yes, let us earnestly hope that it all terminates here, for your sake and every one else's. Mervyn will be master of Carne's Hold now."

"Not of Carne's Hold, thank God!" the girl said with a shudder. "There will be nothing left of Carne's Hold to-morrow but a heap of ruins. The place will be destroyed before he becomes its master. It all ends together, The Hold and the direct line of the Carnes."

"Let us turn and walk away, Mary. This is too dreadful."

"I can't," and Mary shook her head. "I wish I could, father, but it has a sort of horrible fascination. Look at all these upturned faces; it is the same with them all. You can see that there is not one who would not go if he could."

The doctor again went forward towards the house.

"Carne, my dear fellow," he shouted, "jump off at the end of the house into the shrubs on the beds there, it's your only chance."

Again the mocking laugh was heard above the roar of the fire. The flames were breaking out through the roof now in several places.

"It will not be long before the roof falls through," Mr. Armstrong said. "Come away, Mary. I will not let you stay here any longer." Putting his arms round his daughter, he led her away. She had not gone ten steps when there was a tremendous crash. She looked back; the roof was gone and a volcano of flame and sparks was rising from the shell of the house. Against these the figure of the madman stood out black and clear. Then a sudden puff of wind whirled the flames round him. He staggered, made a half step backwards, and fell, while a cry went up from the crowd.

"It's all over, dear," Mr. Armstrong said, releasing his hold of his daughter; and then with Jacob Carey and three or four other men, he ran forward to the house, lifted the body of Reginald Carne and carried it beyond danger of a falling wall.

Dr. Arrowsmith, the clergyman, and several of the neighbours at once hurried to the spot.

"He is not dead," Jacob Carey said, as they came up, "he groaned when we lifted him; he fell on to one of the little flower beds between the windows."

"No, his heart is beating," the doctor said, as he knelt beside him and felt his pulse, "but I fear he must have sustained fatal injuries." He took out a flask that he had, thinking that a cordial might be required, slipped into his pocket just before starting for the scene of the fire, and poured a few drops of spirit between Reginald Carne's lips.

There was a faint groan, and a minute later he opened his eyes. He looked round in a bewildered way, but when his eyes fell on the burning house, a look of satisfaction passed over his face.

"I have done it," he said. "I have broken the curse of Carne's Hold."

The doctor stood up for a moment and said to one of the grooms standing close by: "Get a stable door off its hinges and bring it here; we will carry him into the gardener's cottage."

As soon as Reginald Carne was taken away, Mr. Armstrong and his daughter returned to the village. A few of the villagers followed their example; but for most of them the fascination of watching the flames that were leaping far above the shell of the house was too great to be resisted, and it was not until the day dawned and the flames smouldered to a deep, quiet glow, that the crowd began to disperse.

"It has been a terrible scene," Mary said, as she walked with her father down the hill.

"A terrible scene, child, and it would have been just as well if you had stayed at home and slept comfortably. If I had thought that you were going to be so foolish, I would not have gone myself."

"You know very well, father, you could not have helped yourself. You could not have sat quietly in our cottage with the flames dancing up above the tree tops there, if you had tried ever so much. Well, somehow I am glad that The Hold is destroyed; but of course I am sorry for Mr. Carne's death, for I suppose he will die."

"I don't think you need be sorry, Mary. Far better to die even like that than to live till old age within the walls of a madhouse."

"Yes; but it was not the death, it was the horror of it."

"There was no horror in his case, my dear. He felt nothing but a wild joy in the mischief he had done. I do not suppose that he had a shadow of fear of death. He exulted both in the destruction of his house and in our inability to get at him. I really do not think he is to be pitied, although it was a terrible sight to see him. No doubt he was carrying out a long-cherished idea. A thing of this sort does not develop all at once. He may for years have been brooding over this unhappy taint of insanity in his blood, and have persuaded himself that with the destruction of the house, what the people here foolishly call the curse of the Carnes would be at an end."

"But surely you don't believe anything about the curse, father?"

"Not much, Mary; the curse was not upon the house, but in the insanity that the Spanish ancestors of the Carnes introduced into the family. Still I don't know, although you may think me weak-minded, that I can assert conscientiously that I do not believe there is anything in the curse itself. One has heard of such things, and certainly the history of the Carnes would almost seem to justify the belief. Ronald and his two sisters are, it seems, the last of those who have the Carnes' blood in their veins, and his misfortunes and their unhappiness do not seem to have anything whatever to do with the question of insanity. At any rate, dear, I, like you, am glad that The Hold is destroyed. I must own I should not have liked the thought of your ever becoming its mistress, and indeed I have more than once thought that before I handed you over to Ronald, whenever that event might take place, I should insist on his making me a promise that should he survive his cousin and come into the Carnes' estates, he would never take you to live there. Well, this will be a new incident for you to write to him about. You ought to feel thankful for that; for you would otherwise have found it very difficult to fill your letters till you hear from him what course he is going to adopt regarding this business of Ruth Powlett and Forester."

Mary smiled quietly to herself under cover of the darkness, for indeed she found by no means the difficulty her father supposed in filling her letters. "It is nearly four o'clock," she said, as she entered the house and struck a light. "It is hardly worth while going to bed, father."

"All right, my dear, you can please yourself. Now it is all over I acknowledge I feel both cold and sleepy, and you will see nothing more of me until between ten and eleven o'clock in the morning."

"Oh, if you go to bed of course I shall not stop up by myself," Mary said; "but I am convinced that I shall not close an eye."

"And I am equally convinced, Mary, that in a little over half an hour you will be sound asleep;" and in the morning Mary acknowledged that his anticipation had been verified.

CHAPTER XX.

CLEARED AT LAST.

Reginald Carne was laid down on the table in the gardener's cottage. The doctor could now examine him, and whispered to the clergyman that both his legs were broken, and that he had no doubt whatever he had received terrible internal injuries. "I don't think he will live till morning."

Presently there was a knock at the door. "Can I come in?" Mr. Volkes asked, when the doctor opened it. "I have known the poor fellow from the time he was a child. Is he sensible?"

"He is sensible in a way," the doctor said. "That is, I believe he knows perfectly well what we are saying, but he has several times laughed that strange, cunning laugh that is almost peculiar to the insane."

"Well, at any rate, I will speak to him," said Mr. Volkes.

"Do you know me, Reginald?" he went on in a clear voice as he came up to the side of the table.

Reginald Carne nodded, and again a low mocking laugh came from his lips. "You thought you were very clever, Volkes, mighty clever; but I tricked you."

"You tricked me, did you?" the magistrate said, cheerfully. "How did you trick me?"

"You thought, and they all thought, the dull-headed fools, that Ronald Mervyn killed Margaret. Ho! ho! I cheated you all nicely."

A glance of surprise passed between his listeners. Mr. Volkes signed to the others not to speak, and then went on:

"So he did, Reginald, so he did—though we couldn't prove it; you did not trick us there."

"I did," Reginald Carne said, angrily. "I killed her myself."

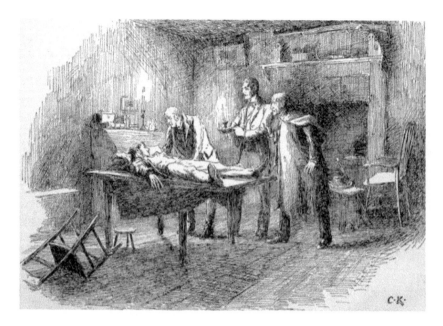

"'I did,' Reginald Carne said, angrily—'I killed her myself.'"

An exclamation of horror broke from the three listeners. Mr. Volkes was the first to recover himself.

"Nonsense, Reginald, you are dreaming."

"I am not," he said, vehemently. "I had thought it all out over and over again. I was always thinking of it. I wanted to put an end to this curse. It's been going on too long, and it troubled me. I had made up my mind to kill her long before; but I might not have done it when I did if I had not heard Ronald threatening her, and another man heard it too. This was a grand opportunity, you see. It was as much as I could do to sit quietly at dinner with that naval fellow, and to know that it was all right. It was glorious, for it would be killing two birds with one stone. I wanted to get rid of Ronald as much as I did of her, so that the curse might come to an end, and now it was all so easy. I had only to drop the glove he had left behind him on the grass close below her window, and after that quarrel he would be suspected and hung. Nothing could have worked better for me; and then, too, I thought it would puzzle them to give them another scent to work on. There was another man had a grudge against Margaret; that was Forester, the poacher. I had picked up his

246

knife in the wood just where he had killed my keeper, and afterwards I heard him telling his sweetheart, who was Margaret's maid, that he would kill Margaret for persuading her to give him up; so I dropped the knife by the side of the bed, and I thought that one or other of them would be sure to be hung; but somehow that didn't come right. I believe the girl hid the knife, only I didn't dare question her about it. But that didn't matter; the fellow would be hung one way or the other for killing my keeper. But the other was a glorious thing, and I chuckled over it. It was hard to look calm and grave when I was giving evidence against Ronald, and when all the fools were thinking that he did it, when it was me all the time. Didn't I do it cleverly, Volkes? I hid her things where the gardener was sure to find them the first time he dug up the bed. They let Ronald off, but he will not come back again, and I don't suppose he will ever marry; so there is an end of the curse as far as he's concerned. Then I waited a bit, but the devil was always at my elbow, telling me to finish the good work, and last night I did it. I put the candle to the curtains in all the rooms downstairs, and stood and watched them blaze up until it got too hot to stay any longer. It was a grand sight, and I could hear the Spanish woman laughing and shouting. She has had her way with us for a long time, but now it's all over; the curse of the Carnes is played out. There, didn't I cheat you nicely, Volkes, you and all the others? You never suspected me, not one of you. I used to keep grave all day, but at night when I was in my room alone I laughed for hours to think of all the dogs on the wrong scent."

His three listeners looked at each other silently.

"It was a grand thing to put an end to the curse," Reginald Carne rambled on. "It was no pain to her; and if she had lived, the trouble would have come upon her children."

"You know that you are hurt beyond chance of recovery, Carne," the magistrate said, gravely. "It is a terrible story that you have told us. I think that you ought to put it down on paper, so that other people may know how it was done; because, you see, at present, an innocent man is suspected."

"What do I care? That is nothing to me one way or the other. I am glad I have succeeded in frightening Ronald Mervyn away, and I hope he will never come back again. You don't suppose I am going to help to bring him home!"

Mr. Volkes saw that he had made a mistake. "Yes, I quite understand you don't want him back," he said, soothingly. "I thought, perhaps, that you would like people to know how you had sacrificed yourself to put an end to the curse, and how cleverly you had managed to deceive every one. People would never believe us if we were to tell them. They would say either that you did not know what you were talking about, or that it was empty boasting on your part."

"They may think what they like," he said, sullenly; "it is nothing to me what they think."

There was a change in the tone of his voice that caused the doctor to put his hand on his wrist again.

"Let me give you a few drops more of brandy, Carne."

"No, I will not," the dying man said. "I suppose you want to keep me alive to get some more out of me, but you won't. I won't speak again."

The others held a whispered conversation in the corner.

"He is going fast," the doctor said. "It is a marvel that his voice is as strong as it is. He certainly won't live till morning. It is likely he may die within an hour."

"I will ask him another question or two," Mr. Volkes said. "If we could but get something to corroborate his story, it would be invaluable."

But Reginald Carne spoke no more.

He heard what was said to him, for he laughed the same malicious laugh that had thrilled the crowd as he stood on the parapet, but it was low and feeble now. In hopes that he might yet change his mind, Mr. Volkes and the clergyman remained with Dr. Arrowsmith for another hour. At the end of that time Reginald Carne startled them by speaking again, clearly and distinctly:

"I tell you it's all over, you witch; you have done us harm enough, but I have beaten you. It was you against me, and I have won. There is nothing more for you to do here, and you can go to your place. Carne's Hold is down, and the curse is broken."

As he ceased speaking the doctor moved quietly up to the side of the stretcher, put his finger on his wrist, and stood there for a minute, then he bent down and listened.

"He is gone," he said, "the poor fellow is dead." The three gentlemen went outside the cottage; some of the people were standing near waiting for news of Reginald Carne's state. "Mr. Carne has just died," the doctor said, as he went up to them. "Will one of you find Mrs. Wilson and tell her to bring another woman with her and see to him? In the morning I will make arrangements to have him taken down to the village."

"What do you think we had better do about this, Dr. Arrowsmith?" Mr. Volkes asked as he rejoined them. "Do you believe this story?"

"Unquestionably I do," the doctor replied. "I believe every word of it."

"But the man was mad, doctor."

"Yes, he was mad and has been so for a long time in my opinion, but that makes no difference whatever in my confidence that he was speaking truly. Confessions of this kind from a madman are generally true; their cunning is prodigious, and as long as they wish to conceal a fact it is next to impossible to get it from them; but when, as in the present case, they are proud of their cleverness and of the success with which they have fooled other people, they will tell everything. You see their ideas of right and wrong are entirely upset; the real lunatic is unconscious of having committed a crime, and is inclined even to glory in it."

"I wish we could have got him to sign," the magistrate said.

"I am sure he could not have held the pen," Dr. Arrowsmith replied. "I will certify to that effect, and as we three all heard the confession, I think that if you draw it out and we sign it as witnesses, it will have just as good an effect as if he had written it himself."

"There was one part, doctor, that surprised me even more than the rest—that was the part relating to the man Forester. I don't believe a soul suspected him of being in any way connected with the crime. At least we heard nothing of a knife being found, nor, of course, of the quarrel between Forester and the girl; Ruth Powlett, was it not?"

"No; that is all new to us," the doctor said.

"I think the best way would be to see her in the morning. She may not like to confess that she concealed the knife, if she did so. Of course, if she does, it will be an invaluable confirmation of his story, and will show conclusively that his confession was not a mere delusion of a madman's brain."

"Yes, indeed," the doctor agreed, "that would clench the matter altogether, and I am almost certain you will find that what he has said is true. The girl was in my hands a short time before Miss Carne's death. They said she had had a fall, but to my mind it seemed more like a severe mental shock. Then after Miss Carne's death she was very ill again, and there was something about her that puzzled me a good deal. For instance, she insisted upon remaining in court until the verdict was given, and that at a time when she was so ill she could scarcely stand. She was so obstinate over the matter that it completely puzzled me; but if what Carne said was true, and she had the knowledge of something that would have gone very far to prove Ronald Mervyn's innocence, the matter is explained. The only difficulty before us is to get her to speak, because, of course, she cannot do so without laying herself open to a charge—I don't mean a criminal charge, but a moral one—of having suppressed evidence in a manner that concerned a man's life. I think the best plan will be for us to meet at your house, Mr. Volkes, at eleven o'clock to-morrow. I will go into the village before that, and will bring Ruth Powlett up in my gig, and if you will allow me I will do the talking to her. I have had her a good deal in my hands for the last year, and I think she has confidence in me, and will perhaps answer me more freely than she would you as a magistrate."

"Very likely she would, doctor. Let the arrangement stand as you propose."

The next morning, at half-past ten, Dr. Arrowsmith drove up in his gig to the mill. Ruth came to the door.

"Ruth," he said, "I want you to put on your bonnet and shawl and let me drive you a short distance. I have something particular that I want to talk to you about, and want to have you to myself for a bit."

A good deal surprised, Ruth went into the house and reappeared in two or three minutes warmly wrapped up.

"That's right," the doctor said; "jump in."

Ruth Powlett was the first to speak.

"I suppose it is true, sir, that poor Mr. Carne is dead?"

"Yes, he died at two o'clock. Ruth, I have a curious thing to tell you about him; but I will wait until we get through the village; I have no doubt that it will surprise you as much as it surprised me."

Ruth said nothing until they had crossed the bridge over the Dare.

"What is it?" she asked at last.

"Well, Ruth, at present it is only known to Mr. Vickery, Mr. Volkes, and myself, and, whatever happens, I want you to say nothing about it until I give you leave. Now, Ruth, I have some sort of idea that what I am going to tell you will relieve your mind of a burden."

Ruth turned pale.

"Relieve my mind, sir!" she repeated.

"Yes, Ruth; I may be wrong, and if I am I can only say beforehand that I am sorry; but I have an idea that you suspect, and have for a long time suspected, that George Forester murdered Miss Carne."

Ruth did not speak, but looking down, the doctor saw by the pallor of her cheeks and the expression of her face that his supposition was correct.

"I think, Ruth, that has been your idea. If so, I can relieve your mind. Mr. Carne before his death confessed that he murdered his sister." Ruth gave a start and a cry. She reeled in her seat, and would have fallen had not the doctor thrown his arm round her. "Steady, my child, steady," he said; "this is a surprise to you, I have no doubt, and, whatever it is to others, probably a joyful one."

Ruth broke into a violent fit of sobbing. The doctor did not attempt to check her, but when she gradually recovered he said, "That is strange news, is it not, Ruth?"

"But did he mean it, sir?" she asked. "Did he know what he was saying when he said so?"

"He knew perfectly well, Ruth; he told us a long story, but I will not tell you what it is now. We shall be at Mr. Volkes's in a minute, and we shall find Mr. Vickery there, and I want you to tell us what you know about it before you hear what Mr. Carne's story was. I do hope that you will tell us everything you know. Only in that way can we clear Captain Mervyn."

"I will tell you everything I know, sir," Ruth said, quietly; "I told Miss Armstrong five weeks ago, and was only waiting till she heard from some one she has written to before telling it to every one."

The gig now drew up at the door of the magistrate's house, and Dr. Arrowsmith led Ruth into the sitting-room, where Mr. Volkes and the clergyman were awaiting her.

"Sit down here, Ruth," the doctor said, handing her a chair. "Now, gentlemen, I may tell you first that I have told Miss Powlett that Mr. Carne has confessed that he killed his sister. I have not told her a single word more. It was, of course, of the highest importance that she should not know the nature of his story before telling you her own. She has expressed her willingness to tell you all she knows. Now, Miss Powlett, will you please begin in your own way."

Quietly and steadily Ruth Powlett told her story, beginning with the conversation that she had had with Margaret Carne relative to her breaking off the engagement; she described her interview with George Forester, his threats against Miss Carne and his attack on herself; and then told how she had found his knife by the bedside on the morning of the murder. She said she knew now that she had done very wrong to conceal it, but that she had done it for the sake of George Forester's father. Lastly, she told how she had gone to the trial taking the knife with her, firmly resolved that in case a verdict of guilty should be returned against Captain Mervyn, she would come forward, produce the knife, and tell all that she knew.

Her three hearers exchanged many looks of satisfaction as she went on.

When she had finished, Mr. Volkes said: "We are very much obliged to you

251

for your story, Miss Powlett. Happily it agrees precisely with that told us by Mr. Carne. It seems that he was in the wood and overheard your quarrel with Forester, and the threats against Miss Carne suggested to him the idea of throwing the blame upon Forester, and to do this he placed the knife that he had found on the scene of the poaching affray a short time before, in his sister's room. After this confirmation given by your story, there can be no doubt at all that Mr. Carne's confession was genuine, and that it will completely clear Captain Mervyn of the suspicion of having caused his cousin's death. We shall be obliged, I am afraid, to make your story public also, in order to confirm his statement. This will naturally cause you much pain and some unpleasantness, and I hope you will accept that as the inevitable consequence of the course—which you yourself see has been a very mistaken one—you pursued in this affair."

"I am prepared for that, sir," Ruth said, quietly; "I had already told Miss Armstrong about it, and was ready to come here to tell you the story even when I thought that by so doing I should have to denounce George Forester as a murderer. I am so rejoiced that he is now proved to be innocent, I can very well bear what may be said about me."

"But why not have come and told me at once when you made up your mind to do so?" Mr. Volkes asked. "Why delay it?"

"I was waiting, sir; I was waiting—but——" and she paused, "that secret is not my own; but I think, sir, that if you will go to Mr. Armstrong, he will be able to tell you something you will be glad to know."

"Who is Mr. Armstrong?" Mr. Volkes asked, in some surprise.

"He is a gentleman who has been living in the village for the last four or five months, sir. I do not think there can be any harm in my telling you that he knows where Captain Mervyn is to be found."

"That is the very information we want at present. We must get Ronald Mervyn back among us as soon as we can; he has indeed been very hardly treated in the matter. I think, Miss Powlett, we will get you to put your story into the form of a sworn information. We may as well draw it up at once, and that will save you the trouble of coming up here again."

This was accordingly done, and Ruth Powlett walked back to the village, leaving Mr. Volkes and the two other gentlemen to draw up a formal report of the confession made by Reginald Carne.

Ruth Powlett went straight to the cottage occupied by the Armstrongs.

"What is your news, Ruth?" Mary said, as she entered. "I can see by your face that you have something important to tell us."

"I have, indeed," Ruth replied. "I have just been up to Mr. Volkes, the magistrate, and have told him all I knew."

"What induced you to do that, Ruth?" Mary asked, in surprise. "I thought you had quite settled to say nothing about it until we heard from Captain Mervyn."

"They knew all about it before I told them, and only sent for me to confirm the story. Mr. Carne, before he died last night, made a full confession before Mr. Volkes, Dr. Arrowsmith, and Mr. Vickery. It was he who in his madness killed his sister, and who placed George Forester's knife by the bedside, and Captain Mervyn's glove on the grass, to throw suspicion on them. Captain Mervyn and George Forester are both innocent."

The news was so sudden and unexpected that it was some time before Mary Armstrong could sufficiently recover herself to ask questions. The news that Ronald was proved to be innocent was not so startling as it would have been had she not previously believed that they were already in a position to clear him; but the knowledge that his innocence would now be publicly proclaimed in a day or two, filled her with happiness. She was glad, too, for Ruth's sake that George Forester had not committed this terrible crime; and yet there was a slight feeling of disappointment that she herself had had no hand in clearing her lover, and that this had come about in an entirely different way to what she had expected.

Mr. Volkes and the clergyman called that afternoon, and had a long talk with Mr. Armstrong, and the following day a thrill of excitement was caused throughout the country by the publication in the papers of the confession of Reginald Carne. Dr. Arrowsmith certified that, although Reginald Carne was unquestionably insane, and probably had been so for some years, he had no hesitation in saying that he was perfectly conscious at the time he made the confession, and that the statement might be believed as implicitly as if made by a wholly sane man. In addition to this certificate and the confession, the three gentlemen signed a joint declaration to the effect that the narrative was absolutely confirmed by other facts, especially by the statement made by Miss Powlett, without her being in any way aware of the confession of Reginald Carne. This, they pointed out, fully confirmed his story on all points, and could leave no shadow of doubt in the minds of any one that Reginald Carne had, under the influence of madness, taken his sister's life, and had then, with the cunning so commonly present in insanity, thrown suspicion upon two wholly innocent persons.

The newspapers, commenting on the story, remarked strongly upon the cruel injustice that had been inflicted upon Captain Mervyn, and expressed the hope that he would soon return to take his place again in the county, uniting in his person the estate of the Mervyns and the Carnes. There were some expressions of strong reprobation at the concealment by Ruth Powlett of the knife she had found in Miss Carne's room. One of the papers, however, admitted that "Perhaps altogether it is fortunate now that the girl concealed them. Had the facts now published in her statement been given, they would at once have convinced every one that Captain Mervyn did not commit the crime with which he was charged, but at the same time they might have brought another innocent man to the scaffold. Upon the whole, then, although her conduct in concealing this important news is most reprehensible, it must be admitted that, in the interests of justice, it is fortunate she kept silent."

The sensation caused in Carnesford by the publication of this news was tremendous. Fortunately, Ruth Powlett was not there to become the centre of talk, for she had that morning been carried off by Mr. Armstrong and Mary to stay with them for a while in London. The cottage was shut up, and upon the following day a cart arrived from Plymouth to carry off the furniture, which had been only hired by the month. The evening before leaving, Mr. Armstrong had intercepted Hiram Powlett on his way to the snuggery, and taking him up to the cottage, where Ruth was spending the evening with Mary, informed him on the way of the strange discovery that had been made, and Ruth's share in it.

"I trust, Mr. Powlett," he said, "that you will not be angry with your daughter. She was placed in a terrible position, having the option of either denouncing as a murderer a man she had loved, or permitting another to lie under the imputation of guilt. And you must remember that she was prepared to come forward at the trial and tell the truth about the matter had Captain Mervyn been found guilty. No doubt she acted wrongly; but she has suffered terribly, and I think that as my daughter has forgiven her for allowing Captain Mervyn to suffer for her silence, you may also do so."

Hiram Powlett had uttered many expressions of surprise and concern as he listened to the story. It seemed to him very terrible that his girl should have all the time been keeping a secret of such vital importance. He now said in a tone of surprise:

"I don't understand you, Mr. Armstrong, about your daughter. What has Miss Mary to do with forgiving? How has she been injured?"

"I don't know that upon the whole she has been injured," Mr. Armstrong said. "At least, I am sure she does not consider so. Still, I think she has something to forgive, for the fact is she is engaged to be married to Captain Mervyn, and would have been his wife a year ago had he not been resolved never to marry so long as this cloud remained over him."

Hiram Powlett was so greatly surprised at this news that his thoughts were for a moment diverted from Ruth's misdemeanours. Captain Mervyn, the owner of the Hall, and now of the Carne estate also, was a very great man in the eyes of the people of Carnesford, and the news that he was engaged to be married to the girl who was a friend of his daughter's, and who had several times taken tea at the mill, was almost bewildering to him.

"I dare say you are surprised," Mr. Armstrong said, quietly, "but you see we are not exactly what we appear. We came here somewhat under false colours, to try and find out about this murder, and in the hope we might discover some proofs of Captain Mervyn's innocence. Now we have been successful we shall go up to London and there await Captain Mervyn's return. I have been talking it over with my daughter, and if you and Mrs. Powlett offer no opposition, we propose to take Ruth away to stay with us for two or three months. It will be pleasant for all parties. Your girl and mine are fond of each other, and Ruth will be a nice companion for Mary. The change will do your daughter good. She has for a long time been suffering greatly, and fresh scenes and objects of interest will take her mind off the past, and lastly, by the time she returns here, the gossip and talk that will arise when all this is known, will have died away."

"It is very good of you to think of it, Mr. Armstrong," Hiram Powlett said, "and it will be a fine thing for Ruth. Of course, she has been wrong, very wrong; but she must have suffered very much all these months. I told you I thought she had something on her mind, but I never thought it was like this. Well, well, I shan't say anything to her. I never was good at scolding her when she was a child, and I think she has been severely punished for this already."

"I think so too," Mr. Armstrong agreed; "and now let us go in. I told her that I should speak to you this evening, and she must be waiting anxiously for you."

When they entered, Ruth rose timidly.

"Oh! father"—she began.

"There, don't say any more about it, Ruth," Hiram interrupted, taking her tenderly in his arms. "My poor girl, you have had a hard time of it. Why didn't you tell me all at first?"

"I could not, father," she sobbed. "You know—you know—how you were set against him."

"Well, that is so, Ruth, and I should have been still more set against him if I had known the rights of that fall of yours upon the hill; but there, we won't say anything more about it. You have been punished for your fault, child, and I hope that when you come back again to us from the jaunt that Mr.

255

Armstrong is going to be good enough to take you, you will be just as you were before all this trouble came upon you."

And so the next morning Mr. Armstrong, his daughter, and Ruth went up to London.

Two months later, Mary received Ronald's letter, telling of George Forester's death, and of his own disappointment at finding his hopes of clearing himself dashed to the ground. Mary broke the news of Forester's death to Ruth; she received it quietly.

"I am sorry," she said, "but he has been nothing to me for a long time now, and he could never have been anything to me again. I am sorry," she repeated, wiping her eyes, "that the boy I played with is gone, but for the man, I think it is, perhaps, better so. He died fighting bravely, and as a soldier should. I fear he would never have made a good man had he lived."

A month later, Ronald himself returned. The war was virtually over when he received the letters from Mary Armstrong and Mr. Volkes, telling him that he was cleared at last, and he had no trouble in obtaining his discharge at once. He received the heartiest congratulations from his former officers, and a perfect ovation from the men, as he said good-bye to them. At Plymouth he received letters telling him where Mary and her father were staying in London, and on landing he at once proceeded to town by train, after telegraphing to his sisters to meet him there.

A fortnight later a quiet wedding took place, Ronald's sisters and Ruth Powlett acting as bridesmaids, an honour that, when Ruth returned home immediately after the ceremony, effectually silenced the tongues of the village gossips. Ronald Mervyn and his wife went for a month's tour on the Continent, Mr. Armstrong joining them in Paris a few days after the marriage; while the Miss Mervyns went down to Devonshire to prepare the Hall for the reception of its owner. Colonel Somerset had not forgotten his promise, and two or three days after Ronald's return, the letter stating how Captain Mervyn had distinguished himself during the Kaffir War under the name of Sergeant Blunt went the round of the papers.

The skeleton walls of Carne's Hold were at once pulled down, the garden was rooted up, and the whole site planted with trees, and this was by Ronald's orders carried out so expeditiously that when he returned with his bride all trace of The Hold had vanished.

Never in the memory of South Devonshire had there been such rejoicings as those that greeted Ronald Mervyn and his wife on their return home. The tenantry of his two estates, now joined, all assembled at the station, and scarce a man from Carnesford was absent. Triumphal arches had been erected, and the gentry for many miles round drove in to receive them, as an expression at once of their satisfaction that Ronald Mervyn had been cleared from the cloud that hung over him, and, to some extent, of their regret that they should ever for a moment have believed him guilty.

Reuben Claphurst's prediction was verified. With the destruction of Carne's Hold the curse of the Spanish lady ceased to work, and no trace of the family scourge has ever shown itself in the blood of the somewhat numerous family of Ronald Mervyn. The tragic story is now almost forgotten, and it is only among the inhabitants of the village at the foot of the hill that the story of the curse of Carne's Hold is sometimes related.

THE END.